LONESOME HEART

EMMANUELLE

USA TODAY BESTSELLING AUTHOR

SNOW

Smart Lily
Publishing

Lonesome Heart
Emmanuelle Snow

First edition - January 2023 (V_1) - 2025 update

ISBN eBook: 978-1-990429-24-8

ISBN paperback: 978-1-990429-84-2

This book is a work of fiction. Any references to historical events, real people, or real places are used fictitiously. Names, characters, places, and incidents are products of the author's imagination. Any resemblance to actual events, locales, organizations, or persons, living or dead, is coincidental.

The publisher and author acknowledge the trademark status and trademark ownership of all trademarks, service marks, and word marks mentioned in this book.

Editors: Shalini G. and SLE

Cover: SMART Lily publishing inc.

Published by SMART Lily Publishing inc.

———

Emmanuelle Snow
emmanuellesnow.com

CARTER HILLS BAND UNIVERSE
(SUGGESTED READING ORDER)

Carter Hills Band series
False Promises

HEART SONG DUET
Blindsided
Forevermore

Whiskey Melody series
Sweet Agony

SECOND TEAR DUET
Cruel Destiny
Beautiful Salvation

BREATHLESS DUET
Wild Encounter
Brittle Scars

Upon A Star series
Last Hope

Midnight Sparks

Love Song For Two series
Lonesome Heart Duet
Fallen Legend
Rising Star

Two of Us Duet
Snowbound

Wicked Love

All titles available at
emmanuellesnow.com

For the best experience, read in the order as shown above

WHAT THE REVIEWS SAY

- "5 huge stars from me for this gorgeous and brilliant book! I cannot wait for the next installment in this series!" (Goodreads)

- "This slow burn pulled me in from the very first page. I felt all the tears, heartbreak, smiles, chemistry, and love while reading." (Tanja, OMGreads)

- "This was so good. I love this series so much and always think it cannot get better but it does." (Goodreads)

- "This story that will have you reaching for your tissues and possibly cursing Ms. Snow a couple times will leave you with a happy heart when it is all said and done!" (Goodreads)

- "This book takes you on a roller coaster ride of emotions that had me in tears so many times but I still couldn't put it down as it was a real page turner and totally addictive." (Goodreads)

TRIGGER WARNINGS

Disclaimer

My books are realistic and emotional love stories.

I'm an advocate for mental health, and some topics could be sensitive for certain readers since they are portrayed as close to real life as possible.

I've listed the potential trigger warnings for each title on my website.

Be advised that those trigger warnings could potentially be spoiler alerts for the storylines.

Those sensitive topics have been written with the utmost care and respect. Please reach out if you have questions or comments.

All books contain sexuality, mature content, and language not intended for people under 18 years of age.
For other readers' sake, please avoid spoilers in your reviews.

Thank you and have a wonderful day!

Emmanuelle

emmanuellesnow.com

To life
A few times you've given me a
shitty hand to deal with.
But now that the sun shines brighter,
I can thank you,
Because I wouldn't be here today
if you hadn't shown me,
How strong and resilient I could be.
I'm sorry it took me a long time
to understand the lesson.
But now I'm finally happy to be
where I'm supposed to be,
And I'm grateful for the bumps
you put in my road.

BECOME A VIP

TO NEVER MISS A THING

Snow's VIP

Join **Emmanuelle Snow's VIP newsletter**

Be the first to know about new releases, giveaways, sales, and special events. And step into a space where big emotions are celebrated, love is messy and beautiful, and stories linger long after the last page.

emmanuellesnow.com

Snow's Soulmates

Join Emmanuelle Snow's Facebook VIP group, **Snow's Soulmates**, to chat with her and other readers, get updates, and more bonus content.

facebook.com/groups/snowvip

KISSED BY AN ANGEL

I've been turned to stone long ago
I can't feel the sun warming my skin
I can't feel the raindrops on my face
I'm numb. So numb.
My heart is locked up in a cage
No one is allowed inside
I've been hurting bad. So bad
It still haunts my dreams
I don't know days from nights
    anymore
I am just being alive right now
I have forgotten how to live

[CHORUS]

The sight of you jolts my heart back
    to life
Your smile thaws every layer of ice I
    hide behind
Your touch soothes my sorrows

It heals my pain
Your lips taste like freedom
Your skin feels like passion
Let me love you, girl
Let me shine in your light
Let me breathe in your air
With you, I'm living again
With you, I'm myself again

Hope has made its way to my heart
Now I can see the colors around me
Now I can smell the lilac flowers
And hear the birds chirping in the
     trees
I'm a mere country boy
And you're an angel from the sky
Please shower me with your light
Please let me love you tonight

[CHORUS]
I've been broken and sad
Until there was no place to hide
I bled until I died
A million times

I stepped back
Not ready to open my heart to you
There were too many things
Pushing us apart
Too many winters
Icing our hearts
But spring came this year
And shattered the ice around my
     frozen heart

Now summer is here, melting the
    last restraints
Leaving my heart raw and exposed
Filling it with renewed hope
Ready for you to make it yours
Ready for you to love and kiss me

[CHORUS]
I'm ready to fight for you
Ready to fight for us
There're no more clouds shadowing
    us from above
Nothing stands in our way anymore
I'm a country boy
And you're an angel
Please shower me with your light
Please let me love you tonight

And kiss me
I crave the kiss of an angel
Of an angel
A kiss from my angel

Music and lyrics by Sam Stevens

1

SAM

Fisting my hands at my sides, I paced the room, a ball of lightning bouncing around in my chest. This was a nightmare. A disaster about to happen. How had I not seen this one coming? How could I have been so blind?

My nails dug trenches into my palms, drawing pinpricks of blood, but I would keep my composure. I had to.

The lump in my larynx rubbed against the chaffed walls of my throat.

I reeled in some of my wrath and tried another approach. My voice came out a ragged whisper, but calmer this time, as I put my pride to rest and urged my sanity to stay in the game. "Lisa, you can't be serious. Listen, there must be something *I* can do. Can we talk about it first? And what about the kids? How am I going to explain any of this to them? We'll get help... You can't just leave like this."

No emotions—rather not the ones I wished to see—

crossed her hardened features. No *I'm having second thoughts.* Or *you might be right, we'll get help.*

My wife had turned to stone, unmoving and unreadable.

Hoping the pain would numb the one ripping my chest in two, I tugged at the roots of my hair. How could I have been so clueless about the woman I'd been married to for the last four years?

She pushed another shirt into her bag, ignoring my words.

Maybe I could reach out to the mother inside her. "Lisa, your leaving will fuck them up for the rest of their lives. Abandoning your own children, really? That's not what motherhood is all about." I halted and turned around to face the woman, who I thought I knew so well, zipping up her royal-blue suitcase. The one that had traveled around the world with us for years. Yeah, what a joke.

She finally raised her gaze, and I saw determination pass through her eyes this time. She wasn't doubting her decision to walk away from us, her family.

I studied her for a long minute, wishing I could see tears glistening somewhere in them, or regret marring her features. But there were none.

She was done.

When did my wife harbor a rock in place of her heart?

"Is it about the miscarriages?" I asked, praying she'd say yes and that I could call her doctor and set up an appointment to discuss her psychological distress. "I know how difficult it's been on you, but it's been hard on me too. We can get through this. Together. We're a good team. We love each other."

She sighed and shook her head, her eyes still showing no sign of hurt or sadness. Or anything. "That's the thing,

Sam. I don't love you. I did. Once. But both miscarriages were eye-opening. I need to find myself. I'm twenty-eight. For the last six years, I've followed you around the globe. I liked that. For the last four, I've played wife and mommy. And I enjoyed it...at some point. Being a parent is your thing. We had babies because you wanted to be a daddy... I never asked to be a mother. In all honesty, I thought it'd grow on me..." She shrugged. "But it didn't. I crave fresh air. To be free to do whatever I want. Whenever I want it. And being a parent isn't just what I hoped it would be. I'm sorry, but I'm over it."

I blinked. What? Was she serious right now? *She's over it?*

I was having one of those crippling nightmares that felt too much like reality. This was it. No woman in her right mind would say such horrible things about her own children. About her family.

Her flesh.

Her blood.

My Adam's apple bobbed, and bile rose in my throat, tinted with disgust and disdain.

My wife was delusional.

Who should I call to get her some help?

Could her state of mind be ruled a mental breakdown? Did she need to see a psychiatrist? Or go on a vacation? No matter what I told myself, she looked sane.

Lisa smiled at me as if quitting on us was just a daily occurrence and not something about to wreck our entire world.

My shoulders fell, and so did my heart. I inched closer when she moved to her feet. "Can we talk about this? Please. You at least owe me that. We've been through so much together. Did you forget everything?" I asked, forcing my voice to sound even and trying my best to keep my anger under wraps.

She offered me another twist of her lips. This time, she looked diabolical. Who was this woman? Where did my wife go? "I owe you nothing, Sammy. The ride has been fun, but I'm not playing this family game anymore. I'm out. Oh, and I'll send you the divorce papers in a week or two."

My eyes sprang wider.

What the actual fuck?

"Divorce papers? Don't you think it's a little early to talk about divorce? We haven't even fought about anything serious in the past, and now you're talking about dissolving our marriage. Tell me you're kidding. Where are the cameras? The crew? Is it for a celebrity prank TV show?"

My wife—or soon-to-be ex-wife if she had her way—huffed, as if anything I said sounded childish. Asking her to stay seemed to get on her nerves.

"C'mon, Sammy. I'm moving to the other side of the world. I won't return. Ever. Come to terms with it. Nothing you do or say will change anything." She sighed again and shook her head, looking desperate. "I. Am. Not. Coming. Back. Ever. This"—she pointed around the room with her finger—"is over. You and I, we're done." A car honked outside. "Now move, my cab is waiting." She pushed past me, rolling her suitcase behind her.

I stood there, frozen. None of this made sense. The dream had lasted long enough. I could wake up now. *Please, someone, make this nightmare go away.*

My heart stuttered, and the sound of little feet padding near our bedroom snapped me back to the present. I spun around and watched Lisa as she stood in the doorway, a mask of annoyance painting her frigid face.

My heart froze. Ice frosted the blood inside my veins, and I held my breath.

Mikaella, our four-year-old, ran our way in her one-piece unicorn white PJs, her wild, curly light-brown hair looking like a bird's nest, a fluffy baby-pink blanket hanging from her tiny hand.

She stopped before Lisa, her round golden eyes traveling from her mama to the suitcase beside her. "Going on a trip, Mama?" Sparks shone in our daughter's eyes, and she lifted a finger. "I love going on the plane. *Nneeeaowww*," she said, her hand imitating the aircraft. "The ladies always gimme chocolate. Justine *lovvvves* chocolate too. She always eats mine. Can I bring Miss Froggy with me? She's never been on a plane. She wanna come. You said she could come next time. You promised."

Lisa looked at our daughter, her gaze empty and back held taut. I prayed to see an emotion crossing her flat gaze. None made an appearance.

Mikaella tugged at her hand. "Mama, can I pack by myself? I'm a big girl. Can I bring my purple dress? And my ballet shoes? Can Boa the raccoon come too? And Holly? She always misses me when I'm gone. She hates being a doll. She wants to be a real baby…or a lady. And drink tea."

Lisa finally said something. My ears scorched the moment the words left her mouth. "Mama is going on a trip by herself, Mika. To Thailand. You can't come, I wanna be alone."

Tears pooled in our baby's eyes. She tugged at her mother's hand once again. "But I wanna come. Justine wants to come too. She'll be sad if you leave without her. Mama, we'll be good, good girls. And be silent if your head hurts."

Lisa ruffled her hair. "Sorry. You're not coming. I gotta go. Be nice to your daddy. And take care of Justine. Can you be a big girl, Mika?"

Our daughter nodded, a wide smile now brightening her sweet face. Lisa ignored her and stalked away when the cab honked a second time. My heart sank deeper in my chest at the sight of my wife walking away from our baby girl.

Once at the top of the staircase, she pivoted to face me. "Bye, Sammy. Have a good life." She removed her wedding ring and placed it on the banister.

My heart tumbled down my chest until it hit the hardwood floor. Smashed and bleeding.

I stood there, acid filling my throat and dissolving the words I wanted to speak.

Mikaella's sobs brought me back to her. "She didn't kiss me goodbye. Mama. *Mammma.* Come back. I'll be a good girl."

I rushed to my daughter and lifted her in my arms, both of us needing each other's love and affection now more than ever.

I brushed her hair with my fingers, dried her tears, and hugged her closer so my heart could soothe hers. Because I had no clue how to heal her pain with words.

I followed Lisa down the stairs. My eyes zoomed in on the front door. My head pounded, and my chest cavity filled with piling rocks as the sound of the revving engine outside faded away. What had just happened?

Two hours ago, everything was fine. Or I thought it was. We bathed the girls, read stories in bed… Where did it go wrong?

My stomach heaved. Lisa left. She fucking left.

"Shhh, sweet pea. It'll be okay. We'll be okay… I'm here…"

In that instant, I didn't even believe my own words.

I fished my phone out of my back pocket to call my wife. We needed to talk—before she left for good. Before she regretted any of it. Before it was too late to fix that rift keeping us apart.

Beep. Beep. Beep.

The last thread of hope holding me together burned to ashes.

Chills lined my back.

Lisa had disconnected her number.

Reality hit me. It wasn't a prank or a spur-of-the-moment decision. It was premeditated.

How long had she been planning her escape?

How long ago had she decided the girls and I were inconveniences in her life?

Oxygen could barely make the journey from my lungs to my brain anymore.

My wife had vanished in the night without giving me any kind of explanation. Or a way to reach her.

I buried my face in the crook of Mikaella's neck, hiding my numbing emotions from her.

My head spun. A weight I'd never carried before grew in my chest, crushing my organs. How would I ever be able to tell my baby girls their mama had ditched them for a reason I still didn't get?

The last fragment of my heart broke free as my baby's sobs doubled, now heart-wrenching, coming from some place deep down her little body, her sadness drenching my shirt. "I want Mama. I love the plane. She didn't kiss me. I want a hug…from her."

My eyes glazed over.

My little girl tilted her head back and stared at me, her lower lip trembling and her face a map of confusion and sorrow.

She cupped my cheeks with her hands and blinked. "Daddy, why are you crying? Do you miss Mama too? Did she forget to kiss you goodnight?" She wrapped her baby arms around my neck and fastened her hug around me. "Don't cry, Daddy. I'm here. I love you. Don't cry, okay?"

I pulled my daughter against my heart. "I love you too, sweet pea. I'm not going away. Ever. You hear me, Mika? I'll never leave you. I promise."

We held onto each other until she relaxed in my embrace, and sleep claimed her.

I tucked my daughter in, doing my best to avoid waking up Justine, my two-year-old, sleeping in the adjacent bed. In one corner of their bedroom, sitting in a rocking chair, I watched my children fast asleep, their steady breathing acting like a bandage around my hemorrhaging heart.

With a slow look around, I took in the pastel-pink walls, the glittery matching unicorn bedspreads, the dolls sitting around a small wooden white table with tiny porcelain teacups in front of them, the net with over twenty stuffed-animals hanging across the ceiling, the fairy lights casting a golden glow wrapped around the princess-inspired headboards.

Would we ever be okay again?

My eyes landed on the family picture framed on the wall we had taken last Christmas.

Our smiles looked so genuine.

I studied Lisa. Was she faking being happy the entire time?

I slouched forward, my face landing in my hands, my shoulders heaving as sobs rocked my body.

The fresh wound ripping my chest in two widened. How did I go from having a picture-perfect family at dinner time to being a single dad mere hours later?

How did I not see my world crumbling? There must have been signs leading to this moment. How did I miss all of them? How could I have been so blind?

That's the thing, Sam. I don't love you. I did. Once.

My life was built on a lie. It was a fucking illusion.

Lisa had faded into the night like she had never existed.

That was when the truth hit me, like a ton of bricks weighing on my fractured heart. I was on my own and had no one to connect to on this journey.

My daughters had become motherless. Not because their mama had died, but because she chose to leave them behind.

Not because she was incapacitated, but because she couldn't love them the way they deserved to be loved.

I cupped my thundering organ with both hands. Every cell in me hurt as the truth of my new reality, *our* new realities, crashed on me and settled in my soul.

My girls' lives would never be the same.

My life would never be the same.

Tonight, I'd lost not only the mother of my children, but also the woman I loved. The one I'd been sharing the last few years of my life with. The one I had traveled the world with, went through great moments of joy and hardships with. The one I had promised forever to. The one who'd said in front of our dearest friends and family I was her only true love.

I perused the bedroom for the final time, my eyes locking on my babies fast asleep.

They had no idea that by the morning, nothing would ever be the same.

That the light of a new day would carry a truckload of sorrow in its wake.

How would I ever be able to do this on my own? Be a single dad.

How would I ever be able to explain the harsh truth to my girls without shattering their hearts in the process?

Closing my eyes, I let darkness descend upon me because right now, I had no clue how to do this by myself and survive the heartbreak at the same time.

2

SAM

Two years later

"I'm not wearing this." Mikaella folded her arms over her chest, giving me some not-so-welcome morning attitude. "Daddy, you have a horrible taste in clothes. I'm too old to wear pink and ribbons." She huffed, and I oscillated between laughing at my life and wanting to kill myself.

Raising two daughters on my own had proven to be a greater challenge than I'd ever expected.

Two years later and we were still dealing with the aftermath of Lisa's departure. The weight of anger I'd nursed for the longest time had receded, but I still found it hard to juggle all the responsibilities on my own.

For a full year, I never had time to heal my own heart, too busy trying to patch every hole in Justine and Mikaella's lives, wishing every night before falling asleep that their mother's abandonment wouldn't screw them up in the long run.

Playing mommy and daddy had been hard, and it had taken its toll on me. Both physically and psychologically.

I never hit the gym anymore and barely ever took an evening off or hung out with grown-ups.

For the first few months after Lisa had walked away, I even forgot to shave or shower most days. I lived in a state of detachment. Going through the motions, staring at the front door, expecting her to walk in, smile, and say it was all a big misunderstanding and that she was back. For good. Something that never occurred.

Then things got a bit better. We found our rhythm. After I had gone through every stage of grief until I fostered no more hatred for the woman I had been married to. Until I was kinda content with my life. And my kids were thriving…for the most part.

These days, I often went to bed in stained clothes or dozed off while watching the credits of yet another princess movie rolling across the screen. But it was a small price to pay after what we had endured.

My kids had become my anchor, my reason to live. The reason I woke up every morning and refused to give up.

Not wanting them to suffer because of their mother's absence, I refused to be away from them—except when they were at school. I had the conviction that if I were around, they wouldn't fear I would leave them and never return.

During weekdays, I did grocery shopping and laundry, cooked and cleaned the house so my weekends were free of chores or any distractions, and I could be just a father, fully involved in my kids' lives. I also squeezed in about thirty hours of work per week at the hardware store belonging to my uncle not far from here.

It kept me sane. A real job. Forcing me to focus on something other than my ruined career and lack of personal life. Faking I'd turned into some sort of social creature. If I believed it strongly enough, perhaps one day it would become true.

After Lisa had left, my parents had come over every weekend to help me out—and to pick up the scattered pieces of me. But since they moved to Florida eighteen months ago, trying to enjoy their new semi-retired lives, I'd been doing everything on my own. Working a full-time job while raising kids all by myself was exhausting.

Rewarding, but tiring.

In the process, I had ditched my own career. At first, it was supposed to be a six-month hiatus until I wrapped my head around being a single dad. But six months became a year that bled into two. Anyway, working at the hardware store provided regular hours and stability that a career in the limelight never would. Not that I needed the money so bad, but the store had become my little sanctuary over the years. Nothing there reminded me of Lisa. Her ghost didn't haunt me with painful memories of a previous life while I was there. A more-than-vital reprieve since every-thing at home brought back recollections of the life we once shared, the four of us together.

Over the last year, I had removed most signs of her from the walls and replaced them with new memories we were creating along the way.

Lisa had left with not only a piece of my heart that night, but also my dreams. She disappeared, taking the husband in me and leaving behind nothing but a father—and some hollow shell of who I used to be. Sure, I loved being a daddy. These little girls were parts of my soul and owned every chunk of my battered heart. But I missed being a man too.

Some days, I missed my wife. I missed the idea of her. Of us. Of what we had been for years—companionship, and maybe love. I wasn't even clear on the specifics yet… I just missed being a family.

How many times did I have to drill into myself that Lisa fucking abandoned us to believe it?

I sighed. Too many to recount.

Until every part of me gave up those slivers of hope and finally came to terms with the fact a year ago. One day, the weight pressing on my shoulders dissolved and set me free.

Returning my focus to my daughter, I lifted my hands in surrender. "Fine. You know what, sweet pea? Wear the black skirt and a black top if it makes you happy. I'm sorry I forgot you were six, and old enough to pick up your own outfit."

Mikaella tipped her hip and frowned, her arms still folded over her chest, before sighing and storming to her room.

My sweet girl had turned sixteen the day she realized her mother wouldn't be coming back.

She had transformed into an opinionated six-year-old teenager who only dressed in dark colors. Only laughed on rare occasions. Enjoyed confrontations. And some days, preferred shade to shiny lights around her.

Lisa had stolen her smile the night she bailed out on us —along with her innocence.

I missed my daughter. I missed her bubbly side. Her *it will be okay Daddy* enthusiasm and her hugs.

Two years later and she still cried herself to sleep sometimes and kept high hopes Lisa would return.

Her therapist told me not to worry, but clouds regularly invaded my little girl's eyes, and darkness swirled around her more often than not. I lacked ideas on how to bring the sunshine back into her days. God knew I'd been trying. Hard. So far, I'd been hitting a wall. Every single time.

On the worst days, her temper could erode every string of patience I still possessed. On the best days, she'd battle with me for everything. From the food on her plate to the color of her nightgown or the music I played in the car.

Overwhelmed, I could barely hold it together myself. How was I supposed to deal with a moody child always at war with anything I said or did? One who challenged every decision I made? She treated me as her enemy most days, and I couldn't help but wonder if she blamed me for Lisa abandoning her.

Justine, now four, was the antipode of her sister. She sparkled and brightened every corner of my dark existence. Nothing seemed to bother her, as if her role in life was to bring peace and calm to those around her.

My baby girl had only scarce memories of her mother, which I was sure helped her neither resent me nor be swallowed by the pain of what used to be. Sure, Lisa's absence wasn't easy on her, but her wounds weren't as visible as her older sister's. She rarely talked about her mama anymore. Justine seemed content to have a daddy wrapped around her little finger. I knew one day she'd ask questions, and I already dreaded the moment we'd have a heart-to-heart that might unearth the scars she had no idea were there, carefully tucked away for now.

Just thinking about all this sent my heart into a frenzied mess.

"Come on, girls, we must go. You don't wanna be late for school."

Justine traipsed my way, her contagious grin lighting up the few slices of my heart still alive.

I lifted her into my arms and kissed the tip of her nose. "Baby, you look pretty today," I said as I carried her to my white SUV.

Her smile widened. Her blonde pigtails—the ones I

had to learn to make—bounced at her sides as she made some sort of dance move with her head.

"Mika is mad at you, Daddy." I leaned forward, studying her to learn more. "She said it's stupid you don't want her to dye her hair black."

I pinched my lips together to avoid smiling. This was a debate Mikaella and I had been having for three weeks now. "I know, Justine. But little girls aren't allowed to dye their hair. It's a grown-up thing. We'll talk about it when Mika is much, much older."

"Like an *adulst*?"

"Adult, baby. But yes. Don't worry, she'll get over it."

Justine shrugged. "She also says she'll *slave* her head to prove her point." She snickered, and I rolled my eyes. Great. Damn perfect. My six-year-old teen now wanted a bald head.

I swore I'd aged twenty years in the last two.

"It's shave. Not slave. Shave her head. And no, Mika won't do anything to her hair."

I buckled my youngest daughter in her car seat just in time to witness Mikaella walking toward us, now dressed in all-black, her hair tied into a ponytail, and wait—? What the hell had she put on her eyes? Makeup? No, there was none in the house. She stopped inches away from me, her chin tipped up, daring me to object, a frown darkening her visage. Resting her fists on her waist, she tapped her foot with growing impatience. "What?"

For a second, I closed my eyes and inhaled, trying to calm the raging storm building inside me.

Swallowing my imminent burst of anger, I squatted in front of my daughter, doing my best to keep calm.

I reached for her hands, but she jerked them away, so I rested my palms on my knees instead. "Honey, tell me. What did you do to your eyelids?"

Mikaella muttered something I didn't quite catch and cocked her head to the side with a pout.

"Sweet pea, I need to know what you used to draw those black lines. It looks…huh…interesting. I'm not mad, okay?" *No, I'm fucking dumbfounded. And tired. And I have no clue what I'm doing.* "You should never use whatever you used on your face without checking with me first. It could be harmful."

I inched closer and grabbed her upper arms. She flinched under my touch but didn't step back. Another fragment of my heart crashed and burned. My baby was hurting.

"Mika, tell me. Is it a marker? Paint? Or something else?"

She bit her lower lip, and her eyes glistened, but she remained silent.

"Look at me, sweet pea. I'm not angry. I'm concerned. Because I love you."

Could she give me a break? Just one morning of reprieve?

After a long minute, she relaxed and met my gaze before dropping her eyes to the ground. "It-it's the marker you use to label boxes. I…I saw a girl doing it in a video the other day at Stella's. I just wanted…I just wanted to try. I know I'm not allowed to wear makeup, but Stella's mama lets her borrow hers. I-I don't have anyone to try it with—" Her lip quivered, and her eyes filled with fat tears.

My chest cracked in two. "Oh, Mika. It's okay, sweet pea. I'm here. I'm so sorry about your mama. I wish she were here too. I know it's been hard on you, but I *am* not going anywhere. You can talk to me. Always. Maybe we could buy some makeup and try it together. You could paint my face, and we'd be rock stars. Or maybe we could ask Stella's mama to show you how to apply it. No, you can't wear makeup every day, but it doesn't mean we can't put it on for fun or on special days. What do you think?"

Her eyes flared, and a hint of a smile graced her lips. "You sure?"

I nodded.

"I…I'd like that."

I blanketed my daughter in my arms, the visceral need to protect and infuse her with infinite love running deep. "I love you, sweet pea. Now let's try to remove this marker from your eyelids, okay?"

She nodded. "I love you too, Daddy." Her little arms closed around my neck, and for a moment, I felt like we were back to being the father-daughter duo we used to be. Before the earthquake that had shattered our lives. Before the heartbreaks. Before everything had gone to shit that night.

I rose to my feet and held out my hand for her to take. "Come on, Justine. Let's get you out of your seat. We're on a mission to help your sister."

With both my girls at my sides, we made our way inside, not a care in the world if they'd miss school today or that I would have to call in sick.

We needed this. To connect. The three of us.

Our makeup removal session didn't go as well as planned, and the marker on Mikaella's eyelids was still apparent, even after a few attempts to remove it with a warm cloth and some soap.

We all changed back into pajamas, built a castle with blankets in the den, and spent the day binge-watching TV and eating nothing but pizza and ice cream, not caring about food groups and nap time.

I loved our home. Maple hardwood floors, off-white walls, nine-foot-tall ceilings, black trims and doors. It was a

Scandinavian-inspired farmhouse. A mix of light and dark decor accents, sleek lines, and soft-colored wood.

The exterior, made of steel-blue clapboard siding, gave the place a rustic and cozy charm. While the front and two carriage-house garage doors were made of natural wood and had been handcrafted by a local artisan.

These days, the den had become our favorite room. The place where the girls could let their imaginations run wild. An arts and crafts station was set in one corner next to a tan leather couch buried under fluffy colorful blankets and half a dozen pillows. An oversized rectangular black rug occupied most of the flooring area, and a comfy armchair facing the stone fireplace completed the decor.

We had redecorated the space last year—erasing all traces of Lisa and making the room fully ours—and I felt at peace here. When we spent time here, the ghosts of the past had no hold over us.

Around seven, both girls were fast asleep in our castle, passed out from a junk food coma.

My phone went off, and I tiptoed out of the room to avoid waking them up.

For the first time in months, my daughters and I had fun together—for more than just a few hours. The three of us, without any drama or interruption. We laughed. We cried when the dog in the movie ran away from home. We sang along with the princess when she swept the floor with her animal friends. We cuddled on the couch.

Yeah, it was a great day. A perfect day.

The face of Riley Burns, country music manager extra-ordinaire and mogul in his own right, flashed on my phone screen.

"Hey, Stevens. How is it going? Still holding the fort by yourself?"

"Hey, man. It's been a while. Yeah. Trying hard at

least. Not sure if the fort is sturdy, though. Some days, I think it could fall apart with just one blow our way. Anyway, it's not like I have a choice. What's going on? You miss me already? How was the tour?" I said, trying to put some spirit into my words.

The truth was that I missed him even more than Riley could miss me. We'd been friends for years, both of us running in the same circles.

When everyone had deserted me because I preferred loneliness to their look of pity, he'd stayed by my side. Even though, for a while, I tried to keep him at arm's length like everyone else, he just persevered. Now I was grateful that he did.

After the first year, when I showed no sign of going back onstage or booking studio time for the album I was set to record, my label had dropped me. The awards I'd won, the double-platinum albums I'd sold, the stadiums I'd filled didn't seem to matter to them anymore.

At first, I didn't care. My days were full, and I couldn't envision embarking on a world tour ever again or living my life the same way I had in the past.

Now, every day, I missed it a little more. The crowd. The adrenaline of singing in front of tens of thousands of fans. Writing songs. Playing music. It all seemed like they belonged to a previous life. To another version of me that I'd lost touch with.

My country music career didn't work with my full-time daddy lifestyle, and I had chosen my daughters over my own dreams. No regrets.

Dwelling on the past would do me no good. Anyway, I was happy—or at least getting there.

Far down in my chest, a spark refused to die. Maybe one day I'd go back there again. Once the girls were old enough. A stubborn part of me refused to give up hope in the future.

"I'm like ten minutes away from your place. Can I come over?"

My eyes traveled all over the space around me. Stuffed animals, toys, princess costumes, empty pizza boxes. It looked like someone had thrown a rager here and had forgotten to clean up after themselves. Well, we sorta did to be honest.

"I…hmm…" Why not? I missed the company. Having a friend over would get me out of my head for a couple of hours. It was about time I started socializing with more grown-ups again. My mental health begged for this too. We were both struggling. With my phone squeezed between my ear and shoulder, I put away the remnants of our day. "Sure. Can I ask you something, though?"

"Anything."

"Can you bring beer over? I have none here, and I'm dying for a cold brew tonight."

"Don't say another word. I have you covered. I'll see you in a bit." He exhaled a huge breath as if he'd been waiting anxiously for my answer. "Stevens, I'm glad we're doing this. Spending time together."

"Me too."

The last time we saw each other was about five months ago. Riley had been busy with Aisha Jones's tour, his latest protégée, and gone to Europe and Asia on and off, following her around for months, making sure everything ran smoothly. He only came to town for days at a time to deal with stuff at the office and be with his ladylove. With our busy schedules, we never found time to meet.

We hung up, and I rushed to my room to change into a pair of dark jeans and a simple black T-shirt. In the mirror of the en-suite bathroom, I combed my dark hair with my fingers and ran a hand over my stubble. In the last two years, I had slackened on my shaving routine. Lisa loved me clean-shaven. In a way, wearing a scruffy jaw was my way of enjoying the freedom to do things my way, without compromise. A big "fuck you" to her preferences about my look. A reality it took me a while to realize. I attempted to tame my mane one last time and gave up. This would have to do. Not that I had to impress my friend, but greeting him in pajama pants was a big no-no. Even for me. At least, now I looked decent.

Downstairs, I filled the dishwasher and carried the girls to their bedroom, praying they would stay asleep for the rest of the night.

The doorbell rang as I closed their door after turning a night-light on.

I couldn't remember the last time I had friends over. We usually met at barbecues or the park whenever they were in town.

Nowadays, most of my guests were under ten and either lived down the street or came from Mikaella's class or Justine's dance lessons.

———

Riley handed me a bottle of beer once we sat in loungers on the back deck. The night was warm, the sky painted in pink and orange stripes. Summer was a month away, and already I could feel it in the warm breeze sweeping across our faces and the moisture thickening the air.

I sighed as I enjoyed the calm and peace surrounding me.

From the corner of my eye, I scanned the yard. We had no back neighbors, only acres of woods the kids loved to explore. Last year, with a little help from my father, I had built a castle treehouse for them to play in, that we had painted a vibrant hue of bubble-gum pink. It was the girls' corner in this world that only belonged to them, where they could be children and forget about everything else for a moment as they transformed into princesses.

Riley and I clinked our bottles, and I enjoyed the coldness of the brew as it slid down my throat. It'd been so long since the last time I had a drink—an adult drink.

"So, Ry? Are you going to tell me what brings you here? It's been months since you parked your ass in one of those chairs," I said with an arched brow.

"The tour had been consuming but overall amazing, but I'm glad to be home. Back at the office. I'll miss the adventure in no time, but for now, it's good to sleep in my own bed and see my woman every day." He shook his head, a tiny smile tugging at the corner of his lips. "Let's just say I'm not sure you're ready to hear what I have to tell you."

"Try me. Hurry before I start talking about dolls or playdates. Man, if only you had kids. We could schedule daddy-and-me afternoons together. Learn new ways to braid hair or apply French manicures. Such a shame."

Riley laughed, and I joined in.

More steel coils relaxed around my heart.

I felt better today than I'd felt in a long time. As if the ripples of everything that happened in the last two years were wearing off, and for once, I could just enjoy the ride without worrying about everything else. Or the future.

My friend set his bottle down on the wooden table between us and turned around to face me, his elbows propped on his knees and his hands joined together. "Listen, man. I know Lisa walking away fractured your world. And I know how hard it's been. I've witnessed the change in you from day one. I also know being a father is your top priority and the most important job you'll ever have…but there's more to life than playing daddy twenty-four-seven, all year-round. You must thrive in life. And I know you're miserable, Sam. I—"

"She fucking quit on us. Without a warning. What was I supposed to do? Tour the world one stadium at a time with toddlers as if nothing happened? With no one to watch over them or tuck them in bed? Fuck their lives by taking them to a different hotel every night, by removing them from their home, the only stability they had left?"

"Tell me. Did becoming a boring version of yourself really solve all your problems?"

"Whatever you wanna think. I'm happy just being a regular father to my girls, Ry. They never asked for their dad to be chased by groupies or splashed across every gossip magazine because he got caught in fame when all he ever wanted was to get on a stage and play music for a living. Why can't you see that? You were the kid with the famous-as-hell dad growing up. You told me multiple times it wasn't easy when he left on tour, whether you and your mother followed him around or not. If there's one person who should get it, it's you."

Riley raised his hands. "Let me finish. I know it wasn't what you had planned. Those little girls will never be able to accuse you of not taking over when their mama walked out on them. But wouldn't you all be happier if you were happy too?"

I shrugged. "I'm not unhappy."

"But are you happy?"

"Yes. No. That's not the point. How should I know? I've forgotten what my life before this"—I motioned to my house with a wave of my hand—"felt like. Now I'm exhausted all the time. And Mika is giving me a hard time. She struggles. It's bad, man. It breaks my heart. I have no clue how to help her. This is so fucked-up." I dragged a hand over my face, trying to control the emotions swirling inside me, overshadowing the progress I'd made. "I can't get through to her. Every time we take two steps forward, she retreats into herself, and we end up back four steps."

"She'll get better. Allow her more time. Kids are resilient."

"I guess."

The old me, the guy from two years ago, would have thrown a fit, broken in tears, kicked something, or screamed at the world that all of this was unfair. For a long time, I had resented Lisa for what she'd done, holding her responsible for everything that didn't go my way.

But last year, after a particularly bad day, I'd chosen to forgive her. I couldn't keep living in a permanent state of anger. It exhausted me and wasn't good for me or the girls. We deserved to be set free.

"What do you have in mind? You wouldn't be here if you didn't have something planned."

Riley let out a heartfelt chuckle. "Am I that obvious?"

I shrugged. "That woman of yours is turning you into a softie. It suits you. You've lost some of your legendary grit. Your *nothing will stop me* drive. But you look happier. Calmer."

"I won't tell Devon you said that because I'll never hear the end of it." He chugged the rest of his beer and fished another one out of the crate. "Listen to me, Stevens. It's time for you to get back out there. I have waited long enough and bided my time. By the way, I'm not taking no for an answer. It will do you good. A change of air. To live like a man again. It'll be better than any therapy. Even if it's just for a couple of months."

My arm froze halfway between my chest and my

mouth, the bottle hanging from my fingers. I blinked. One. Twice. Three times.

"You can't be serious. I don't even have a label anymore. I'm the guy who refused big money to take care of two motherless children. I can't leave my kids, Ry. You know I can't. They count on me. I'm all they have left." I slouched in my seat, my shoulders slumping forward. "We already had this discussion…a few months back. Before you left. My answer is still no."

"Who said you'd have to leave them? This time, it's different. Hear me out. I wouldn't be here if I hadn't hatched some plan for your big comeback. And by the way, fuck your old label. Like I told you the last time, I'll be the one in charge. I'll take care of everything. You won't have to worry about a single thing. The girls will be in good hands. I swear." A smile spread across Riley's face. "My cousin owns a nanny agency. She interviewed this woman who also has a teaching degree. I talked to her over the phone. She could go on tour with you and take care of the girls whenever you're not available, teaching them at the same time. This woman, Madison, comes with an impressive number of references. Last year, she was on a yacht, crossing the Atlantic Ocean, with a family of four kids. She even did some voluntary work a summer in Africa, teaching kids when she was eighteen. I'm supposed to meet up with her next week. This could be a great opportunity. This woman is a rare gem. If we don't get her on board, someone else will snatch her up, and it could take months to find another candidate as qualified."

"Fuck. You thought of everything. It even sounds good when you say it out loud… Almost perfect. It can't work, though. It's not that I don't trust you, but the girls need a stable environment." I sipped my beer, thinking about how to explain the situation to him. How to refuse his generous and enticing offer. "It'd be selfish of me to ask them to change their newfound daily routine because their daddy's gotta fulfill his dreams. I'm sorry, Ry. For a moment, you got me thinking it'd be possible. I'm not saying never, but right now, the time isn't right."

My friend gave me a lopsided smile. "Told you, I'm not taking no for an answer. Not yet at least. I want you to think about this. For real. I'll meet with this Madison girl, and if she's as great as she sounds, we can have a talk with her. Grill her. Both of us. Together. Then, and only then, you'll give me your final answer."

I snickered. "You're wasting your time, but I love how persistent you are. Do your homework first and we'll see. But you know what? Thanks for making me believe for a moment I wasn't dead inside. For making me see I still have it in me. The fire to do what I love. I haven't dreamed in a very long time, and I like how it makes me feel."

I clinked my bottle with his.

We sat there, side by side, enjoying the sunset in silence. Every word my friend had said twirled around in my head. Sending frenzied *what-if* jitters to my heart. If only it could be that easy. If only I could go back out there and have the certitude it wouldn't affect my children, then I'd do it without hesitation.

If only.

3

SAM

"**I** want the blue glass. Not the red one. The blue. I want the *bluuue*," Justine yelled at the top of her lungs. "Gimme the blue, Mika. You had it *yesthursday*. Now it's *my* turn. I want the blue glass. Blue. Blue. Blue."

"Justine, you had it twice last week. Don't be a baby. Now it's my turn to have it twice. Stop whining. Daddy, tell her to shut up."

My eyes rounded.

Did I hear her right?

"Mika, when did you learn to use those words? It's not fine. You can't talk to your sister like this," I barked. "Or anyone else for that matter. I don't want you to use grown-up words." I scratched the side of my face and dialed down my sudden burst of anger. "Use nice words. *Please, I'm sorry, thank you*…huh… whatever."

"Whatever."

I blinked again. My insides were tied in a series of knots. If Mikaella had this much attitude now, how on

Earth would I survive her teenage years? She'd be the end of me.

"Mika, language. Talking like that isn't allowed in *this* house. Now say you're sorry to your sister."

"Sorry," she mumbled so low I barely heard her myself.

"Louder. You can do better than that."

"No. I already said it once. I'm not saying it again."

"Mika," I warned, my tone harsher this time.

"Okay. Fine. Sorry, Justine." My eldest daughter turned her head my way. "Happy, now?"

I fisted my hands at my sides, doing my best to disintegrate the fresh wave of wrath bubbling inside me. *Don't say anything,* I told myself, repeating the words Mikaella's therapist advised me to. *She's just trying to get a reaction out of you. Ignore her attitude.* Yeah, well, I'd like to see the therapist dealing with her this morning. And every other morning.

I breathed in and finished packing their lunch when my eyes landed on the empty beer bottles Riley and I had drunk last night. Our conversation replayed in my head. If only I could make this work. If only it could be that easy.

I was tired of being a household fixture.

My eyes traveled around our home. I used to adore this place. Our little family nest…

We'd built it when Lisa found out she was pregnant with Mikaella.

Over the years, I had framed some of the girls' artworks on the walls, next to the staircase, bringing a touch of color to the room. This morning, though, the entire house seemed dull. Faded. Boring and sad.

Same as me.

I'd become all those things too.

I used to be fun. Happy. Joking around. Having barbecues with friends every other weekend. Having date nights with my ex-wife once a week to keep the flame burning strong, as we liked to call our little alone time. Yeah, that one failed. Miserably.

I craved a change. Perhaps selling the house would do it for me. But the girls weren't ready for something so drastic. They had lost too much already. They needed their safe haven.

Could a few months on the road do us some good, though?

Why was I letting Riley's words take a front seat in my mind? Damn it. He'd planted a seed, and now it was begging to grow into a tree. A cherry blossom. Tall, fierce, and beautiful. Fucking, Ry.

My heart throbbed in my chest.

With my back resting against the kitchen counter, I sucked in a breath.

"Girls, can we talk?" I asked, my tone so serious they both stopped bickering over that stupid blue glass. The one about to live its final days in a trash can. "Remember when I told you daddy used to sing songs for a living?" They both nodded, their fight long forgotten. "It's just an idea, but would you like to someday…live on a big bus and travel around the country with me? It would be like going camping, but for longer periods of time."

My emotions clogged my throat. I couldn't breathe. Why was I opening that door?

My head spun, and I gripped the edge of the counter to keep my balance.

"I like *clamping*," Justine exclaimed, jumping to her feet and squeezing her doll against her heart. "Can I sleep in a tent?"

The tension in me lessened—a tad.

My youngest daughter neared me, and I lifted her in my arms, relishing the scent of strawberry shampoo lingering in her hair. It acted like a calming balm.

"Justine, it's camping, not *clamping*. You two would have a bedroom. Maybe a bunk room to share."

"With pink walls? And a giant unicorn?"

I shrugged. "Why not? We could do whatever we want. It would be like a big vacation. Except that, some nights, Daddy would have to work."

"Work?"

"Yeah, baby, work. Like parents usually do. You know when I spend my days at the hardware store Uncle Jim owns?"

They both nodded.

"It would be like that, but a different kind of work."

"But who's gonna kiss me goodnight? Or hold me when I have *nightlemares*? Or tuck me in? Mika and I are going to be alone when you go to work."

I fastened my grip around her tiny body. "Nightmares, baby. Not *nightlemares*." A smile stretched my lips. "No one would be alone, baby. You would have a nanny. Someone super nice to take care of you and tuck you in the nights I wouldn't be available."

Mikaella walked toward me and raised her arms, asking me silently to pick her up too. With both my daughters nestled against my chest, I answered all their questions.

"When?" Mikaella asked. "Because no way am I missing school."

"You'd be doing schoolwork during the day. The nice lady would teach you everything you have to know. Don't worry about it."

"What's the name of the lady?" Justine asked.

"I don't know yet."

"Where is she going to live?" Mikaella inquired.

"Again, I don't know. We'll have to figure this one out. I'm sure we can find a solution we all agree on."

"Will the lady be our new mama?" Justine asked with big expectant eyes. "I want a new mama."

A lump, hard as a rock, settled in my throat. I swallowed around it and shook my head.

"No, baby. The lady would only take care of you. Make sure you're safe and sound. And play with you when I'm onstage."

"But who will take care of you, Daddy?" Justine asked, her blue eyes drawing me in, in a way only she could.

"Know what? I'm sure I can take care of myself. Anyway, I have you girls. I'm the luckiest man on Earth because I'm surrounded by so much love. Don't worry about me, okay?"

They both bobbed their heads, and Justine kissed my cheek.

My grin widened.

"What do you think, girls?" I knew I shouldn't put them in the middle of this, but now that I'd realized it could be a possibility, the idea of going back on the road started to grow on me. And no way would I ever consider Riley's offer if the girls weren't on board—one hundred percent.

"I wanna go *clamping* with you, Daddy." Justine squirmed until I lowered her to her feet. "Now can I go play?"

"Sure, baby." Once she exited the kitchen, I turned to face my eldest daughter. "What do you think, sweet pea?"

She shrugged and avoided my eyes. "I don't know. Will Mama be able to find us if she comes back and we're gone?"

My heart plummeted down, pooling at my feet. Mikaella, always worrying about Lisa and her antics. My ex-wife didn't deserve her concern. I sat my daughter on the counter and framed her face with both hands. I inhaled through my mouth to keep my emotions on a leash.

"Honey, I'm not sure Mama will be back before long. She's not keeping me updated very often." The truth was, she never did—but Mikaella didn't need to know that I hadn't spoken to Lisa since the day she left, and that the only exchange we'd had since was through our lawyers, when she voluntarily gave up all her parental rights. No, my babies didn't have to learn the ugly truth of our divorce, or their motherless status. "If she ever visits, I'm sure she'll give us a call beforehand."

"Will you still play with us? Or will you be too busy working?"

"Sweet pea, you'll always be my priority. You and Justine are what matters the most in my life. If you girls don't wanna go, then we won't. It was just something I was wondering about. That's all. Anyway, if we do this, it wouldn't be so soon. I would have to get an album out first."

Mikaella jumped off the counter. "It could be fun. Can I tell Stella?"

"Not right now. Let's think about this for a little longer before we give it a go, okay?"

"Okay." She looped her arms around me and squeezed me tight. "I love you, Daddy."

I returned her hug, kissing the top of her head. "I love you too, sweet pea."

And just like that, for a moment, my little girl tossed her rebellious mask aside and became a child again.

Hot tears welled up in my eyes, and I blinked them away.

For the first time in so long, I could envision a future doing what I loved and being a daddy, all at the same time. A dormant energy woke up inside me and shook my foundations. Excitement and apprehension tangled inside me. How hard would it be to juggle both?

————

With one arm folded under my head, I lay on my back and stared at the dark ceiling of my bedroom. With a wooden king-sized bed, a matching dresser and two nightstands, and an armchair in the corner by the window, my bedroom was decorated simply. Like the rest of the house, it missed a little spark these days. It felt blah. Perhaps I should've accepted my mother's offer to update it last fall. To inject it with a touch of vibrant colors and spice up the decor. I'd been up since five this morning, unable to fall back asleep. My brain was overexcited with all the possibilities Riley's visit had planted inside my head. It'd been a week since he came over, and I'd turned restless since, unable to stay still, my mind hyperactive, and my heart galloping.

Every day, the girls asked me at least once if we would go camping next fall. I still had no answer to give them. I had made countless pros and cons lists in the last few days, the recycling bin in my music studio slash office that I barely used nowadays, overflowing with crumpled pieces of paper.

It used to be one of my favorite rooms in the house. With a wooden ceiling, a dark carpeted floor, and steel-blue walls, it had an industrial yet country chic vibe. Enlarged album covers and framed photos of concerts I had given in the past lined the walls on one side. A cream leather sofa, a desk, and a wooden arched floor lamp offering a soft glow tied the decor together. A glass partition divided the small recording booth, its walls lined with sound-absorbing panels. In the center stood a microphone, a headset, and a stool—waiting to see if I'd ever be ready to record a song again.

Even if I tried, I couldn't remember the last time they had been of any use.

In an attempt to busy myself in the last couple of days, I had even updated the decor. Unlike my bedroom, my music studio inspired the creative side of me. New picture frames, drawings on the walls, and a plant I hadn't killed so far. The additions had transformed a stagnant office into a living space—where I prayed I could get inspired.

The most amazing thing to come out of this new possibility was that I had started writing again. I wrote about love. About loss. New beginnings. And hope. I wrote about my babies. About my life. And my broken heart.

The words flew on the paper so easily that I wondered why I hadn't written a single song in the last two years. No therapy could equal the profound sense of peace that swirled inside me as the lyrics spilled over the pages. My guitar, thick with dust, seemed almost happy to see me again. Long-lost friends reuniting after circumstances tore us apart. The instrument had never failed or wronged me. It had always been my most loyal companion.

Every night, I'd sing the girls the songs I wrote during the day, and they would learn some of the lyrics to sing along with me.

Music brought joy back into our lives.

Mikaella hadn't argued about dyeing her hair black or shaving her head in five days.

Justine hadn't tiptoed to my room or woken up screaming in three nights, which was unusual. She had been having nightmares almost every day for the last two years and bed wetting episodes for the first ten months following Lisa's departure.

Could Riley be right? Could his crazy idea be the salvation we'd all waiting for to start living again?

Even the air in our house seemed lighter these days. Filled with excitement and fervor. With sparks and laughter.

As if Lisa's ghost had finally left us. For good.

Everything looked better and brighter now, optimistic and possible.

Jitters rolled in my stomach, and I rose to my feet to get dressed. Every now and then, I eyed my phone as if it could catch fire any second. Riley had called yesterday before he went to meet up with that Madison woman. He'd even asked Devon, the love of his life, to join him so she could use her woman's instincts, as he had said. Since then, no news. Nothing. Radio silence. My patience ran thin nowadays, and I was desperate to know how their meeting went. What to expect.

Half of me hoped Madison was the gem Riley had described. That she had agreed to this scheme of his.

The other half wanted her to be found crazy and unfit to care for my children, forcing me to put this silly idea of going back on tour to rest.

With a coffee mug in my hand, I paced the living room, relishing the scorching heat burning the walls of my throat. The girls were still asleep. I fought the desire to wake them up so my brain could keep busy instead of anticipating and making up scenarios.

Unable to wait any longer and lacking distractions, I shot a message to the man who could become my manager and change my journey.

ME

Hey, it's me. How did it go last night? Keep me updated.

He took an eternity—well, five minutes—to reply, and I spent the whole time pacing the kitchen, rubbing my nape raw.

RILEY

Good. Why?

I squeezed the device in my hand. How much fun was he having, messing with me like this?

RILEY

How's your blood pressure, Stevens?

I typed. And erased. And typed again. Only to delete it.

I groaned and bit my tongue to avoid cursing out loud.

RILEY

You like the idea?

Was he kidding right now? Was he playing with my patience on purpose?

I blew out a puff of air. My blood fired in my veins.

My fingers itched to ask about the meeting, but I wouldn't play his childish game. If I did, Riley would see that I was hooked on the idea. Right now, I wasn't ready to let him know just how much it had me worked up.

Proud of myself for resisting the temptation to question my friend, I put my phone away and went to wake up my daughters, ready to jumpstart our day and feel useful. And escape the madness of Riley dodging the silent questions calcifying in my bones.

On our way to school, I played the song I'd written last night on my phone, and the girls and I practiced the chorus together until they both nailed it. I'd titled it "Summer Nights," and it was about our lives, the three of us, and the freedom we were aiming for. The girls applauded, and peace rooted under my skin, spreading through me. Once again, my friend's idea didn't appear so insane in the morning light.

On my way back, I pulled into my driveway and noticed him leaning against his red sports car, arms folded over his chest, a smug grin splitting his face.

"What are you doing here?" I asked as I neared him, scowling to mask my reaction to the devilish tilt of his lips.

Riley ran a hand through his dark hair and flashed me another smile, a glint in his eye.

Jerk.

He was well aware I loved the idea of going on tour. He had me all tangled up inside, playing with me and trying to get me to admit it out loud. Still, it seemed too good to be true.

"Stevens, you think I don't know you?" he asked with a quirked brow. "If you think I'm obvious, then you haven't looked at yourself in the mirror in a long time. I saw it in your eyes the other night. You like the idea of going back out there. No. Scratch that. You love it. You crave it. Since I came over, you haven't been the same man. I hear it in your voice each time we talk on the phone. And right now, I can tell you're dying to know how it went with Madison so we can talk real business, you and I. Don't even try to deny it. You know I'm right."

I offered him a pointed look, but my lips curled up, unable to hide the excitement pouring out of me any longer. Yeah, I loved the idea. Who could blame me?

With a sigh, I waved a hand between us. "Okay. Fine. You got me. I wanna know. Spill it already. Doesn't mean I'm on board, though." I paused. "Can't you see I'm too old to extract the information out of you?"

"We're the same age. Find a better excuse," he bantered, the smirk on his face definitely not a good look.

Nah. In that instant, it drove me nuts.

"Stop smiling like that and just get to the point. You know what? Forget it. I've changed my mind. Don't tell me. Your loss." I was heading for the house when he spoke again, forcing me to turn around.

"How many songs have you written in the last week?" His grin stretched wider—as if it were possible. Fucker.

"Ok, fine. Seven. I've written seven songs. Are you happy now? You can hide your stupid smile now. I've seen enough of it, and it's"—I fished my phone out of my back pocket—"not even nine o'clock. You wanna come in, or do you want to have this conversation on my front lawn?"

"I'm not staying. Just came here to see your face." He shrugged, and for a moment, I felt like punching that smug look off his face. "Tonight, I'm picking you up at six. We're meeting with Madison in my cousin's office."

"But I—"

He waggled a finger. "Before you find a million excuses to refuse, Devon will watch over the girls while we're gone. She loves your children and can't wait to spend time with them. Do you mind if she"—he lifted a finger—"just a sec." He unlocked his phone and read something. "Oh, yeah. Do you mind if she paints their nails and bakes chocolate chip cookies with them? She wanted me to ask you that."

I chuckled.

Riley was so deep into his relationship with the woman who stole his heart the first time they met. It took him over a year to meet her again, but since that day, they hadn't left each other's side, except when he went on Aisha's tour. Even I, with my heart filled with grudges, had to admit they made a perfect pair. They complemented each other in every possible way.

"Once again, you hatched a plan behind my back. Should I be afraid?"

"You can thank me later. Be ready. We'll be here at five. I wanna spend time with the girls too before the big meeting. Then you and I we'll have dinner afterward. Carter is in town."

"Fine, I'll be there, man." I gave a shake of my head. "Carter Hills is visiting? I haven't seen him in a long while. Count me in. For what it's worth, thanks for getting me out of my cave. And tell Devon I'll owe her one."

"I will. See you later, Stevens."

Riley hauled himself behind his wheel and drove away as I stood in my driveway, speechless, my heart doing a million weird flips in my chest and my head dizzy from all the crazy ideas swimming in it.

4

SAM

I rummaged through my closet. What should I wear to this meeting? A suit seemed too formal, but a pair of jeans and a cotton T-shirt seemed a bit too casual. Nowadays, I mostly owned a daddy's wardrobe. Comfy and versatile options: jeans, T-shirts, and hoodies.

After changing for the third time, I put on dark jeans and a cobalt shirt and pushed my hair, the same shade as Mikaella's, away from my forehead. That would do.

Justine jumped on my bed—dressed in a long, glittery purple skirt with a faux-fur yellow sweater, and a neon-pink boa draped around her neck—and I caught her mid-flight.

"Come here, you," I said, nuzzling her neck and sniffing her like a puppy would do. My youngest daughter giggled while I carried her downstairs. "Uncle Riley will be here soon, baby. Devon will watch over you and your sister tonight."

Justine flashed me an adorable grin, highlighting the dimples on each side of her mouth. The doorbell rang at the same moment. *"Debon, Debon, Debon,"* she chanted as she hurried to let our guests in.

"Devon, baby. Her name is Devon."

"*Debon*," I heard my baby girl repeat as she opened the door.

My shoulders slouched and I sighed. Devon would have the entire night to teach Justine how to pronounce her name correctly.

"Hey, guys. Come on in," I greeted them, Mikaella in tow, curious about the commotion. I grabbed the bags from Devon's arms. "What's all this?"

"Ammunition," she said, flipping her blonde curls over her shoulder. "I brought everything required for a perfect girls' night. Don't worry, we won't miss you guys. The girls and I will have so much fun." She lifted Justine in her arms before leaning forward to drop a kiss on Mikaella's cheek.

My eldest daughter's eyes filled with sparks. "Did you bring makeup?" she asked, glancing at me sideways, as some silent approval traveled between us.

"No, but I brought something better. Nail polish. I have at least ten different shades we can try on. I'll do your nails, and you'll do mine. Then we'll vote on who has the coolest mani-pedi."

"Yay," Mikaella said, her face lighting up with a smile.

Nothing was more amazing than seeing my girls beam.

"Nobody is glad to see me? I thought I'd get a full red-carpet greeting, trumpets and all," Riley teased with a pout, stepping beside his woman in the doorway.

Justine chuckled, and Mikaella rolled her eyes dramatically.

"You're silly," my baby said, holding out her arms so he could pick her up from Devon's arms.

"You didn't bring girly stuff. Sorry," Mikaella told him as she started running, and Riley chased after her.

My gaze followed them until they turned the corner

and disappeared into the living room, their laughter making its way to my heart.

Devon grabbed my elbow. We hadn't seen each other in months—the last time being Justine's birthday—but I still could read the worry in her eyes. "How is it going? For real, okay? Not the bullshit you serve Riley every time he calls you." Oh yes, her woman's instincts as her man called it.

I inhaled a shaky breath and dropped the bags at my feet on the entryway floor after kicking the front door shut, resting my shoulder against the wall. I stuffed my hands into my pockets—a habit I'd picked up after Lisa left, whenever I felt uncomfortable.

"Last week has been good. Really. Before that, it was on and off."

"Mika still giving you a hard time?" Compassion filled Devon's gray-blue irises. She'd been through a lot herself. If someone could understand family trauma, it was her. She went through hell for years before Riley appeared in her life.

"Most days, she's hurting, Dev. She misses her…or the memory of her… She puts up a strong front, but behind all this crappy attitude, I know her heart is in pieces. She still believes Lisa will come back someday and play mommy again as if nothing happened. It crushes me." I blinked, doing my best to calm the emotions simmering inside me. "I don't wanna feed her beliefs that she'll come back, but at the same time, I don't want to smother her hope even more by telling her she will never come back, you know?"

"It's an impossible situation. Imagine how confusing it must be for her." She gave my arm a reassuring squeeze. "We're here, Sam. Whenever you need us. Or when you need a break. Riley is a big fan of yours, and all he wants is to help you out. The only way he knows how. I think his grand idea isn't as crazy as it sounds. The change of scenery could do you guys some good. All three of you. Like a new adventure. Something to put the past behind for good. The beginning of a new chapter. A new life."

I hung my head low. "Maybe."

"By the way, Madison is great. The girls will love her. I have no doubt. She's sweet and smart. She'll fit right in with you guys. I can already tell."

I breathed out. "Perhaps you're right. The girls are excited about it. We'll see."

"Trust me. I'm around if the girls need a woman's presence in their lives. Don't be afraid to ask. It's always been my pleasure to be there for you three."

———

"You ready?"

I swallowed the bitter taste sitting in my throat, firmed my back, and nodded. "Yep. Let's do this." I blew out a breath. "I can't believe you convinced me to go through with it."

Riley clapped my shoulder. "You'll see, man. Madison knows her shit. You'll want her on board, I promise. It's a match made in heaven. All the puzzle pieces are now coming together. Trust me."

I rubbed my jaw, trying to dissipate the tenseness in my chest. Coils of steel crushed my organs in tight grips.

"You're lucky I do. I wouldn't do this for anyone else, man. I can't believe we're actually going through with it."

"I know. And I'm thankful you put your trust in me. It means a lot. Have faith. It's a good call to make. You'll see. C'mon, follow me," Riley said as he opened the door of his cousin's nanny agency to let me in.

I sucked in some much-needed air. I could do this. He was right. This could work. This could be the beginning of something new as Devon had said.

A petite woman in her early forties greeted us. "You must be Mr. Stevens. I'm Janice," she said, offering me her hand to shake. "Riley told me a lot about you. I'm glad you agreed to meet with us."

"It's nice to meet you too. Thanks for having us."

Through a hallway painted in vibrant shades of blue and green and a purple carpet, we followed Janice to her office. Dozens of pictures of smiling kids were framed along the ten-foot-high walls.

The whole place looked cheerful and inviting for families.

I clenched and unclenched my fists at my sides. The room felt ten degrees warmer since I'd come in. Sweat beaded on my nape. "You have a lovely office." Could Riley and Janice sense how nervous I was? I wiped my clammy hands on my denim-clad thighs, forced another breath in, and relaxed my shoulders.

My eyes wandered, trying to distract my mind from overthinking the decision to be here.

A large window, overlooking a park, let the fading daylight filter through. The walls were painted in the same shade as the hallway. A tall plant sat in one corner, beside a children's powder-blue table with a stack of coloring books and a bucket of pencils.

The girls would love it here.

We all turned around to face the door when we heard a soft knock.

Janice let the woman in, smiling. "Hi, Maddie. Come meet Mr. Stevens."

Madison entered the room. I inhaled a sharp breath, her arrival stealing every bit of air from the room, leaving me breathless. I took a step back, solidifying my stance. If I'd been sitting, I would've fallen off my chair.

A surge of misplaced heat washed through me.

A sense of annoyance spiraled in my core, intertwined with an inexplicable fascination whose source I couldn't trace.

I blinked. Once. Twice. A million times. The woman before me had nothing to do with all the nanny images I'd constructed in my head. She looked nothing like the middle-aged women starring in children's movies or the ones we often heard about.

At about five feet eight inches, with dark hair braided over her shoulder and wearing a knee-length red wrap dress, she looked too young to be the girl with all the credentials Riley had praised about.

It was a mistake.

Her smile directed at me warmed my insides when I extended my arm to shake her hand. It overcast my underlying irritation. A tingling sensation raced up my spine when our palms met. We stared at each other for what felt like forever, both sizing each other up, the weird tension between us thickening with every passing second.

Her lips trembled, and for a short instant, I wished I could tug the bottom one with my teeth. I shook myself out of the daze that had held us both captive. What the hell was wrong with me? Where were these thoughts even coming from? My lack of a social life had clearly messed with my head more than I'd realized. I had become a sick fucker.

I cleared my throat, my vocal cords feeling heavier, her sea-green irises locking onto mine. I couldn't look away. "You must be Madison. It's nice to meet you. I…I've heard great things about you." Did my voice quiver? *You must be Madison.* Oh geez. Like it wasn't a given already. Great, I must have looked like a complete dork and sounded like an airhead. In my career, and even at the hardware store, I was used to meeting new people all the time, but it had been so long since I'd had one-on-one meaningful interactions that I felt rusty.

This woman, by her proximity alone, threw me off my game—for a reason I couldn't decipher. Except that she didn't fit the profile of a live-in nanny, and the green pools of her eyes hypnotized me. So did the curve of her lips.

"It's nice to meet you too. Mr. Burns…huh…Riley"—her gaze traveled to my friend before returning to mine—"couldn't stop bragging about you yesterday. It's nice to finally put a face to the name. He said amazing things about you and your family." She blushed a little, and I found it fucking adorable.

Yeah, adorable, because Madison wasn't the grown-ass woman I'd pictured in my head, but a kid. Not the severe yet caring woman I'd imagined when I had agreed to this meeting. Or the years-of-experience-candidate Riley had sworn she'd be. She didn't look a year older than eighteen.

How could she have any work experience?

Did she even graduate college? Or even have a high school diploma?

I blinked again, my eyes unable to flicker away, her hand still locked in mine, fumbling with my sanity. And my whole body.

I took in the straight line of her nose, the heart-shaped lips, the angle of her chin, the slender neck.

Yeah, to make things worse, she looked beautiful. No, stunning—for a young woman. One I shouldn't have these kinds of thoughts about. One I was here to interview, not crush on.

My two-year-long dry spell was now making me all hot for a college girl. One with delicate shoulders and a body sinful enough to drive any man wild, even underneath that demure dress.

It wasn't sexy or short or anything like that, but it still had an effect on me. A big one. One I had no control over and that filled my pants. That spiked my heart. And that fucked with my brain.

An invisible vise closed around my heart.

Steel bands tightened around my stomach.

I wasn't here to get my dick back in the game, but to hire a nanny. Someone to watch over my kids.

This Madison girl wouldn't do. She looked too naive to be qualified enough for the job. Too young to be in charge of small children. Too sweet to… Why bother? It wouldn't work anyway. It couldn't.

She eyed me, and I felt as if she could read my soul and every word that didn't cross the rim of my lips. My dirty inner reflections. I broke eye contact, praying the discomfort in my lower self wasn't too obvious and that it would subside quickly.

Another breath in and the pressure rising in me decreased. Once I regained some of my composure, I risked another glance at her.

My stance hadn't changed. No way could Madison be experienced enough to care for my little ones. I bet she still lived with her parents. Or that she shared an apartment with half-a-dozen roommates because none of them had a job steady enough to pay the full rent by themselves, too busy hitting bars every night and working shitty hours for little-to-no money while juggling college classes during the day.

Anger rose inside me. My features hardened, despite myself.

I closed my eyes and balled my free hand at my side.

Was Riley shitting me right now? How could a college kid be the one whom I'd rely on to care for my daughters? This girl wasn't even old enough to run a household in my absence and follow my kids' school curriculum next fall. How could he and Devon have vouched for her? They must have known she didn't fit the requirements. What were they thinking? Clearing my throat, I removed my hand from Madison's grasp. This whole thing was a lost cause. A clump of false hopes.

The moment her palm slid out of mine, something deflated inside my chest, and I missed the warmth of her touch and the prickles raiding my body. Not willing to let her notice my uneasiness and misplaced attraction, because yes, I was feeling things that were not allowed in a business meeting, I shoved my hands into my pockets.

The air in the room stiffened, and I withdrew into myself.

Riley and Janice exchanged a glance, and when my eyes drifted back to the woman fucking with my head again, she busied herself picking the nail of her thumb, a faint blush still tinting her cheeks. I flexed my jaw, grinding my teeth. Inside me, every one of my organs spasmed with foreign awareness. I had no recollection of my heart trying to flee my ribcage before in my life.

With an exhale, I tipped my chin up. All eyes were on me. Expectant. Inquisitive. Apprehensive. I found my voice, deciding not to release my position on the subject. "This meeting was a mistake. I'm sorry if I made you all waste your time. You can bill me for an entire hour." I fished a business card out of my wallet and placed it in Janice's hand.

She watched me with wide eyes, probably thinking I was a rude jerk for walking out on her and her teenage recruit.

"Now, if you'll excuse me, I have little girls I must go back to." I whirled around and hurried out of the office.

Oxygen made its way back to my brain once the door slammed behind me and the distance between Madison and me increased.

My pulse calmed down, and I could breathe again.

My entire body loosened up.

With long strides, I reached the front door in no time. Just when I was about to exit the agency, Riley caught up with me, and his hand connected with my shoulder from behind, stopping my retreat.

"Where do you think you're going, Stevens?"

I unleashed the ball of fury bouncing around in my chest, jumbling together all my mixed feelings. With a roll of my shoulders, I freed myself from his grip, readying myself for a fight. "Are you kidding me right now? How could you even think I'd agree to this? You set me up with a kid, man. You made me believe I could do this whole career-tour-children thing and that you had my back. I believed you. Trusted you even. I fucking put my confidence in you. And it was hard for me to do so, but I had faith you wouldn't let me down and that you understood where I was coming from."

I tightened my fists.

Anger sliced my words.

I shouldn't be angry with Riley. After all, he'd only tried to help me out, but I couldn't help it. I felt tricked.

All the remnants of the bottled-up anger I thought I'd already dealt with over Lisa abandoning us surged all at once. Everything I wished I could have told her, and never did, spewed out of my mouth.

"You have any idea how hard it is for me to trust someone? Mostly around my kids? Do you know how I struggled for the longest time, trying to make sense of the life that was forced on me without my consent? It imploded, and I was alone to pick up the pieces—and I still am doing so. Every fucking day. This single-dad thing is hard enough as it is. I thought you said Madison has a teaching degree and lots of experience. How could another kid be the right fit? Tell me, please. Enlighten me. Because, right now, I can't see your big plan unfolding perfectly. I thought we were meeting a mature woman with years of experience caring for children. I thought you had it all figured out. I thought… I don't know what I thought, but it wasn't this." I pointed to where the office was located down the hall. "It wasn't fucking this… Another kid? Really? As if I'm not already drowning under everything on my plate. I. Can't. Do. This. Nope. It's asking too much of me. Maybe I'm not meant to follow this road anymore… It was a mistake." I sighed. "I feel stupid for wasting every one's time. Forget the idea of a tour, Ry. I'm out. For good this time. I don't even know why I agreed to this in the first place. Deep down, I always knew it wasn't meant to be. God, how could I have been so clueless? I'm done." My words sat in my throat, heavy as a ton of bricks. "For life."

How could I ever let myself imagine this would work out? I was the butt of my own joke.

I spun around in a hurry to leave when he squeezed my forearm. "Stevens, where do you think you're going?"

I swallowed my rage before facing him. "Home. To my children. Those tiny human beings who are my whole world and who expect everything from me."

"Did you forget I drove us here?"

I shrugged. "Who cares? I'll take a cab. Or I…I'll walk. Yeah, it could help to diffuse my anger. I'm furious, man. If I were you, I'd step back because I'm about to explode. You don't wanna stand in the crossfire."

"Sam, you're not going anywhere. Listen to me before

doing something foolish you may regret later. Grant me five minutes. If I haven't convinced you to give Madison a chance by then, I'll call the meeting off myself, and we'll leave."

I blew out a breath, fighting the pros and cons in my head.

I came out short of reasons why I shouldn't trust my friend, and finally agreed. "Okay. Fine. Five minutes. You'd better do exceptional, or I'm out of here, and we'll never talk about my going back on tour ever again. Am I clear?"

Riley nodded and motioned for me to follow him through a door leading to a small conference room. A long white table filled most of the space, surrounded by a dozen teal chairs.

We sat next to each other, and I leaned back in my seat and folded my arms across my chest, waiting for my friend to explain himself. Tension rippled through me. I hadn't felt this much anger in a long time. In a crazy way, the overbearing sentiment reminded me I was alive. That I still could feel passion—whether positive or negative. That I hadn't turned into a rock. A small part of me rejoiced at the thought. I wouldn't dare show it in front of him, but I couldn't deny the fire blazing in my veins.

Riley muttered something I didn't catch, caught up in my own internal battle, and shot a text—probably to Janice. He turned off his phone—something I didn't remember him ever doing—then tossed it on the table and swiveled to face me. "Now just listen. Don't interrupt me. I want to make the most of the five minutes you're allowing me."

I nodded, my posture stoic.

"I didn't tell you Madison's age beforehand because I knew you'd freak out. Sure, she looks young, but she's twenty-one. She graduated early with honors, one year ago. She was homeschooled most of her life and is very smart. Anyway, she owns a degree. And it's legit. She also passed the background check. Hands down. Not even a single speeding ticket in her life. Right now, she's not teaching a regular twenty-five-student class because she loves adventure. She told me so herself. I'd never lie to you, man. You have to believe me. We've been friends a long time, you and I.

"Since Carter has decided to stop going on extensive world tours and is mostly doing low-key concert stretches here and there, and Aisha just came back from a tour, I have a lot of free time on my hands. I have one other group I'm managing, but they aren't as big a deal as you, Aisha, and Carter are… Not yet at least. I'm not doing you a favor or doing it for the money because you know I don't need it. Sam, you gotta get back out there. You're dying a slow death. You're miserable. I'm doing it for your kids, man. Ever since I came to your house the other night with my not-so-wild idea, you've been looking ten years younger. The smiles I saw on your kids' faces tonight were genuine. It was about time those girls started thriving again. It's like ever since I planted that idea in your head, you've decided to enjoy life. You've been rising from your ashes. You guys looked happier tonight than I've seen you in the last two years. Gone was the tension that has been choking all three of you. You were at peace. It wasn't a front…or the mask you usually hide behind."

I closed my eyes to prevent the emotional storm building inside me from erupting. The one about to transform my ire into tears.

Was every word Riley said accurate? Even if I wanted to deny it, they rang true, shook me to my core, and spoke to my soul.

Did my girls need this as much as I did? Could he have been right all along?

A calmness spread through me. The kind that comes when it's paired with a sense of belonging.

A treacherous smile threatened to slip out, but I pressed my lips together, not ready to let him see how much his words had affected me.

As silly as it sounded, my friend's idea had lodged itself in my heart ever since he drilled it in.

A door I'd kept locked inside me swung open. Air filled my lungs more easily. How could Riley know what was best for my family better than I did? Was I really struggling as much as he suggested? Yet, I couldn't deny it.

"You all right, man?" he asked, forcing me to snap back to the present.

"Yeah….huh…was just thinking. All your words sound great, Ry, but don't you think I'm too old to take care of a college student? I'll be turning thirty soon. I'm not looking for another kid to raise."

My friend burst into laughter. "Stevens, I'm pretty sure Madison can take care of herself. Stop calling her a kid."

"She looks like one."

"She's not. She's an adult, independent, and reliable. Meet with her. For real this time. Trust me, for fuck's sake. I'm telling you, she's the real deal, okay? You two will get along just fine. I swear."

I shook my head. "Why do I feel like I'm gonna regret this?"

"Because you'll tell me I was right to insist, and you'll realize you've been acting like a big baby since we got here. Who's acting like a kid now?"

My warning glare had no effect on him.

"Now let's go. Madison and Janice must be worried we'll never come back."

I released my smile. "*Touché.* Lead the way. I hate it when you're right."

He snickered. "It's love, man. You and I, we fight, then we make up." He pushed me forward, his hands splayed across my back. "Not my fault I was born to be right all the time."

I bowed my head and shook it. "I won't buy you flowers." I joined in on the humor as laughter exploded between us.

Seconds later, he knocked on Janice's door, and I followed him inside the office, closing the door behind me, a grimace forming on my face as shame wrapped around me.

Both women's eyes shot in my direction. Janice offered me a shy smile, and Madison stared at me with glossy eyes. Did I make her cry when I stormed out of here earlier? I scrunched up my nose, feeling responsible for her distress. Did I mess things up already? No wonder Lisa left if I was that bad at reading her emotions all these years. Did I convince myself we were in love instead of seeing the signs that proved she didn't love me back? I raked my fingers through my hair. I shouldn't let Lisa inside my head. It never did any good. I had done nothing wrong in my marriage except love her. She was the one who had run away. I shouldn't doubt myself—now wasn't the place or the time.

I brought my hands in front of me, my palms open before anyone could say anything. "Hey, I'm sorry for leaving like I did. I panicked, and it's nobody's fault but mine. Thinking of going back on tour is a huge deal for me. It-it's something I thought I'd never do again. It doesn't excuse my behavior, but that's the truth... Now I'm ready to listen to everything you tell me. This won't happen again, I swear."

My gaze returned to Madison, and we exchanged a nod as I stuffed my hands into my pockets to quiet the brewing agitation I felt deep in my bones. Our eyes connected. For longer than required. She swept her lip with her tongue, appearing nervous.

This time, I kept my dirty observations to myself and switched to a business mindset.

Janice clasped her hands in front of her, breaking the spell. "Great. Let's all take a seat then." The four of us sat in the colorful chairs surrounding her desk.

She led the meeting, good and persuasive at why I needed to hire Madison as my children's nanny and teacher.

When Madison started talking, she avoided my eyes. She looked between Janice and Riley, but barely at me. I hated myself for making her feel uncomfortable.

But then her eyes, glistening and alluring in the light, found mine, and I lost myself in their depths.

I sucked in a breath, afraid I would drown in her irises if I weren't being careful.

"What are Justine and Mikaella like?" she asked me.

Wow, she knew my daughters' names already. Impressive. My jaw went slack, and I had to force it shut. This small detail was important enough in my heart that my professional interest in Madison grew.

"They are lively little girls. Justine is four, and she thinks she's a princess and can't wear enough glittery stuff or sparkling dresses. She loves to ask questions and can't seem to say people's names or everyday objects the right way. It's a part of her charm, I guess. Mika is more rebellious, but she's only six, so I haven't lost faith just yet. Her mother's leaving, abruptly in the middle of the night, affected her the most." A cloud passed through Madison's gaze. I paused, wondering if what I said triggered it. She blinked, and it dissolved, so I continued. "Mika thinks she's a grown-up and wants to be treated like an adult. I know she's struggling, and I get her all the help I can. Anyway, she's doing amazingly at school. Her bad attitude is mostly directed at me. She's a great kid with a huge heart. Justine and she are inseparable. Even when they fight for the most trivial reasons."

"If it's okay with you, I'd like to meet them. But only if you think your family and I could be a great fit. I don't want to impose, but I always like to make some sort of test run. Spend time with you guys and see if there's chemistry. The last thing you need is a nanny your children are hostile to. Nobody yearns to be unhappy."

Those words resonated with me. Yeah, I was done being unhappy too.

"I agree," Janice said when I didn't speak up, lost in my thoughts.

Who was this Madison Prescott, and where did she come from? One more point in favor of Riley being right all this time.

I scratched the side of my head.

Everything Madison said sounded smart—and logical. Could she be wiser than her young age? For everyone's sake, I hoped so.

The entire time I told her about Justine and Mikaella, she stared at me. As if she could swallow my words. As if I spoke some wisdom she craved the secret to.

Riley nudged me in the ribs.

"What?"

"Are you okay, Stevens? Janice has been talking to you, but you totally blacked out."

My face heated up. "Sorry. What were you saying?"

Janice offered me a warm smile. "No problem. I was saying that if you agree, Maddie could come to your house next weekend, and she could spend some time together with the girls and see if you all get along. And then we could meet up next week and discuss the details if you decide to go forward and hire her. How does that sound?"

I coughed to clear my throat, too many words trying to come out at the same time. "Sounds good to me."

"Me too," Madison echoed, her hands linked together in her lap, her general demeanor less strained than before.

Janice rose to her feet. "Great. I'll send both of your contact info in a joint email, so you'll be able to set up a date to get together." She held out a hand and I shook it. "It was great meeting you, Mr. Stevens, and I hope to see more of you soon." She circled her desk and kissed Riley on the cheek. "See you, cousin. Don't be a stranger."

"Take care, Janice. We'll keep in touch. Madison, I'm sure we'll see each other again soon. Thanks for giving this grumpy fellow another chance. I knew you two would hit it off, even if it got off to a bit of a bumpy start."

Madison offered him a lopsided smile before turning toward me. She fidgeted with the ring around her middle finger before her eyes caught mine and halted there for long seconds. She opened her mouth to say something but seemed to refrain. My gaze followed every movement of her lips when they bent at the corner as she said, "Thank you for giving me a chance."

"Sure. Let me know when you're available, and we'll set it up."

She returned my hesitant smile as we exited the office, and I made eye contact with her one last time over my shoulder.

Once out on the other side of the door, I exhaled and rotated my shoulders. The tension in my upper back dissolved bit by bit, and air didn't struggle to oxygenate my brain anymore.

I did it. I took the first step toward reviving my dying dreams. I was doing it—the gears finally in motion. I didn't know whether to feel excited or cautious. It all felt so surreal.

"Drink and dinner?" Riley asked as we walked to his car.

I fished my phone out of my back pocket to look at the time.

"Stop worrying. The girls are fine." My friend flipped his phone so I could see the screen. Devon had sent a picture of the three of them with rainbow pedicures, and another one of them baking cookies. By the giant grins on their faces, my daughters looked more than fine. "See? I told you. Carter is waiting for us at Wild and Country."

"Oh, how's the partnership with that Tucker guy going?"

"Great. It's a passive investment on my part. I only jump in when he has technical questions about music or is looking for the next best opening numbers for special nights. For a bar, the food he serves is freaking delicious. I'm telling you, it's the most popular new spot in town. The guy knows his shit."

"Any big names playing there these days?"

"Yeah, a guy I met a few times. Sam Stevens. You should hear him when he's onstage. People call him *The Legend*. You should come to see him play when you have some free time. He's worth the buzz. And soon he'll rock that stage. Give him a few weeks. Three months at the most."

"Tell me again why you never were my manager before?"

"Because you were too stubborn to see a great opportunity—aka me—when we met. You went with the big sharks, and they tossed you like an old pair of shoes the moment you didn't play by their rules anymore. It's never too late to recognize I'm the best in the business. Don't tell me now. Wait until you're at the top again, then I'll be all ears when you chant my praises and tell me how fabulous I am." Riley winked at me as he unlocked his car.

"Yeah, yeah. Keep dreaming, man." I shook my head, unable to hide my grin this time. Deep down, I'd always known my friend was the best in the business. I was just too stupid back then to recognize it.

We entered the bar. My eyes fought to adjust to the semi-darkness. This place had become an institution in Nashville since its opening. Back in the day, this used to be a pub where I met my friends regularly. When life was simpler and we still had dreams of making it big one day. A guy name Tucker Philips had bought the building, renovated it, and turned it into a hit venture in a short amount of time. When he asked for Riley's professional opinion about sound systems and acoustics, my friend offered to invest, swearing he could already see the potential of the place.

Tucker and Riley had friends in common, including Dahlia Ellis—Carter Hills's ex-bandmate—and her husband Nick. They became fast friends, bonding over investments, stocks, real estate, and good whiskey, as he'd once told me.

Riley Burns would do just about anything for his country family as he called them. Carter, Dahlia, Stud Burgess—the third ex-bandmate of the Carter Hills Band —Aisha Jones, his newest artist, and all their partners and children.

A family I wasn't a legitimate part of yet but aspired to be. Rightfully.

Carter waved from a booth at the back when he spotted us. Riley's phone went off, and he gestured for me to continue as he moved toward a room on our right, the device still glued to his ear.

My fellow country music star rose to his feet to pull me into a hug. "It's been a while, Stevens. I'm glad Ry convinced you to join us."

Rubbing my jaw, I sank into the black leather seat. "He has made it his mission to get me out of the house lately. He's adamant I should go back on tour, but I'm sure he's already told you all about his new plan. Anyway, why are you in town? You're barely ever here, now that you're living full-time in Green Mountain."

The first time I met the members of Carter Hills Band was when I'd just turned twenty-three and we both played at Green Mountain Fest. We all landed record deals and kept running into each other at every award show and music event after that. Carter, Dahlia, Stud, and I got along easily from the moment we first met, and a friendship quickly followed. Even if we didn't see each other as often these days, we were still close.

Carter brought the glass of water to his lips and took a sip before answering. "Had to go over some concert dates with Ry. And I wanted to see June. I missed her. We talk on the phone all the time, but it's not the same. April is with her right now. They planned a shopping date or something."

June was Riley's assistant and Carter's go-to person in his professional life. She worked almost exclusively for him.

"Where are the kids?"

"With their grandparents."

"April's parents?"

"No, her in-laws."

My eyebrow twitched. "April's in-laws? Which I'm

pretty sure should be your parents... What am I missing here?"

"Remember the Bensons?"

"Yeah, the ones organizing that charity event every year in New York. What about them?"

"They're April's in-laws," he said.

"Let me recap. Mr. And Mrs. Benson are babysitting your children? How did you make that happen? Sure, you are a country superstar, but this is big. Even for you."

Carter snickered. "It's a bit complicated... April and they go way back. The time you canceled your appearance at the fundraiser because of Lisa's miscarriage, well... I replaced you, and they bumped into each other that night and rebuilt their relationship. It has progressed from there."

The mention of my ex-wife didn't hurt anymore. A sense of serenity spread through me at the realization I was done with that chapter of my life. She didn't own my heart anymore. Or my sorrow.

"Anyway, they are her family. So, by association, they're mine too. Where were you when it all went to shit? It was all over the news for weeks. When the media chased April away. Anyway, the Bensons gave that interview. They protected her...vouched for her... It was something else."

"Geez, I missed a whole chapter of your life. I've been living in some sort of cave for the last few years, and clearly I'd forgotten how entertaining your existence could be."

Carter Hills had been nicknamed the bad boy of country music. He had an attitude, could serve a mean left hook, and had had his face plastered on gossip magazines too many times due to a previous relationship. He was nothing like the media made him out to be. You had to be part of his inner circle to see the real version of him. The one he kept hidden from strangers.

A server approached us. "Can I get you anything?"

I ordered a beer, and then he turned to face Carter. "Another Smoky Stream, sir?"

My friend nodded. "Yes, please."

"Smoky Stream? Even water sounds fancy with you, man."

He shook his head and smiled. "The guy keeps calling it that, and I love it. Sounds almost like a high-end cocktail. Have you met Tucker yet?"

"No. Heard great things about him, though."

"Yep. Nick and he go way back. The three of us have become quite a trio over the last couple of years. Who would have thought? Let's say Nick sweeping Dah off her feet at first didn't sit well with me. But, in the end, I'm grateful, because I wouldn't have met April if I hadn't survived all the pain of unrequited love and the betrayal of the evil witch who made my life a living hell… Whoa, I haven't thought about her in a long time. All along, April was the one I was destined to be with. Anyway, I'll introduce you to Tuck later. He must be around here somewhere. You two will get along." His gaze fused to mine. "Now tell me you're really thinking of going back on tour. Country music misses some new Sam Stevens material. It's been too long. You're *The Legend*, and I can't hold the fort all by myself."

"Look who's talking, Mr. *Every One of My Songs Is Still a Hit*."

Carter shrugged, not an ounce of smugness shadowing his face. "It's not about me. I'm happy for you, and I hope it all works out. You deserve it. I walked away by choice. You didn't. That's a big difference."

The server brought us our drinks, and Carter swirled the water in his glass, the ice cubes clinking. "I don't have any real competition when you're taking time off, Stevens.

I used to love competing with you for the top spots on the charts. I haven't retired, just doing smaller crowds instead of stadiums now… It suits me better. So…your return…is this serious or not?"

I inhaled, trying to put some order into my jumbling thoughts. "Yes. No. I don't know. Now that the possibility is real, I guess I'd like to give it a try. There's so much to think about, though… So much at stake. The girls… I gotta make sure they won't suffer because of it."

"What about that girl Ry set you up with? The nanny?"

"Yeah, what about the nanny, Stevens?" Riley asked as he took the seat next to Carter after they hugged, a tumbler of whiskey in his hand.

I dragged my hands over my face. "I'll give her a chance. I'm not agreeing to anything yet. We'll see how it goes."

A voice in my head told me there was no going back, whether I was ready or not.

"Yeah, we'll see how it goes," Riley echoed, his tone teasing, and a grin stretching across his face, practically begging to be punched.

5

MADISON

Emily, my older sister, was waiting for me when I returned from my meeting with Sam Stevens at the nanny agency. We had both moved to Nashville to attend college and never went back home to Kentucky. Emily was studying to become a surgeon. We shared the townhouse she was renting in East Nashville with two other doctors. Since I was always in and out, due to my work, she offered me one of the guest rooms to stay in every time I was in town or between jobs. It suited my hectic lifestyle since I wasn't ready to commit to a nine-to-five career just yet.

"How was it? Did you get the job?" she asked after I dropped my purse on the table, kicked off my shoes, and slumped onto the couch beside her, resting my head on her shoulder.

"No clue. That was the weirdest interview ever."

I straightened and rubbed my throbbing temples with my fingers as I felt a paralyzing headache coming my way.

"I thought you said it was a done deal after you met with his manager and his wife." I could hear all the questions in her voice and imagined the wrinkles around her eyes without even looking at her.

"I did, but the guy shook my hand, studied me for a few seconds, and announced it was a mistake, then bolted out of the room as if it were on fire." I sighed and risked a glance at her.

Emily coughed, her eyes widening. "He left? You're kidding, right?"

"He stormed off. I swear, it felt like I'd injected poison into his bloodstream with a handshake… He couldn't get away from me fast enough." She gasped her surprise as I continued, "But then he came back a few minutes later, said he panicked and was sorry, and now we agreed to meet again next weekend so I can spend time with his daughters."

"And you're okay with that?"

I blew out a long and loud breath. "The truth is, I really want the job. Riley made it sound so much fun. So different from what I've done in the past. Deep down, I feel for the kids. Their mom left without saying goodbye…or something like that. It's heartbreaking. With what you and I went through when we were their age, it's like I'm even more qualified for the job." To understand what they were dealing with.

My sister nodded her agreement. Nowadays, we were both at peace with our childhood trauma. Over the years, we had become more than just sisters. Best friends who always had each other's backs.

I let out a long sigh, and Emily watched me with a puzzled expression. "High tension swirled between us, but I think I can handle it. I won't be there to care for him, but for the girls. His manager said he has trust issues. So, it might explain his cold reaction toward me at first. I checked him up online. Most articles are from before he stepped down. In the past two years, he hasn't given a single interview—at least, none that I could find. It's like he vanished from the limelight entirely, shutting out the rest of the world. The man I saw in the old pictures had an edge that the one I met today lacked…eyes that seemed to burn into the soul. It's hard to explain, but I have a good feeling about this. Imagine, going on tour with someone who once topped all the music charts around the world. This feels too good to be true. And yet, they picked me. I'm trying not to look too much into his past and just skim the surface so it doesn't influence how I act around him. The last thing I want is for him to think I'm some sort of groupie. Anyway, I'd love to live on a tour bus. See what the fuss is all about. Most kids my age are still in college or have just graduated. I'm not ready for a steady teacher's position just yet. I love my lifestyle."

"You've never loved things most kids your age enjoyed anyway. You're weird, but a good kind of weird. You're way too intelligent and mature for your own good. You know that, right? I could tell when you were like nine that you'd do great in life. That fire in your eyes, that will, it was already shining bright." Emily nudged me with her shoulder. "Let's be serious for a minute, though. What if the guy turns out to be a dickhead and you're in the middle of New Mexico with no cell phone reception for me to come to your rescue?"

"Like I said, I'll be there for his daughters. As long as I get along with them, the rest will be just fine. Remember Mr. Cruz at first when I lived on the yacht with his family last year? He warmed up to my presence after three months. It can't be worse. I don't scare easily."

My sister rested her palm on my thigh. "You're right. I just don't want you to end up hating the guy if he messes with your opportunity to live a great experience, that's all.

We should go out tonight. To celebrate your potential new job. It's still early, and I have the day off tomorrow. Please say yes. I'm putting in an official request to have some fun with my little sister before you're too busy to hang out with me. And since you're still unemployed as of right now, drinking on a Wednesday night is no big deal. Plus, it's ladies' night, so we'll drink for cheap. Are you in?" My sister's eyes clouded for a moment, and she sighed before looking away.

"Ems, what's going on? Talk to me."

She shook her head. "Nothing. I just need a change of air. Long shifts at the hospital are weighing heavy on me. My entire existence is dedicated to my job right now. Some days, I find it dreadful. Don't worry. Plus, I think Becks is playing somewhere on Broadway. Could be fun. To be young and carefree for a night."

She tugged at my dress sleeve giving me puppy dog eyes.

"Why not? We haven't gone out together in a long while. Let me change, though. This dress isn't suited for a night out," I said with a huff, recalling the earlier interview that had left me with a sour taste.

Two hours later, I was leaning against the counter in an overcrowded downtown bar with a glass of sangria in my hand when a guy about my age neared me.

"Hey," he said, aligning his body with mine, making me the center of all his unwelcome attention. His red T-shirt, a size too small, clung to his broad shoulders, biceps, and defined chest. And he smelled like he'd bathed in after-shave and hair gel.

I scrunched up my nose and stepped aside to avoid the overwhelming fragrance.

"Hey," I replied, giving him my most fake smile that screamed *stay away*.

He clearly couldn't read between the lines—or my facial expressions—because he moved closer. I leaned back. I hated this. I wasn't the type of person who made small talk with strangers in a bar.

"You wanna go somewhere?" Biceps Guy asked.

I winced. "Sorry, not interested." I sipped my drink and pivoted to my right, putting an end to our conversation.

"C'mon, let me at least buy you another drink."

Chills ran down my spine while he edged closer.

I took another step to my left, escaping his suffocating presence. My eyes scanned the crowd for my sister and her friends. They were supposed to head to the ladies' room and come back, but it had been a while, and there was still no sign of them. Maybe they'd gone upstairs. The bar had three stories, including a rooftop terrace on the third floor.

Biceps Guy clutched my elbow as I moved further away from him. "Let's have some fun, baby."

I cringed and wrenched myself free from his grip. He'd just called me *baby* and fucking touched me.

I discarded my cocktail on a nearby table, the taste making my stomach churn. Amazing. He was ruining my night.

Fishing my phone out of my pocket, I called my sister. *Please pick up. Please pick up. Please, please, please... Where are you?* It rang five times before going to voicemail.

Fantastic, I had no money and no way to get home since my wallet and keys were in Emily's purse.

Biceps Guy leaned even closer, his breath brushing the shell of my ear. Too much. Too close. He was too...everything. Icky. My pulse raced and I breathed fast. My insides coiled. I retreated until my back touched the wall. "Don't be afraid, baby. I won't bite you. Not yet at least."

Everything in me screamed to run away.

He trapped me between his arms. At least a foot taller than me and twice my width, I felt tiny in comparison.

To appear taller and stronger than I really was, I straightened my back and lifted my chin. I wouldn't let this guy intimidate me. "Move," I said, my tone leaving no room for argument, my voice firm.

"Don't be afraid, baby. I'll take care of you."

I raised my hands, ready to push him back when a voice behind me stopped me mid-action.

"Here you are. I've been looking everywhere for you. Don't get out of my sight again, honey." A guy in black jeans, a white T-shirt, and motorcycle boots, with an eyebrow piercing and brown hair, closed in on us. He arched one dark brow, smiled at me, and moved closer to take my hand. I wanted to be looked at like that for the rest of my life. As if I were the sun, the moon, and the entire universe.

What was going on? Who was this guy?

"Honey, is this man giving you trouble?" the mysterious stranger asked. High cheekbones, angular jaw, turquoise eyes, and thin lips. He looked like a fashion model. The ones you gotta to look at twice to get the complexity of their beauty.

Biceps Guy raised his hands in surrender. "Sorry, man. I had no idea she was yours. I'll go now."

"Yeah. Do that. And don't creep out the ladies. It's sick, man."

Biceps Guy muttered something and slinked away, leaving me with the fake boyfriend who had saved me. I tried to avoid his eyes, but they were like two abysses swallowing me whole. And I loved that. A little too much. We studied each other, neither of us able to look away.

"I'm Jacob. You are?" he asked, his fingers still laced through mine, his warmth spreading through me.

"Maddie."

His grin widened. "Well, it's nice to meet you, Maddie."

"Thanks…huh…for that. That guy, he—" Why was I unable to form a complete sentence?

"I know. I've been watching him from the other side of the bar. He's a douchebag. I'm glad I was there this time around."

"Me too. You come here often? Is saving ladies hit on by jerks your night job?"

Jacob smiled, and I got hypnotized.

"My first time. I wish I could be that kind of hero."

"You should consider it as a side hustle. So far, your track record is impressive."

We shared a chuckle. Somehow, Jacob and I clicked, and we spent the next twenty minutes talking about everything and anything.

"Hungry?" he asked after a while.

"Famished." After my interview with Sam Stevens, I'd barely eaten dinner, my stomach too tied in knots.

"There's a food truck outside, and they served the best Southern chicken fries in Nashville. My treat. You in?"

I bobbed my head, a stupid grin spreading across my lips, completely entranced by everything Jacob was. He took my hand in his. We were about to leave the bar when I remembered Emily. Where was she? I'd been so caught up with him that I'd completely forgotten my sister had gone MIA a long time ago.

Digging my heels into the wooden-planked floor, I spun in his direction. "Wait. We can't go just yet. I gotta find my sister. She's here. There…huh…somewhere." I gestured around the crowded bar with my hand.

"Let's find her then."

Hand in hand, we squeezed through the patrons,

dancing and mingling, though I wasn't tall enough to spot my sister.

"What does she look like?" Jacob asked, speaking close to my ear so I could hear him over the music.

My body vibrated at the sound of his deep voice.

"About my size, wavy brown hair reaching past her shoulders, yellow tank top, and a mole on her right cheek. Oh, and she has my eyes. Other than that, you wouldn't guess we're related."

"Copy that," he said with an irresistible grin. One I wished could stay anchored to his face all night.

We searched the third and second floors. No trace of her anywhere. I was about to tell Jacob we had to come up with another plan as we returned to the first floor when I bumped into her.

"Hey, Ems. Been looking everywhere for you. Even tried to call you. Are you okay?"

She squeezed my upper arms. "Oh, Maddie. I thought I'd lost you. I'm so sorry. Cecilia drank too much tequila, and I had to hold her hair while she was puking her guts out. She's fine now, but we have to go. We'll drop her at her place on the way home." She moved closer and spoke into my ear while pulling me into a hug. "Who's that?" she asked, pointing to Jacob, who was busy watching the live band, with her chin.

"Someone I just met. We were going to grab a bite. Go with Cecilia. I'll stay here."

"You sure? You don't even know this guy."

"His name's Jacob. And I have a good feeling. Don't worry about me. I'll be fine."

Her gaze traveled between Jacob and me for a moment. She offered me her big sister's *be careful* look and smiled. "Maddie, you gotta have some fun. Doctor's orders. Enjoy yourself for once. Don't be too serious for a night, okay?"

"I'll try."

Growing up, Emily and I had been homeschooled by our mother until she got too sick after I turned fifteen. For as long as I could remember, my sister and I had always fended for ourselves and been more mature than most kids our age. It all explained why we'd both graduated early from high school and college. Our father had taught us to save our money, to be responsible. And self-sufficient. Sometimes, I felt more like a *thirty going on forty* girl than a *just-turned twenty-one-year-old*. People my age bored me. I'd never really connected with them the way I should have. No wonder I had such a hard time making friends.

In the short time we'd known each other, I realized Jacob got me. I could tell he was similar to me in that way.

Emily dropped a kiss on my cheek and pushed two twenty-dollar bills and my credit card and keys into my hand, then spun around to face my new friend. "Take care of my sister. Don't make me chase you down 'cause I will. Now gimme your phone."

His eyes flared, but he said nothing and handed her his device.

She typed fast and gave it back. She grabbed her own phone and nodded. Seconds later, a deep frown appeared across her forehead, and she brought her fists to her hips. "Be warned. I have your phone number, so don't try anything, or I'll hunt you down."

"No worry, ma'am. I'll take good care of Maddie."

Emily sighed. "Fine. And don't *ma'am* me ever again. Second warning."

Jacob winked and interlocked his fingers with mine, leading me away. "Is your sister a psycho, or does she take great pleasure in intimidating men?" he asked, amusement clear in his voice.

"Believe me, you don't want to find out." I plastered my most devilish grin on, and he pretended to be spooked.

In a half-empty parking lot, we sat on the pavement against a red-bricked wall, drinking soda and sharing a plate of the best Southern chicken fries I'd ever had.

"Gotta say, you were right. I can't believe I've never tried these before," I said, licking my fingers.

Jacob smiled. I could watch his expression all night. It fascinated me. He looked like a boy with the dimple on his chin and glints in his eyes. A great contrast to his dark biker appearance.

"You know you're beautiful, right? I can't keep my eyes off you."

Was my face fire-engine red right now?

I wasn't used to getting compliments. And I wasn't used to flirting with strangers either.

"Don't be shy, Maddie. Your energy is contagious. It drew me in the moment I laid my eyes on you in the bar."

My heartbeat picked up. I didn't know how to react. Should I run for my life or savor his words?

Jacob cast a glance down and brought another piece of fries to his mouth. I zoomed in on his lips. They looked soft and were the perfect shade of pink.

Nothing about him screamed "serial killer." I just hoped my instincts were sharp and not off.

"Sorry. Didn't mean to freak you out. I just had to tell you." He shrugged, and I relaxed.

"It's okay. I'm not used to this," I said, motioning the space between us and around with my hand. "I don't go out a lot, and I'm dedicated to my work, so meeting new people and getting compliments isn't something that happens often to me."

"It should be." He sipped his drink, looking in the distance. When he turned his head and his irises met mine, nothing existed but us. "You said you're dedicated to your work, so what do you do when you're not eating with a stranger in a deserted parking lot at night?"

"I'm a teacher…sort of. And a nanny. I enjoy going on adventures with families and teach their kids while they're away from home. I spent a year on a yacht across the Atlantic last year. In a couple of months, I'll be on a tour bus for six months…if it all works out."

"Wow, I'm impressed. I wouldn't have pictured you as the adventure-seeking type. I like that. A lot."

I shut my eyes, trying to calm the flutters inside me and keep my expression blank—and breathed out.

"Tell me something not a lot of people know about you," he probed.

"Let's see." I hesitated for half a second. "I often feel like I can't find my place in this world. That's why I love to try new experiences. I rarely connect with people my age. I guess I'm trying to find out my true purpose… See where life takes me… It's a confusing process sometimes."

"Aren't you too young to think about all this?"

"My parents have always said I have an old soul. My friends have always been older than me. Instead of running around and pinning donkey tails at birthday parties, I was the kid chatting with the parents. Sorry, it's weird."

"Nah, I like that you can be vulnerable with me and able to speak about things honestly, as they really are."

"Trying to get the most from this life, I guess. And be authentic," I said.

"No one wants to live a life built on lies. I can relate to this. Honesty is something I value a lot."

"What about you? What do you do for a living?"

"I'm a biologist. I work at the university lab. We're testing ways to decontaminate soil using bacteria. It's quite captivating, and so far, our research is promising."

"You're a scientist? I had pegged you as an artist." I let out a weird giggle.

"Yeah. Most people do. I don't exactly have the geek vibe going on for me. I just love sciences. Always have." He raked a hand through his mass of brown hair, messing it up, and for a second, images of Sam Stevens doing the same gesture earlier flashed through my mind. I pushed them away and brought my attention back to the man beside me, losing myself in his gaze once again.

"Ready to go?" he asked, jumping to his feet and holding out his hand for me to grab.

"Where?"

"Wherever you want. I'm not ready to let go of you, Maddie." I could've freaked out, but the manner he said it sent a wave of calm through me. Jacob had a way of making me feel comfortable around him. There was some-thing peaceful about him. Something that put all my demons to rest. Like I didn't have to pretend or be anyone else around him.

Without a word, I slid my palm into his, and we strolled through Nashville. We stopped midway across the pedestrian bridge, pausing to admire the city's night skyline from a distance.

Leaning on the banister, we listened to a country music concert in the open-air amphitheater below. Jacob circled one arm around my waist from behind, and I tilted my head back until it rested on his shoulder as we let the music soothe our souls.

"I don't want this night to end," I whispered, not sure if I wanted him to hear my confession but hoping he would at the same time. I loved the freedom our time together had given me so far. Closing my eyes, I etched it into my memory.

"Me neither," he said, his cheek pressing against my temple.

"Can we stay like this forever?"

"Yeah," he said, pulling me closer to him, curling a hand around my hipbone.

"We should do this again. Spend time together. You and I," he said.

I whirled around to face him. "I'd love to."

The chime of my phone broke the moment. I grabbed my device and smiled at the screen.

EMILY

Hope you're having fun. Don't be an idiot.
But enjoy every second. I love you xx

ME

I am. Love you too xx

"Everything's okay?" Jacob asked.

"Yes. Everything's perfect. I have a serious question to ask. Hope you're up for the challenge. What's your opinion about ice cream?"

"Swirled. With a waffled cone."

I grinned. "You passed the test. Let's get some."

Two hours later, I hauled my tired self into a cab as Jacob kissed my cheek.

"Good night, Maddie. Are you free this weekend?"

"I have a job meeting, but I don't know the specifics yet. We could meet again Friday night, though."

"Have dinner with me," he proposed.

I nodded, smiling like a fool.

"It's a date then." He closed the door after me and hit the cab roof twice to signal it could pull away.

Jacob watched me go, his eyes following me until the

vehicle turned at the next intersection, and our gazes lost their connection.

Lying on my bed a bit later, I replayed the entire night in my head. My awkward meeting with Sam Stevens earlier. The heaviness of his stare as he had studied me. Almost powerful enough to rip my dress to shreds. For a moment, I had believed he liked what he saw until he ran away as if I suffered from a contagious disease. The guy was both fit and hot, but he clearly lived behind a thick fortress, keeping people at a distance. I could tell from the moment our eyes met together for the first time. No matter how aloof he became, I felt an instant pull toward him. With his square jaw, short stubble, and straight nose, he was the living picture of my definition of a perfect man. Even the conflicting energy radiating from him appealed to my senses. On top of that, he still projected confidence in his nervous state. Yes, I could read the anticipation in his body language. The warring thoughts as he battled with himself about the meeting.

And then my brain traveled to Jacob. In a way, he resembled a younger and more grunge version of Sam Stevens. Dark hair, similar poise, manly energy, self-assurance. Easy-going, just a tad mysterious, and way less broody than his counterpart. I felt attracted to him the instant I laid eyes on him.

My mind zigzagged between the two men, so similar and yet so different all at once. How could I be attracted to both? I was way over my head and being ridiculous, so I shoved my silly thoughts away. Soon, sleep claimed me, and I forgot all about the encounters of the day.

———

On Friday, I woke up early to indulge in some yoga before starting my day. I was still unemployed, but Sam Stevens had reached out last night, and we'd agreed to meet on Saturday at his house so I could meet his daughters. I fixed my hair in a knot at the top of my head, rolled out my mat, and positioned myself, ready to start my practice, but my mind kept drifting back to the possibility of this new job. I had a hunch about this position, and the idea of living on a tour bus for months got me excited. It was unlike any job I'd had before. Cramped living quarters, random schedules, and a different city every night. How could I not be curious about experiencing life on the road for a while? Usually, yoga helped quiet my overactive mind, but this time, it barely did anything.

Draped in a towel thirty minutes later, I exited the shower, and a notification flashing on my phone screen caught my eye.

Jacob.

Since we spent the evening together strolling around Nashville two days ago, we'd been messaging each other nonstop. At twenty-five, he had a sense of humor matching mine, and my instincts were right the night we met. We got along, and I enjoyed our blossoming friendship. I wasn't the kind of girl with a huge circle of girlfriends…or even many friends at all. I usually hung out more with Emily's friends than with people I went to college with. Being away for work most of the time made meeting new people even more challenging. But I was fine with it. I was good at being on my own. Still, something about Jacob made me yearn to see what we could become.

JACOB

Good morning. About to leave for work.
Just wanted to know if tonight still works
for you. We talked about lots of things
yesterday but never actually made plans.

My apartment is a ten-minute walk from
downtown. We can meet there or
someplace else. Let me know if it's still
good for you.

Have a great day. Can't wait to see you
again.

I cracked the widest smile, unable to tune out the flutters in my stomach at the idea of spending time with him
again.

I typed a fast reply, already thinking about later.

ME

Yes, works for me. Your place is fine. Send
me your address.

How about Billy's? We can eat out on their
covered deck. Nobody serves better pulled
chicken in this town. We can walk there.
Together.

Or there's the Music City Market. Always
wanted to try their renowned turkey legs.
Never visited since they opened last fall.

My chest swelled at the sight of the three little dots
bouncing at the bottom of my screen.

JACOB

Billy's. I'll make a reservation. Seven?

ME

Perfect. I'll meet you at six.

JACOB

It's a date.

Have a beautiful day, Maddie.

The day passed in a blur. Emily and I shared the house with two other med students working with her. They were barely ever here due to their hectic schedules. I spent my day running errands and tidying up the place so my sister and her roommates could relax once they got home.

At six, I rang Jacob's apartment buzzer from the sidewalk. Before I could even announce myself, he appeared in front of me. The warm late-spring breeze tousled his hair. Dressed in black jeans and a Henley shirt with the sleeves pushed up to his elbows, a leather band around his wrist, and boots, he looked even more handsome than I remembered. Especially in the daylight.

The dimple in his chin gave him a boyish charm.

He scanned me from head to toe, and when he stepped closer to press a kiss to my cheek, I caught a whiff of his mountain-fresh cologne. "Maddie, you're beautiful."

"Thanks," I murmured, warmth rising to my cheeks. His compliment had me giddy all over again. "You're pretty nice-looking yourself."

"Shall we?" he offered. "Our reservation is in fifty minutes. Let's go for a walk first." Grabbing my hand in his, he led the way.

Jacob was everything I loved in a guy, and I enjoyed the easy comfort we'd been sharing since the moment he saved me in that bar the other night.

Strolling by the river, we eased into more conversation after we finished dinner.

"When will you know if you got the job?" he asked, smiling at me, never releasing my hand. The kind of smile that heated my core.

I shrugged. "Hopefully tomorrow. I'm meeting with his daughters. We'll see how it goes. I really hope it works out. I'm not sure this kind of opportunity will present itself more than once."

"I think it's admirable what you're doing. Those kids will be lucky to have you in their lives."

We exchanged timid smiles. All night, we had grown closer, our chemistry impossible to ignore. We paused to watch the opposite shore when he traced the side of my face with his knuckles, sending addictive shivers through me. I felt his gaze burning into my skin.

The flutters I had felt before mushroomed in my stomach.

"Can I kiss you?" Jacob asked after what felt like forever.

I turned, rested one hand against his chest, and nodded. "I'd be really unhappy if you didn't."

Tilting my head back, I met his lips. Careful and warm.

My head spun.

My heart cavorted in my chest.

With my hands locked around his neck, I drew him closer and deepened the kiss. Jacob entangled his fingers in my hair while his other hand wound around my waist.

Neither of us required fresh air anymore.

Someone wolf-whistled behind us, and we pulled apart.

Jacob skimmed my lips with his thumb, then traced his own, as if to make sure it had really happened.

A satisfied smile brightened his features, and I was sure I wore one just like it.

We resumed our walk, our fingers now intertwined, and no gap between our bodies. Whenever we paused at a street corner, he pressed his mouth to mine in a slow, intoxicating kiss that made my toes curl.

The breeze picked up, sending a chill through me. Jacob held me closer, casually tracing the skin beneath the strap of my summer dress with one finger.

"Thank you for tonight," I whispered, rising to my tiptoes to kiss his lips once we reached his building.

"Wanna come upstairs?" he asked. Before I could reply, he pulled me to him, and I buried my face in his chest. "I'm not ready for the night to end."

"What's on your mind?" I tilted my head back to meet his gaze and blinked.

"We don't have to do anything other than cuddle. I kinda want to hold on to you for a bit longer."

"I'm not ready to go either," I admitted.

As soon as we stepped inside his apartment, Jacob gripped my hips and lowered his mouth to mine, claiming it in a kiss that weakened my knees.

We kissed for what seemed like hours. Until my lips felt too sensitive to continue.

"Make yourself at home," he said once we broke apart. "Snack? We could watch a movie."

"Movie sounds awesome. Want any help?"

"Nah, I'll be right back. Beer?"

I shook my head. "Can't. I'm a lightweight, and I'm driving. Better not."

While he busied himself in the kitchen, the scent of freshly popped kernels tickled my nostrils. I perused his living room. Jacob lived in a one-bedroom apartment in a five-story brownstone. It was small but cozy. The walls were painted white, and most furniture was black. The place looked a lot like its tenant. Classic and mysterious. Science books occupied most of the bookshelf along the wall opposite the TV. A couple of thriller and fantasy fiction titles I hadn't read yet were in the top section.

"You're an Avery Davis and Tessa Salinger fan?" I asked from where I stood, my back turned to him.

"Yes. I love the worlds Avery Davis creates. Salinger, I've been a fan since I got a copy of *Spite* on my sixteenth birthday. Are you?"

"Kinda. I've only read two of Salinger's books so far. I'm more of a Brandon Clifford type of girl. Avery Davis, I've heard of her but never read anything she's written. I think her husband, Carter Hills, is a friend of Sam Stevens, my *fingers-crossed* future boss. Who knows, maybe I'll meet her someday if I get that job."

Jacob didn't reply, and seconds later, his warmth coiled around me and so did his arms while his lips grazed my nape. "You and I, we're already a great match." His smile caressed my skin, and I swiveled between his arms to press a quick peck to his lips.

It wasn't even midnight, and I struggled to keep my eyes open as the credits rolled across the screen.

"Spend the night," Jacob offered.

I straightened, and the gears of my brain engaged. I enjoyed the comfort he brought me. I felt safe in his arms and relished the connection we shared. But would I hate myself for spending the night with him?

"Sorry, I didn't mean to scare you. I just spoke my mind. I should have added that we can just sleep. Nothing more."

The frantic beating of my heart calmed down.

I inhaled and relaxed, folding my legs beneath me. A yawn passed my lips. *Be a grown-up, Maddie. You can go back to being a mature twenty-one-year-old in the morning.* I splayed my hand across his chest, feeling every thump of his heart under my palm. "I'd like to stay."

His brows shot up. "You would?"

I nodded and moved to my knees to kiss him. His scent enveloped me, and I felt good about my choice.

"No pressure, okay?" Jacob tipped my chin up with a finger, as if to make sure I knew he was speaking the truth.

"I wanna stay. I'm not used to having sleepovers, though."

He grimaced. "Me neither."

I let out a nervous smile. "Cool. Because it's a first."

"Are you—? Have…huh…have you ever been with anyone?"

"I had one boyfriend. We dated for a couple of months. It wasn't meant to last… I think we were too different… We expected opposite things from life."

Jacob cradled my face with one hand and searched my gaze. "For the record, I don't either. Invite women over, I mean. I'm not a people person, so I usually prefer being on my own. I had one serious relationship. And one…well… less serious. With you, it already feels different. Not only new, but like it could be the beginning of something."

We exchanged knowing glances that carried a lot of weight. We were both trusting someone we barely knew and getting out of our comfort zones. Together.

Jacob and I were much more alike than I had ever thought.

Knitting his fingers through mine, he led me to the bedroom. "I was serious before. I only want to sleep. And to cuddle. Nothing more. There's something special about you, Maddie. I have no intention of spoiling it. Everything about you is beautiful."

"Can I kiss you?" I asked, repeating his own words, feeling bold for once in my life.

His eyes darkened. "Yeah. Then we'll stop, because if we don't, I might have a hard time resisting you."

I nodded, not wanting to risk the moment by saying something stupid.

With my eyes shut, I quieted my breathing and my thundering heart when his lips molded to mine, deciding not to miss a second of how amazing he made me feel.

Breathless, we both pushed apart at the same time.

"Okay, bedtime," Jacob announced, his voice husky.

We grinned at each other, our foreheads pressed together, oxygen flooding our mushy brains.

Feeling the flush on my cheeks, I followed him to the small bathroom. Black tiled floors and ceiling, white walls, and a touch of orange in the towels and square rug. It was all masculine, jut like him.

"There are toothbrushes in the first drawer, and I'll bring you a shirt to sleep in." He watched me, waiting for an answer.

"Sure. Sounds good." Was I really having a sleepover at a guy's place? Remembering my sister's warning from the other night, I sent her a text. Including the address we were at. It would prevent her from going ballistic. Yes, Emily had a tendency to be a bit overprotective of me.

EMILY

Enjoy your night *smiley face*

A stupid smile peeked out as I slid my phone back into my pocket after setting the alarm.

Jacob knocked on the door at the same exact moment. "Can I come in?"

"Yes."

"Here, I brought you two. Pick one."

Once he left, I undressed and slipped on the white T-shirt. It fell to mid-thigh. His perfume lingered on the fabric, and I found myself hooked on the masculine scent, feeling at ease as it wrapped around me.

With soap and water, I removed most of my makeup and joined him in his bedroom. I gasped at the sight of him—shirtless, wearing only his unbuttoned pants.

He twirled on his feet, catching me ogling him.

"Sorry," I said with a lopsided smile.

Jacob inched closer, kissed my forehead, and disappeared into the bathroom.

Not sure what to do, I slipped under the covers, wondering whether he slept on the left or right side. I felt inexperienced in that moment. This was all new territory to me.

The bathroom door opened, and our eyes locked onto each other like magnets, unable to resist. "I love the image of you in my bed," he said, with mischief lighting up his features, only wearing pajama pants that hung low on his hips. He turned off the lights and slid under the covers, pressing his body against mine from behind, his face nuzzled into the crook of my neck.

He wrapped one arm around my waist, his hand resting on my stomach at the junction of my T-shirt and the waistband of my panties. He traced circles on my bare skin with his thumb, sending shivers of pleasure through me.

With a sway of my hips, I scooted closer, his hard-on now nesting between my ass cheeks.

"Good night, Maddie."

I swallowed. "Good night."

Unable to fall asleep, I listened to his steady breathing and stared into the darkness. I'd missed this.

Affection.

It'd been too long since someone held me like that.

As if I was his.

As if I was precious.

I felt every thump of Jacob's heart between my shoulder blades.

His hand ventured to rest on my hip. I wriggled on the bed as one of his arms held me tighter against his chest.

My eyelids fluttered close.

His breathing steadied.

And I dozed off in no time.

6

SAM

Why was I nervous like going on a first date? Madison wasn't here to interview me, for Christ's sake. She was here to meet the girls.

When we had talked yesterday, we decided to spend an hour or two at the house, then go to the park at the end of the street to have a picnic and talk about logistics and expectations while my daughters played around.

Dressed in faded jeans and a black T-shirt, freshly shaved, I joined my kids downstairs as they watched cartoons.

"Oh, you smell good," Justine said as I squeezed myself between them on the couch.

Mikaella leaned in and sniffed my shirt. "Yes, you smell *gooood.*"

Busted. I might have used cologne. Did I overdo it? Would I scare Madison away? Why did I put it on in the first place? What was I thinking? I just wanted to look presentable. Nice. Was that a crime? Okay, I was being ridiculous. My rustiness with people—and women in particular—ran deeper than I'd realized.

"Maybe I should change."

Justine climbed onto my lap and hooked her arms around my neck. "No, Daddy. I love when you smell good." The smile she offered me melted all my fears, and I chased away my apprehension with a deep inhale.

"Okay, fine. You win." I tickled her belly, and the sound of her giggles filled the room.

"Is *Mallison* here?" she asked once I stopped the torture.

"Not yet. Her name is Madison, with a *D*, like *dinosaur*, and she should be here in about ten minutes. What are we watching?"

"Something stupid Justine chose. I don't like it. It's for babies," Mikaella whined, her arms crossed over her chest, giving me a pointed look. Yep, her teenage years would be so much fun.

"I'm not a baby, Mika. You are the baby," Justine replied.

I placed a hand on both their thighs. "Stop. No one is a baby. Justine is allowed to enjoy this…this… What is it anyway? Are those pink kangaroos even talking, or are they only making those weird sounds?" I asked, my eyes now glued to the TV screen. "Don't tell me. It doesn't matter." I shook my head. Mikaella was right. This looked awful. The sight of the kangaroos alone gave me a headache. "Madison will be here shortly. I'd like you girls to be nice, okay? Can you do that for me?"

Justine nodded.

Mikaella shrugged.

I cursed in silence.

"What's wrong, sweet pea? We've already talked about this. You promised you'd give Madison a chance, remember?"

"I changed my mind. I don't want another mama. I

already have one. And one day, she'll come back to get me."

The already fractured pieces of my heart turned to dust.

I wrapped an arm around the shoulders of my eldest daughter until she rested her head against my chest. "Mika, you're not getting another mama. No one is. Madison will only help us so Daddy can go back to the work he loves to do. If you want to live on the big camping bus like we've talked about and travel the country, then we need Madison to come with us. Either that or we're not going. I need some help. I'm sure you'll like her. She's nice and—"

The doorbell rang, and Justine rushed to the door before I could tell her to wait.

"*Mallison,*" she said as she yanked the door open, jumping around. "Daddy, *Mallison* is here. *Mallison* is here. *Mallison* is here. Daddy. Daddy, come."

"Hey, you must be Justine, right? You can call me Maddie," Madison said as she kneeled to level her face with my little girl's. "I've heard so much about you. And if I remember correctly, you're a princess. Am I right?"

I watched the exchange from a safe distance.

Justine's face brightened up. "You can tell I'm a princess? For real?"

Madison smiled, and a chunk of my heart that was dead came back to life. "Oh yes. Look at your purple dress. It's really princess-y. Later, I'll want you to show me around your kingdom if that's okay with you?"

Justine bobbed her head, her smile widening, happiness radiating from her.

My heart melted a little more, filled with an exciting buzz.

She slid her little hand into Madison's and pulled her

forward. "Come. Mika is not a princess. She thinks pink is only for babies. She only wants to wear black clothes, and the other day she put marker in her eyes. She looked scary."

"Marker in her eyes? Are you sure? It sounds painful."

Justine snickered and closed her eyes, sliding a finger across her eyelids. "Not in her eyes, silly. Black lines here and here."

"Oh, I see. Your daddy must have had a great time removing it." Madison's eyes met mine for the first time, and I shrugged, offering her a slight smile that she mirrored.

My heart flipped a little. Just a tiny bit. Maybe this could work after all.

"Come on. Mika is in there," Justine told our guest, pulling her toward the den.

I followed close behind, letting Madison introduce herself to my six-turning-sixteen-year-old daughter.

"Hi, Mikaella. I'm Maddie. It's nice to meet you. I've heard great things about you. What are you watching?" She took a seat on the opposite side of the couch where Mikaella sat.

My daughter said nothing, ignoring the woman conversing with her.

"It's fine. You don't have to talk to me. We can just watch this show together if it's okay with you. Do you mind?"

Mikaella shrugged.

Justine neared Madison and climbed onto her lap, twirling the loose strands of her dark hair around her fingers. "You look like a princess too. Your hair is pretty. I love pretty hair. Princesses love pretty hair too. You're missing a crown. Wait for me." My daughter jumped to her feet and disappeared, only to come back a minute later with two sparkling plastic crowns. "Here," she said as she fixed one on Madison's head. "Now we are both princesses."

From her end of the couch, Mikaella studied them. I could tell she wanted to join in but refused to break her walls. Nowadays, I wasn't the most trusting guy myself, so I couldn't blame her for having trust issues too. My heart bled some more for the pain Lisa had inflicted.

"Now that you're a real princess too, want to visit our castle?" Justine asked. "It's back there," she said, pointing to the back door.

"Sure," Madison said, rising to her feet, and holding out her hand to take Justine's. "Do you want to come with us, Mikaella?"

"It's Mika."

"Oh, sorry. Are you coming with us, Mika?"

My daughter shrugged but finally nodded. Her curiosity would get the best of her. No way would she ever be able to resist Madison for too long.

"Great. Show me the way then."

Madison and I exchanged another hint of a smile as she walked past me. This was awkward. Having another woman in this house. No, a college-aged girl. Anyway, I wasn't sure how I felt about a stranger spending a lot of time in our day-to-day lives yet. All of us would have to get used to this new dynamic.

Leaning against the living room archway, I watched the three of them as they exited through the back door and emptied my lungs, the knots around my stomach tightening, instead of loosening, once space separated us.

My brain started making up scenarios.

Could this really work out? Going back on tour? Madison taking care of the girls? Our being a happy family once again?

Or was all this just a mirage? A fake sense of possibilities I had no right to expect anything from.

The three of them laughed, already at ease with one another. Even Mikaella couldn't refrain from joining in. The sight and realization that my little girls had missed so much in the last two years while I was busy mending my own heart hurt as much as they fixed a broken string inside me. For the longest time, I didn't infuse laughter into our household, and it pained me to come to the same conclusion as Riley did. That all three of us needed this new experience. Together. A new opportunity to connect and move on with our lives. For good.

I shut my eyes, exhaled, and busied myself in the kitchen, watching Madison interact with my eldest daughter and giving Justine a piggyback ride, through the bay window. She said something, and the girls laughed their hearts out. Madison grabbed her phone, and the girls started dancing. Did she put music on? From where I stood, I couldn't tell for sure.

At some point, I couldn't contain the smile that broke free on my face. Madison looked like she belonged here. With them.

Tension rolled off me in waves.

For a moment, I could see the clouds over our heads parting and the sun shining brighter upon us. Yes, perhaps Riley's crazy idea could work out after all.

Peace tinted the air and calmed my worries.

———

"Okay, girls. You'll spend the day with Madison. Daddy has a meeting with Uncle Riley, and I'll be gone until the evening. Promise me you'll be nice."

"Yes, Daddy," Justine said as I lowered her to her feet.

"Here," I said to Mikaella after I finished braiding her hair. "What about you, sweet pea? Will you be a good girl with Madison?"

She glanced away. "It depends."

I sat on the edge of the mattress and pulled her closer. "Give her a chance. A real one. Do it for me. Madison really likes you, and she's been nothing but great with you guys so far. You always have fun when she comes over. I know two weeks is not a long time to get to know someone, but I'm positive you'll enjoy your time together. She has a whole day of activities planned for you two. We already talked about it. School is over, and it's time to enjoy your summer."

"Fine," she said, forcing a smile.

In the past two weeks, since Madison came over the first time, we'd spent six full days with her, and she had dinner with us twice. So far, the girls got along with her just fine. Even though Mikaella acted as if spending time with her annoyed her, she always let her guard down within five minutes of being around her. Madison had a way of reaching my daughter through the glass cage she had built around herself. My six-going-onto-sixteen sported happy grins these days. And that was worth more than any performances I'd give in my life. Worth more than any amount of money I could ever earn.

In the end, I had warmed up to Madison looking after my daughters in my home faster than I thought I would.

Springing to my feet, I scooped Mikaella over my shoulder, tickling her at the same time. "Come on, sweet pea, stop brooding. Put on your cheerful face now. Do it for me."

We rolled onto the bed, laughing. My little girl cupped my cheeks. "I will. I love when you put your cheerful face on too, Daddy. *Grinchy* isn't a good look on you."

Fog clouded my vision, and I blinked my emotions away. I swallowed the boulder in my throat as her words wound their way into my heart. Yes, joy and giggles were more frequent these days in the Stevenses' household. And lightness had invaded our home too.

Justine joined us, sitting on my stomach.

"Girls, listen." I caught a wheezing breath in. "I'm sorry for everything. The last two years have been hard on me too. I'm ready to change things up around here. For us to have a fresh start. To be cheerful and smile more, so much that our lips are stretched forever and our happiness can't be erased."

Justine leaned forward and pulled my cheeks out, creating a huge, ridiculous exaggeration of a smile. "Like this?"

I had to laugh at that. "Yes, baby girl."

Mikaella shook her head. "No, please, you look scary. Don't grin too much. It's freaky."

"I'll stop smiling if you stop with the moody attitude. *Grinchy* isn't a good look on you either," I said, repeating her own words. "Do we have a deal?" I sat and held out my hand.

Her eyes darted from my palm to my eyes for a long beat. An I-mean-business frown appeared across her forehead. My daughter already possessed way too much backbone for her young age. She'd be a tough opponent growing up.

She groaned, putting her best game face on. "Deal."

We shook on it, and Justine climbed onto my back. "Let's get ready then because Madison will be here in fifteen minutes."

With Justine still clinging to me and Mikaella in my arms, we made it downstairs, the three of us laughing.

We were done with breakfast when the doorbell rang.

"*Mallison* is here, Daddy," Justine screamed as she ran toward the front door, her sister in tow.

I put the dishes away and wiped the kitchen island as they sauntered back in my direction.

"Good morning, Mr. Stevens," the nanny said. Coming from her mouth, Mr. Stevens made me feel like my old man. Damn it. I was older than her, sure. But I wasn't *that* old.

"We've already talked about this. Sam is fine. Don't Mr. Stevens me. Please."

"Then it's Maddie. No more Madison."

I ran a hand through my hair, taking in the woman before me. Dressed in black shorts and a cream tank top, she looked even younger than I remembered. Dewy complexion and rounded eyes. With hardly any make-up on, only her lips painted in a soft shade of pink. A few strands of her hair had drawn loose around her face from the low ponytail she was sporting.

She bent over to pick up Justine, and I got a peek at the swell of her breasts.

A fuzzy feeling worked through me.

I hadn't been close to any woman, except for my friends' wives or the girls' teachers, in two years. Having one in my kitchen, nonetheless, had a weird way of making my testosterone spike.

I cleared my throat before my mind wandered to uncharted territories. "I should be back after dinner. There's chicken in the fridge I made last night. And snacks in the pantry. My phone number is by the sink in case you erased it by mistake from your phone, and I made a set of house keys for you. Also, all the emergency numbers are on there," I pointed to a paper on the countertop, "and—"

Madison inched closer and put her hand on my forearm. She barely brushed my skin, and I almost shot my load in my pants. I really was a sick motherfucker.

"Mr. Stev…Sam. Stop. We'll be fine. I've been here almost every day in the last week. You don't need to worry. We've been over this more than once. And no, I haven't erased your contact from my phone, and I can dial 9-1-1 from memory."

She offered me a sweet smile, and I stepped back, desperate to move out of her magnetic field. All my poles were off. I had to get them back in check.

"Yeah, you're right." Warmth swirled inside me. I must have looked like a complete lunatic, not a father of two who had all his shit together and who was about to leave on tour for months.

Mikaella walked into the kitchen and broke the sort of daze I'd fallen into.

Thank you, sweet pea.

"Can we bake a cake? You said last time you'd show me how to ice one."

Madison's grin widened. "Sure. I even brought little sugar flowers I made to decorate it."

"You did? Can I see them?"

Justine came running. "Cake," she cheered with her adorable, overflowing enthusiasm, a trademark of hers.

Madison fished a small container out of her bag and showed the girls. They both screamed with excitement. They'd be fine.

From my office slash music studio, which I had reclaimed as mine, I grabbed my guitar case, ready to get out of here.

When I walked back into the kitchen, the girls were already deep in baking mode.

Justine sat on the counter, cracking eggs, a white—did Madison bring it?—paper chef hat on, and Mikaella was propped on a stool, wearing a banana yellow apron, busy pouring flour into a measuring cup, white powder sprinkled all over her. Madison stood between them, a priceless, pride-filled grin stretching her face, her eyes sparkling, giving them instructions.

They'd be more than fine.

Why was I so worried about leaving them for a few hours? Standing in the kitchen doorway, I felt silly.

For a long minute, I watched them. The three of them looked at ease working together. The kitchen consisted of an island with an oversized butcher block countertop, stainless steel appliances, and a large window overlooking the backyard. The room had been neglected over the years. When the girls were little, Lisa and I used to bake pies on Thanksgiving together and cookies on Christmas day. On Sunday mornings, she made hot chocolate while I flipped pancakes, to my daughters' greatest enjoyment. Our own family traditions that had gotten lost after her departure. A fleck of nostalgia hit me, followed by a draft of happiness that took root in my chest. I relished the sight of this room, that contained so many good memories, being animated once again.

"What are you baking?" I asked as I landed a kiss on Justine's head.

"*Crotchcolate* cake, Daddy. Your favorite." Joy radiated from her.

"You mean chocolate," Madison said before I could correct her.

"Yes. *Crotchcolate.*"

I sighed, and Madison snickered behind her hand.

"We'll practice it, sweetie," she told my oblivious baby girl.

I leaned forward, careful not to get flour all over me as

I kissed Mikaella's cheek. "Mika, you're doing good. I can't wait to taste that cake tonight."

"Can we stay up until you come home to eat it together?"

"Absolutely. I wouldn't have it any other way."

"Justine, we'll make Daddy the most beautiful cake he's ever seen. Careful. Don't drop the eggshells into the batter."

I spun around to leave but bumped into Madison, squeezed between Mikaella's stool and the refrigerator behind us. My eyes darted to her chest, rising and falling, for a quick second before I brought my gaze back to hers.

"Here," I said, wiping the flour from her cheek with the pad of my thumb unable to help myself.

Her breathing picked up. So did mine.

High-voltage electricity gushed through me, and I yanked my hand back. I scowled to avoid sending her the wrong signals about a nonexistent attraction between us. Our relationship wasn't about this. I'd hired her to care for my daughters. Nothing more.

"Thanks," she whispered, eyeing me as if she were trying to understand the switch in my demeanor.

"I-I gotta go. You call me if you need anything, okay?"

She nodded. "I will. And we'll wait for you to eat that *crotchcolate* cake." A flush appeared on her face as she used my baby's word.

"I'm counting on it."

Before I could say something stupid and my brain started making double-meaning jokes, I walked away. Outside, with my back resting against the shut door, I breathed in and out, trying to find a reasonable explanation for my sudden lack of boundaries.

Coming short, I shook my head, pushed the thought

away, and climbed behind the wheel of my SUV, ready to get far away from here.

7

MADISON

Why was Sam looking at me with a frown? As if I'd done something wrong. Nothing had happened. The girls and I were baking a cake when he walked in. At first, he had looked relaxed and happy. What had changed? His eyes had darkened when he'd glanced at me from up close, his pupils stealing the color of his eyes.

I had tried to swallow but failed when his heated gaze landed on me.

No matter how I flipped around our last encounter in my head, I couldn't come up with a reason why Sam Stevens would have been suddenly annoyed with me.

Justine spilled milk on the countertop as she lifted the measuring cup.

"Justine, you're making a mess," Mikaella complained.

The little girl's bottom lip quivered, and tears pooled in her eyes.

"It's all fine. Don't worry, okay? You're doing a great job, sweetie," I said, patting her head once she poured the remaining white liquid into the bowl.

"Like that?"

I nodded, and her cheerfulness returned. The girl's delight was contagious, and a wide grin split my face.

"Can I add the *crotchcolate* now?"

"Chocolate, dummy," her sister said.

"No, Mika. Enough. Don't use this word around your sister. Be nice and help her out instead." I crossed my arms over my chest, and Mikaella studied me for a moment, probably wondering if I was being serious. "What do you have to say to Justine?"

She muttered something under her breath.

"What did you say?"

"Sorry." She spoke so low that I wasn't even sure I heard it right.

"Come on, Mika, you can do better than that."

"Sorry, Justine. I am sorry I called you dummy. You're not. Happy now?" she asked, angling her body until we faced each other.

I clasped my hands together. "Better. Now let's finish this cake because we're going to the park before lunch. I brought a swimsuit, and we can play in the fountains."

"The fountains? I love the fountains," Justine singsonged, her happiness fully restored now.

"You're coming in with us?" her sister asked, stopping midway as she poured the batter into a mold.

"Sure. Why not? I like to have fun too."

"Daddy never comes in. He always watches from the side. Says he's too old."

"I'm not your daddy, girls. Age is just a number. Anyway, I wanna play in the fountains with you two. It's hot outside, and no way am I staying on the sidelines. What about a picnic? We could eat there."

"Yes," they both screamed at the same time.

———

When Sam came back, looking his usual mix of handsome, serious, and sexy but more tired than usual, the girls and I were in the backyard, tossing water balloons around.

Even though he wasn't always the most pleasant man —someone who ought to smile more often—he had everything women swooned over. Tall, a couple of inches over six feet, I bet he hid delicious chest muscles underneath his clothes. The ridges of his body, visible through his T-shirt, had me hot and bothered. His broody attitude made him mysterious and inaccessible, and his voice, rough and low with a Southern drawl, added to his magnetism, husky enough to melt panties.

No doubt he was a country music superstar. Just his presence could steal the breathable air from a room.

Did women throw their bras at him when he gave concerts in the past? Did they follow him to his hotel room and try to seduce him? Did they tattoo his face on their backs or ask him to autograph their breasts?

A twinge started in my toes and reached my skull.

I shouldn't think about my boss this way. I was the hired help. Nothing more. Nothing less. My job was to take care of his two adorable daughters, and I'd never do anything to jeopardize that. Ever.

My mind wandered to Jacob. His hooded eyes and sexy bed hair in the morning, the intensity of his gaze each time it roamed over me, the softness of his kisses, and the strength of his arms that one time he held me at night. Our friendship was blossoming, and neither of us was in a hurry to take it to the next level. We enjoyed each other's company, and for now, it was more than I could ask for. We hadn't discussed it, but since I was leaving in the fall, we were both aware that a relationship would only complicate things between us.

Our easy friendship, common interests in literature and music, and our introverted lifestyle, added to our burgeoning attraction and made us a perfect match.

It also prevented me from entertaining a forbidden crush on the man who had hired me, one that had the potential to hurt me and screw with my job.

The other night, curious about him, I'd watched a video from three years ago of Sam rocking a stage. His hair had been longer back then, and his eyes glinted with joy—something missing nowadays. The present version of Sam Stevens always sported dark circles under his worry-filled eyes, and a permanent sadness lingered in his gaze. No matter what he did, it was always there, tinting his irises.

"Oh, you're home already?" I asked him, pushing the wet hair glued to my forehead back to clear my vision. "What time is it? We haven't had dinner yet."

Sam stepped closer, his hands floating between us. "It's only four. My meeting ended early, and I didn't feel like eating out, so I just came home instead. I prefer a night in to fancy restaurants or clubs anytime." He shrugged. "It was a no-brainer."

His eyes lowered to my red bikini top and snapped back to my face quickly.

"Sorry. I-I usually don't parade half-naked around you…people. I usually…you know…wear clothes. I had them, huh, I had them on earlier, then I got hot and undressed when I decided to get wet." *Uh-oh, that's coming out all-wrong.* I sounded like a lunatic. And a sex-crazed exhibitionist. Dear God. I paused, trying to regroup my thoughts and stop my rambling.

Sam watched me, his lips pinched together, barely

containing the smile that threatened to burst out—*jerk*. It was clear from the crooked smile uplifting the corners of his mouth, he wouldn't help me out of this one. I was on my own.

I gave a loud, theatrical sigh as if he was forcing me to give an explanation and wasting my time. "I should use a towel now. I'm still dripping all over your deck. One slip and you might end up sliding right into my puddle… and me."

Sam cocked an eyebrow.

Gosh. Why were all my words sounding like innuendos while talking to my boss, half-undressed? My brain was either on strike or defective. These words didn't even sound like mine. *Geez…someone please kill me right now.* "I'm soaked, and being drenched isn't comfortable. Sorry, I'll get changed. And…huh…shut up." Oh, for crying out loud. Every time I opened my mouth, it got worse. "I'll go now." *Smooth, Maddie, real smooth.* I felt my face heating up.

He studied me a little longer, pleasure written all over his face.

"Daddy, watch out," Mikaella warned as she and Justine ran toward us and shot water balloons at Sam, dousing him in no time.

I pinched my lips together to fight the fit of giggles stirring deep inside me.

Sam stood there in his damp jeans and shirt, an unreadable expression overtaking his face and chasing his amusement away.

The girls froze, water balloons still in their hands.

I stopped breathing.

Would he get mad? I wrinkled my nose, waiting for his reaction. Instead, he grabbed a handful of ammunition from the bucket beside me and tossed them at his daughters. They both started running around, laughing and screaming for more.

His eyes twinkled and I exhaled, relishing this playful side of him.

From the lounger, I picked up a towel and wrapped it around myself, ready to leave.

My job here was done.

Just when I was about to open the back door, Mikaella caught up with me. Her eyes rounded as she stared at me. "Are you leaving?"

I kneeled before her. "Yes, I am. Your daddy is back. I'll let you spend time with him. I'm sure he missed you today."

She tugged at my hand. "But I like it better when you're here. You could have dinner with us. You can't leave without tasting the cake. We worked hard to make it pretty for Daddy."

My heart expanded in my chest. These little girls already owned my heart. "Maybe you could save me a slice, and I'll taste it tomorrow."

She shook her head. "No. I wanna taste it with you tonight like we were supposed to. I'll tell Daddy to come back later." She twirled on her feet, but I grabbed her wrist before she could rush to him.

My eyes followed Sam, now completely soaked, being chased by Justine, both of them zigzagging across the back-yard and giggling. The sight of them brought a curve to my lips. "Mika, it's better if I go now. We'll have many more occasions to eat together. Go play with your daddy."

She shook her head. "I don't wanna play anymore if you leave."

Pieces of my heart cracked, and I pulled her into my arms. "Mika, listen to me, I—"

"What's wrong, sweet pea?" Sam asked, closing in on us, his hair falling over his eyes, giving him a rakish look.

My entire being pulsed at the sight of him, free of all the icy control he usually kept close around him.

"Why don't you play with us?"

Mikaella pushed away from me and firmed her shoulders, her attitude back. "Maddie is leaving. I'm not playing anymore if she goes. We were supposed to eat our cake together. She was supposed to have dinner with us. You were supposed to be at your music work. It's not fair. I want Maddie to stay."

"You leaving?" Justine asked as she moved between all of us, her eyes big and full of question marks. "Why? You don't wanna play with us anymore?" Her lips shuddered, and another fragment of my heart cracked.

"I love spending time with you two, but your daddy is back home, so it means I must go. I'll see you both tomorrow, okay? Don't be sad. We'll have a great time, I promise."

Justine circled my neck with her arms. "Can we go to the fountains again?"

"Sure, I'd love to."

"Can Maddie stay, Daddy?" Mikaella asked, her eyes bright with hope.

Sam cleared his throat and took a step in my direction. He locked his dark gaze on mine, swallowing me in. "Why do you have to go? The girls are right. Why don't you stay? You guys were having fun. I intruded on your game."

A shiver ran through me. "I shouldn't. It's your time with the girls."

"I brought everything for a barbecue on my way home. We can eat outside and—" He shrugged. "We can taste that chocolate cake you promised this morning. I've been looking forward to it all day. What do you say?"

"I…" Why wasn't I able to come up with a good enough reason to walk away?

Sam's heavy stare pinned me on the spot, and my brain lost the ability to think clearly.

"Say yes," Justine pleaded.

"Please," Mikaella added, giving me puppy dog eyes.

Sam took one step closer, and before I could add something, he popped two water balloons over my head. "Oops. You're soaked again. I guess you can't leave just now and must stay a little longer so that you don't ruin the floors when you go in, dripping wet. You know because if you're drenched, I could slide into you…or your puddle."

"Ohmygod. No, you can't do this. It's unfair. Using my previous humiliation against me in a battle of words is a cheap shot."

He winked, and I nearly melted into a puddle right there on his deck. How bad was the flush on my face right about now? That word again. I should never, ever think or say 'puddle' again. From now on, it would always be tinged with memories of this moment—with him—and my utter humiliation.

"Your words, not mine," he said, lifting his arms in surrender.

A fit of laughter escaped both our lips. I supposed the ice was broken between us. Maybe it would help melt the tension that always swirled between us whenever we stood close—the same tension that had been there since the day we met—for good.

"I can't believe I said that." I shook my head, trying to get rid of the moment.

Oblivious to the exchange, the girls laughed at my dripping face. Sam looked like he'd already forgotten my little embarrassing moment because he tossed missiles at his daughters before running after them.

With a sigh, I discarded my towel. "Girls, I think we should come up with a revenge plan." They both bobbed their heads, still laughing their hearts out as we devised a scheme to get back at their father.

For the next twenty minutes, we threw all the remaining balloons we had at Sam, now rolling around on the lawn, grass stains on his jeans, his arms folded over his head like a shield, begging us to stop our attack.

The girls helped him to get to his feet when we were short of projectiles before disappearing into their castle in the woods.

"You're sure it's okay for me to crash your family dinner?" I asked, still unsure if it was a good idea.

Sam busied himself removing the bits of grass stuck to his wet shirt. "I'm sure. I'm the one who disrupted your plans."

I nodded, avoiding his eyes.

"And Madison—"

"Maddie," I replied, savoring the sound of my name rolling off his lips. *Focus, girl. Enough with the misplaced crush. Grow a spine and get over it. Not happening.*

"Yes, *Maddie*. Thanks for bringing joy to my little girls' lives. Thanks for putting smiles on their faces. They haven't had as much fun as they should have had in the last two years. It-it's all my fault… For over a year, I was in a very dark place. I'm grateful you're here to show me what I've been missing. And how I can get better."

"Stop it. You're a great father."

"Yeah. Well, I try to be. But I screwed up. A lot. My life was a mess, and it impacted my children's happiness. Without you around, I'm not sure I would've realized it soon enough. So, thank you. For everything you are doing for our family. I don't say it often enough."

I bowed my head, at a loss for words. Vulnerability looked good on him. Almost dangerous.

The air between us heated up.

When I tilted my head back, I met his eyes, dark and cryptic. He watched me for a beat as if deciding whether to tell me something or not, before breaking eye contact.

"I should get changed."

"Me too," I said, following him close behind toward the house but making sure to keep enough space between us. "Careful. Don't get the floors wet," I teased.

He watched me over his shoulder, choking on a laugh. The air charged around us. Sam blinked, cracked a tiny smile, but said nothing as he stared ahead and retreated inside.

———

"They're both fast asleep. I don't know what you did today, but I'll buy your recipe. Neither one complained when I told them it was bedtime. Mika, who usually always has something to argue about, stayed quiet."

"I can't tell you my secrets, or they won't be secrets anymore. All I can say is that we ran around all day. And can you believe Justine napped for an hour and a half this afternoon? Mika didn't, but we rested anyway."

He nodded and motioned to stand. "Drink?"

"No, thanks. I'll stick to lemonade. I'm a lightweight. I don't drink and drive. One is enough to get me dizzy."

Sam fetched a can of beer and resumed his seat across from me on the back deck.

The terrace ran almost the entire length of the back of the house. Accessible from the kitchen door, the outdoor cooking space—featuring a grill, a sink, and an under-counter refrigerator set into a stacked stone structure—was to the left of the dining area. Matching loungers and a set of dark couches were two steps up on our right, positioned by the door leading to the den and dining room.

Both side neighbors were far enough, and the thick line of mature trees bordering their land created natural fences, allowing enough intimacy.

The girls' castle was nestled in the woods that outlined the far end of the backyard, surrounded by an expanse of manicured green lawn. A wooden swing set with a corkscrew slide and a guitar-shaped covered sandbox were on our right, where the back deck ended.

"Listen," Sam said. "I was thinking… Before the big tour, I'd like to throw a party for the girls. With their friends. Something special. I might ask for your help. You're amazing with kids, so your intake would be useful. I know it's months away from now, but I'm putting it out there…so I don't forget."

"Let me know what you have in mind, and I'll be happy to brainstorm ideas with you and help out."

"Are they giving you trouble?"

"The girls?" I asked.

"Yeah. Mika can be stubborn sometimes."

"Nah. They're good kids. And let me tell you they love baking. It doesn't seem like it, but cooking is a mix of literacy, math, and sciences. It's a great way to teach kids without them feeling like you're trying to force knowledge into their brains."

"Whoa. I'd never seen it like that before, but it makes sense."

"Plus, it's fun since we can eat our creations afterward. It's great for their self-esteem. Has Mikaella told you about Stella's birthday party on Friday? They stopped by earlier to drop off the invitation. It's from late afternoon till the evening at the park. Justine is invited too, but you gotta be present."

"Mika said nothing. We're auditioning musicians to form the band on Friday. It's usually a long and exhausting process. I'm not sure I'll make it on time."

"I can go if you want," I offered. "The girls are really looking forward to it. Stella's mom said there would be a magician and a petting zoo."

"You don't have to. I can talk to Stella's mom. She'll understand."

"I insist. Since Mika will be away for six months, she should enjoy time with her best friend while she's still in town, don't you think?"

Sam sipped his beer, drumming his fingers on the table, appearing to debate the idea in his head. "I'm still not comfortable asking you to put in more hours."

"When we first met, you and Riley told me there would be evening and night shifts. I'm prepared for all eventualities. I'm telling you that I'm happy to go if you agree."

Sam huffed. "I won't fight with you over this. Just make sure you still get some free time too before we leave. Because once we're on the road, it will be intense. Fun, but tiring sometimes."

I flipped my phone over on the table to check the time. "It's late. I should leave. Thanks for dinner. You didn't lie. I gotta say, those ribs were spectacular."

We both rose, and Sam shoved his hands into his pockets, looking a lot younger and vulnerable in the sunset. In the last few hours, some of the creases around his eyes had receded. "We'll see you tomorrow?"

"Sure. I'll be here at nine." I waved at him as I walked to my car, a vehicle I'd bought with the money I'd piled up, working two jobs at eighteen.

In the safety of my car, I blew out a long breath.

Why was the air tense every time Sam and I were alone in the same room?

My imagination was playing tricks on me. That had to be it.

I pulled away from the driveway and parked on the side of the road to text Jacob.

ME

I'm done with work. Want to hang out tonight?

His answer came within a minute.

JACOB

Wanna come over?

ME

I'll be there ASAP.

After Jacob buzzed me in, I climbed the stairs to his apartment, two at a time.

"Do you wanna go out or stay in?" he asked me, locking a hand around my waist and tugging me closer.

I leaned back and studied his face. "Night in would be awesome, but I kinda have somewhere to be later tonight. I was hoping you'd join me."

"Do we have time before leaving? There's something I'd like to try with you first."

I raised an eyebrow. "What is it?" I asked, the air molecules around us charging with possibilities.

"Do you trust me?"

"I do."

"Close your eyes then."

I heard a door being opened—or closed. Something

that sounded like a zipper. And plastic on plastic rubbing together. The suspense was killing me.

Jacob fixed something on my head. Was it a helmet? Or a hat? My pulse kicked up a notch. Should I be worried?

"Okay, look now." He spoke in that pleased tone he only ever used around me, mostly shy with everyone else.

My lids fluttered open, and my hands flew to cover my overexcited heart. I mirrored his gorgeous smile. "Ohmygod, you got these for us?"

"Nah, I borrowed them from a girl at work. She actually gave me a lesson during lunchtime so I wouldn't break my bones and would be able to stand for more than thirty seconds straight."

"You roller-skated in the lab during your lunch hour?"

"Kinda. I have to be able to care for you if you have a hard time staying upright. These are way tougher to manage than inline skates."

I took in the retro white roller skates. The ones people wore in eighties movies.

Without a word, I jumped into his inviting arms. "This is the best idea ever. I love it. I would break my neck with you any time, Jacob Williams. Only with you, though."

He fixed the helmet properly over my head. "Promise me you won't put them on without this."

I nodded, and he kissed my forehead.

"I promise. When can we go? Tonight? I always wanted to try roller skating. I used to watch old music videos when I was a kid and pictured myself skating around a rink, wearing them."

"I remember your eyes lighting up when you saw those girls skating around in that clothes ad the other night. Thought you might be onboard."

Jacob was always noticing the small details about me.

Things I didn't say out loud, from my expressions alone. It amazed me how well he could read me.

"Thursday. There's a vintage-themed night at the rink. Black lights. Laser beams. Disco music."

I fastened my grip around him. "I'm so ready to fall on my ass and be the worst skater on the face of this Earth if I'm doing it with you."

"I was hoping you'd say that. If we like it enough, maybe it could become our thing. Rocking the skating rink to old pop songs in mismatched, vibrant clothes once a week."

I bobbed my head. "Yes. I'm glad we're doing this together. Speaking of tonight, Becks—one of Emily's friend—is playing at a bar downtown. His set ends at eleven thirty. It's almost ten, but would you join me? It's a big deal for him, and I'd promised a while back I'd make an appearance."

"Let's go then. I'm always more at ease around people when you're beside me."

"I know. I am too. Before we leave, can I try those skates for just a minute?" I asked, batting my eyelashes, my hands linked together in a prayer—or a plea.

"I was wondering why you hadn't begged until now. Come on, let me give you a quick lesson. I'll move the couch and table while you get set. And don't be scared. I won't let go of your hand."

His contagious smile turned my chest into a firework show.

Our friendship was the highlight of my days. With Jacob, I could just be myself. No pretense. No complication. We connected on so many levels. I had never experienced a relationship like this with anyone else before. Except for my sister, but that didn't really count. I never had a best friend before him.

I put the skates on, unable to hide my happiness overload.

"Need help to tie those?" he asked.

"Nah. I think I'm good." I winced. "Oh, maybe you could tighten the left one. It feels a bit loose."

Jacob kneeled before me and got to work. "Earlier I was thinking… When you get back from tour, I'd love for us to go somewhere."

"What do you mean?"

"I've never traveled the world. If I go on a plane and visit another country for the first time, I want it to be with you. It would be out of my comfort zone, but backpacking in the jungle or climbing a mountain sound like things you would enjoy. If we do this together, I bet I'd love it too." He shrugged. "I don't know. I always feel braver when I'm with you."

I rested my hands on his shoulders, and his gaze found mine. "You do?"

The tilt of his lips got my heart racing. "Yeah."

"Jake, I'd love to go on an adventure with you. And for what it's worth, I feel more courageous around you too. I never told anyone about my childhood. You're the first person I ever confided in. I don't know… It seems right. Thanks for saving me in that bar. I can't imagine a life where we never met."

His lips brushed mine. "Then let's do this. Get up and show me your skills." He extended his arms, helping me to my feet.

When I rolled backward, his hands secured my waist, preventing me from falling.

"Ready?" Jacob asked.

I exhaled and firmed my back. "Yes."

For the next ten minutes, like a baby giraffe learning to take her first steps, I roller-skated around Jacob's living room, laughing so hard my abdominal muscles hurt and my eyes leaked happy tears.

For the first time in years, I felt content. And light-hearted.

8

SAM

I came home in the middle of the afternoon, exhausted. Rehearsal had lasted forever, and the band and I had made so many adjustments to three of the songs, I could no longer decide which version I loved best. All I craved was some quiet time and a cold beer. Something I started buying again, now that I'd decided to reclaim my *Sam Stevens, the man* title and not just be defined as *Sam Stevens, the single father of two.*

The last month had come and gone in the blink of an eye. It felt like it was just yesterday when I had walked in on Madison and the kids running around and throwing water balloons in the backyard.

Madison's presence in our lives had turned out to be a blessing after all. Every day, Mikaella laughed a little more —and smiled a whole lot more. I had no idea if it was due to the fact there was a woman in our house most days of the week or if Madison just possessed some magical power that appealed to my daughter, but I noticed the subtle changes every time we were together. Even her psychotherapist asked me what I did differently that brought her out of her shell. A few weeks with her nanny had achieved what almost two years of therapy couldn't.

Like a magnet, my eyes found Madison the moment I stepped into the kitchen. Dressed in denim cut-offs and a loose white T-shirt, her back made an enticing picture. Her hair was tied in a knot at the top of her head, and colorful bracelets dangled around her wrist. She looked like a vision I could easily fall for.

A *too-young-for-you vision*, I chastised myself.

On her tiptoes, she tried to grab a pan from the cupboard. Cursing under her breath, she stretched to her full length, still unable to reach the upper shelf.

Feeling like it was my duty to help her, I neared her from behind and placed my hands over hers. "Here," I said. "Let me get that for you."

She gulped a sharp intake of air, nodded, and stepped back.

My body powered up at the proximity, her citrusy fragrance whirling around me, but I ordered it to shut down.

"Thanks," she said in a soft voice I had a hard time resisting. "I didn't hear you come in."

"Where are the girls?"

"Napping. I put them to bed for a nap a bit later than usual. I'll wake them up in about thirty minutes. We had an active morning."

I grabbed a can of beer from the fridge and took a seat on a stool, facing her across the island.

She studied me. "You're home early."

Something was different between us. Madison was different. Distant. Something had changed in the last couple of weeks, and I couldn't pinpoint what it was exactly. Gone were the sideways stolen glances and the easy connection we'd once shared.

"Everything fine?" she asked

I shook off my questioning thoughts. "Yeah. All good. Just tired." I chugged half the beer in one gulp, relishing the coldness down my throat, and watched her pour a mixture of something chocolaty into the pan. "What are you baking?"

"Brownies. You guys always devour them within the hour every time I make them. I thought you'd like to have some for dessert tonight. I also told the girls they could have a piece after their nap."

"Are you staying for dinner? I'm sure the girls would love you to," I said, trying to sound casual. Since the day we had a water-balloon fight and I'd barbecued, Madison had refused all our requests to stay for dinner on the days I was home early. In all honesty, I missed the company. Her company. She possessed some special power—not only with my kids, but with me too—able to put my mind at rest. To keep my annoyance simmering low instead of overpowering.

She shook her head. "Sorry. I already made plans for tonight."

"How are you going to make it home? I noticed your car isn't in the driveway. Need a ride?"

Was I being too inquisitive? Was I overlapping boundaries? No. I was just caring for her safety. Nothing more.

"Nah, thanks. I have someone picking me up later."

A light pink flush crept up her neck and cheeks. She looked like a little girl caught doing something naughty.

"Wanna hear something funny?" she asked, leaning forward and resting her forearms on the countertop to stare at me.

"Always."

"The girls and I talked about New York, and I showed them pictures of the Statue of Liberty. Justine decided she looked pretty and spent almost twenty minutes with a blanket tied around her shoulders and one arm over her head, holding the TV remote, pretending to be her."

"She did?"

Madison nodded. She showed me a picture of my baby girl on her phone. "She lowered her arm when I served lunch and couldn't resist my mama's mushroom chicken recipe."

"Rewind a sec. Mushrooms?" She bobbed her head as I scratched my forehead in awe. "Once again, you gotta tell me your secret. How did you get her to eat those? She's a picky eater. She never even takes a bite when I serve them."

"We pretend they are fairy's houses, and they sprinkle magic dust in her stomach. I'm telling you, she can't resist then."

She returned to her pan and placed it in the oven. After using a dishcloth to wipe her hands clean, she twirled on herself, ready to exit the kitchen. "Be right back. I'll go check on the girls."

Why did I have the feeling she was avoiding me? Did something happen? Did I do or say something that had bothered her? I raked my mind. No, I couldn't think of anything.

Before she could get too far away, I grabbed her arm. Why was I always drifting toward her…always fighting not to touch her? What was wrong with me?

She's your children's nanny. My conscience jumped in, trying to berate my kindled, traitorous body once and for all. Easier said than done. Something about Madison was waking up the primitive side of me. *Me. You. Cave. Babies.*

With a deep breath, I shook my head, trying to erase the intimate images of us forming in my mind.

I'd been alone for so long. It was the fact she was a

gorgeous woman, and I was a man, single and lonely, that was messing with my hormones. Nothing more. I was only receptive to her feminine charms. It had nothing to do with her, per se. After all, she was the only woman I saw almost daily. We were always around each other. Breathing the same oxygen.

Madison halted and stared at me.

Why did she have to look at me with those sea-green eyes of hers? Like she could swallow any word I'd throw at her.

Trying to ease the air surrounding us, I broke the charged silence. "Mika and Justine are fine. If they wake up, they'll come downstairs."

She nodded, looking away, her teeth imprinting on her lower lip as she chewed on it.

I took a deep breath. "I'm gonna ask you a question." Her eyes darted back to mine as I stared at her face. "Did I do something that…huh…hurt or annoyed you?"

She glanced down to where my hand still clutched her arm, and I released her.

My heart went off-beat the moment we broke apart. Why was my body so responsive to hers?

"Every time I'm home, you-you can't leave quickly enough. We'll be living together on a bus for months. If you've changed your mind or if something is bothering you, you have to tell me. We must be honest with each other. That's the only way we'll get through this without harboring murderous thoughts about each other. Tour life isn't always easy. People cramped together for long periods of time with no room to catch a break more often than not. It can get ugly fast. I'm speaking from experience."

Before she could answer, Justine came barreling down the stairs, wearing a glittery pink princess dress, and rushed toward me. My heart burst from too much happiness at the sight of her happy demeanor. I pulled my baby girl into my arms, spun her around, and nuzzled her hair.

"Daddy. Daddy."

"Baby, oh, I've missed you so much. Where's your sister?"

She cupped my cheeks with her small hands. "Sleeping. She sounds like a monster. Why is she making weird noises?"

I fought a smile. "She must be snoring. That means she's really tired. Aren't you tired too?"

"No. I want to eat *browkinies*. And play in the castle. And draw."

"First, it's brownies, and they're not ready yet. Second, why don't you draw something I can hang in my studio? Third, when Mika is up, you two can play outside. Sounds good?"

"Yes, Daddy." Those two words. They could melt my heart and heal every broken piece. Justine jumped from my grip and hurried into the den where her pencils and coloring books were stacked.

As soon as she scurried away, I brought my attention back to Madison to continue our conversation, but she was nowhere to be seen. Well, we'd have to do this some other time.

I emptied my beer and went to find my daughter. Sitting in the chair by the fireplace, I fished my guitar out of its case. "Wanna sing with me?" I asked her.

"Yes." She abandoned her coloring books to sit at my feet. "Doo-doo-la-la," she said, referring to a part of the chorus of "I Belong," the first song I'd written this summer.

...You and me (Doo-doo-la-la)

**Are meant to be (Doo-doo-la-
   la)
This is where you'll find me
Because this is where I belong,
   baby**

While I sang the last verse, I watched Justine, grinning, and said, "Solo, baby."

Goose bumps bloomed on my arms at the sound of her small voice. She took her time to articulate every word the best she could while following the melody.

**...You and me (Doo-doo-la-la)
Are meant to be (Doo-doo-la-
   la)
This is where you'll find me
Because this is where I belong,
   baby**

My eyes caught Madison listening to us from the archway. Her eyes weren't on my daughter, but on me, cold and unreadable. Not a single hint of a smile touched her face. She watched me with an intensity that sent a surge of heat to my core. My throat worked as the song ended.

She neared us, clapping. "Wow, you guys. You two were great."

"You heard my song?" Justine asked as Madison sat beside her and pulled her into her lap.

"Yes. And you were the best." Her voice turned to a whisper. "Don't tell your daddy, but I think you're even better than him. You are the star, sweetie."

My baby girl sprang to her feet, running away, "Mika, Mika. Maddie said I'm a star and I sing better than—" The distance drowned her words.

"Ever played music?" I asked.

"No. It's not something I've ever been inclined to learn. My mom and sister play the piano. Growing up, I preferred to sit and listen to them than to give it a try."

She moistened her lips with a quick swipe of her tongue, and my attention drifted there for a brief second.

I cleared my throat. "Wanna try?"

She hesitated for a second. "Not sure I'm talented."

I shrugged. "You won't know unless you give it a shot."

"Yeah… Makes sense."

On my knees, I settled next to Madison and handed her my instrument.

"What do I do now?"

"Place your hand here," I arranged her digits, "and your fingers here and there. Yeah, like this. Now your other hand should be positioned like this," I said, shifting it into place. "Let's try it."

In a hesitant motion, she strummed the cords. "Oh, I did it. It almost sounded like I know what I'm doing."

"You did. You played your first chord," I said, smiling at the contagious grin stretching her face. "If you'd like, I could give you lessons now and then."

"That would—"

The sound of stomping little feet interrupted us. A barely awake Mikaella neared us, a bouncing Justine in tow.

"I wanna sing too," my eldest daughter said.

Madison handed me the guitar back.

"Pick a song, sweet pea."

For the next half-hour, we all sang any song the girls came up with. Laughter filled the room. Madison turned out to be quite a singer. If she weren't so shy, she'd be really talented.

"This is fun," she said as I put my guitar away. "I

understand now why the girls can't stop raving about it. Thanks, Sam, for giving me a peek into your life."

"Anytime. You can bake one hell of a cake and sing in tune. I'm impressed."

"Don't worry, I won't go after your job. I would be petrified to stand on a stage in front of so many people. I'll stick to teaching and baking instead."

"I won't object to any of those," I said.

Justine linked her hand with mine and grabbed Madison's with the other as we made it to the kitchen.

The four of us were eating brownies, positioned around the kitchen island, when the doorbell rang. Who could it be? I wasn't expecting anyone. Mikaella and Justine raced toward the front door, debating who would open it first. This was such a bad habit. One I should forbid. Running after them, I caught up just in time when they yanked the door open.

A man, about twenty-five, with messy dark hair, dressed in black clothes, stood there, his hands stuffed into his pockets. Didn't he get the message that it was summertime and it wasn't some goth party? Without a word, we eyed each other. A hunch in me told me I should give him all my attention.

"Who are you?" Mikaella asked. "Are you a friend of Daddy?"

"*Yesss*. Who are you?" Justine echoed, pressing her tiny fists to her hips.

"I'm… My name is Jac—" His eyes landed on something, or rather someone, behind me and lit up. I could see the whole galaxy shining in them. What the hell did that mean?

"Hey, you're here," Madison exclaimed from behind me. "I thought you were supposed to call when you arrived."

The guy, whose name I still ignored, frowned. "I was, and I called you, but you never picked up."

I turned as slowly as possible to study Madison's reaction, her face now bright red as all eyes were on her. She patted the back pockets of her cut-offs. "Shoot, I must have forgotten my phone in the castle in the backyard. Wait for me. I'll go get it." She left us all in the entryway as we studied one another some more.

"Castle?" the guy asked, looking confused as he scratched his temple.

"It's a treehouse Daddy built for us," Mikaella chimed in.

Justine tugged at his hand. "Are you Maddie's special friend?" The guy, who still didn't have a name, smiled. Even I had to agree he looked kinda mysterious and handsome as his face brightened up. "If you are her friend, I want to be your friend too. I'm a princess. And Maddie is a princess too. What's your name? Do you want to play with me?"

I pressed a hand on her shoulder. "Easy with the questions, baby," I said, when all I wanted to do was beg her to get every truth out of this guy using her four-year-old irresistible, charming power nobody could resist.

The guy raised his hands. "It's okay. My name is Jacob. And yes, we can be friends. I think princesses are awesome. And I'd like to play with you and visit your castle one day."

"Do you love pink?" Justine asked next. "It's my *favoritite* color. Do you wear princess crowns too?"

Rocking on his heels, Jacob focused his attention on her. "Pink is nice….huh…I guess. I've never worn a crown before. Think it would look good on me?"

Justine bobbed her head fast. "Mika doesn't like—"

Before she could continue, the door opened, and Madison joined the party, a lightness in her steps I had never noticed before. I let out a relieved breath—and so did Jacob. A huge grin parted her lips, her eyes shooting sparkles all around her, dissipating the suffocating tension that had permeated the air.

She positioned herself between all of us and kneeled to pull the girls into her arms for a hug. "I'll see you two tomorrow, okay? Be nice to your daddy." She touched Justine's nose, grazed Mikaella's cheek, and stood. "Bye, Sam. Thank you for the music lesson. I'll be here at nine."

I unfroze. "Sure. See you then."

Her gaze met Jacob's, and they exchanged a smile.

She returned the girls' waves as she traipsed away.

I rubbed the back of my neck, watching them pull away. A foreign emotion swirled inside me. The skin there felt raw and sensitive, and only then did I remove my hand.

The girls' chatting reached my ears. They both tugged at my hands.

"Daddy, are you okay?" Mikaella asked.

"You look like a statue," Justine added. "The *Libersilly* Statue."

I shook my head, still hanging low. "All fine, ladies. Let's prep dinner. And it's Statue of Liberty, Justine."

Armed with glue sticks, a bucket of glitter, and paper, I set my daughters and the arts and crafts supplies on one side of the kitchen island while I chopped vegetables to make chili on the other side. Glitter required constant supervision because it often ended up in places even the vacuum couldn't reach. Complete chaos.

Lost in my mind, my thoughts wandered to uncharted territories. I attributed my angst to the upcoming tour and my growing loneliness. Since Madison had started to care for my daughters, I had more time on my hands, and more time to think about the next chapter of my life. Lately, the idea of meeting a woman took more space inside my head each day. Madison's appearance in my life had triggered my ache for company. Love and sex. With the new album consuming my time and the rehearsals and tour fast approaching, a steady relationship was out of the question for now. Maybe a consensual, part-time friends-with-benefits agreement could be an option…or not. There were so many changes happening in my life right now, and I had to focus on what mattered the most. My children and the tour. There was too much at stake here, starting with my daughters who shouldn't get mixed in the clusterfuck of my non-existing love life.

———

"Daddy, you have your angry face on. Why are you mad?" Mikaella asked as I placed the pizza I had ordered in the middle of the table. In the last couple of hours, my mood had downgraded from great to awful. I sighed and pushed some of my anger down. My daughter was right. I'd been a grump since Madison had left two hours ago. I was furious with myself, the circumstances, and the whole fucking world for things I had no control over—and the glitter bomb that had exploded all over my kitchen.

"Daddy is no fun," Justine added. "Daddy is mad, mad, mad."

"I'm not mad," I said, trying to defend myself when I knew deep down, they were both right.

Every time I tried to chase away the memory, my anger returned with a vengeance.

I'd burned dinner. Then I'd dropped a pitcher of lemonade that had mixed with the *glitterification* of my floor.

It was impossible to clean up, so it would be sticky and shiny forever. Justine had dumped my phone in the toilet—luckily for me, she had flushed seconds before—so it had been sitting on the kitchen counter, covered in rice, for over an hour. Perfect. Amazing. Incredible night so far.

"*Mushy-brooms* are yucky," Justine said, pushing her slice away. "I like just cheese on my pizza."

Mikaella, the teenager in the making, rolled her eyes. "Don't be stupid. You gotta have sauce too."

"Mika, don't call your sister stupid. Say sorry."

"Sorry," she said with her mouth full, giving me a *that's the best I can do* look. Little devil.

"Justine, they are fairy's houses. They sprinkle magic dust in your belly."

"No, they're yucky. Yuck, yuck, yuck."

"You sure? They look delicious."

"No, they don't. I want just cheese. *I wantjustcheese. Justcheese.*"

I pinched my lips together to avoid getting angrier than I already was. "Fine. Gimme your plate. I'll fix it. See? I removed all the yummy things you don't like. All gone. Don't be mad if *I* turn into a fairy."

She offered me a grin big enough to split her face in two. "Love you, Fairy-Daddy. I hope your wings are pink."

Some of my annoyance vanished. How could children heal your heart with just three words?

I sat opposite them, and my shoulders slouched forward as I exhaled. "Girls, I'm sorry for being grumpy. It has nothing to do with you." I forced a curl to my lips and relaxed as I took a bite.

"Daddy, can we invite Jacob over?" my eldest daughter asked.

"Who's Jacob? A friend of yours? Was he in your class?"

Mikaella rolled her eyes again, and Justine snickered, cupping her mouth with both hands, her shoulders and the set of purple butterfly wings strapped to her back bouncing.

"Daddy is funny," she said. "Do you think Daddy is funny, Mika? I love Jacob."

"You know Jacob too?" I traced the length of one eyebrow with my thumb. They had never spoken about that kid before today. "Does Jacob live down the street? Did you meet him at the park?"

Both my girls shook their heads, looking annoyed.

"What?" What did I miss?

"Daddy, Jacob is Maddie's special friend," Mikaella whispered as if I were in on the confidence. Oh, *that* guy. "I think he's pretty. Can he be my special friend too?"

"You're silly, Daddy. Mika, is Jacob Maddie's *bote-friend?*" Justine asked with a snicker.

And now even my kids were smitten with him. Perfect.

Craving some alone time in my home studio, I put the girls to bed early. Me. My guitar. My music. It always transported me into a new universe far away from the rest of humanity.

Feeling inspired, I penned, in less than an hour, the lyrics to a melody I'd been working on.

The more I played it, the more the storm inside me lessened. Confident about how it sounded, I adjusted it until I was fully satisfied.

Unable to come up with a title, I put my guitar on its stand and lay back on the cream couch, one arm folded under my head and the other resting on my stomach, staring at the high wooden ceiling. It usually helped me clear my overactive mind and see the situation from a different perspective. As predicted, my thoughts traveled far from here. They went back to the last time I gave a show, to the night Lisa quit on us, to my first encounter with Madison at the nanny agency, to tonight, when I came back from work and she looked at home in my kitchen, baking. It traveled from the four of us singing in the den to the girls and me sharing a pizza and practicing my newest song at bedtime.

Images of Madison were conjured in my head. For a reason I failed to explain, I had a hard time not thinking about her whenever she wasn't around.

I'd never survive six months on a tour bus around her if my fascination with her didn't die. This would just complicate my life. All our lives. How did my existence go from boring to messy in just a matter of weeks?

Resigning from the tour now made no sense. Even less for a forbidden crush I had no intention of pursuing. This opportunity was my chance to get my life back on track, to prove to myself I could do this. And decide if the two sides of me, the father *and* the artist, could co-exist together.

The other option would be to find a replacement for Madison. A dude or a lady old enough to be my parents.

Nah, Madison fitted in our lives, and the girls loved her. I'd never be able to extract her from their existence. If I chased her away, I feared they'd never trust another grown-up woman ever again.

Now that she had infiltrated our lives and made a huge impact on us, I believed no one else would ever be good enough for them, except for her.

Why did everything have to be so complicated?

Without Madison around, I couldn't embark on this six-month adventure.

With a loud sigh, I shut my eyes, my mind drifting to my resurrected career and the new song I'd just written.

"Sam?" A pause. "Sorry to bother you."

Was I dreaming? I struggled to open my heavy eyelids.

"Sam?" The voice, filled with softness, spoke my name. The voice that had been haunting my dreams lately.

Was I dreaming? A hand landed on my forearm, and I jumped awake. My pulse quickened. It wasn't a dream after all. God, I really had fallen asleep.

The guitar. The song. My messy thoughts. Yeah, I must have dozed off in the middle of this.

Oh, right. The title. The last thing I remembered was trying to come up with a title for the song I'd just written.

My lids fluttered open.

There she was, crouched beside the sofa, watching me. A twinkle shone on her face, and her hair fell loosely over her shoulder in waves, the copper highlights from days spent under the sun adding a glow to her aura. Madison looked ever more angelic in the low light than I had pictured her in my head. Her lips parted, and she smiled. At me.

How much would I give to be kissed by an angel?

The title. It fit. I loved it.

"Hey," she said in a gentle tone. "I'm so sorry to wake you up."

I propped myself up on my elbows, scanning the room, urging my brain to return to the present. "What time is it?"

Her smile widened. "Ten. I forgot my purse here earlier, and my sister is working a night shift, so I couldn't get home. I didn't want you to think there was a thief or whatever, and that's why I decided to let you know I was here. Again, sorry I disturbed your sleep."

"How did you get in?" I remembered locking the front door earlier.

"The back door. I hauled myself over the fence." She grimaced. "Sorry. I texted you and knocked, but you didn't hear it and never replied. I didn't want to ring the doorbell in case it woke the girls up. I-I'm rambling. I have my stuff now, so I'll get going."

Madison motioned to stand, but I circled her wrist, the pad of my thumb resting over her frantic pulse point. What was I doing? Why was I touching her—again? We held each other's gaze, neither of us looking away.

As they did so many times before, her sea-green irises sucked me in.

Her bottom lip trembled.

I breathed in, fighting the urge to trace its length with my finger. My attention darted back to her eyes, and I coughed to clear my airways, breaking the moment that had settled between us. "Stop saying you're sorry. You did nothing wrong."

A strand of her hair fell over her eyes when she tilted her head, and my fingers itched to tuck it away.

"I should go."

"Do you need a ride home?" Could I slap myself? If she said yes, I'd have to call her a cab. Waking up the girls wasn't a viable option.

A flush spread across Madison's cheeks, and she avoided looking at me. "No, my…huh…Jacob is waiting in the car."

I nodded.

Her scent, that citrus blend, tipped all my senses. Could I bask in it for just a little longer? Her heart rate synced with mine. I felt every beat under my touch. In a jerky movement, I let go of her wrist and jumped to my feet. With the heels of my hands, I erased the remnants of sleep from my eyes. "I'll walk you out then."

She bowed her head and followed me.

The air in the house warmed up and became a heavy blanket enveloping us.

Oxygen barely reached my brain, and I got dizzy.

"My phone… Justine…huh…she dropped it in the toilet earlier. I'm trying to save it. I didn't *not* reply to your message on purpose." For a reason I couldn't justify, I wanted to explain myself. To let her know I'd never ignore her by choice.

"Oh no."

I offered her a noncommittal shrug. "It goes hand in hand with the night I had."

"That bad?" she asked.

I exhaled. "Yep. It was awful."

"Sorry to hear that. Tomorrow will be another day."

"I suppose."

We stopped by the front door.

"I should go," she said, pointing to the idling car.

Neither of us spoke for a whole minute.

"Yes," I finally said.

"Night." She traipsed away and approached the car where her friend was waiting. "See you tomorrow," Madison said, her voice strained.

My gaze followed her movements. Before she got too far, her head twisted in my direction, and I captured her gaze for a couple of endless seconds.

"Good night," I repeated, mostly to myself.

Jacob waved at me, and I returned the gesture.

His lips connected with hers before they drove away.

Standing in the dark for a little longer, I wondered what the nagging feeling that crawled over my vertebrae meant. "Probably nothing," I muttered before retreating inside.

9

MADISON

Wearing a silver cocktail dress I'd borrowed from my sister, I kept my gaze trained on the entrance. Beside me, a man in his sixties was going on and on about the Neoclassism influence of artists from the eighteenth century, something I really had no interest in.

I sipped my champagne, trying to forget how much the strapped heels on my feet hurt. Why did I agree to wear those? Oh yes, because I wanted to look pretty for my date. The same date who was almost half an hour late.

I closed my eyes for an instant, the alcohol already bubbling through my brain and making me unsteady on my feet, to block out the voices around me.

I hated large crowds. For no reason other than I disliked feeling like I lived in a cage. Being surrounded by too many people just didn't sit well with me. Another thing Jacob and I had in common. Living on a yacht for months had been the perfect setup last year. I was aware going on tour would probably force me to deal with a lot of people at times, but I'd decided I was ready to tackle my aversion and face it once and for all. With the girls or Sam around, I believed it'd be easier. For some reason, I felt at ease around them. And it calmed my nerves.

I inhaled through my mouth and reopened my eyes.

"Miss, are you even listening to what I'm saying?" the man asked.

"Sure." I faked a smile and brought my focus to the rim of my glass where my lipstick had left an imprint. I wasn't that girl. Pretending to be interested wasn't who I was. "You know what," I said. "I'll be right back. I need some fresh air and to call someone."

"Oh, okay," he replied, looking dejected.

"I'm sure a lot of people will be interested in your theory about *The Enlightenment*. If you'll excuse me." I discarded my half-empty glass onto a tray as a server passed by.

Threading through the patrons, I finally made it onto the sidewalk.

The thick summer air did nothing to ease the pressure in my lungs, but at least I could breathe on my own here. To my left, a group of people was having an agitated conversation. In front of me, two parking attendants dressed in black were joking around. The wide poster announcing the museum's newest exhibit glowed in white light on the building's facade.

"Jacob, where are you?" I asked no one, checking my phone screen for the umpteenth time.

Just when I was about to put it back into the fancy purse Emily swore I had to carry around tonight, his face flashed on the screen.

"Maddie. Ohmygod... Sorry... Supposed to meet like thirty minutes ago... Car broke down on the highway... Waiting... Towing...Presentation in Memphis... Be back… Afternoon… Middle of nowhere and… Reception is bad." His voice sounded distant, and I could catch only about half of what he said.

"Oh no. I was getting worried. You're always so on time, and running late is so unlike you. Can I do something? I can't drive because I had champagne, but I can call a cab to come get you."

"Nah… State patrol with me. I'll call you later… Better reception. Again, I'm—" The line cut before he could finish his sentence.

"Great. All this," I said, looking at my outfit, "for nothing."

I opened the app on my phone to call a cab when a silhouette I recognized strolled in front of me and stopped mere feet away.

"Maddie?"

"Sam?"

"Wow, you look stunning," he exclaimed, before rolling his lips over his teeth and glancing down as if he'd said something wrong. His eyes returned to mine. "What I meant is…huh…what are you doing here? Not that you don't look great…but… Okay, let's start over. Hi, it's nice to bump into you. Are you here for the—?" His eyes traveled behind me. "Are you here for the inauguration of the new exhibit?" He frowned. "Sorry, I know nothing about museums."

I let out a snicker. "Me neither. I guess you can call it that. Jacob got invited by one of his peers at the university, and I was supposed to be his plus-one, but his car broke down, and I'm here, figuring out how to get away from this place as quickly as possible." I lowered my voice. "I really don't feel like I am in my element in this cesspool of art intellectuals."

"Yeah, I understand the feeling. A few years ago, I gave

a performance at a museum in Texas, and I felt out of my element too. I can tolerate the children's museums and the natural history ones because they're fun, but this"—he pointed to the building behind me—"I cannot. Where are you going now? Anything I can do to help?"

I sighed. "Home. I got all dressed up for nothing." My shoulders dropped forward. "One thing I'm excited about, though, is removing these blistering pumps. They are killing my feet. I'm not drunk enough to forget they are skinning my feet alive every time I take a step."

"I'd give you mine, but not sure they'll fit you." He gazed down. "And those will definitely not fit me."

He laughed, and I relished the deep baritone of his voice. Sam Stevens looked handsome when he let his guard down and laughed without restraint. Tonight, he appeared younger than usual. He had a calm about him, hard to ignore, and it drew me in like never before.

"I have a question," I said. "Where are the girls? How can you be out on your own tonight? A night off is unusual for you from what you've told me in the past."

"My parents are in town for the weekend. They arrived last night. Surprise visit. They insisted I go out and enjoy some me-time. That's what I'm trying to do. It's all new to me, and I'm not sure I'm doing it right. Was on my way to a small hotel bar to watch the game. I know it sounds pathetic. I'm just a little rusty when it comes to social inter-actions. It's been so long that I'm not sure how to proceed. How do we meet people these days, other than through an app? How does anyone?"

I shook my head. "You're not asking the right person. I'm such an introvert. Somehow, I think it's just a question of timing."

A chime on my phone announced the cab was a

minute away. When it pulled along the sidewalk, Sam scratched the side of his neck and averted his gaze before speaking again.

"I know it's spur of the moment and all, but do you… do you want to maybe grab a bite or something? The night is still young, and I could use the company. You won't have wasted your night and dressed up for nothing." He stuffed his hands into his pockets. "What do you say?"

The idea of sitting alone in front of the TV at home didn't appeal to me. And I'd never hear the end of it if my sister found out I came home at seven on a Saturday night.

"Why not? Could be fun," I said.

Sam opened the passenger door and said something to the cab driver who drove away.

He winced. "I shouldn't have sent him away," he said. "Your feet. Can you walk the three blocks from here?"

I bent down, and soon my heels dangled from my fingers. "Problem solved. For three blocks at least."

We exchanged small talk for the first few minutes. It was different. Being here with him on our night off. It didn't feel like I was with my boss, but just a guy friend.

"I'm not gonna spend the night going on and on about the girls, but I did try feeding Justine mushrooms, and it backfired. Big time."

"For real?" I asked, giving him a sideways glance, a grin threatening to form on my lips. "How so?"

Dressed in a casual button-up deep frost-blue shirt and a pair of dark jeans, Sam looked both relaxed and sophisticated tonight. He wore brown cowboy boots and a matching belt. Beside him, minus the heels, I didn't feel *that* overdressed. Just a tad.

"They were on her pizza. She complained she hated them. I told her, like you said, that they were fairy's homes, and they would spread magic dust in her belly. It didn't do the trick. She started screaming and pushed her food away."

I couldn't help but burst into a fit of laughter. "She did not?"

"Yep. And when I told her I would be the one turning into a fairy, she said she wished my wings were pink."

I used my fingertips to wipe the tears building in the corners of my eyes. "Oh no. She's the best. Your children are so adorable."

He shrugged. "Guess so. At least, when they put their minds to it."

We kept talking, not giving the world around us any attention.

"Oops, we passed it," Sam said after a moment. He spun around. "I think it was like five minutes that way." He pointed to where we just came from. "Well, this is embarrassing. We can either go back or we——"

I surveyed the city around me. "There's a country bar two minutes from here. I used to go there when I was in college and pretended to have fun getting wasted for the three months it lasted. Wanna go? Unless you think people will come to you and ask for pictures and stuff."

"Nah, it's fine. People here are laid-back and rarely care."

At the entrance, I slipped my heels back on and winced as I stepped forward.

"That bad?" Sam asked.

"Yep. Heels should be illegal. I never found a pair I could wear without wanting to rip them apart." I took another cautious step, feeling—and probably looking—as if I were walking on a bed of nails.

Sam offered his bent elbow. "Hold on to me. It might take some pressure off your poor feet."

"Thanks."

We exchanged a soft smile and entered the establishment. Country music blared from the red jukebox on our left. A few pool tables were set in the far back. In front of us, a wide bar dominated the space, shelves of alcohol bottles lining the wall behind the bartender—an old man with thick glasses. A makeshift dance floor, surrounded by high tables and stools, took up most of the room to our right, with a small stage holding a single microphone and two chairs in one corner. The rest of the bar was filled with wooden tables and chairs for those coming here to enjoy a meal.

It was everything I remembered, just older than the version in my memory.

The host led us to a table and set down the menu after listing the night's specials.

Sam and I sat across from each other. The table was so small our knees brushed underneath the surface. With the dim-lit chandeliers casting a soft glow, the setup almost looked romantic.

Tilting sideways, I slipped off my heels, sighing in relief.

"Better?" Sam asked.

"Yeah. My feet are relishing their freedom."

"I'm lucky I'll never have to endure such torture," he said with a wink that got me smiling way too big. "Hungry?" he asked as he perused the laminated two-sided piece of paper.

"*Yesss.*" I said it with too much enthusiasm before I could rein in some of my excitement. "Sorry. I haven't had dinner, and the champagne went straight to my head."

The server came to take our orders, and we both asked for a beer. "Do you want a bit of everything?" Sam asked me.

"Sure. Why not?"

"You okay to share?"

I nodded and mirrored the faint curl of his lips. Gone was the pain masking his face most of the time. Tonight, Sam Stevens appeared relaxed. And happy.

"We'll have the large nachos, extra guacamole, a plate of chicken wings, potato skins, the mozzarella sticks, a side of raw veggies, a plate of mini-burgers, shrimp tacos, and the fries with gravy and brisket."

"Anything else?" the server asked.

"Ohmygod, no," I let out. "I think we're good."

We handed our menus back and settled in as we waited for our drinks.

"Can I ask you a question?" I asked Sam.

He nodded.

"How do you deal with fame? How weird is it to have strangers call your name or tell you they love your stuff?"

"Truth?"

I nodded.

"I don't think I'll ever get used to it. Those two sides of me live in the same body, but it's like they're different identities. In my everyday life, I'm a private person. I love the anonymity. When I'm onstage, this other side of me lights up. Takes over. I crave the music. The energy only an amphitheater full of people can provide. It's hard to explain. I have a friend who can't tolerate the limelight that comes with the job. It gives him anxiety. I guess we all deal with it differently. For me, it's really about separating those two versions of me. The regular guy, single dad, and the musician slash celebrity or whatever name you wanna call it."

"I could never do what you do. Having all those people, obsessed with me, scrutinizing my life as if I was a social experiment, voicing any opinion they deem fit about me and my character."

"It took me a while to develop a thick skin. When I was younger, other people's opinions of me mattered…a lot. Well, I thought they did. Until I realized looking up my name online and reading those heinous reviews was only hurting me and my self-confidence. Now I don't care anymore. I do my own thing. People like my sound, fantastic. They hate it, I won't miss sleep over it. They're entitled to their own opinion. There are people out there who seem to be born to always find negativity in everything other people do. Not sure they're happy, though. If they were, they wouldn't feed on the high they got from bad-mouthing others."

"Wow, that's impressive."

"What?"

"Your vision of things. I like that. And you're so right. So many people nowadays feel free to say anything they want about anyone, without giving it a second thought. It can be hurtful. They forget they are addressing their heinous comments to human beings…people with feelings. Criticizing their lives, their choices, their careers. But those same people would never accept themselves being ripped apart for the sake of entertainment. It's sad. It's frustrating how some people choose to be mean just because they think their voice gives them the right to project their insecurities onto anyone trying to do what they love. It's nobody else's business if they're unhappy in their own lives." I paused. "Sorry about my ranting. Human beings are a weird species. They should lift other people up instead of finding ways to belittle their work or character. Encourage them. Cheer them on. Help them get better. We should all have each other's backs. Spread happiness instead of hate. I love that you can block the negative out and feed on the positive." I shrugged. "It's inspiring."

Sam sipped his beer. "It's much more empowering to tell someone *keep going, you're doing a good job* or *I love your stuff, you inspire me* than to break their spirits and call their stuff mediocre or any other detrimental adjective. I'm trying to teach my kids to be empathetic, to think with their hearts. We all have it in us…you know…what it takes to be mean. It's a choice we make to opt to be better than the greater majority."

"And it's rewarding," I agreed.

"Yep." He pushed his drink toward me. "Let's drink to that."

We clinked our glasses just as the server brought our food.

"Whoa, that's a lot. Do you think we can eat it all?"

Sam stared at me, amusement dancing in his irises. "Guess we'll find out. I have all night. I'm free tonight. For once, I don't have to be anywhere."

I clinked his glass again. "Let's drink to that. A free night."

"Cheers," he said.

We talked about our families as we indulged in our food. I hadn't had a proper junk meal in a long time. After licking my fingers, I wiped my hands on a napkin.

"How was it?" he asked next. "Teaching kids in Africa."

I clasped my hands together. "One of the most rewarding experiences of my life, without a doubt. Children in developed countries take school, and learning in general, for granted. Those kids… Their eyes lit up every time I walked into the classroom. They were thankful. I had an all-girls class. They have so much to learn from us, but we have just as much to learn from them—their strength, their resilience. It's hard to believe we live on the same planet, yet our lives are so different. I was only eighteen back then but could sense how what we were doing was important to them. These little girls were thriving. I would love to go back one day and try to see where they're now."

"It's amazing what you do. I'm here, being paid big money and being adulated because I can play the guitar and sing songs. What you do means so much more for our world. Our children are the future. There shouldn't be distinctions between them, no matter their background or where they are born."

"Thanks. For recognizing the value of my work. It means a lot."

"Maddie, I've witnessed the changes in my own daughters. It's amazing what you've succeeded in accomplishing with them in such a short amount of time. Mika is back to being a kid. She laughs, smiles, and is happy again. This is priceless. I don't know how you do this, but your talents are underrated."

I could feel a blush taking over my face. I returned Sam's smile. "Thank you."

"No," he said, shaking his head, his eyes glued to mine. "Thank *you*."

Hours later, we enjoyed more beer as people started line dancing on the makeshift dance floor.

Barefoot, I tapped along to the intoxicating rhythm. Despite my efforts, I couldn't conceal my love for the group dance.

"You love that song?" Sam asked.

I leaned back, angling myself toward him. "I love *the* dance. Do you know the steps?"

He massaged his temples. "I used to. A long time ago. Do you?"

"Yep. It was part of my three-month *let-loose* challenge in college, to tour bars and play drinking games. All in the name of experience. To understand why people love it so much." I blamed the booze for the next few words escaping my mouth. "Wanna give it a try?"

He pointed at his chest with his thumb. "Me?" I nodded. "Nah, I think I'll pass."

"Come on, you're called *The Legend* of country music and you're afraid of some line dance?" I waggled my eyebrows as if to prove my point.

Sam exhaled sharply. "Don't you dare me. I'm super bad at resisting those. I used to always get in trouble as a teen because I was the dare king."

"Dare King, show me what you're made of." I poked my tongue out playfully.

Sam frowned. "Maddie, are you being serious?"

"I got dressed up. Better enjoy the night, no?"

On wobbly feet, thanks to the champagne and beer I'd drunk tonight, I kicked the heels I had removed when we got seated further under the table and reached for his hand.

"I'm too old for this," he teased.

"Age is just a number. You're twenty-nine, not seventy-five. Come on."

We reached the dance floor and stood side by side. After a few seconds, the steps came back to me, and soon I was dancing in perfect sync with everyone, laughing my heart out. Sam tried to follow me, off-tempo and mixing the steps. Concentration etched across his features as he kept trying until he got it right. When the song ended, I lost my footing, and strong arms coiled around my waist to steady me.

"Thanks." I swiveled to face him, his arms still

wrapped around me. A soft ballad began to play, and couples paired up all around us.

Sam shifted me so we faced each other. We locked eyes for a long beat. His Adam's apple worked, and I followed the movement with my gaze, entranced.

"Wanna go back to the table?" I asked, feeling like he was still standing here because of me.

"Not really. I'm having fun. Are you?"

A wide grin broke free on my face. "I am."

Without overthinking everything, I splayed my palms across his hard chest and closed my eyes, letting the slow tempo of the music control my feet.

Sam's scent—musky, woodsy, and entirely him—clung to all my senses.

When I opened my eyes, he was staring at me with an unreadable expression.

The song eased into another, and before we knew it, we spent over an hour on the dance floor, breaking apart just long enough to take sips of our beers.

"Where does *The Legend* moniker come from?" I asked.

"When I released my second album, I sold a million copies within forty-eight hours. Back then, it was a big deal. Not many artists had done that before me. The nickname passed the test of time. I don't really like being called that. It just puts unwelcome pressure on me." He shrugged. "Why would I enjoy being put on a pedestal? I'm just a regular guy who enjoys a low-key life. There's nothing legendary about me."

"Don't be so hard on yourself. You're allowed to be the best at something. Nothing to be ashamed of. For what it's worth, I like it. It's flattering. Don't put too much thought into it, but I think it's fitting."

"Maybe. Still, I don't consider myself special in any way."

"Be proud of what you have achieved. Sometimes, it's okay not to be humble and to acknowledge what we've accomplished. This is the perfect example. Everyone is special in their own way. You are too."

"How can you be so smart at your age? You see the good in people—and in life. It's a great quality. Never lose it. It's precious."

"Born this way." I shrugged. "Are you excited to go on tour? It must be an adrenaline rush to come back into the spotlight after two years."

"I am. But parts of me fear I'll be rusty. Or that I'll forget how it's done. It sounds silly."

"It's not silly. It's normal to have doubts. But you're *The Legend* after all, so I'm confident you'll be fine." An idea hit me. "Do you still consider yourself the dare king?" I asked.

"Not sure. I haven't thought about it in years. Why?"

"Because I dare you to ask the barman for a guitar—I saw one behind the bar when we walked in—and to play a song. Here and now. On that small stage. I'll be the judge of whether or not you've lost your title."

"You're kidding, right?"

"Try me," I said. Yep, the beer should be blamed for my newfound confidence tonight.

Sam's voice was a soft murmur against my skin when he said, "Maddie—"

I stepped back. "Sam, time to prove yourself you still got it. You said earlier you can't walk away from a dare. This, right here, is me challenging you."

"Maddie—" he repeated.

I pushed him back with both hands. "Impress me."

Our eyes were transfixed on each other, a conversation of unspoken words that I couldn't vocalize but understood. It awakened something deep in my heart. Sam's irises went from shiny to dark, a hidden emotion simmering in them. One that lured me in. And stole my breath away.

He twirled me one last time on the dance floor before letting go of my hand and sauntering away, shaking his head.

With his back straight, chin tipped up, and a newfound determination pouring out of him, he neared the bar.

When he stared at me over his shoulder, I saw a glint in his eye I'd never witnessed before.

"Show time," I murmured.

10

SAM

With steady steps, I reached the bar. I still had a hard time comprehending how Madison had ended up challenging me. Tonight, I had discovered a new side of her, and for the first time in years, I felt free. Like I could do anything or be anyone and nobody expected anything from me. With Lisa, I used to always walk on eggshells. She had expensive tastes, demanded and expected a level of commitment from me that always seemed exaggerated.

Other than Riley's trick to send me back on the road and with my own children, I hadn't been challenged by another person in a long time. Deep down, I relished the feeling and the adrenaline rush that came with it. I didn't lie earlier when I'd told Madison I was the dare king as a teenager. Running down the street bare-assed, climbing the tallest trees, going to school dressed like a cheerleader, I had done it all.

Right now, I missed the version of myself I once was— the carefree guy. Responsibilities, a quickly ascending career, and heartbreak had buried that Sam. Madison had just dug him out earlier when she had convinced me to line-dance with her.

If I were being honest with myself, I hadn't laughed this much in years.

It felt good to feel alive. To just be. And have an honest conversation with someone. In the past two years, I had closed myself off a lot, not letting people in. Talking with Madison felt different. As if she could understand me. Without judgment. As if she got the whole fame thing without making too much out of it. Tonight, I was presented with the side of her I'd only ever witnessed around my daughters. Her caring side that she had never extended to me until now. The woman in her. The funny, beautiful, and easygoing person she was inside and out. I already knew her heart was made of gold, but I had the certitude tonight she was genuinely a wonderful human being.

One thing was certain: she cared. And she was a lot more perceptive than most people I knew.

As I walked away, I caught her gaze over my shoulder. She watched me traipse away, her hands clasped in front of her and her chin jutting forward as if she believed I needed encouragement to go through with the dare.

For the first time since we'd met, I could see she had taken off her responsible-adult suit too, enjoying the night, without questioning anything.

"Hey, man. Listen, I was wondering… Is there a possibility I could borrow that guitar for a song or two?" I asked the bartender, pointing to the instrument resting against the wall.

"What for?"

"See, I'm going back on tour in a couple of months and my friend back there," I gestured behind me with my thumb, "the one in the pretty dress, thinks I should prove to myself I still have it in me."

"Have what?" he asked.

Okay, he's not going to make it easy for me, is he? The last thing I wished for was to use my name to convince people to give me a chance.

"The stage presence. The jitters. The excitement."

"What are you? Another guy trying to make it big? Over the years, I've seen enough young men your age arrogant about their talent when they couldn't sing for shit. If you're booed, please walk down that stage, even if you're not done. I'm telling you, this industry is overcrowded. Don't expect too much from it."

"Thanks for the advice. I'll remember it when I am on tour. So, can I?"

"Sure." He grabbed the guitar and handed it to me. "Be careful. And good luck."

"Thanks." I saluted him with one hand as I adjusted the keys with the other.

I climbed the four steps up and sat on a chair in the middle of the stage. I waited until the song from the jukebox ended and reached for the microphone after I turned it on.

"Hi, folks. I was challenged by the brunette down there," I gestured to Madison, who was standing so close that, even in the low light, I could see the pink hue coloring her cheeks as people turned to look at her, "to sing a song tonight."

I heard people whispering my name, but I chose to ignore them, continuing to pretend I was that eighteen-year-old Sam Stevens, praying that one day he'd be able to play his music for a larger audience and make a living writing love songs.

Someone wolf-whistled as I strummed the first chords of "When You're Far Away."

More people cheered and clapped. Standing in front of me, never blinking, stood Madison. Her contagious smile rubbed off on me, and I started grinning like a fool while I played.

"Again," a group of women hollered once I was done and about to climb down the stage.

"Okay. If I do this, though, I'll need some help." Many patrons lifted their hands. "Sorry, guys, only one person knows this song. Maddie, come on up here."

She shook her head, her cheeks now bright red.

"She might require a little encouragement from you guys. Everyone, please welcome Maddie to the stage."

Sam, she mouthed. *Why?*

I offered her a one-shoulder shrug. "You know the lyrics," I said, my hand covering the microphone, as I bent forward. "Plus, you're all dressed up. You made me dance earlier. It's the pendulum swinging back. Pretend it's just me and the girls like we rehearsed the other day. I'm the king of dares, remember? And I'm daring you to do this with me. You'll see, it's not as intimidating as it seems. You'll be able to decide for yourself if it's as scary as you believe up here." I held out my hand in invitation.

Muttering something under her breath, Madison exhaled in a dramatic fashion and squeezed my offered palm as she stepped up the stairs and settled next to me.

After I adjusted the microphone between us, I added, "Forget about them. No one is listening. You have a beautiful voice. Sing with me, okay?" I squeezed her hand for an infinitesimal instant, and a shiver passed through her before she nodded her agreement. I let go of her and strummed the first few notes.

We sang "I Belong," the song I had played with Justine the other day. Madison joined me on the chorus. Her voice quivered as the words initially escaped her lips. We locked eyes, neither of us breaking the contact, and soon enough, confidence coursed through her, and she looked more at ease. We exchanged smiles, and I relished watching her come alive beside me. No doubt, people were falling under her charm too. How could they not? Madison had a magnetic aura. One that made it painful to leave once she cast her attention on you.

When we finished the song, I jumped down the stage and helped her back to the floor.

"See? It wasn't that bad," I teased, bumping her shoulder with mine.

She blinked. "You're joking, right? I did it. I faced a fear of mine." She spun on the balls of her feet and looped her arms around my neck. Heat crawled where our skin connected. "Thank you, Sam." She detached from me and averted her eyes for a split second, as if she feared she'd crossed some lines.

Trying to push away the sensations rising from deep within, I handed the guitar back to the bartender.

"You should have told me, son, you were *The Legend.* Sorry I didn't recognize you. My sight is not so great these days. Cataracts are a shame."

"I loved being anonymous for the time it lasted. It reminded me of my younger days."

He offered me two beers. "For you and the lady. Thank you for singing at my bar. It means a lot to an old fellow like me who's been following your career since the beginning. I'm excited you're getting a new album out. It was about damn time."

I thanked him with a nod.

Madison and I returned to our table. "I'm still floating in the air," she said. "Now I understand the adrenaline rush you get from being onstage. I still wouldn't do it, given a choice, but I loved it for the length of one song."

We cheered to that.

"Ready to go?" I asked later.

"What time is it?"

"Around two in the morning."

"Two?" Madison exclaimed with round eyes.

"Yep. We'll share a cab ride. I'll feel better knowing you get home safely."

"Sam, you don't have to."

"I insist." She fished her credit card out, but I stopped her with a hand. "Let me. You saved the night. Trust me, it's the least I can do."

She grabbed her heels and grimaced as she put them on.

"Still hurting?"

She shut her eyelids and tilted her head back. "It's awful. You have no idea."

"Sit," I ordered.

Confusion took over her gaze, but she did as I said.

I leaned down, removed both her shoes, and turned around. "Jump on."

"Sam, what are you doing?"

"Doing my part to heal your feet. Come on."

She shook her head. "I can't."

"Come on. It's already too late. Our picture is probably already plastered all over the internet as we speak. You're the one who challenged me earlier. Just don't read the news for the next week. The press will insinuate lots of things. Ignore it. Soon, they'll fabricate stories about other people. The gossip never lasts. There's always some more riveting news to cover in the entertainment industry."

"Huh…okay…all right."

Perhaps giving the nanny of my kids a piggyback ride

wasn't super ethical since technically, she worked for me, but right now, I just didn't give a shit about it. Tonight, we were just two friends watching out for each other.

When the cab halted in front of Madison's townhouse that she shared with her sister, she turned toward me and hesitated. She held out a hand, then pulled it back. I leaned forward to kiss her cheek but decided it would be awkward. In the end, we waved at each other.

"Thanks for tonight," she said. "I had fun."

"Me too. See you on Monday."

"I'll be there."

For the next minute, my eyes stayed trained on her as she made her way inside and closed the door behind her.

Madison had opened a portal in me in the last few hours we'd spent together. I now felt energized and ready to conquer the world.

When we had danced tonight, her touch had woken up something in me. It made me want to be better. I did my best not to make a big deal of the electricity her hand in mine sparked through me. This couldn't mean anything. We already had a couple of drinks, so it was probably my imagination playing tricks on me. Yeah. I glanced down at my palm and massaged it with my thumb, stretching my digits to remove the memory of our connection.

"Sir, you can go now," I told the cab driver who pulled away from the driveway. Through the back window, I noticed the curtains moving on the second floor and wondered if, just like for me, the deception that the night was over filled her too. A tinge of nostalgia hit me. My stomach knotted at the thought of stepping back into our roles when we'd see each other again on Monday. I couldn't remember the last time I had felt completely like myself, or when the weight pressing on my shoulders had finally receded.

I wished it never came back because I loved the freedom my night with Madison had provided.

———

"What the hell, man," Riley said as I took his call the next morning. I cracked my eyelids open and decided it was too early to deal with him at eleven in the morning. I hadn't slept in…in, huh, forever. Nope, I couldn't remember the last time I had done so.

"Can we talk later?" I asked, burying my head under a pillow. "I'm tired."

"Nah. I need an explanation. Why are there pictures of Maddie and you looking cozy all over the web? Singing together. Dancing together. What did you do last night, Stevens?"

I scrunched up my face. Damn. I had forgotten all about it. "It's nothing. Just the press making up a story for the sake of it. Don't worry."

"*Who is Sam Stevens's new love interest? Is Sam Stevens in love again? Sam Stevens is coming out of his retirement and paraded his girlfriend all over town.*" He huffed so loud that I could hear his lungs deflating. "I'll ask the question again. What happened last night, Stevens? Because there are pictures of you two singing together, of you two looking intimate on the dance floor, of you giving her a piggyback ride. A piggyback ride, man. Are you serious? What is this all about?"

I sat on the bed and rubbed my eyes with a finger, trying to shake off the grogginess. "Ry, you should know that nothing in the press is ever what it seems. Why are you even grilling me about last night's whereabouts right now?"

"June is overwhelmed with calls and emails. I just

wanna hear the truth from you. No doubt Janice will ask for an explanation too when I talk to her later."

For the next ten minutes, I described my night to my friend.

"Madison is not used to this kind of attention. What were you thinking? You should be aware ending up on a cover of a magazine can break someone. You're aware what happened to Carter and April. It almost destroyed them. She didn't want to be known as Carter's girl. The media painted her as a gold digger. They spread lies to sell copies of their trash. Be careful. Madison is inexperienced with fame. The last thing we need is for her to panic and back out of the tour. I'm not mad at you two… Just concerned."

I dragged a hand over my face. "I'll talk to her. I warned her last night. Kinda. Geez, I'll meet with her and explain. Make sure she stays away from any gossip rags."

After a hot shower, I made my way downstairs. My parents had taken the kids to spend the night at a hotel with a pool and a waterslide, so I had the entire house to myself.

Last night had long-lasting upsides. I felt refreshed. For once, I didn't feel ten years older than I really was.

The doorbell rang as I was pouring myself an oversized cup of coffee.

"Coming," I said, nearing the front door in nothing but a pair of lounge pants. I had ditched the shirt, thinking I'd be alone most of the day. "Maddie?"

She stood on the front porch, her hands linked before her, dark shadows under her eyes, wearing a look on her face I wished I could forget.

"Come on in. I was just about to call you," I said.

"Sam. We gotta talk."

11

MADISON

"Coffee?" Sam asked after he closed the door behind me and led me through the house as if I'd never been here before.

As I followed him, I did my best to avoid looking at his naked torso.

"Yes. Please." Caffeine would help settle my nerves.

After he put on a faded black T-shirt from a past world tour, Sam carried two mugs to the kitchen table as we took a seat next to each other.

My pulse hastened, and I wrapped my palms around the mug, entranced by the billowing steam instead of the man studying me from up close. I could feel the weight of his gaze on my skin, and I wondered if I'd dreamed of the connection we shared last night. Or if my boozy brain had conjured the ease and familiarity with which we challenged and confided in each other.

"So, I suppose you searched the internet?" he asked, going straight to the topic that brought me here on a Sunday morning.

"About that... I...I know you said to ignore the rumor

and to avoid it. But…huh…even though I've tried to, people I love and care about sent me links to multiple outlets that shared pictures of us and insinuated we're a couple. Even my mama called me first thing in the morning to ask questions."

Sam said nothing for a minute. I risked a glance at him. His face had lost his easy composure, a somber mask tightening his features.

"Listen, Maddie, I'm aware of how this looks. Trust me, I never meant for your face to get plastered all over gossip rags. It was never my intention to put you on the hot seat. For what it's worth, I'm sorry. If you want, I'll give an interview or ask June to write a press release. But in my years of experience, it's better to let the story die. It will… Eventually."

I drummed my fingers, and Sam reached for my hand, putting my fidgeting to rest.

"Stop. It will be all right, Maddie. I promise. You can trust me. I'll make sure of it."

I abandoned my hand to his comforting squeeze. After a moment, I realized something was off and scanned the room around me. "It's oddly silent in here. Where are the girls?"

"They spent the night at the hotel with their grand-parents."

"Wow, you're really going all in for your first me-time weekend."

"Trying to. Since I went to bed too late, I was glad to have the morning to myself."

Sam released my hand as if he'd just noticed he was still holding it in his.

"Huh…do you really think those pictures will go away?"

"Yep. They may resurface at some point, but we did

nothing wrong. All they show is two people having a great time. They can come up with the narrative they want, but you and I both know the truth."

I finished my coffee and rinsed and placed my mug in the dishwasher. "I'll go. For what it's worth, I trust you. It was just weird to wake up to my face splashed all over the internet. Not sure I'd ever get used to it. Sometimes, it's hard to remember people actually know who you are. Strangers speaking about you like they're part of your everyday life." I sighed. "This is surreal. Anyway, thanks for reassuring me."

"Anytime."

I turned to leave when I spotted the half-built structure at the far end of the backyard, in the corner across from the girls' castle. "What is it?" I walked toward the window, which offered a view of the green lawn, to try to make out what it was.

"A greenhouse. To grow herbs and veggies. I thought you and the girls would love it. A project to tackle this summer. I'm supposed to finish setting it up today. My father and I did most of the work yesterday."

"For real?"

"Yeah. I thought it could be fun to teach the girls how nature works."

"Ohmygod, I love DIY projects. Can I give you a hand?"

Sam neared me, angling himself so we faced each other, a perplexed expression overtaking his face. "You sure? It's your day off."

"Unless you wanna do it on your own, I have nothing planned today, and I really like working with a hammer. I used to do all kinds of construction projects with my daddy when I was little."

"In that case, gimme a sec. I'll never refuse help. Let me gather the tools we need and I'll be right back."

For the next few hours, Sam and I finished assembling the greenhouse. While he painted the exterior walls in a sky-blue hue, I used the small paintbrushes to add embellishments of fake grass, butterflies, and flowers, sitting cross-legged on the lawn.

"Other than being the king of dares, were you more like Mika or Justine growing up?" I asked.

"Neither one. For the longest time, I was a shy kid. Then I started playing music, and I was good, like really, really good. It gave me confidence. I was thirteen when I wrote my first song and nineteen when I signed my first record deal. Since then, I've never stopped working."

"Do you feel like you missed out on things by working full time from an early age?"

"Whoa. I never actually asked myself that question. Would I do things differently? Hmm… Not sure. It brought me to who I am today. In the grand scheme of things, I consider myself lucky." He paused. "Do you feel like you're missing out on something?"

"Not really. I'm doing exactly what I've always dreamed of. If I didn't, I'd be scared to wake up one day and feel like I didn't follow the little voice in my head begging me to go for it. Even when it's out of my comfort zone."

"Like singing on a stage in a country bar?"

I burst out laughing, and Sam joined in. "Yeah. Well, I'm glad I did it. What are the top three craziest things that have ever happened to you in your career? Any women throwing their panties at you or asking you to marry them?"

"Let me see… I've seen a lot of crazy over the years." He paused. "Top incident for sure was this one. I was twenty and signing autographs at a VIP event. A woman I never saw before waited for over two hours in line, and when she walked up to me, she handed me a newborn. I thought it was for a picture, but it turned out he was supposed to be my son and I was to recognize and accept my paternity. The woman had a fair complexion and red hair. And the baby, let's just say his skin was so dark there was no way anyone would have assumed we were related. She started screaming I was an egotistical jerk and refused to feed my own child. Security had to escort her out. It was…surreal."

"I thought such stories were rumors. The ones we heard sometimes."

Sam shook his head. "Nope. I can assure you there are some weird people out there. Second was when a fan wrote lengthy posts online and wouldn't stop bashing my new album because he didn't like the title of a song. He said it reminded him of his cheating ex. He went on and on, writing on blogs, social media, and anywhere he could post his words, insulting me. It's insane how your work can trigger people, and instead of dealing with their own pain, they mirror it back to you, calling you out for things that have nothing to do with you. He even threatened to sue me for psychological distress."

"Geez. I'm not sure I'd be able to deal with haters. What's the third?"

"This one you'll like. A guy reached out to a friend of mine. He wanted to ask his girlfriend to marry him, and they had tickets for my show in Cleveland. I called him one night, and he explained his plan. We set everything up, and during the show, he came onstage, and in front of an entire stadium, he asked his high school sweetheart for her hand. It was so emotional. Turns out the guy had been fighting cancer for years and had just learned he was in remission. I sang at their wedding a year later and offered them tickets to Fiji for their honeymoon. We're still in touch. They live in Spain now and have two kids. They named their son Samuel. Those are the stories that stick with you."

Moisture dampened my eyes. "Wow, this is beautiful. I'm…wow. Thanks for sharing with me."

"What's your best memory?" Sam asked.

"When I was around eight, we adopted a dog. A stray. I was having nightmares, and Cooper, that was his name, slept in my bed at night. We had so much in common. He became my confidant. Other than my sister, he was my best friend. We shared a deep connection, he and I. Did you ever have a pet?"

"When I was a kid. A cat named Peluche. One day, I'd like to get one for the girls. I'm just not convinced the timing is right. I may reevaluate the idea after the tour."

I finished the last touches to my design and studied the flower pattern I'd just painted. "I think we're done here." Back on my feet, I admired the work we just did.

"It looks great. It exceeds my expectations," Sam said, pride radiating from him. He smiled at me, and something swelled in my chest. I loved being on the receiving end of his happiness. "I've also bought everything we might need to build a garden in there."

"I can't wait."

Once we put all our tools aside, he stood next to me, and we high-fived. "It really does look sharp," I stated. My phone chimed in my pocket, and as I swiped the screen to unlock it, I realized it was almost four. "Oh shoot, I gotta go. I have dinner plans tonight."

"Go," Sam called after me. "Thanks for the help."

I waved at him over my shoulder, crossed the house, and hurried down the three steps leading to the cobblestone pathway. Once in my car, I slid my shades down over my eyes, ignited the engine, and pulled away. Sam Stevens's front yard was more like a big parking space, separated from the street through a curved driveway, making the house almost invisible from the main road. In the rearview mirror, I noticed him standing next to the alley leading to his backyard, watching me with a serious expression and his hands stuffed in his pockets. Had Sam and I become friends in the last twelve hours?

———

"Hey, how is it going?" I asked as Jacob let me in. His face didn't reveal the signs of the easy cheerfulness he usually carried around me. "What's going on?" I stepped closer to kiss him, but he yanked away from my touch. "Talk to me. What did I miss?"

His eyebrows bunched as he eyed me with an expression I'd never seen before.

"Jake…"

"Maddie, what's going on between Sam Stevens and you?"

I blinked. "What?"

"Don't play the innocent. I saw the pictures. The entire world saw the pictures. You both looked lovely together. Are you leading me on?"

"Me?" I said, gesturing to my chest. "Am I leading you on? Are you being serious?"

"I'm not blind, Maddie. The guy's a catch. And from what I've seen online, riding on your boss's back doesn't exactly scream a professional relationship."

"Wow, I can't believe you're accusing me of something that never occurred. Nothing went down. I was outside the museum, talking to you, worried because you never showed up, and the next thing I knew, I bumped into him.

I was disappointed about going home after putting in the time and effort to look pretty for our date. He was alone and planning to watch a game at the bar, but we decided to grab a bite instead and ended up at that country joint. I dared him to play a song. People recognized him, and he played two. By then, my heels had wrecked my feet, so he offered to carry me until we caught a cab. End of the story. See? Nothing worthy of gossip websites or mass-media magazines."

"You'd tell me if it meant something more?"

"Yes. And by the way, I freaked out when Ems woke me up with the links to pictures of me online. They were taken and posted out of context."

"I sounded like a jealous asshole before. Sorry. I know we're not even officially dating and you don't owe me anything. For a moment, I felt played. It's silly." His lips claimed mine. Slowly. With care. "Just be honest with me. That's all I'm asking."

I nodded against his chest as he pulled me into his embrace.

"You have no idea how much I love this movie," I told Jacob a week later as we strolled toward the park where there was an outdoor presentation of the movie *Catching Up With You*. "I think I watched it a thousand times when I was a kid. That scene with the dog, it's the best."

Jacob reached for my hand as we neared the entrance. He did that every time we were surrounded by many people. As if I could ease something in him just by being by his side.

"I can't believe you've never seen it," I whispered in his

ear as we followed the crowd, all of us on the lookout for the best spot.

"I was a book nerd as a kid." He pressed a kiss to the tip of my nose. "Come on, for once, I'll even sit in the middle of all these people so we're front and center." He handed me the rolled blanket tucked under his arm. "Go wild. I'll head over to the concession stand."

I scanned my surroundings. "See that free patch of grass over there?" I pointed through a sea of families and couples. "Meet me there."

"It's a date," he said, his smile lighting up his handsome face.

"Before I forget, don't make plans for Saturday night."

He cocked his pierced brow. "Why?"

"Remember when you said you missed the opportunity to see the monster truck show when you were sixteen because you got food poisoning?"

Jacob nodded.

"Well, they're in town for a night, and I got us tickets."

He blinked. "You did?"

I nodded and offered a half-shrug. "I thought you might like it."

He looped his arms around my waist in a tight embrace. "You thought right. This is very sweet of you." He stepped back. "Now go, or you'll miss that perfect spot."

"Oh yeah, sure." We broke apart, and I returned my focus to my mission. "Sorry," I said, weaving through the crowd and trying not to bump into anyone or step on their toes, heading for the green patch I had set my eyes on. Just as I was about to lay down the blanket, someone crashed into me from behind, and I fell to my knees.

When a hand reached down for me, my eyes lingered on the long fingers, slowly tracing the corded forearm, muscular shoulder, and finally resting on the handsome eyes trained on me.

I blinked. "Sam?"

"Maddie?"

"Hi." I anchored my hand in his, rose to my feet, and brushed dust off my knees with my free hand.

He frowned. "Are you okay?"

"Yeah. All good. Okay, this is so weird. We gotta stop meeting like this."

"What are you doing here?" he asked.

"*Catching Up With You* is my all-time favorite movie. I wouldn't miss the screening for anything."

"It is? I watch it at least once a year. That dog scene gets me every time."

I blinked, speechless. Was he for real? "Wow, I didn't—"

"Girls, let's get ready to watch this movie," Riley announced, nearing us with Justine in his arms and Mikaella holding Devon's hand in tow, cutting our discussion short. He stopped when his eyes landed on me and gave Sam a puzzled look. "Hi, Maddie. I had no idea you were joining us tonight."

"Maddie," the girls hollered. Justine wiggled to get down, then both of them ran into my arms as I squatted, holding them to my heart.

"I'm so happy to see you." I glanced at the others from above their heads. "Actually, it wasn't planned," I told Riley. "Sam and I were battling for the same patch of grass to lay out a blanket."

"Now that you're here, you gotta watch the movie with us," Devon chimed in.

"Actually, I'm here with my friend."

"Jacob?" Mikaella asked.

I patted her head. "Yes. He went to get us popcorn. He should join me any minute."

"I wanna watch the movie with Jacob, Daddy." Justine bounced on her feet. "Please, please, please."

"You two are invited to join us if you'd like," Sam offered at the same time Jacob reached us.

"What's going on?" Jacob asked, his eyes darting across everyone, stopping on me.

"Huh, we happened to—" I began.

Justine jumped in. "Daddy and Maddie want to sit together, and Mika thinks you're pretty. Wanna watch the movie with me?"

Mikaella's cheeks reddened as her little sister bobbed her head, unapologetic about revealing her innocent crush.

I shrugged as Jacob asked me a silent question. Sam's daughters owned my heart. Even though I wanted to spend my night alone with Jacob—despite being surrounded by strangers—I could never refuse them time with me.

Justine curled her tiny body around his leg. "Please," she begged.

I cupped my mouth with one hand to stifle a laugh and noticed Devon doing the same.

Justine batted her eyelashes. How could anyone refuse her anything?

Jacob's arm slid across my waist, and he nodded. "Fine. The more the merrier, I guess." I could tell by his sudden rigid demeanor that the idea of spending our night with other people didn't please him. I leaned in so only he could hear me. "We can sit elsewhere if you prefer."

He breathed out. "No. It's okay. At some point, I gotta meet them. They are important to you, so they are important to me too."

I grinned way too big at the sound of his words. "Thanks. Girls, it's settled, we'll watch the movie together."

"Yay," they both cheered.

The moment we all sat down, Justine perched herself on Jacob's lap, her tiny arms circling his neck, and Mikaella curled herself under my arm while I brushed her hair back with my fingers. This, the concept I belonged somewhere, filled me with warmth.

Sam's gaze caught mine, and he shrugged, shaking his head.

They're perfect, I mouthed, at which he nodded his approval.

He offered me a lopsided smile, and I mirrored it. I loved this new friendship we had going on.

About forty minutes into the movie, Justine fell asleep. Sam set her beside him, using his hoodie as a blanket. Mikaella moved between Riley and Devon, snuggling with Hope, their dog. Jacob used his newfound freedom to scoot closer to me and wrapped an arm around my shoulders, and I sank into his embrace.

Minutes later, he nuzzled the side of my neck and kissed my temple. He was usually not a very PDA kind of guy, and this sudden urge to claim me in front of everyone else felt out of character for him.

"What are you doing?" I asked in a whisper.

"Enjoying the movie." He leaned in to silence me with a kiss, but I pulled away.

"What's going on?" I asked. We had agreed not to *date* date because I was leaving for six months soon, and if we got too invested in a relationship before my departure, leaving would break both our hearts. I didn't want to complicate or jeopardize the tour—and my heart—or feel homesick the whole time. So far, being just friends had worked well for us, even though I could tell Jacob yearned for more. But I wasn't ready to fall in love if it meant being heartbroken shortly after.

"Just enjoying the night," he said, tracing the contours of my face with his fingertips.

I pushed further away from his touch. "No. Stop. We're not making out here."

He toyed with the tendrils of my hair that fell down my back. "I'm tired of pretending we're not together when we both know we are. Why are you so scared?"

"Can we talk about it later? Now isn't the time or place."

Jacob slid to the left and folded his legs before him, a frown creasing his forehead. His eyes stayed glued to the giant inflatable screen positioned between mature trees in front of us. From the corner of my eye, I noticed the tick in his jaw and the hurt hardening his features. Tears prickled my eyes, but I blinked them away. I hated fights and the feeling I had deceived someone I cared about. Since the day Jacob had confronted me about the pictures of Sam and me in those tabloids, he'd been acting insecure. I was done reassuring him that they were just pictures meant to insinuate and provoke, and nothing more. I understood where he was coming from and why he was questioning me, but I was twenty-one, single, and free to hang out with whoever I wanted, without having to explain myself. We had agreed, Jacob and I, that we were friends. Who kissed sometimes. But friends, nonetheless. No label. No sex. Nothing to blur the line until I came back from the tour, and we decided if we wanted to give it a real shot.

I cocked my head to the side, and Sam's eyes reeled me in.

Are you all right? he mouthed.

I shrugged. Not really. But I wouldn't confide in him about my messy, nonexistent love life.

For the rest of the movie, I felt his heavy stare on me. I could tell he wasn't convinced by my act. More than once, I caught him watching Jacob intensely, a frown marring his forehead.

Since Jacob had shifted away from me, he'd kept his hands to himself and remained distant.

I placed a hand on his shoulder in a tentative attempt to bridge the gap. "Can we not fight here?"

He shook his head and sighed. "Sorry. It's stupid. It's weird for me to spend the night with your boss and his family and friends."

I leaned against him. "I know. It wasn't planned. Thank you for agreeing, though. It made the girls happy. I'll never hear the end of it. They'll chant your praises for weeks to come."

We exchanged tentative smiles.

"They love you," he said after a stretch of silence. "I'm glad they have you in their lives…because I'm glad I have you too."

The movie ended, and Sam lifted a near-comatose Justine in his arms. Riley picked up a tired Mikaella, who complained that her legs were asleep and she couldn't possibly walk back to the car on her own.

Devon grabbed my hand. "It was so good to see you again, Maddie. I hope we'll see more of each other soon." She waved me goodbye and followed her man, who had stopped to strike up a conversation with a couple he seemed to know.

Jacob left to look for the portable potty, and then it was just Sam and me—and a sleeping Justine. Like he did every time he was nervous, Sam stuffed his free hand into his pocket. "So, I was wondering if—"

No idea why, but I could finish his sentence. "I'm…

huh…okay… Jacob and I just had a disagreement." I decided to be honest. "He's not over the pictures…"

"I see." He sighed. "If I were in his shoes and saw my girl online with all those headlines, I'm sure I would've reacted too."

I lowered my shoulders. "We're not really…dating. We're just friends."

"Oh." He took a step forward, and skimmed my upper arm with his fingers.

The air around us charged. Time seemed to stop. All I could hear was the pounding of my own heart.

"I believed…" He never finished his sentence. Dropping his arm to his side, he backed away from me.

I swallowed, pretty sure I'd imagined something that never existed, and tried to return to my previous train of thought. "All I'm saying is—" I stopped. Why was I breathless?

Sam's throat worked, and he watched me, waiting for me to continue.

"I…huh…I understand his concern. I do. About the… about the pictures. It's legitimate. Why wouldn't it be?" And now I was rambling. "But…" I didn't remember where I was going with that. "Anyway, I'm free to do whatever I want. I'm aware those pictures weren't ideal, but we did nothing wrong. So why would I get carried away? We had a great time. I chose to do as you said and let them be. With the ugly, multi-million-dollar celebrity divorce going on in Hollywood right now, you and I are already old news. You were right. Those things get swiped away pretty quickly."

"See? I told you so." His amused expression made him look boyish, and I relished the sight of it.

"I should go," I said, pointing over my shoulder. "Jacob will be back. And you gotta put the girls to bed so…"

"You'd tell me if you weren't fine, right?" He raised one dark brow. "As your *friend*." Was it me, or had he put too much emphasis on the word *friend*?

"Yep. No worries."

Our eyes fixated on each other for a bit longer. Why was it so hard to move away from Sam's energetic field? Since the first time his eyes had roamed over me at the nanny agency, Sam Stevens's attention always sent flutters to my belly. It made me feel special—in a way I had never felt with anyone else. I had no explanation for it.

I pushed the thought away, knowing I was, once again, overthinking everything.

"I'll go now." Recalling the awkwardness in the cab the other night, I leaned forward, unsure if we should shake hands or kiss each other's cheeks. And, like that night, I decided against it and waved instead. Sam nodded his agreement but didn't budge, watching my retreat. I could tell because I felt his eyes on me. They burned my back.

Jacob joined me, and when I risked a look back, I noticed Sam hadn't left, a serious expression painting his face. A small knot twisted my stomach. Was he worried I had faked being all right seconds ago?

Whatever his expression meant, I preferred to be on the receiving end of his smiles. That I knew for sure.

12

MADISON

"Will Daddy be home before bedtime?" Mikaella asked, her hair still damp from her bath, dressed in a pastel-blue nightgown with a grinning, pink-glazed donut printed on the front. The one I'd gotten her the other day when we all went shopping together because she argued her father had no sense of girls' fashion. The memory of it sent a bolt of warmth through my heart.

Back then, we were fine—all of us. Or at least, I believed that was our reality.

In the last month, since that movie night, Sam had been colder around me. Even more than usual. His broody attitude had made a full comeback, reminding me of the man I'd first met at the nanny agency. His annoyance seemed solely directed at me, though. His patience ran thin these days. He argued with the girls more often too. Up until that night, we were getting along great, and our working relationship had even evolved into a friendship. Or I thought it did... Now, I didn't know what to think anymore. For a week, I'd blamed it on the anxiety of going back on tour, but now I wasn't so sure.

In the midst of everything, my relationship with Jacob had also gotten complicated.

He was asking for more. For commitment. A voice inside my head was telling me to be careful and to give it more time. To wait and see. And thus far, in my life, my intuition had been mostly right, so I usually chose to listen to it.

Many question kept me up at nights these days, and I often wondered if Sam was rethinking my presence on tour? That was the only logical explanation I could come up with for his iciness toward me.

When we were alone in a room, he always found a reason to leave. He never struck up a conversation with me anymore, just for the sake of it, nor did he ask random questions to get to know me or look me in the eye. My ego was hurt, and I feared what would happen with the girls if he decided my presence on tour wasn't necessary anymore. No way would I leave them of my own volition. Never.

I had been that kid—the one who felt like the adults in her life had turned their backs on her at some point. I would never subject Mikaella and Justine to the same treatment. They had already been deceived once. I wouldn't be the next adult in line to disregard them.

Needing more than a grown-up's bad temper to ruffle my feathers, I swallowed the whirlwind of emotions rising in me and kept giving my full attention to those two little girls, who had become my entire world over the past few months.

No matter how hard I tried to forget him, my troubled mind always swirled back to their father whenever I was left alone with nothing to occupy my thoughts.

Sam and I had spent a great deal of time together

before the movie night, and on each occasion, I'd felt we were getting closer…understanding each other on a deeper level.

The night I went back to his house after forgetting my purse, I was certain we shared a moment in his music studio. I'd bet my life we did. Supercharged electricity had infiltrated the room....and the intensity with which he'd stared at me… Whoa, I thought I would melt right there on the carpeted floor. I remembered I could barely breathe, my brain starved for oxygen.

Then we shared food in that bar, danced, and sang together. Though I'd tried to convince myself otherwise, I knew I hadn't imagined the powerful connection we'd shared. That night, I saw a new version of Sam Stevens— the man who enjoyed his freedom for a few hours, a man rather than just a single father. The one who thrived and shed all the walls around him.

He hadn't faked happiness that night. Sue me, but I could tell. I knew it deep in my bones.

At that point, my feelings for him had become conflicted. Once back home, I'd watched him leave through my bedroom window, my heart fracturing at the thought that it had been a one-night-only thing between us. Nothing more. Just a glimpse of a laid-back life—one where we could be ourselves, without anything or anyone standing between us. A man and a woman, simply enjoying each other's company for a few uninterrupted hours.

When I'd gone to bed afterward, I concluded it wasn't mere attraction we shared but undeniable chemistry. I had convinced myself that being friends with him was enough. Things were simple between us. Nothing was forced. We got along great.

But now, over a month later, I'd realized I had completely misread the situation back then.

Gone was the easy familiarity between Sam and me. Every time we were around each other, he spoke as if I were just another employee, the warmth behind his words nonexistent. These days, he didn't grab my arm when I said something he disagreed with. We shared no eye contact. In fact, Sam had shut me out entirely. If the greenhouse hadn't stood as concrete proof that we once made a great team, I wouldn't have believed it myself.

I hurt as the rip separating us became a canyon. Wide and deep.

Mikaella tugged at my shirt. "Maddie, you're not listening. Will Daddy be home before bedtime?"

"Sorry, I got lost in my head for a minute." In one swift movement, I flipped my phone over on the countertop to look at the time. "He should be here within the hour." I cringed. "I…think. He didn't go over the day's plans with me this morning. I'm sure we can push bedtime a tiny bit to wait for him."

Justine met us, dressed in an almost-identical nightgown as her sister, but hers was pink with a toothy ice cream cone printed on the front. "I wanna dance. Can we do a *partly*? With music."

"A party, sweetie," I said with a smile. "You want to throw a party?"

The four-year-old nodded. "*Partly. Partly. Partly*," she repeated, jumping around the kitchen.

I wiped my hands on the dishcloth hanging over my shoulder. "Okay. Let's put some music on. Help me move some furniture around in the den, okay?"

Both girls bobbed their heads with unconcealed glee and infectious giggles.

We cranked up the volume of a pop song they adored,

and Justine and Mikaella started dancing around. The room soon filled with laughter, and my heart brimmed with delight.

Lifting Justine in my arms, I spun her around only to grab Mikaella's hands next to twirl her too, swaying to the rhythm of the catchy melody.

"Again," Justine said once the song ended.

I put another song on, and this time, we held on to one another's hands in a circle and danced, laughing our hearts out.

This, right here, was why I would never be able to walk away from those girls unless I was forced to.

"I'm thirsty," Mikaella said, breathless, her cheeks crimson, after the third song.

"Keep dancing. I'll get you some water. Be right back." I put another song on, and the girls did all kinds of acrobatic moves, jumping, swaying their hips, spinning.

I watched them, unable to stop grinning as I walked away.

In the doorway, I bumped into a wall—a human wall —and lost my balance. Two strong hands clamped around my waist, and I nearly melted under the searing heat coursing through me.

I raised my head, meeting Sam's eyes. They fixed me in place, darkening more and more with every heartbeat. My throat felt dry and itchy, and I swallowed through a maze of sharp edges.

Trying to regain control over my senses, I blinked twice.

As if someone had nailed me to the floor, I couldn't move, his gaze pinning me in place.

My deafening pulse drowned out Mikaella's and Justine's laughter, its thudding all I could hear besides Sam's heavy, fast, shallow breathing.

Maddie, say something. Anything.

"I…huh… We-we've been… I mean, hi." *Real smooth, girl.*

Sam cleared his throat, and his voice sounded rougher than usual, pulsing through all my cells. "What are you doing?"

"Getting water."

His fingers dug into my skin, his grip tightening instead of loosening.

My head hovered just above his heart. Could I hear its drumming if I closed my eyes and listened closely? Would it beat in time with my own?

"I said, what are you doing?"

I leaned back, my brows bunched together, not sure I understood the meaning of his words.

"The girls should be in bed by now. It's almost eight thirty."

I met his gaze, my face probably betraying my bewilderment. Was he kidding right now? Since when did he become so stiff about bedtime hours?

It wasn't like I kept them up late often. It only happened once or twice in the past. And both times, he was glad they stayed up until he came home.

"They missed you. They wanted to wait for you. I'm sorry if I overstepped here. I thought you'd be glad to tuck them in yourself."

A storm rumbled in his irises. I parted my lips, but no words came out.

Would he lose his cool over this? What was going on with him? Where was the guy I got to know in that bar? The king of dares who enjoyed a good time.

His tone turned icy, sending chills through me. "You can't decide what's best for them, Madison. I'm their father. I call the shots." His words sounded lethal. What?

We were back to Madison? What was happening? What did I do to deserve his unconcealed wrath?

I blinked again. Once, twice. A hundred times.

Fragments of fury formed inside me. How did I ever think Sam Stevens and I were on an equal level of friendship?

In the past, when I barely knew him, this grumpy side of him allured me. Not this time. The time, it affected me instead…a lot.

This version of the man I worked for didn't sit well with me.

I straightened my back and glared right back at him with the same fervor. He had no right to belittle my character or my judgment. No matter who he was or what he wanted, he had to trust me to know what was best for his kids when they were under my care. No, Sam Stevens couldn't stand there and intimidate me just because he was in a sour mood or had a bad day. Whatever was wrong with him had nothing to do with me and everything to do with him. It would be better if he kept his wrath for someone else—someone who had truly hurt him and deserved this angry side of him.

"I'm sorry if I kept the girls up fifteen minutes past their bedtime, Mr. Stevens. Won't happen again. You have my word."

His face flushed, and some of his anger evaporated as he studied me, blinking, as if taken by surprise, the storm in his eyes dissipating and switching to surprise. "Mr. Stevens? Are you being serious? What is this all about, *Madison*? Explain."

Why was it that every time my name fall from his lips, it sent waves of heat through me? I felt like a popsicle in the sun whenever he called me by my full name. I sighed. Somehow, tonight, it even eased my irritation.

"You called me Madison so I'm calling you Mr. Stevens. Only fair."

Breathing the same air, neither of us looked away as we indulged in a staring contest. Tension ran high, swirling around us, taking us hostage in its claws.

We faced each other.

"It's a bit childish, don't you think? If I remember correctly, Madison is your name." He arched one dark brow in a sexy slash infuriating manner.

My ire clothed my heart, leaving knots crushing my stomach in its wake.

Using my most innocent tone, I mocked, "Mr. Stevens is *yours* too, no?"

If looks could kill, I'd be dead right now. Our gazes stayed locked, neither of us stepping down. Sam's nostrils flared. His eyes transformed into weapons, powerful enough to vaporize every inch of me. A new flame ignited in my lower belly. Great. Now desire and hate mixed together. Because, like some idiot, I relished the fervor of our exchange.

He watched me but said nothing, so I continued, "You told me once we needed to be honest with each other. Right now, I feel like you're upset with me for some unknown reason. You're the one acting like a petulant child." I clamped my mouth shut as soon as the retort escaped. Why was I engaging in a war of words with my boss? *No, no, no.* This was bad. I was crossing a line that couldn't be uncrossed. "Sorry. I…I…huh…didn't mean to be disrespectful. Won't happen again." In a twisted way, it felt good to get it out there and to express myself without restraints.

His somber expression morphed into amusement. A crooked smirk appeared on his face, and it disrupted my flimsy resistance. "I must say I'm impressed. I—"

"Daddy," Justine and Mikaella screamed as they ran in our direction. Sam released his grip on me, and my knees wobbled. I used the wall to hold myself upright as I regained my composure.

What had just gone down?

Once my legs steadied, I stepped back, creating space between us, determined to break free of Sam's gravity and reclaim my self-control.

I resumed my breathing, shaking away every lingering morsel of our heated encounter. Whatever I did, I didn't deserve his rant. But the way his stare had burned into me was hotter than any confrontation I'd ever experienced, making my confusion even more overwhelming.

"Daddy, we're having a dance *partly*. With music," Justine said as he lifted her in his arms and spun her around before she peppered his cheek with kisses.

"Maddie said we can go to bed later because we wanted to wait for you," Mikaella said, raising her arms to be picked up too. "We missed you."

"She did, didn't she?" he asked, his gaze slowly finding me. His Adam's apple bobbed, and I pushed down whatever heat his unyielding attention provoked inside me.

For a moment, I forgot how to breathe, intoxicated by the hostility raging in the room. My body overheated, and prickling sensations surged through me.

Gasping with each intake of air, I spun around and fled to the kitchen, desperate to create space between us.

I poured myself a tall glass of water, fighting my emotions down and cooling all my misplaced attraction. I was mad at Sam. And upset at how he'd addressed me. But I also couldn't deny our altercation had woken up something in me that I had no words to define.

Tilting my head back, I tried to put a name to that rapture vibrating between us. The push and pull. That forbidden attraction we had felt in the past that had flared up again just seconds ago—more potent this time, more explosive.

The cold liquid eased some of the fire down my throat.

Not in the mood to have another face-off with my boss —since when did I start referencing him as my boss again and not Sam?—and fearing that for some reason I'd read the situation wrong and he wasn't rethinking my place in their lives, I gathered my stuff, ready to bolt before I combusted. My mind drifted to Jacob. I missed the comfort he provided me. His arms. His kisses. And the way he made me feel like I was the most important person on Earth. How he never took pleasure in submitting me to a battle of wills.

My heart changed its tempo as more thoughts of him filled my mind.

I wiped the tears pooling in the corners of my eyes with the hem of my shirt and sent him a text.

ME

Can I come over?

He replied within a second.

JACOB

Just got home. I was hoping I'd see you.

ME

I'll be there soon.

JACOB

Can't wait. Dessert?

ME

Yes.

I had dinner with the girls earlier, but dessert sounded great right now, as chocolate and ice cream always helped me sort out my troubled emotions.

I slid my phone back into my back pocket and poured two cups of water for the girls.

They were still in the den, telling their daddy all about their day. The twinkles in their eyes soothed some of my doubts. They healed the cracks Sam's earlier accusations had carved into my heart. Now that the heaviness suffocating us had lessened and my common sense had returned, I couldn't wait to flee the scene.

"Are you leaving?" Mikaella asked as I leaned closer to hug her goodbye.

"Yes. It's time for me to go." I coughed, my emotions lacing my voice, trying to erase all traces of my meltdown.

Still in her daddy's arms, Justine looped her small arms around my neck, pulling me forward. "Why are you sad, Maddie?" Why did she have to be so perceptive at such a young age? She was connected to people's emotions. All the time. She cupped my face and studied me for a moment, her eyes boring into mine as if she could read my soul.

I blinked, not ready to let her see through me. "I'm okay, sweetie. I just have to go. I'll be all right. You should go to bed now. It's late."

"I love you, Maddie," she said, burying her face in the crook of my neck. "Don't be sad."

Tears filled my eyes and rolled down my cheeks. Her compassion broke the dam I was trying so hard to contain. I fastened my grip around her tiny body, my shoulders heaving. She moved from her father's arms to mine, and I squatted to level my face with a worried Mikaella.

"Did Daddy do that to you?" she asked.

I sniffled. Could I hold on to these girls forever? I

wasn't ready to let their father see how badly our interaction had overwhelmed me.

"Girls, go brush your teeth. I'll be right up to tuck you in. Say goodnight to Madison."

His clipped tone propelled another wave of hot tears down my face. Great. Now I'd look like a mess. Just like a kid unable to face any criticism. Because when he confronted me tonight, Sam Stevens had treated me like a kid. He had talked to me like an entitled jerk. One I refused to acknowledge anymore for the time being.

I pulled away from the girls' embrace and wiped my tears with my fingertips. "I'm fine, sweethearts. Just a bit tired. I'll go to bed and be all good in the morning, okay? It's bedtime for you two."

They both nodded, hugged me one last time before walking away.

"Come on, Justine. They wanna have a grown-up conversation," Mikaella whispered to her sister. She huffed and stretched her arm to grab Justine's hand in hers and led her away.

I watched them go. They reminded me of how Emily had looked after me a long time ago, and it eased some of my emotional overload.

Sam held out his hand, helping me to stand up. He searched my eyes, shoving his hands into his pockets, looking less lethal than he did minutes ago. "What's wrong?" His tone softened. Kinda. "Was Mikaella right? Did I do that to you?"

I shrugged, avoiding his gaze.

"Fuck. I'm sorry. I overreacted earlier. You didn't deserve my anger." He hung his head low, chin nearly touching his chest, and burrowed his hands deeper into his pockets, an unmistakable sign he was uncomfortable. "I… I'm bad at this." He rubbed his scruffy jaw with a hand.

"I'm trying hard to do the right thing here." I had no clue what his cryptic words meant. "Maddie, I-I didn't wanna make you cry. I swear. There's a lot going on in my head right now, and you paid the price. Again, I'm sorry for anything I might have said that hurt your feelings. It was never my intention. You do a fantastic job with the girls."

His words twined around my heart. They spread pride and warmth throughout my being.

When regretful, Sam looked vulnerable and charming all at the same time. A deadly combination. One that appealed to the caring side of me, and to some extent, to the woman in me too.

Again, it messed with my feelings. And my will to leave.

I was hurt—and sad—but I craved his devoted attention, nonetheless. How every time he smiled at me, it lit up my days and reminded me I was his equal. Not just the hired help or another employee. How when we'd had openhearted conversations in the past, I saw beyond his celebrity or daddy status and just witnessed the guy hiding behind those labels. They didn't define him. There was so much more to Sam Stevens than people could see. You had to work backstage and be in his inner circle to grasp a hint of it. Deep down, I was grateful I did. More than once. Yet there were times when he went back to being a jerk for reasons I still couldn't comprehend.

Without thinking it first, my hand moved to rest on his forearm, my fingers grazing the skin there. His annoyance dissolved. Sam blinked, avoiding my eyes for the longest time. I sucked in a shallow breath, trying to keep my composure.

His eyes darted back to mine. This time, gone was the aggravation. He looked at me with respect and reverence, and a new surge of never-experienced-before sensations bubbled up deep in me. Messy feelings I'd been trying for months to conceal returned and amplified. They went against all logical reasoning.

"Are we okay?" he asked.

I retracted my hand, praying it would kill the longing knotting my stomach.

This just didn't compute. Right now, I was attracted to Sam—more than ever before—but I was also attracted to Jacob. Intellectually, we were a perfect match. We enjoyed nights in and a laid-back way of living. Sam did too, but he was more complex. He and I connected on another level. Family, his children, music, and reaching for our deepest dreams in life while facing our fears. On the physical level, the resemblance between them was striking.

I was sick. How could someone sane be attracted to two completely different people?

This was bad. How would I ever be able to do my job if I had a crush on my boss? This situation had to go away. It needed to be resolved, and fast.

Sam's voice, like a drug I couldn't escape, brought me back to him. "…hear me out, okay?" Great, I'd missed most of what he was telling me. "I hate the tension between us. It's not good for the girls. They sense it. We should talk. Once they're in bed."

Still under the shock of my inner revelations, I folded my arms over my chest, trying to raise a barricade between us and hoping my heart would get the memo and leave it at that. "Another day. I'm not feeling well right now." My words sounded weak as they left my mouth. I had to retreat and assess my complicated feelings far away from here.

He shook his head. "No, I wanna clear the air tonight. It's the right thing to do. Let's not draw this out. There's a weird tension between us. It's unhealthy. Let's hash it out once and for all and move on." He touched my upper arm for a split second, his finger tracing the length of my triceps, leaving me spellbound.

I stood there, hair standing on end on my arms, a storm of inner chaos swirling in my stomach, and closed my eyes. What should I do?

Taking advantage of the time I had while Sam tucked the girls in bed, I hurried to the bathroom to splash cold water over my face and gave myself a pep talk.

"Go out there and face him. First, no getting all emotional when someone criticizes you. Second, he's your boss. Just. Your. Boss. Drill that piece of information into your head. Third, grow a spine and face the man, Maddie. He wasn't upset at you earlier. He overreacted and said he was sorry. You did nothing wrong. If he's had a bad day, it's not your job to fix it. Or to fix him. Nor to be on the receiving end of his annoyance."

I rolled my shoulders back and exited the room with a new resolve.

Sam Stevens wouldn't break me—or my spirit. I wouldn't let his vulnerable and handsome self get a grip over my heart.

After I poured two glasses of water, I took a seat on a stool at the kitchen island, waiting for him to join me.

Meanwhile, I sent Jacob a text.

ME

Will be running late. Have something to deal with here first.

JACOB

Noted. I went to get ice cream. Just in case that's the mood you're in right now. And a raspberry and cream cake in case I'm wrong.

Jacob's thoughtfulness made me smile, and it made my heart rate peak.

ME

Be there ASAP.

Sam joined me, and I flipped my phone over, hiding the screen, as if he'd just caught me doing something bad.

I relaxed my stance when his lips bent into a shadow of a smile.

He didn't sit down. Instead, he leaned against the opposite countertop facing the kitchen island.

"About earlier, again, I was wrong. And I'm sorry. I had no right to bark at you. Since you've come into our lives, the girls can't stop talking during bedtime, telling me all they did and all they learned during the day."

His shoulders relaxed, his stance softened, and I emptied the air stuck in my lungs. The one I kept in, in case I required a reserve if our conversation went south.

Repeating my pep talk over and over in my head, I lifted my chin and decided to get to the bottom of this. The source of this tautness between us that hadn't existed before. "Something's wrong. I feel it. It's been going on for weeks. I thought we were getting along just fine, the four of us."

Sam looked away, his upper back going rigid. He shut his eyes and breathed out, pinching the bridge of his nose. Gone was the easygoing posture.

I had no idea how to read the man. He was so closed off most of the time that every once in a while when he got out of his shell and laughed or played with us, it felt like a small victory.

The girls and I didn't deserve his shitty attitude, though. I couldn't tell him that without overstepping, especially since I had reminded myself that Sam was my boss, not my friend.

"There's so much going on—"

"Stop. It's not that. I can tell. It's not about tonight. You're mad at me, and it's been going on for a while. Did I do something wrong? Did I say something that bothered you? Are you rethinking the tour? My position?"

My heart lurched into my throat, and my airways constricted as I spoke the words I feared the most out loud.

Chills moved along my spine.

An acidic taste filled my mouth.

Sam's gaze snapped back to mine. He moved toward me, as if an invisible string connected us, stopping just a foot away.

"No. Maddie, don't say that. We need you. The girls need you." The column of his throat rippled. "I…I need you." He glanced down, rocking on his heels. When his irises found mine again, they were darker than I'd ever seen them, and the sight had a powerful effect on me. His voice cracked as he spoke. "Are you…are you thinking about quitting?"

I parted my lips but couldn't speak.

"Are you second-guessing the tour, Maddie? Are you looking for an out?"

I shook my head, feeling myself softening like molten clay beneath his heavy stare.

"Y-you need me?" Why was my voice suddenly so raspy? Somehow, all I'd heard was his need for me. The rest of his words didn't even register in my conscious mind.

The room temperature shot up by a thousand degrees.

Sweat lined my back.

My breath caught in my lungs.

Sam blinked and stepped back with a head shake, breaking the moment.

"We all do…" Not '*I* need you' this time… but '*We* need you.'"Your presence is essential for me to go on this tour. If you're not coming or are not fully committed to it, then I can't go. I won't let anyone else but you around my daughters. If you're having doubts, you must tell me now before it's too late and we can't fix things."

Back to business. The heart-to-heart had evaporated. Gone was the moment. The air cooled. He only needed the professional me to pursue his career, not the personal me to appease his heart or speak to his soul. I was wrong all this time when I believed we were friends.

How could he think that his newly raised barrier protected him from real talk? From opening up? From feeling anything?

Sam Stevens stood a couple of feet away from me but appeared much farther away.

My fingertips followed the condensation on the glass, caught by its quiet pattern. Would it be out of line to fight with him? To show him he could drop the false pretenses and speak his mind—be honest, like he had been in that bar? That being himself, not that robotic version, would benefit not only his daughters but himself too? I had seen that version of him, so I knew it existed somewhere inside him.

I weighed my words before speaking again. "No… I'm not quitting…or thinking about quitting. Unless that's what *you* wish. And even if it is, I'm ready to fight for my job. I don't back down from my responsibilities and engagements easily."

Something passed in Sam's eyes. A glimpse of his hurting soul. His lips twitched. Clouds shadowed his face. It had been a while since I'd seen that expression etching his features, and I had forgotten how it twisted my insides when it faded away.

"Good," was all he said, his voice lacking warmth. "In that case, it's settled. We go on tour as planned. End of discussion. Unless you have something else you wanna say. Now is the time."

I bit my tongue, choosing to avoid a battle I was certain I couldn't win—at least not tonight. I was drained and longed to be somewhere far from his orbit.

"Nope. All good." My words sounded insipid, not even convincing myself.

"And for the record, I'm not angry at you. If I made you believe I was, it's not the case. I'm mad at myself for different reasons." He turned around and busied himself with making coffee. "Want some?"

"No. I should go. I'm sure you have plenty to do. I'll get out of here. It's getting late."

"Yeah. Sure. Go. Do your thing." He did not even bother to turn around to look at me while I saw myself out. "Good night."

The more space I put between us, the cooler the air turned. As if an arctic breeze had replaced the chinook that had swept the room when we had our face-off earlier and minutes ago when he admitted to needing me.

With my hand around the knob and about to open the front door, I rethought my escape. Sam was hurting. I could tell. The friend in me should find the courage to go to him and offer him a way to vent it out. But again, I had decided earlier we weren't friends per se because it was safer for me to only see him as my boss. I hated the idea of leaving when things were still awkward between us. My heart hung by a flimsy thread in my chest. I debated my options in my head. Before I could come to a conclusion, his muscular hand pushed against the panel over my head, preventing me from leaving.

I jumped at the abrupt movement. My pulse spiked.

I swiveled around, trying to decipher Sam's mixed expression.

His irises, fixated on me, shone darker. Midnight abysses I couldn't flee from. They captured mine, and I swallowed to ease the tightness in my throat.

We stood too close for comfort. I could smell the hint of coffee on his breath and the lingering notes of his cologne.

My head spun. I backed against the door, my eyes still linked to his. His looming posture was anything but professional. It was dominating. I had become the prey he'd caged with his entire being.

He started talking, his voice rough, sending shivers through me. "Before you go, I just want to tell you I'm having some people I care about over for a barbecue on Saturday. Friends. For my birthday." His tone, still hardened, reverberated through me. "I'd like you to join us…if you're free. As a guest, not the nanny or anything else. There'll be plenty of food, good wine, beer, cocktails, music, and… Anyway, the girls made me promise to ask you to come."

My mouth went dry, and my heart thudded. A new wave of anger blossomed inside me.

"You're only inviting me because Mika and Justine asked you to. I'm no one's pity invite." No way would I be an imposter at this party and feel like a stranger amongst all his probably rich and famous country music friends. Never. Anyway, why would he want me there in the first place?

Sam swallowed, taking his time to answer, his gaze fleeting away.

He cleared his throat, still not looking fully at me, but not moving back.

He spoke again, his tone gentler this time. "Maddie, is this what you believe? That I'd invite you out of pity?"

In the scant room between us, I folded my arms. "It sure sounded like it. Like it hurt you to invite me. Like you're only dealing with my presence because you don't have any other option and you'd rather stand anywhere else but here, in front of me."

He stepped closer. The slim gap separating us shrunk. "Maddie, I want you there. You and I... I-I consider you my friend. I wouldn't have asked if that wasn't the case. I'm sorry if it sounded rude. Believe me, it was never my intention. I swear. And I'm far from being annoyed by your presence. On the contrary... You call me out on my bullshit, and it's unsettling. *Petulant child. Pity invite.* I'm not used to people defying me when I go off track or when I'm wrong."

He finally met my eyes. I noticed the pleading in them. The apology. Fire ignited around us. What was this force messing with my whole self when we stood close? Was I the only one feeling the sparks?

Sam leaned in as if he couldn't evade the magnetism too.

"Saturday, I already—"

"If Jacob is around, he's invited too," he added before I could refuse. "Since that movie night, the girls have been talking about him nonstop. I'm sure all of us will get along just fine. When he visits you on tour, it's better if we're already acquainted."

"You'll let him come visit me?"

"Maddie, you're not going to jail, but to live a life not a lot of people are lucky to experience in their lifetime. Your friends and family are welcome anytime."

And now he was back to being the generous and caring man I had uncovered under his tough exterior. The one he was around his children—and around me when he wasn't pretending.

After the realization that had hit me earlier, mixing my personal and professional lives didn't appear to be a good idea. It screamed disaster in big bold letters. Jitters invaded me at the thought, and I could feel my will to stay away from him off the clock slipping away bit by bit. Would the nagging voices in my head just shut up for a minute so I could gather my thoughts?

I exhaled a shaky breath, racking my brain for a smart reply. "I, huh, gotta check with him because we had plans to go to this astronomy convention in Chattanooga. Can I give you an answer tomorrow?

Sam dropped his head, looking deflated, his confidence gone. "Sure." Why was he looking so defeated right now? "You're into galaxies and stars and planetary orbit things?"

I sighed. "Not really, but I said I'd accompany him. The road trip part will be fun. Perhaps we can go on Sunday… I'll have to ask him."

Sam backed from me and released the door. "Night, Maddie."

"See you in the morning," I blurted as I hurried outside, welcoming the summer breeze as it tickled the tip of my nose.

There, I could finally breathe.

With my back resting against the door, I tried to find an explanation for the complicated emotions that had invaded me tonight. Soon I'd be screwed if I didn't find a way to untangle the mess I was slowly creating inside me.

———

"Is everything all right?" Jacob asked after he greeted me.

I forced a smile, not wanting to worry him. "I'm fine. Just tired. Had a long day and it was kinda weird."

"Wanna talk about it?"

I shrugged. "Not really. Just my boss being his grumpy self for no reason."

We sat on opposite countertops in the kitchen, bowls of cookie dough ice cream in our hands.

"Maddie, I gotta tell you something, and it can't wait."

My spoon hung, suspended midair, just below my mouth as I waited for him to speak. From the looks of it, I feared the words that would leave his mouth. I could tell they would just add another layer to the entanglement I was already dealing with.

"You occupy every corner of my brain all the time. I want more with you." I parted my lips to protest, but he kept going. "I know what you're gonna say. That you're leaving and don't want ties here so you're not heartbroken because you'll want to be in two places at once and it will be difficult to enjoy the experience of the tour if your heart is here." He paused and sucked a long breath in. "We're already in a relationship....whether you like it or not. Knowing you'll come back to me after those six months are over is all I'm asking for. Please say yes. I want you in my life. I'm all in."

I stopped breathing. Ohmygod, I was pretty sure I stopped breathing. Yeah, I did.

I blinked, trying to jolt my lungs back to life.

My heart danced in my chest, its throb echoing through every fiber of me.

A fuzzy feeling filled my chest.

I blinked again.

Would I pass out or start breathing on my own soon?

Jacob jumped from the counter and inched closer. He studied me, waiting for me to say something.

All the words died on the tip of my tongue.

I blinked some more.

"What do you say? Maddie? Are you okay?"

I nodded. "I hear you, but…the thing is, it's not what we discussed. I know me," I said once I regained control of my speech. "If we do this, I'll never be able to walk away."

"Think about it. We're spending the weekend together. Let's give it a try. See what it would look like if we were together for real." He cradled my face with his palm. "I'm falling for you. Hard. There's nothing I can do to stop it. We're amazing together. Why wait? When you know, you know."

"You'd wait for me while I'm gone?"

"Yep. Because you make me happy, Madison Prescott. Now that I have you in my life, I don't want to let you go."

Jacob looked at me with reverence. Everything he said sounded good. Why was I so afraid to commit to a relationship?

"I'll be the lucky one you come back to when it ends. I'll hold the fort while you tour the country."

"O-kay. We'll give it a try." As I spoke the words, an uneasy feeling woke up inside me. Knots wrapped around my stomach. I wished to do this, but a part of me kept telling me I shouldn't agree so fast. For once, could I ignore that voice in my head?

Jacob's mouth claimed mine, and I lost myself in his love. It silenced all those unwelcome voices in my head that knew nothing about what I desired.

Breathless, we broke apart.

"I can't wait for this weekend," he said, smiling like a fool.

"About that, can I meet you there on Sunday instead?"

His brows pinched together. "Why? We both have the

weekend off. We planned this weeks ago. You know how hard it was to get tickets."

I pushed away to look at him. "I've been…well, we've been invited to a barbecue at Sam's place. All afternoon and probably all evening on Saturday."

A frown creased his forehead. "I don't understand. Are you working or not?"

I shook my head, chewing my bottom lip. "They're having friends over, and Sam invited me. As a guest. Well, he invited both of us, but I told him you already had plans. It's his birthday."

"*We* already have plans," he corrected with a sharp tone. I could read all the hurt painting his face. "Your country music superstar of a boss wants me at one of his infamous birthday parties with his friends?"

I nodded and remained silent.

"You sure? Our last encounter was a bit strained. Not sure he appreciates my company."

"I told you already. He's broody sometimes. Don't make too much of it. He's nice—well, most times—and has a huge heart once you get to know him. When he's in a good mood… Did you forget he walked out on me the day we met?"

Jacob tilted his head back and let out a warm chuckle. "God, you're too good. I can't believe you gave him a second chance after he stormed out without a valid reason. Only a dick could do that to you."

I shrugged. "Anyway, he probably had his reasons. Or maybe not… Remember, he said he was sorry because he panicked. It doesn't matter anymore. We get along fine now. Most of the time." I paused and stared at him. "The girls and I will be happy to have you over."

"You're really going?"

"You already met Riley and Devon. Since I'll be spending months with him on a tour bus, it's better if I get to know his friends beforehand, no? At least, I'll know what to expect. The underside of the country music industry is all new to me. I won't have this chance twice. I wanna immerse myself as much as possible in it. It's a huge opportunity for me." I studied his face. "If you don't wanna come, like I said, I can drive to Chattanooga early on Sunday morning and meet you there. Or take the bus if you want us to drive back together."

"Gimme the night to think about it."

I nodded.

Jacob's eyes drank me in as he gave me a slow once-over. "I was really looking forward to spending the entire weekend together."

"I'm sorry."

He huffed. "Don't be. We'll make it work. Somehow." He flashed me a pearly-white smile.

Jacob looked so sure of us. Why couldn't I share his optimism? I really wanted to. I was desperate to. The chatter in my mind wouldn't stop, no matter how much I tried to block its murmur.

"Are you staying over tonight?" he asked while he refilled our bowls.

After the night I'd spent here on our first date, I'd never stayed over again. Ever. Why was he asking me tonight of all nights?

I fixed a curl to my lips. "Nah. I should go, it's getting late."

Anyway, I still needed to sort out my feelings, and fast. I couldn't be attracted to two guys at once. With Jacob, I knew it would be safe and easy. On the other hand, Sam woke up something potent inside me. It was the worst-case scenario.

Once I showered and slid under my covers an hour later, I prayed the night would erase all my doubts and things would look so much clearer in the morning light.

13

SAM

"When will Maddie be here, Daddy? She's better than you at braiding my hair."

"Sweet pea, I can do it." I emptied the grocery bags on the kitchen counter. "Gimme ten minutes."

Mikaella shook her head with enough velocity to detach it from her neck. She had a much better attitude when Madison was around. Her occasional bad moods were still mostly directed at me, but her therapist told me my little girl had made lots of progress in the past few months. I could only thank Madison for helping my girl through her struggles.

"Maddie's here?" Justine asked, bouncing our way. "I *loooove* Maddie. Maddie? Maddie? *Maaaaaddie?*"

I fought a smile while she looked around sporting a glittery emerald-green dress with lime-green satin ribbons and a yellow cape. A blinding combination of colors. For a second, I wondered who had gifted her that piece of ugliness. No matter how awful it looked, my youngest daughter glowed in it, and it was all that mattered.

"Maddie's not here, baby girl. She should arrive later this afternoon. At the same time as everyone else."

"But she gotta braid my hair," Mikaella argued.

"And I want Maddie to make pancakes," Justine said.

"Girls, I can do all this. If you'd give me ten minutes."

"NO," they both screamed at the same time.

"We want Maddie, Daddy," Mikaella said, not breaking her stance. "We need her. She's better at this than you are. She's a girl. She gets us. You're a boy, so you can't get our women complexities."

"Women complexi-*what*?"

She rolled her eyes. Great. "Women complexities, Daddy."

"Women complexities? Who taught you that?"

"Stella's mama told her daddy the other day after she got mad, and he said she was overreacting. See? Women complexities."

Oh wow. I hadn't seen that one coming. I huffed and tried a new approach. "Doing your hair and prepping lunch are two tasks I can manage on my own."

"Doesn't matter. We want Maddie to do it."

"Yes, Daddy, we want Maddie," Justine echoed. "She cooks special bunny pancakes. You don't."

"Girls, you want breakfast for lunch? I was thinking pasta."

"No. Bunny pancakes. It's *Saturnday*."

I kneeled in front of my little girl. "Saturday. And you'll have round and boring pancakes today. I'll ask Maddie to teach me how to make special bunny pancakes for next time. Deal?"

Justine frowned and stamped her feet on the floor. "No. No *dweal*. I only eat Maddie's pancakes."

"Since when?" I asked.

"And Maddie *has* to braid my hair. Not you," Mikaella chimed in.

When did my daughters team up against me? I usually had at least my youngest daughter on my side.

I should get a dog. Some old fellow—not a puppy who'd be all over the girls—too rusty to run around, who'd agree to be in my corner. Then it'd be two against two. Fair fight.

This house was lacking testosterone.

I'd be overrun by the time they were both old enough to go out and get into trouble.

Mikaella led her little sister away and whispered something to her. Justine bobbed her head, her smile reaching her ears.

They giggled some more before joining me.

"Fine, Daddy. We'll wait for Maddie," Mikaella said, her eyes bright with devilish sparks.

"Sweet pea, what did you tell your sister?"

"Nothing."

Justine snaked her arms around my legs, tugging at my shirt.

I squatted to level my eyes with hers. "What's up, baby girl?"

"I *loooove* you, Daddy," she said, mischief in her gaze.

"What are you girls up to?"

"Nothing, Daddy," Justine said, batting her eyelashes at me. "I love you *verrry* much."

I ran my fingers through my hair.

They both had me wrapped around their fingers. This was bad.

I shook my head and chuckled. My daughters would be the end of me. One day. They would team up for real, and I'd be defeated.

"I love you too."

She ran after her sister, leaving me confused as I continued emptying the groceries.

The front door was yanked open less than twenty minutes later, and I jumped at the sound. I looked at the time. My friends should be here in three hours. Whoever arrived hadn't called beforehand.

"Ry?" Who else could it be?

A flustered Madison entered the kitchen instead, her hair in a messy knot at the top of her head, dressed in black shorts and a teal shirt, looking fabulous. Distressed. And in a hurry.

"What's the emergency?" she asked, panting.

I ditched the vegetables I was cutting and moved closer to her. "What emergency? I have no clue what you're talking about."

She sighed. "The girls. They called. They told me you were having an emergency and requested my help and to get here as soon as possible." She raised a brow, studying me.

"They what? I—"

"Maddie," they both exclaimed as they stormed into the kitchen, with matching, satisfied grins on their faces.

"You made it," Mikaella said with a crooked smile. "That was quick."

"Special bunny pancakes. Special bunny pancakes. Special bunny pancakes," Justine chanted, pulling her forward.

"There's no emergency?" Madison asked, a frown of confusion crossing her brow.

My daughters both shook their heads. At least they were honest.

"Not really. We just need you. A *lotttt*. Can you braid my hair?" Mikaella asked in a low voice, expectation dripping from each word.

"And cook pancakes," my baby girl added, looking at her with her big eyes and curled lips, still wearing that eye-bleeding dress.

Madison's expression softened. She sat on the floor, and both my daughters climbed onto her lap, caressing her face and her hair with their hands. The picture of the three of them cuddling on my kitchen floor offered me a glimpse of how different our lives would have been if their mother hadn't left. Would she have taken the time to just be with them? Comfort them? Throw water balloons on a weekday afternoon only because it was fun?

"Girls, listen. Emergencies are serious. You can't just call me behind your daddy's back to tell me something is wrong when it's not. I thought something bad had happened. That you guys were hurt. Do you understand what I'm saying?" They both nodded. "Next time, tell me you need my help, and I'll still come. I'll always be there for you two. You own my heart, and I love you. Just don't make me lose my mind, okay?"

They all hugged and kissed, everything forgotten.

Madison came back downstairs after tackling the girls' hair and helping them change into sleeveless summer dresses.

"I'm sorry. I had no idea they'd stolen my phone. I don't even know how they got hold of the password."

"I'm sure they have their ways. Ever heard of voice command? Anyway, they are kids, and technology has a sweet spot for them. Don't worry. It's fine. I just pictured the worst-case scenarios in my mind as I drove here. I'm glad everyone is safe and sound. Need a hand?"

"Sure."

"By the way, happy birthday."

We exchanged a smile. "Thanks."

"Oh, I almost forgot. Be right back." I heard the front

door open and close, and seconds later, Madison set a square white pastry box on the counter.

"What is it?"

"It's for you."

I removed the tape securing the lid and opened the box. Inside lay two dozen chocolate-glazed cupcakes.

I blinked. It had been so long since someone had baked me a birthday cake that I couldn't even remember when. "You baked them?"

"This morning. Thought it would be weird for you to make a cake to yourself."

Emotions washed through me. "I'm touched. Thank you." I almost pulled her into a hug, because with anyone else that was what I would have done, but I refrained just in time. I didn't need to make whatever this was, awkward between us. Since our heated exchange a couple of days ago, things had been less tense, and I intended to keep it that way.

That night, after she'd left, I had stayed awake for hours, trying to figure out why I was so annoyed by her presence lately. I'd realized that over the last few months, Madison had taken over a huge part of my life. I enjoyed every moment we spent together. For reasons beyond my understanding, she appeared to get me better than anyone else. With her, I could let go of the control and social expectations and talk openly without fear of judgment. I could speak from my heart and be entirely myself. To be honest, this bond between us scared me. Fascination with a woman had become a rare occurrence for me these days. I met plenty of them in meetings, rehearsals, and at the recording studios, but at the end of the day, Madison was the one person I wished I could tell everything to. My fears. My dreams. And my hopes. A hunch told me she would understand them all and reassure me whenever I doubted myself. It freaked the hell out of me to be attracted to her this way—to feel like her presence in my life was essential and that she could calm the storm inside me. What would happen if I became dependent on our friendship? It was a scenario I preferred not to think about, because no matter what, it would lead nowhere. Madison and I, we didn't have that kind of relationship. She was my kids' nanny, not someone I could be attracted to. Yet somehow, the thought that we were destined to keep our distance saddened me more than it should have.

Next to me, she made a joke about me teaching her to play the birthday song on the guitar, and it brought me back to the present.

Just like that, we worked side by side, calmness settling between us, as if we'd done this thousands of times before and that it was the most natural occurrence in the world. Every time Madison smiled at me or we locked gazes, my heart did a somersault in my chest.

Beyond all expectations, I was falling for her—hard and fast—and had no idea how to stop the emotional disaster that was about to unfold. I'd never planned for this to happen, and I had no idea when it actually did. Last night, I looked at the pictures of us that the press had published, which I'd saved on my phone. For the first time, I saw what the rest of the world might have seen when they looked at them. Chemistry that couldn't be faked. No matter how much we both denied it.

Even when I was upset and kept her at arm's length in the last month, she had found a way to get past all my restraints and reach my heart.

Madison was my kids' nanny. Why did I have to keep reminding myself of that?

She was also almost ten years younger than me.

All pieces of evidence that proved that I should never harbor a crush on her.

This couldn't be serious. I had to get over it before it jeopardized the tour—and my stupid heart.

"I think we're done," I said, once we finished prepping all of tonight's food, wiping my forehead using the crook of my elbow. "Thanks for your help. I don't know how I would've gotten it done all by myself in time."

She said nothing, but a warm grin spread across her face, and it made me feel like a teenager all over again. When I had a crush on Anastasia Sullivan in high school and couldn't breathe each time we crossed paths in the hallways. Or when she looked at me and my heart threatened to rupture from my chest.

A little while later, Justine came over and wrapped her tiny arms around my thigh. "Daddy, can we do a dance *partly*?"

I looked at my phone. We had a little over one hour before our guests arrived. "Sure." I played a song on my phone.

She wrinkled her tiny face. "No, Daddy. Dance *partly*. With dance."

I drummed my fingers on the countertop. "That's not what we're doing?"

She shook her head with way too much zest. "We need to make a dance floor. And twirl around."

Madison and Mikaella joined us, my little girl beaming.

"What were you girls up to?" I asked.

"Girl chat, Daddy. About girl stuff."

I lifted my hands in surrender. "Fine. Don't tell me more."

Justine pulled at my T-shirt, and I looked down at her. "Yes, baby. The dance party, I totally forgot about that."

"Music, Daddy."

I put another song on.

"No. This is not good."

I was perplexed. What did I do wrong?

Madison fetched her own device and typed something. A catchy pop song played, and the girls started dancing. "See? Wasn't hard," she said with a wink.

We both burst into a fit of laughter.

"Gosh, it's awful. Please, tell me they don't make you listen to this sh—to this all day long."

Her grin widened. "Nope. It's exclusive to dance parties."

Mikaella came to get her, and Madison spun on her feet, laughing so hard with my daughters it swelled a part of my heart I thought had died two years ago. She looked so at home with us. As if she'd been here all along. I watched them, unable to avert my gaze, entranced by the happiness pouring out from them.

Justine neared me. "Daddy, wanna dance with me?"

I scrunched up my nose. "You want me to dance?"

She bobbed her head. "Yes. With me."

I rolled my shoulders back and breathed out. "In this case, how can I refuse a princess?"

I scooped her up into my arms and nuzzled her neck, my feet moving in some kind of dance steps.

Justine wriggled until I lowered her to her feet and wound her small fingers around mine, leading me by swaying her hips.

Soon, I got propelled into the joy emanating from the room.

"Look at you," Madison said. "Dancing. Like you were

born to. I should've guessed the girls would be better at convincing you."

"Hey, I danced with you, no? You dared me, so I couldn't refuse." I shrugged, and we both dissolved into laughter.

My mind went back to the night in the country bar, and for a heartbeat, I wished we could rewind to that moment. Where everything seemed simpler. When I didn't foster a crush on the woman I wasn't allowed to fantasize about.

"Daddy, you danced with Maddie?" Mikaella exclaimed, catching up on our conversation. "When?" She turned toward her nanny. "Maddie, did you dance with Daddy?"

Madison's eyes searched mine and silently asked me to confirm or deny.

"You know what, sweet pea? I did. We ended up at the same place one night, and Madison taught me how to line dance. She was pretty awesome at it."

"Show me," my daughter pleaded.

"Yes, Daddy, do the *lintdance*," Justine agreed.

"Line dance," I echoed. "Maybe some other time."

"No. Do it. Please," Justine pleaded, batting her eyelashes.

How did she always manage to make me change my mind with those? The last time I tried, I'd had a few drinks. They'd injected me with enough liquid courage to ignore the eyes on us...on me. But now, sober and painfully aware of the woman in the room, breathing the same air, my chest tightened, and a wave of uneasiness crashed over me.

"Not sure I recall the steps." A warm feeling spiraled in my stomach, tightening my insides, and my simple black T-shirt and tan cargo shorts felt hot on my skin.

"Daddy, dance," Mikaella said, tugging at my hands.

Madison played a song on her phone, snickering behind her hand.

"You think it's funny?" I asked, waggling my brows.

She pinched her lips together and gave me a head shake. "Nope. Not at all."

"Too bad, because if I'm doing this, you're doing it with me."

"Yes, dance with Daddy, Maddie," the girls cheered.

Her laughter multiplied, and her gaze darted between the three of us. I silently begged her to help me and find a way out of this. "Fine, cowboy," Madison teased. "Man up and follow me." The dark flush on her neck spread to her cheeks. She looked adorable as she positioned herself in front of me.

As if we'd rehearsed this dance many times before, we got in step. I focused on every movement of her legs, trying not to trip over my own feet.

The girls came standing next to me and did their best to imitate us. At some point, Madison pressed pause, taking time to teach us the right steps to follow. "Ready, you guys?" she asked.

The girls jumped and clapped their hands.

"Play it, woman," I said, unable to resist the contagious energy.

For the next half-hour, the four of us line-danced, and my daughters picked up the steps easily.

Madison halted to observe them, stars shining in her sea-green irises.

I watched her watching my children. A foreign sensation invaded me. I could barely breathe. All my senses were attuned to her. Her happiness brightened the entire room. The whole fucking universe. I was desperate to stand in the glow she projected all around her.

She pursed her pink lips, and I quickly cast my gaze downward, forcing my mind to shut out any inappropriate thoughts.

The song ended, and we both were so engrossed in the girls twirling around that we missed when it changed to a ballad. A ballad I had written when I was eighteen—that now played in my house.

The air around us grew heavy, crackling with electric energy we couldn't escape.

Madison swayed her hips to the melody. Mikaella beckoned me with a finger. When I bent to level my face with hers, she whispered in my ear, "Maddie loves this song."

"She does?" We cocked our heads to watch her, now dancing with Justine in her arms. "She told you that?"

"Yes. She always sings it when it plays on her phone."

"Oh." *Ohhh.*

"You should ask her to dance with you."

I frowned. "Not sure it's a good idea."

She rested her fists on her hips. "Daddy, don't be a baby. Man up."

"Sweet pea, where did you learn to talk like this?"

"Maddie said it to you earlier when you were scared to dance, and you did as she told you. And Uncle Riley told someone to man up over the phone the other day. It worked because the man did what he said and stopped arguing."

I blinked. "How do you know that?"

"Because. He. Told. Me." She challenged me with her don't-be-stubborn look. "Now go. Maddie loves to dance. She always dances with us. She never dances with you."

Before I could find the courage in me to ask her, my daughter went to her. "Daddy wants to dance with you. Come on, Justine, you can dance with me now."

Madison's lips parted, and her fleeting gaze zoomed in on me. I was so bad at this. Why did I let my six-year-old drag me into this? Madison waited for me to do or say something. Anything. I wiped my moist hands on my shorts. Before I had the urge to shove my hands into my pockets and pretend none of this ever happened, I held out my hand under my children's watchful eyes. "Dance with me?"

Madison ate the gap between us and linked her hands to mine. "Okay," she whispered, breathless.

I shaped my free hand to the curve of her hip while hers came to rest on my shoulder. Fireworks erupted inside me. I got dizzy. I shut my eyes, trying to calm the storm ravaging my insides. The citrus blend of her perfume permeated my nose. Time stood still. I became aware of every beating of her heart as the pad of my thumb rested on the pulse point of her wrist. Each of our mingled breaths sent shivers through me. My mouth felt dry as desire raged its battle within me. I moistened my lips with a swipe of my tongue, and her gaze followed its movement. A quiver started in hers. We got engrossed in each other, and subtle signs of our longing fought to reveal themselves. I tried to look away but couldn't. I was mesmerized by the allure of her feminine scent and irresistible charms—the one I shouldn't let consume me, yet secretly yearned to.

Madison's lips moved to the lyrics, and I was a dead man. She knew the words to *my* song. We were dancing to *my* melody. "The One." I had written it one night after I'd gone on a date with a girl who turned out to be not what I expected. I remembered it as if it were yesterday. I'd returned home, bummed, thinking I would never know what true love was all about. The one all my country music idols sang about. For hours, I'd daydreamed about how it would be to find the perfect woman to share my life with.

In a way, I believed I had stayed married to Lisa because failing at love was something unthinkable to me, and for a while, I had let myself believe we were *it*. That she would be the one woman I'd spend my life with.

Having Madison in my arms right now felt like nothing I'd ever experienced before. I had no idea what the tingles in my palms meant. Or why my heart felt like it could run away from my chest at any time.

I got lost in the green pools of her eyes.

If I weren't careful, I'd never be able to escape their magnetism.

I swallowed, but the dryness had now reached my throat.

Someone had cast a spell on me. This was the only explanation for how I felt.

All my cells vibrated.

Justine pushed herself between us, breaking the moment. "Daddy, there's someone at the door. They're asking for you."

I stepped back, trying to escape whatever enchantment had descended upon us.

For how long had we been so spellbound by each other that we had lost track of time?

I detached myself from Madison and brushed her upper arm with my fingertips, unable to find the right words to tell her how I felt—or what our connection meant to me. And to think I'd made millions of dollars as a songwriter. Yeah, the irony wasn't lost on me.

We exchanged one last glance. She blinked, and it broke the remnant slivers of rapture that had taken us prisoners.

"Coming," I called out loud to whoever stood on my front porch.

14

SAM

"**M**addie, Maddie, I wanna show you something. Come," Mikaella called out.

Carter, Madison, and I were sitting at the table on the back deck, enjoying a drink while my friend told us all about the latest developments at his foundation. Madison listened to him with laser-focused attention, the teacher in her clearly relishing the stories about the children he helped. She asked dozens of questions, and I simply watched her, amazed by how captivated she was by the way Carter and his wife, April, were helping kids through their art programs.

Madison pushed back her chair and rose to her feet, ready to follow my daughter who was pointing toward something in one corner of the backyard.

"You don't have to," I told her, bringing the bottle of beer to my lips. "I'm sure the girls can survive a few hours without including you in their shenanigans."

Since my friends had arrived, Madison and I had done a pretty good job so far of staying away from each other.

Before we sat with Carter and he entertained us with

his stories, I'd caught her multiple times looking my way in a manner she never had before, and that shouldn't be allowed. And each time, a new whirlwind rose within me—one I prayed wouldn't sweep me off my feet.

She let a shy smile slip through. "It's fine, Sam. Really."

From my perch on the back deck, I watched her walk away. No matter what I did, my gaze kept finding her. Her charm was magnetic.

Madison's lips curled into the kind of smile that could shatter me when Mikaella joined her and tugged at her hand. That same smile could easily make me believe in love again if it were ever directed at me.

I perused the space around me. Riley was busy with Georgia—Carter's daughter—and Justine, chasing butterflies. April, Aisha Jones, and Devon were mixing drinks in the kitchen inside. Tennessee, Carter and April's son, was napping in the guest room inside. The baby monitor they'd brought was set on the table between us.

"Are you fucking her?" my friend asked out of the blue once Madison was out of ear's reach.

I blinked, my attention snapping to him. "What?"

He pressed his hands together, propping his elbows on the table, leaning closer, and lowering his voice. "You heard me. Stevens, are you banging the nanny?"

"No." I cringed. "What makes you think so? She's like twenty, man."

"You're eating her up with your eyes. If you think you're being subtle, you're failing big time. You look like a lost puppy drooling in front of a bone."

I clenched my hands, my tone turning colder. "Stop. Nothing is going on between us. Don't start rumors."

Carter lifted his hands in front of him. "I'm not, but you should see yourself. You're in love, Stevens. I know it because I went through the same denial phase with April." His eyes drifted to his wife through the large window, laughing with Devon and Aisha, tucking strands of her pink hair behind her ears. "She was driving me nuts. I was acting like an ass, as she likes to remind me sometimes. Truth? I was scared. Savannah Prince did a number on me, man. I believed I wasn't good enough for April at first. Anyway, if one person can understand the battle of will going on in your head, it's me. Look at us now."

I ran a hand over my face as knots, big sturdy ones, strangled my stomach. "It-it's not the same thing. She's my employee, and she's…she's like a decade younger than me. We're not at the same stage of our lives. There are kids involved…*my* kids. It's enough to kill my impulses. Everything would be wrong if we got together. Can you imagine? It'd be a total clusterfuck."

Carter lifted his glass of water and clinked my bottle. "So, you thought about it."

I murdered him with my eyes.

"Whatever. If you say so… You can man up, give it a chance to see if she mirrored your feelings, or be miserable. Hard choice." He let out a heartfelt chuckle. "Mm-hmm. Yep. Tough decision."

What's with everyone and that man-up expression today?

"She's a kid." Poor defense, but that was the only one I had.

"Stop. You can't be serious now. She's a grown woman who's all smitten with you. That much is clear from where I sit. She flushes when you two stand too close, and you're acting like a stupid teenager with a crush, sneaking glances her way every chance you get."

"You speak nonsense," I said, my defensiveness doing nothing to deter his suspicion.

"Yeah, sure I am." Carter watched me with a barely-contained smirk.

"Fine. We might have had a moment this afternoon. It's gone now. Over. I won't make a move. Our relationship must stay professional. If I indulge in the attraction and it fails, it will mess everything up. My daughters depend on her. I can't jeopardize that. I-I can't be a selfish prick. Nope… Not this time. They have suffered enough already."

"Whoa, you're stronger than I thought…or just dumber. Anyway, I'd like to be on the road with you and see how you resist her when you are spending six months cramped on a tour bus together. Yeah, I'd pay big money to see *that* unfold. Is it too late to cast you in a reality series about your big comeback?"

"Shut up," I said as Riley joined us.

"What are you guys talking about? Are you okay, Stevens? Your face is all red. You look like you're about to explode," he said.

"Don't worry about his face, Ry," Carter said. "I think it's his heart that's struggling. Maybe, at his age, he should reduce his stress level. Watch out for his blood pressure… or start eating a plant-based diet. Take my example, man. I should be your muse. Your inspiration to aim for bigger and better." Carter winked at me and stood to pick up his daughter from our manager's arms. "I'll go and put this one down for a nap with her baby brother," he said, rocking his half-asleep little girl in his arms. The father's role suited him perfectly.

"Yeah, you do that," I said, chugging the rest of my beer.

"And think about the reality TV series offer while I'm gone," Carter replied.

"What is this all about?" Riley asked. "Stevens, it's true you don't seem so fine."

"I'm good," I protested with a shake of my head.

"Then what was that about a reality TV show? I'm confused right now."

I sighed. "Carter is speaking shit. You know how he is, pushing my buttons. I won't—"

Carter walked inside, his shit-eating grin now reaching both ears when he looked our way. Yeah, I bet he was having the time of his life watching the control of my misplaced attraction dissolve before his eyes.

"Hey, Sam. There's someone at the door," Aisha announced, interrupting us when she poked her head out the back door. "Should I get it?"

"No," I said. "I will. Thanks."

"Who's missing?" Riley asked.

I shrugged. "No idea. Everyone is already here."

I perused my surroundings. My eyes found Madison, still busy with the girls near their castle, followed by Devon, Aisha, and April exiting the house to join Riley as I made my way in.

A funny taste filled my mouth when I opened the front door and found Jacob standing there, a bottle of whiskey and a pack of beers in his arms.

"Hey, man. I thought Maddie said you left for Chattanooga already."

"Yeah, well, change of plans. I'm here now."

"Huh, come on in. Make yourself at home. Everyone is outside." From our two previous encounters, I could tell Jacob was in love with Madison—this much was obvious. My stomach clenched at the thought that we were drawn to the same woman. "Maddie is in the backyard. Huh… somewhere." I gestured to the back door with a hand.

"Thanks. Where should I put this?"

"Here," I said as we crossed the kitchen.

Jacob dropped the booze on the island.

"I'll start the barbecue later. For now, there are snacks outside. You can also hit the bar to make yourself a drink. If you miss anything, ask me. Or ask Maddie. She's familiar with everything in this house."

He grabbed a beer from the pack he brought, and I led him outside. All my friends were now seated at the table around the back deck. April was in Carter's lap, a hand splayed across his chest, laughing at something he said. They stared at each other as if nothing in the world existed but them. A sting of envy stabbed my chest, and the lyrics of "The One" replayed in my head. I'd always been a sucker for love.

My attention traveled to Devon and Aisha, deep in a conversation about Aisha's next album.

"You actually never told us where this man of yours was tonight?" Devon asked her.

"His sister. In Michigan. He had some activities planned with his nephews."

Gavin Moore, Aisha's boyfriend, an art therapist with kids on the autism spectrum, worked with Carter and April at their foundation to give kids access to art programs. Their love story was the inspiration behind many of her hit songs.

Further to our right, Riley was busy on his phone. Nothing unusual since the guy never took a day off.

From the end of the backyard, Madison spotted us. Her gaze traveled back and forth between me and her... huh...boyfriend? I really couldn't tell the status of their relationship.

She neared the house just as Justine called out, "Jacob," before I could introduce him to my friends.

"Hey you," he said, tapping the tip of my baby's nose

with his finger as we reached them, stepping off the deck onto the lawn.

Madison cleared her throat. "Jake…you came? I thought you left early this morning for the convention." Okay, so she hadn't expected him to show up. Hmm… interesting.

He sipped his beer and offered her a shrug. "I went. It felt wrong to be there without you, so I came back. We'll drive there tomorrow morning. Together."

Madison stood still, clearly taken aback. "You what?" she asked when she found her voice back. "You went and came back? For me?"

"Yep. Thought I'd surprise you."

"I love *surpirises*," Justine screamed. "Do you have *surpirises* for me too?"

Jacob shook his head. "Sorry, princess. Next time I'll figure something out."

My baby clapped her hands, oblivious to the tense air surrounding us.

I opened my arms, waiting for her to leap into them. "Baby, let's go and see if anyone needs anything."

"Bye, Jacob." She waved at him as we climbed back the four steps leading to the deck where most of my guests were seated.

While I poured fresh drinks and my little one passed around a veggie platter, my eyes stayed on Madison and Jacob. From where I stood, I could tell they were arguing about something. Madison folded her arms over her chest, looking hurt. Jacob blanketed her in his embrace. Her whole demeanor told me she didn't agree with whatever he was saying.

The caring side of me, the one believing Madison and I had become friends, longed to intervene. The sad curl of her lips made me feel queasy inside. It got my blood pumping in my veins.

Jacob skimmed her cheek with his thumb, and her easy smile returned.

My heartbeat eased, my whole body relaxing now that she didn't seem so concerned anymore.

"Who's that?" Carter asked as I sat in the empty chair next to Aisha.

A strange sound escaped my throat as I popped open another beer. I should have opted for something stronger—whiskey…or maybe tequila—since I wouldn't hear the end of it.

"Jacob. Madison's *friend*."

Carter's eyes flared, and he choked on a bite of food. "You mean boyfriend?"

"Not that I know of."

"Stevens, you're kidding, right? Tell me you are. Earlier you—"

I shrugged. What was the point?

"Fuck, the nanny is banging a rock star?"

I sighed. "He's a chemist…or biologist, or something related to that field. I don't give a fuck, so I don't know." My gaze followed them as Jacob, dressed in all black with motorcycle boots on, leaned forward to kiss Madison's cheek, my daughters now bombarding him with a hundred questions. This time, she didn't pull away.

"Everything makes sense now," Carter said, following my line of sight. He tsk-tsked. "So much sense."

I said nothing and downed half my beer in one gulp. I'd need all the liquid courage I could get to go through the rest of the day.

The kids ate first, and we all gathered around the table as April stepped out of the house, carrying the cupcakes Madison had baked—each topped with far too many lit candles. If I had to guess, I would say she put thirty there. I lifted my daughters into my arms as my friends crooned the birthday song to me.

"Happy birthday, Daddy," Mikaella said, perched on my lap as she kissed my cheek. "Whoa. It's a lot of candles," she exclaimed.

"Yep. I'm turning into an old man, sweet pea," I added with a wink.

"Can I blow the *crandles* with you?" Justine asked, with her arms looped tightly around my neck.

My lips spread wide into a grin. "Sure. Candles, baby. Let's do this. The three of us."

They both cheered.

"Are you ready?"

They nodded.

"On three. One, two, three."

With the two most important people in my life held close in my arms, I celebrated turning a year older.

While the kids sat to eat dessert, I took the time to thank each one of my friends. Months ago, I would've never thought I'd celebrate my milestone birthday surrounded by people I loved. Funny how life turned out sometimes.

I shook Jacob's hand, and when I reached Madison, I kissed her cheek. It was the first time I'd allowed myself to get that close to her. Her loud intake of air when my lips connected with her skin vibrated through me. I schooled my features, trying to dissipate the agitation rising inside me.

Hours later, after the kids had gone to bed, exhausted but with delighted faces and sugary smiles on, we all sat back around the table to eat.

The night was warm, pink and violet stripes painting the clear summer sky.

I relaxed as we enjoyed great food and greater wine.

"April, I just wanted to tell you I'm a big fan," Jacob said, clinking his glass with hers.

My friend cupped her heart, a soft blush tinting her cheeks. "Thanks. Wow, it means a lot."

"Told you, Fairy, you're amazing," Carter said, dropping a kiss on the side of her head, pride radiating from him.

"I was sad when you announced you'd be writing mostly music from now on," Jacob continued.

"I'll try to keep writing novels, but only one title a year or every two years. We'll see."

They continued their discussion while I zoned out and focused my attention on my plate, doing my best not to watch the nanny sitting across from me or notice the charged air ping-ponging between us. Or perhaps it was just the late hour, the booze, and my imagination playing tricks on me.

"So, Jacob. What do you do for a living?" Devon asked next.

Madison, sitting on his left, lifted her eyes and locked them on mine. A small tilt appeared at the corner of her lips.

It stole all the air from my lungs, and I coughed, the bite of baked potato in my mouth tumbling down my throat and choking me.

How could I be so affected by just a hint of a sign from her aimed at me?

This time, we fixated on each other from across the table, neither of us able to break eye contact.

Her face turned scarlet, and she twisted in her seat.

My body tingled, and my heart banged against my ribcage.

My senses shifted to hers. My food tasted weird, and

my nostrils caught the fading whiffs of her perfume. I wasn't so hungry anymore. Madison's lips parted, as if to mouth something meant only for me, but Jacob demanded her attention, leaning closer and whispering in her ear.

She nodded, and I averted my eyes.

Jacob's gaze captured mine. His eyebrows twitched. Not in the mood for a pissing contest over who had the bigger dick, I looked away and asked Aisha about her last European tour. There. Better. Safer. My pulse calmed, and the ties crushing my organs released.

"Guys, we should do this more often. Now that Stevens has joined the family officially, after years of fighting against it, I want all of us to stay close. You're all precious to me, so let's spend more time together. Let's make it a regular occurrence. Also, thanks, everyone, for being here with us tonight to celebrate our host hitting a new decade." Standing, Riley angled his upper body to address Madison and Jacob. "You guys, it's great to have you here with us tonight. And Jacob, thank you for being selfless and letting Madison join this grumpy fellow," he said, pointing at me, "on tour. None of this would be possible without her. She's one hell of a woman. The missing puzzle piece to this whole adventure." He zoomed in on me. "All y'all, raise your glass to Sam turning thirty. Happy birthday, Stevens."

We all cheered.

Madison eyed me from her side of the table over the rim of her glass, the column of her throat rippling as she swallowed. Why did even her throat have to be appealing?

Pressing both hands to the top of the table, she moved to her feet. "I'll go inside. Huh…to check on the kids. I'll be right back."

I discarded my napkin on the table. "Wait, I'll come with you."

We needed to have a chat—to clear the air—before it

caught fire and burned everyone standing too close, us included. I had to be the mature one here and kill whatever sparks were sizzling between us.

Jacob jumped to his feet before I could stand up. "No man, it's your party. Stay here. I'll go with her. I think we can manage." He flashed me a don't-you-dare half-smirk before following Madison inside, his hand pressed to the small of her back.

His possessiveness rubbed me the wrong way, even though I had no grounds to be upset.

I pushed my plate away, definitely not hungry anymore.

15

MADISON

"The guy's in love with you. Are you blind? Is this some prank you two are playing on me, and you're both in on it?"

"What are you talking about?" I asked.

Jacob harrumphed. "Okay, you're smart, but you can't be so clueless."

"You're wrong. Sam doesn't love me. Not this way. I…I would know."

"You're kidding, right? You can't be that oblivious. You spend all your time at his place. You're young, hot, sweet. Why wouldn't he want to bang you? To make you his? Any man in his right mind would want to. I'm telling you. I know I'm one hundred percent right. He's fucking gone for you. That much was evident tonight. He never stared anywhere but at you. The. Entire. Fucking. Time. I. Was There. Get prescription glasses, Maddie. Your sight is cloudy."

I unbuckled my seatbelt and turned my upper body in his direction. We were parked on the side of the road, less than a mile from Sam's house. Jacob had offered to drive me home since I'd had a few drinks, and we planned to pick up my car in the morning. When we'd left Sam's house, tensions ran high between Jacob and me, and it took about five minutes before he parked the car and exploded, unable to keep his wrath to himself any longer. The streetlights cast a golden glow inside the car, softening his otherwise hardened features. Yet I couldn't miss the deep lines fanning from his eyes and the weariness etched across his face.

"Okay, this is getting out of hand," I said in a gentle voice, taking a big inhale to avoid adding fuel to his anger. Instead, I reached for his hand, squeezing his fingers. "My sight isn't defective. And I already wear glasses when I read. Listen, Sam is not into me. Stop projecting. Anyway, who cares? I'm here with you. Because I wanna be."

Jacob dragged his free hand over his face. "Are you serious? I fucking care. A lot. Because we talked about being together. I-I'm in love with you, for God's sake. If you haven't noticed by now, you're really blind." He yanked his hand away and punched the steering wheel with both fists. "This whole situation is a joke. I can't believe I didn't realize it sooner. And here I thought…here I thought I was intelligent. Clearly, not enough. Sam Stevens surpasses me. He invited us over tonight just to rub in my face how much of an idiot I've been, by openly eye-fucking my girlfriend the entire time."

"Jacob, stop. Right now. You are being ridiculous because nothing is going on between Sam and me. I would never lead you on. You and I agreed from the start we weren't going to date until I came back. You're the one asking to change the rules. I'm trying here. I really am. You know me….and my heart. But the thing is, I know myself too. If we get involved before the tour, I won't be able to go. When I love, I love something fierce, and it's hard for me not to feel intense emotions. That's why we set that rule. To keep our hearts safe while I'm gone. Until we decide if being together is still what we yearn for months away from now. If being apart is impossible and we gotta move forward… Together."

"That's the problem, Maddie. I don't think I know you as much as I thought I did. Not anymore at least… You enabled his behavior. You locked eyes with him. Countless fucking times. Do you realize that being someone's girlfriend usually comes with an unspoken rule of exclusivity?" He exhaled, closing his eyes.

A ball of nerves settled in my chest, bouncing around and affecting the rhythm of my heart.

Jacob inhaled, opened his eyes, and fixed them back on my face. Every word that spilled from his mouth was tinged with hurt. "Why did you even invite me to go with you? Or maybe you knew all along I'd be in Chattanooga, and you thought you could play his game and that I wouldn't witness it. If that's the case, I'm sorry I ruined your plans. Even Carter Hills noticed. I was the butt of the joke. At first, I thought I was being paranoid, so I waited to see if it would stop…but it never did. Yeah, the joke is on me."

"Do you hear yourself right now? I'm not a master conspirator. I'm the girl who does everything not to fall for her best friend while trying to keep the peace between all parties."

"Well, best friends are honest with each other."

"Can we talk about it without getting into a fight?"

"Another guy hit on you, in my face, for hours, and I should be all right with that? I swear, at first, I thought I was seeing things I conjured in my mind. When his fingers traced your arms before we left, I saw red. Fire-engine blinding red. You're lucky I don't make scenes in public or that I'm not a puncher because he would have earned at least a shiner."

"He's not in love with me. Stop being possessive—it's not a good look on you. God, I hate this side of you. And stop calling me your girlfriend like you have some claim over me. It just makes everything messier." Was I trying to convince myself right now or Jacob? Could he be right after all?

He blinked as if I had spoken another language, and a fortified wall appeared around him. He rubbed the spot between his eyebrows, strands of his hair falling over his forehead. He looked so handsome—and in pain—all because of me, for a forbidden crush I had no intention of pursuing.

I extended my arm in a tentative gesture to hold his hand and melt the iciness that kept us apart, but he leaned back, shaking his head, a twist of disgust shaping his lips.

Cursing under his breath, he blocked me out as he looked away, tugging at the roots of his hair while he stared out of the window.

"Jake. Don't shut me out. Please. The night we met, you said you liked my adventure-seeking personality." I inched closer and splayed a palm between his tense shoulders. He relaxed at the contact. "I can't believe you're questioning my motives. You gotta respect my wishes."

His breathing accelerated, and he turned until we faced each other, a mask of hurt covering his visage. He studied me with glossy, bloodshot eyes. Then he lifted his hand, reaching for my cheek. His knuckles skimmed the skin under my eyes, and his thumb traced my lips. I shivered under the intimate touch.

"It matters. It fucking matters to me…so much."

Tears now flowed down my face.

Jacob pulled me to him and rested his forehead against

mine, his hand molding to my nape. His ragged breathing mixed with mine."Maddie, I'll ask this question once. Tell me the truth."

I braced myself for the words about to come out of his mouth. He swallowed and leaned back, a grave look carved on his face. "Do you love him? Are you in love with Sam Stevens?"

I gasped. What Sam and I shared, or what I imagined we shared, meant nothing. Nothing. How many times would I need to repeat it to believe it myself?

"Answer me, Maddie. Here and now. Be honest with me. That's all I'm asking. Are you attracted to him? And. Do. You. Love. Him?"

I gulped a large intake of air. "I-I don't... I...I don't know." I glanced down, unable to meet his eyes. "It's just a stupid crush, okay? Or at least, it was."

Something invisible clamped around my heart. Was it shame or the dead weight of the lies I was feeding myself right now? Sam and I had shared a moment earlier today when we danced. I'd felt it. Even if I tried, I couldn't convince myself otherwise. But still, it was a dead end. Those feelings should be kept locked as far as possible.

"Anyway, I won't do anything about it. Our friendship is important to me. It means a lot, and I won't spoil it." I inhaled a shaky breath, desperate to explain myself. "He's my boss. Crossing this line would have consequences. I'm happy when I'm with you. We're so much alike, you and I. You're my best friend, Jake. For now, it has to stay this way. I'm sorry I should've told you. I realize it now."

Jacob pulled away, but I refused to release him. "Fucking friend zone. Maddie, no smart guy wants to be stuck there. Trust me."

"Don't push me out," I begged, my voice colored with despair. The streams down my cheeks intensified. No way could I shut the dam once it broke. "I'm sorry I'm breaking your heart. I love you, but I'm not ready for you…for us to be together like that." My voice was strained, and my sobs drowned my words. "Can we just go back to where we were…for now?"

He shook his head, his fingers laced behind his neck, distress bleeding from his entire being. "Maddie, I know your heart. I can tell you love me. That's the problem. You wear your heart on your sleeve, or your emotions on your face, and you can't bring yourself to hurt those you care about. It's just not in your DNA. But the thing is, you can't love us both…or be attracted to both of us. At one point, you're gonna have to choose. This moment is right now. It's either me or him. If it's me, you resign. You can't be around him if you want us to work out and have a true shot at a lasting future together. One day or another, one of you won't be able to fight this. I'm not risking our relationship for something that can be prevented."

"You're doubting me?"

"No, it's other men I don't trust. I'm a guy, and you're…huh…you're you."

"What does that even mean?"

"Maddie, you're exceptional. One of a kind. A diamond in a sea of rubies. If the guy is intelligent—and I suspect he is—he'll realize your worth sooner or later. Good luck resisting him when that day comes, especially if you already have feelings for him. If you can't decide, I'll let you walk away. I will not be your consolation prize, your second choice…the one you settle for. If you hope for us to last, it should be me—only me—all the way. It shouldn't be a hard decision to make."

"But I can't… The girls… They count on me. I…I promised. I can't just leave. It's more complicated than this.

It's not just about me…or you…or us. What about the tour? What will happen to the tour if I'm not there?"

"Come on, Maddie. The guy is filthy rich in case you haven't noticed. I'm sure he can find another nanny to watch over his kids. He's not desperate."

A cocktail of emotions mixed inside me. More prickling tears overflowed my eyes, as if tiny needles were piercing the backs of my eyeballs.

"No," my voice cracked. "You can't ask me to choose. Not now. I can't leave the girls... It-it's not fair to them. They…they trust me. I'm all…I'm all they've got. You know my story. You know how bad I've been hurt when I was their age. How…how my parents failed me…for years. They're… Jake, they're just kids. They don't deserve to be let down. Not if I can prevent it."

He shook his head, edged closer, and grabbed my upper arms. "I'm not saying you're not good at your job, Maddie. Or that those kids aren't adorable and that you can't bring them peace. What I'm saying is that Sam Stevens has the means to find a replacement to care for his daughters. He's not without resources. You'll find another family. I know how much you suffered, and I wouldn't wish the same on anyone else—but this isn't about you. *They are not you.* You can't be responsible for the choices their own parents made, and for their own mother walking away." He exhaled before continuing, "Don't go back there. Please. I love you, but I…I won't beg for your love. Being together must be what you really desire too."

A curtain of tears blinded me. "Ohmygod, this is an impossible situation. I-I can't walk away. Mika and Justine mean the world to me. I'm not quitting on them… I just can't. Their mother has already done that. I-I've been there. You're the only person I've ever confided in about my past. I never…I never told anyone else. I trust *you*. Why can't you understand?"

Jacob recoiled, throwing his arms over his head. "Fuck, Maddie, you're not their mother. It's not your responsibility to fill in for her. They aren't yours… It-it's just a job. You can't compare their situation to yours. It's not even remotely the same."

I pressed the heels of my hands over my streaming eyes. "I…I can't. I won't abandon them. Wh-what do we do then?"

"If you're going back to his house, then we're done. I also can't be your friend anymore… I-I can't be *just* your friend. I want more. I'm longing for more. Even though you're not ready for me, I am. I *am* ready for you…for us." He turned around, not letting me see the storm of emotions running through his gaze.

Silence fell between us, heavy and unyielding. It stretched on, neither of us daring to speak.

"You should go," Jacob said after what appeared like hours.

"But—"

"Now." Chills ran through me at the finality in his voice. "If you were sure about us and if you were willing to give us a chance, you wouldn't take this long to come up with a definitive answer."

"No, I don't wanna go. I'm choosing *you*, but I'm not resigning. We both have dreams. You're one of the most important people in my life."

"That's the problem. I shouldn't just be one of the most important people in your life… I should be the number one. If the situation were reversed, would you let me work for a woman who's madly in love with me?"

I said nothing.

Jacob shook his head. "See? You've made your choice.

Your silence speaks volumes. I just hope it's the right deci-sion—for all of us."

"Stop. I didn't choose anything. You forced these deci-sions on me. I don't want us to break up. There are two of us in this relationship."

"You can't break up something that doesn't exist, Maddie." Jacob's voice was stripped of all fight.

"And you, you can't decide by yourself what's good for both of us. I have a voice, and I'm using it. What we have, it's precious." My voice weakened. "I'm not letting you go without a fight."

"Well, that's the thing. No way am I waiting while you spend all your time on a tour bus with him. It's not fair to me. You can't ask me to wait for you… We both know I'll be the one with the broken heart in the end."

I scanned the space around me. From driving around town for hours just for the heck of it, to grabbing takeout and confiding about our lives—and our dreams—under the stars, Jacob's car had always been a safe place for us. After tonight, though, it would forever be tainted by a fight I wasn't sure I could win.

My world was crumbling, and I had no idea how to prevent the downfall. Until now, I thought I had everything figured out.

The worst? Sam wasn't in love with me. Jacob was speaking nonsense. I would die of shame if my boss ever found out I'd been harboring a one-sided crush on him. The man had baggage, and with the tour and the new direction his life was taking, a girlfriend was clearly nowhere near the top of his list.

"What do we do now?" I asked Jacob, forcing the words out. "Can we sleep on it and talk about it tomorrow?"

"No." His decisive answer shook me to my core. "Do

whatever you wish, Maddie. We're over. Our friendship isn't salvageable. It would hurt too much to have you without truly having you. Maybe someday we can be friends, but right now, it's asking too much of me."

His eyes darkened, and his lips formed a thin line. This time, the walls he built around himself were high, sturdy, and unyielding.

I stayed still.

"I'll call you a cab to go pick up your car from his place. Wait here until it arrives. I'll go for a walk."

I opened the passenger door. "Stay. I'll walk back to his home." I wiped my tears with the back of my hand.

"Maddie, no. It's unsafe. I can drive you back."

"No. I'm sorry about everything."

Before the door slammed after me, I heard his last words. "Me too. Goodbye, Maddie. I hope you find what you're looking for with him."

Alone, broken, and in the middle of a neighborhood I didn't recognize, I followed the instructions on my phone's GPS, not even bothering to hide from my sorrows.

16

MADISON

I didn't remember the hour-long walk from Jacob's parked car to Sam's house. A foggy cloud had enveloped my mind, my thoughts a jumbled mess inside my head.

A vehicle I didn't recognize slowed down beside me. "Miss? Are you okay? You look lost. Want me to call someone?" the driver, a man in his late forties, offered.

I blinked, rebooting my confused brain. "Huh, no… I-I'm fine," I said, giving him what I hoped looked like a ghost of a smile.

"You sure? You look sad. I bet someone is worried about you."

"I…I can assure you they are not. Anyway, I'm here." I pointed to Sam's long driveway, lined with tall trees on both sides. The house was barely visible from the street. An open forged-iron black gate between stacked-stone pillars bordered the road. I had no clue if he ever used it or if it just served as a decor element because, since the first time I'd come over, Sam had never closed the gate or talked about closing it. "I've arrived at my destination." I flipped my phone so he could read the screen. "See? Even my phone agrees."

"Okay. Have a safe night then." He rolled his window back up and drove away. For a while, I contemplated his taillights as he disappeared into the night.

When I reached my car, my hands were trembling, and I couldn't fish the keys out from my purse. Sobs rocked my body, and I was unable to think clearly. With my back pressed against the steel frame, I slid down to the pavement, dropping my head between my knees.

Tonight, I had lost the best friend I'd ever had—the one person I trusted enough to share every horrible detail of my childhood with, who brought me peace, and made me smile just by being himself.

My broken friendship with Jacob had left a void in my chest that I wasn't sure I'd be able to repair one day. My fingers itched to call him, to tell him our argument was a big misunderstanding, and that I chose him, and would resign to be with him. But I couldn't coax myself to say the words he yearned to hear out loud. Because it would be a lie. A terrible lie.

Time passed.

Jacob and I had left the party at eleven. Then we fought for what appeared to be hours. Right now, I had no idea how late it was.

Darkness descended upon me.

My demons clung to my skin, sucking all the good and hope in me.

I lost my best friend. Just the thought of it sent fresh sobs and tremors through me. I couldn't imagine a life without him in it. His accusing words replayed in my head on a loop, and I had no idea whether what he'd accused Sam of was true or not.

The broken pieces of my heart punctured my chest.

I hurt. My body hurt. And my soul hurt too.

I woke up when two strong arms lifted me up and brought me inside. His scent assaulted me first. Then came the protective embrace of his arms as he carried me.

Sam sat me on the couch, the living room lit by a single lamp in the corner, its golden glow making him appear almost mythic as he stood before me. A figment of my imagination.

Without a word, he crouched down, pushed my hair away from my eyes, and stared at me, concern swimming in his irises. Our gazes fixed on each other for a long moment. He rested his hands on either side of me, and his eyes swept the length of my body as if to make sure I had no visible wounds.

"Since you're not telling me shit, I'm gonna ask. Are you all right, and did someone hurt you?"

I shook my head.

When did my vocal cords stop working?

Even though I tried, no word passed the seam of my lips. Sandpaper lined my throat. A drum fest had taken up residence inside my head. My heart could barely pump blood, bleeding from every crack and tear.

"Where's Jacob?" Why was he saying his name like that? As if it were a disease.

I shrugged.

Sam's eyes rounded. "Come on, Maddie. Help a guy out here. Where is he? Did he leave without you? I thought he was driving you home… He said he'd make sure you get there safely."

I shook my head, glancing down, fidgeting with the bracelet around my left wrist.

"Why are you here? At this hour?" He paused, and when I didn't reply, he asked, "By yourself? Are you sure you're fine?"

I nodded. Moisture returned to my mouth, and I swallowed, shaking my head from side to side. "Ja-Jacob… Huh… Jacob and I… We had a fight." Why was my voice not sounding like mine? "It was bad…very bad…and he left." I buried my face in my hands as a fresh batch of sobs rocked my body. My shoulders heaved. Jacob had left. I would never see him again. The thought shattered me. I already missed him. How would I survive a life where he wasn't a part of it?

"When? Why? I knew you two were close."

"He…he was my best friend."

"Did that punk do something to you?"

I sighed. "He's not…he's not a punk. We love each other." A sarcastic laugh escaped me as I spoke the words aloud. "It's not enough. The timing isn't right."

"You've lost me. I'm confused. Can you be more specific?"

"It's complicated. Anyway, I walked and… My car was here so…" Hot tears ravaged the back of my eyes, and I turned my head to avoid looking at Sam, so he couldn't see the truth. It did nothing to lighten the weight of his stare on me.

"Maddie, you can stay here tonight. Don't cry, okay? I feel powerless when you do." His voice was soft and soothing. Comforting and familiar.

My ache amplified. It burned a hole through my chest.

Sam got up and paced the room before me. "Tell me what I can do. I'm pretty good with broken hearts. I swear, I should get a Master's degree in heartbreak." His humor vanished the moment the last word left his lips. "Or… huh…we can watch a movie, something super depressing, and cry together. I'm a sucker for dramatic, *someone will die at the end*, romance stories."

I dried my tears, and a small smile peeked through my devastated state. "You are?"

"Yeah. Don't tell anyone, though. It's not good for my rep."

I pretended to zip my lips with my fingers. "I won't tell a soul."

"You're in?" he asked.

"Sure. I'd like that. Thank you."

"Let me get some snacks and a blanket. Make yourself at home. I'll be right back."

I blew out a long breath and let the couch swallow me.

In the last few months, the Stevenses' house had become a second home to me—or a third if I counted Jacob's place. More tears welled up in my eyes at the thought of losing him, but this time I wiped them away quickly.

Sam returned and sat beside me, spreading the blanket over us. He placed a bowl of popcorn between our thighs and put on the most tear-jerking movie I'd ever seen.

"Ohmyfreakinggod, this is so depressing," I managed to say, my words lost in tears, halfway through the movie. "How's crying over *their* lost love supposed to help me with *my* heartbreak?"

Sam sniffled and shrugged. "No idea. I-I told you I had a talent for choosing heart-wrenching movies. There's more to me than playing the guitar and enjoying dares."

This side of him called to me, just like it had the last time we had spent quality moments together—building that greenhouse where the girls and I had planted flowers and seeds. Every time I faced him without the broody front, the annoyance, the armor he hid behind, I felt we could connect on a deeper level if we gave it a chance. Since the night at the country bar, this was the most real version of Sam Stevens I'd witnessed. Other than when he played with his daughters. A part of me always relished the easygoing side of his personality. The human not shying away from his flaws and emotions.

"I'm…I'm not denying that you are. You earned your title, fair and square." I scooted out of the blanket and pressed pause on the remote. "Water? I've gotta rehydrate."

I stood and made my way to the kitchen, needing a few minutes alone. The more I got engrossed in the movie, the more I pushed my own feelings aside. For now, it would have to do. Until I could face them and deal with them, instead of pretending they didn't exist. On my own time. Away from my boss's inquisitive gaze.

Sam's voice carried through the house. "Bring something stronger. There's a bottle of vodka in the freezer. Riley left it there earlier."

I stopped by the bathroom and washed my tear-stricken face. Better. I still looked like a mess, but a less afflicted one.

I grabbed two bottles of water and placed two shot glasses in the front pocket of my hoodie. My eyes lingered on the tub of mint-chocolate ice cream as I opened the freezer to fetch the vodka. A leftover treat on the countertop also called my name, and I snatched it too.

I carried all my precious heartbreak cargo back to the living room.

"Wow, did you raid the pantry? What do we have here?" Sam asked as I took my place back by his side, sitting cross-legged on the couch.

I winced. "Hope it's okay… The ice cream was begging me to take care of it."

He let out a warm chuckle that seemed to warm some of the broken pieces of me. "Sure. I love how your mind works. Vodka and mint-chocolate ice cream should be an interesting mix."

"I have something for you first. Close your eyes."

He angled his upper body toward me and frowned, but he obliged.

"Gimme your hand." I put the chocolate cupcake in his open palm. "You can look now. Happy birthday," I said when he did.

"It's past midnight. It's not my birthday anymore."

I shrugged. "Let's just pretend it still is."

Facing me fully, he brought the sugary treat to my lips. "Want a bite? Chocolate is good for the soul. The woman who baked it told me that once."

He was quoting me. What I had said to him when I first started working for him, in response to his question about why I was always baking.

I took a big chunk, relishing the frosting coating my tongue. "Delicious," I said with a mouthful. "Whoever she is, she has great tastes."

Sam took a bite and gave me the last one. "She does." His thumb grazed my lips.

I gasped as the space between us grew charged, the air warm and electric.

"You had a little frosting there," he murmured before bringing the dollop of icing to his mouth and licking his finger clean.

"Th-thanks." To keep awkwardness from creeping in and ruining the moment, I opened the ice cream tub, and armed with spoons and facing each other, we attacked the milky treat.

Sam pressed play on the remote and poured us two shot glasses of iced vodka, offering me one before raising his own. "To heartbreaks."

"Yeah. To heartbreaks," I echoed. "And messy rela-tionships."

The liquid burned the lining of my throat as I chugged it. I blinked. My stomach churned, and I grimaced, trying to keep it down.

"Guess liquor isn't your poison of choice."

I shook my head, my hand pressed against my lips.

"Don't worry, it gets better after the third one… maybe. At least, I think it did when I was younger."

We both chuckled.

"Let's test that theory." I held out my hand, ready for another shot.

Sam poured two more shots and slid one toward me.

Tilting my head back, I guzzled the vodka in one gulp, the taste lingering on my tongue.

"Second one isn't better?" Sam asked.

"Nah. Let's get the third one out of the way." We downed another shot each. "It doesn't taste better, but the burn is more enjoyable…sorta. Crap, we're missing all the movie."

"Madison Prescott, you can swear. Who would have thought?"

I shrugged. "Sometimes. Don't get used to it, though. This side of me rarely makes an appearance, and alcohol is usually to blame."

We sank back onto the couch, shoulders brushing, spoons digging into the melting ice cream, my mind swim-ming in vodka-soaked bliss.

I wasn't sad anymore—just content.

At one point, Sam took the tub out of my reach.

"Hey," I protested. "I need this. I'm the one with the broken heart, remember?"

"I know, but I'm the rightful owner of this delicious snack, so it kinda balances out."

I sighed. "One point for you. Can I at least have one last bite? Just to etch the taste into my memory."

He lifted an eyebrow. "Is this even a thing, or are you fucking with me?"

"For me, it's real." I pressed my hand over my heart. "When something is too good—or too beautiful—I try to burn the feeling into my mind so I can remember it forever." I offered his a half-shrug. "My sister says it's weird."

"It is, but it's also super sweet. I dig it."

I used this moment of distraction to jump over him and dip my spoon into the almost-empty tub like a thirsty girl in the desert who hadn't seen rain in months.

As I brought the spoon to my mouth, I realized my boobs were in his face. His throat undulated, and I pressed my lips together, struggling to maintain my composure and not get flustered.

"Huh…oops." Panic swirled inside me. *Think fast, Maddie.* I tried to shift back in my seat, but the spoon betrayed me, tipping and dumping melted ice cream onto his crotch. I froze. Heat flared in my chest. "Ohmygod… I'm so sorry." My hand shot down to wipe it off before my brain could catch up with my actions.

Sam's very stiff and thick erection vibrated under my touch.

We both went motionless. I was pretty sure the Earth stopped rotating too.

What was I thinking? Gosh, what was I doing? *Retreat. Retreat. Retreat.* My brain screamed the message, but my hand stayed there, glued to his manhood as if it had a mind of its own.

"I didn't…huh…I-I wasn't… It-it's not what you thick… What you *think*. With an *N*. It's not what you *think*. It was just a…a reflex? I…gosh…I didn't mean to rub it off." Kill. Me. Now. "Oh God. Now anything I say sounds awful. At least I'm not dripping wet like that time in your backyard, and this time, you're not at risk of sliding right into me… My puddle. Oh no. Sorry, it sounds terrible. Huh…you know what I mean."

Shut up, Maddie. For once, just zip it.

Our gazes met and fused together. My heart lurched into my throat, and I grew light-headed. Did I stop breathing? My head felt too fuzzy to think rationally. Sam's stare shifted between my eyes and my mouth. We stayed frozen, and I had no idea for how long. Seconds felt like hours.

After a moment, some clarity returned to my numb brain, and I pulled my hand away, slouching back into my end of the couch. I pressed my palms against my face in mortification.

Without a word, Sam poured us two more shots. We gulped them down, both of us desperate to erase the last few minutes from our memories—at least I was—and to return to safer territory.

Thanks to my mishap, my body was now attuned to his proximity, even without trying. His scent. His breathing. The heat radiating from him. I could feel it all, in high definition, enveloping me.

I refused to put too much thought into our little…huh… I had no word to describe what had just happened. Our collision? My head, not functioning at full capacity, couldn't come up with a better word.

Sam stretched his arms across the backrest, casually scooting closer to me, his proximity impossible to ignore.

My heart banged in my chest. All I wanted was to lean in. My head—the part still capable of logic—pleaded with me to move away. The tug-of-war between what I craved and what I should do ended in a draw. As if my body knew I needed someone else—or something else—to take the lead, the alcohol hit my brain and took control.

I turned my upper body toward Sam, my heart thundering in my chest like a wild symphony. He closed the gap between us, and I shut my eyes. The tension between us, now almost palpable, felt like it could catch fire at any moment. My brain disappeared, leaving my heart in charge.

Our lips collided in a breathless kiss.

My mouth opened to welcome his tongue inside. Nothing about it was slow or delicate. No, it was pure carnal need. An urgency, a survival necessity.

I didn't recognize myself. My body responded to Sam as if he controlled it, in a primal, instinctive way.

"We shouldn't… It-it's wrong… So, so wrong." His words were barely audible as his tongue pressed deeper into my mouth.

My head spun, and a series of yelps passed my lips. How could any of this be wrong when it felt so right?

"Maddie, you taste like something I could easily get addicted to. Fuck. What are we doing?"

I shrugged. I had no idea. All I knew was that I was done being afraid. I was burning up. Tugging at the hem of my hoodie, I yanked it off, tossing it to the floor, leaving only a thin cotton shirt clinging to my skin.

"I haven't kissed anyone in two years. I'm…I'm like a virgin all over again. I-I can't stop... You're gorgeous… bewitching."

His words sizzled through me. I wanted more…so much more.

He cupped the back of my head with his hand, deepening the kiss. "How can it feel so right?"

At least we were in agreement about that.

"Shut up and kiss me," I begged, moving to my knees to straddle him. I arched my back as he nibbled the skin of my throat, his teeth grazing me like I was the most decadent chocolate he could indulge in all night.

Tingles. Ache. Heat. They all pooled in my lower belly.

He traced my spine with his fingertips, sending a shiver rippling through my body.

"You're too good, and too young, for me. I'll burn in hell for this." Sam kneaded one of my breasts over my shirt, brushing over my hard nipple, and I became putty in his hand. Gripping the back of his T-shirt at the nape, he pulled it over his head, revealing his sculpted chest.

I watched him in awe, unable to tear my eyes away from the sight of him.

He grabbed a fistful of my hair, guiding my mouth back to his.

"Age is just a number. It means nothing." I leaned back, gasping for fresh air after he'd stolen every molecule of oxygen from me.

His muscular hands slipped under my shirt, familiarizing themselves with my heated skin.

My head spun faster.

My breath hitched in my throat.

The room lit up in a full spectrum of colors.

"Fuck, Maddie. I've never wanted anyone the way I crave you. It's agony having you around every day, knowing I can't do anything about it. You're the only one who gets me… No one else does. Everything about you appeals to me…all of me."

I sank into the kiss, letting everything else fade away. My fingertips dug into his scalp as I pulled him closer, unwilling to process his words just yet.

Could tonight just be about physical pleasure, without all the complications? My brain scrambled to catch up, my thoughts tumbling over each other. I wasn't that girl—the one who could have a no-strings-attached, one-night stand without expecting something more. Yet, this felt too perfect to ruin by overthinking what it meant.

Sam held me against his chest before gently lowering me onto my back, his strong frame hovering over me. His eyes locked onto mine, a raw, thirsty desire radiating from every inch of him.

"I'll have my way—"

"*Daaaddy? Daaaddy? Daaaaaaaddy?* The monster is back. It's under the bed." Justine's heart-wrenching cries echoed from her bedroom upstairs, freezing the blood in my veins.

The intoxicating tension between us cooled in an instant. The promise he was about to make faded into nothingness. We broke apart abruptly.

He pulled the T-shirt I handed him over his head. "I'm sorry. I have to go to her." He flashed me a small, mischievous smile, his gaze sliding over my aroused body, hunger still burning in his eyes.

We both breathed hard.

I bet my face was as flushed as his, and no doubt he could see my diamond-hard nipples pressing through the thin cotton of my shirt.

"Stay here. Don't move. I'll be right back."

He disappeared upstairs, and the gears in my mind sluggishly started turning again, each thought dragging behind the last.

I traced the length of my lips with a finger, not sure if I had dreamed the last hour of my life. What did we do? What did *I* do? Making out with my boss was all kinds of wrong. We'd violated so many rules with that kiss. We had crossed so many boundaries.

In seconds, I sobered up—well, not really, but enough to recognize my wrongdoing. The images of what we'd just done swam in my mind. Rousing. How could I ever look him in the eye again? How could I look at myself?

I slumped onto the couch, burying my face in the crook of my elbow.

I had to go. To leave. To get the hell out of here.

Hours ago, I had told Jacob I'd never act on my crush, and I meant it. Now I had complicated everything.

Before I could move, Sam came back, his hands stuffed into his pockets, his head hanging forward.

"Nightmares. They come and go." He raked his fingers through his hair, looking away for a fraction of a second.

"Is she okay?"

His attention returned to me, and his shoulders dropped. "Yeah. She will be. She's asleep now." He inched closer, his gaze searching mine.

I pressed my cheeks. They burned scorching hot under my palms.

"Maddie. Listen. We… *I*… It was a bad idea. We can't do this." He flicked his hands between us. "We can't risk the tour. It's important to me. To the girls. To Riley. And I hope to you too. We can't be together. It will fuck everything up. It's just… Sex complicates things. We got lost in the heat of the moment. Are we cool?"

I shook my head. Then I nodded. Because everything he said rang true, but I didn't know if I should agree or not, the question blurry in my boozy brain.

"You…you sure we're fine?"

Oh, now I understood the question. "Yeah, we are."

He scratched the skin at the back of his neck. "Good. Huh…I guess. We should go to bed. It's almost four in the morning."

I nodded, not sure what to add. Then reality hit me. "Huh, Sam? I can't drive home."

"Come," he said. "You can crash in the guest room."

We stood in the doorway, inches apart.

Sam twirled a strand of my hair around his finger.

Shivers ran along my back, reaching my toes, and sent tingly goose bumps to my skull.

"Everything you might need is in the en-suite bathroom or the closet. Stay as long as you want to. You're… you're part of this family."

I bowed my head, trying to escape the magnetism of his gaze.

"Good night, Maddie."

"Night."

My heart plunged ten stories down inside my chest.

My shoulders slumped, and I whirled around, desperate to hide the deception I was sure was written all over my face.

"Maddie?"

I turned around and risked a glance at him, bracing myself, ready to swallow every word that was about to leave his mouth.

Sam leaned forward and caught my lips between his for a nanosecond, igniting a new spark within me. "I'm sorry." He turned around and left me there, needy and more lost than I'd been in a very long time.

17

SAM

I woke up, unsure if the crappy feeling inside me was from a hangover or just a major lack of sleep, and a weight across my chest. My head pounded. My eyelids weighed tons. My tongue stuck to the roof of my mouth. And my heart ached in my chest.

"Daddy, are you up?" Justine asked, straddling my torso, prying my eyelids open with her tiny, prickly fingers.

"Baby, stop. Daddy needs his rest."

"And *I* need to eat. I want *bracon*. A mountain of *bracon*. And eggs," she said, clearly more rested than I was. "Do you want *bracon*, Daddy? Like a big mountain?" She giggled, opening her arms wide.

"Ten more minutes," I begged, closing my eyes.

Images of last night flashed behind my eyelids.

Vodka. Ice cream. Madison touching my dick. Her smile. The twinkles in her eyes. The taste of her. Her hands on me. My hands on her. Her boobs. Her neck. The bolt of desire throbbing through my entire self almost to the breaking point.

My dick woke up faster than I did as my pulse raced

and the memories of what we did toasted my body until it combusted with unattained release.

Madison. The sweetness of her lips. The hardness of her nipples. The caresses of her hands.

Fuck, Maddie. She must still be asleep downstairs.

All traces of sleep vanished as I sprang to a ninety-degree angle, setting my giggling daughter down beside me on a pillow. I was so not ready to answer my children's million questions that were sure to follow if they saw Madison had spent the night.

How could I break her out of here before the girls noticed she had slept in our guest room?

Fully awake, I was now a man on a mission. An extraction mission.

"Justine, wake up Mika and get dressed. We'll go eat breakfast somewhere."

My baby girl's enthusiasm reverberated within my bedroom walls, and she hurried to her own room. "Mika, Mika, wake up. We're going to eat *bracon* at the *rest-the-torrent*."

I shook my head. How could she come up with new words for everything?

Dressed in a pair of dark jeans and a plain white T-shirt, I tiptoed downstairs before my daughters had time to join me. I combed my hair with my fingers, trying to tame the locks I knew must have pointed in all directions.

In front of the guest bedroom, I firmed my back and took a deep breath in. I could do this. No reason to make things awkward between us. Last night, Madison and I had fun, but this was it. Nothing more. We could slide back into our roles today. We had to.

Much of what she had said last night turned out to be a foggy memory hours later. Some parts, though, were still vivid, like a movie playing in my head—on a loop. Damn it. I almost fucked my children's twenty-one-year-old nanny. On my couch. And in the heat of things, I'd had no remorse whatsoever. It had just felt like the most natural next step in our relationship. *Relationship?* I bit my own tongue to evade the alternate reality I'd stumbled into since last night. *Work relationship.* I bet I had confused my body and mind quite good last night. It was all on me, though. I was the father. The responsible adult. I should've stopped the kiss at the first brush of our lips.

My dick swelled at the memory of yielding to the temptation I'd been battling for weeks. A warm buzz infiltrated my blood.

I stretched my neck to the side, cracked my knuckles, and took another deep breath in.

The door opened before I could find the courage to knock.

Madison appeared, looking rested. Did she have some special youth power I didn't possess anymore? The words I'd rehearsed vanished. Every single one of them.

With less than a foot between us, we stood still, heaviness tinting the air as we lost ourselves in each other's gaze. It confirmed that I hadn't dreamed of the yearning we'd shared hours ago.

Her bed hair not only made her look younger in the morning light, but it also gave her an irresistible just-been-fucked vibe. Everything I had a boner for. My erection pushed against the zipper of my jeans at the sight of her. She pursed her pink lips. Dirty thoughts flashed before my eyes at the prospect of everything she could do with those plump wonders. Heat, a scorching inflammable fever, coursed along my spine. My balls tightened. My pulse sped up, and my airways struggled to carry oxygen to my brain.

All the images of things we'd never experienced, but I

couldn't stop fantasizing about, had front-row seats in my mind.

This was bad. Before I could assess how screwed I was, I chased the reflection away and focused on the girl standing in front of me, looking vulnerable and so damn gorgeous.

"Hey," I said once I found my voice and blood started flushing my brain again.

"Hey."

"Sleep well?"

"Yes."

Why were we unable to make complete sentences?

"Good." *Enough with the one-word replies.* "Listen, the girls and I are heading out. I'd invite you to join us, but I don't want things to be weird, and it's your day off."

"It's okay." Her gentle tone sent shivers through me. "I gotta get home anyway and figure stuff out." Her eyes glazed over, and she looked away.

My palm molded to her cheek before I had time to assess my actions. "About last night—"

We both breathed hard, and I let go of her.

"Don't worry, Sam. I'm sure we'll be able to put this behind us and move forward. I was emotional, and we drank a lot. Let's not let it affect our working relationship, okay?"

Yes, *working relationship*. At least we both agreed.

I nodded. I fucking nodded, though all I craved to say was that it wasn't a mistake and that I wanted to finish whatever we had started. And kiss her senseless. But Madison was right. We had to get over it.

"Why don't you sleep in? I'm sure you can use the rest. We'll talk later." My eyes traced down her body, each curve pushing the flimsy boundaries of my willpower. I grabbed her hand and traced her knuckles with the pad of my thumb. "You can stay here tonight if you don't feel like going home. I mean it."

Her breathing accelerated, and she jerked her hand away.

"Sorry." I shoved my hands into my pockets to avoid touching her again.

"Thanks, but I'll be fine. I'll get back on my feet." She wiped a lone tear rolling down her cheek. One I'd like to steal away so she wouldn't cry ever again.

"We'll be out of here in ten minutes. Sleep in or make your exit. Whatever you choose, please let me know you're okay later."

She hung her head low. "I will."

"I'm sorry about Jacob and you. I can't understand why he wouldn't wanna be friends with you anymore." She looked past me as I added. "Should I be worried?"

"No. Please don't be. It's on me. We didn't agree… He said what we had wasn't salvageable… I'll…I'll get better. What other choice do I have?"

"Don't drown in your pain. Whatever went down between you two, I'm sure it'll get better."

"It won't. Thanks for caring."

Madison never delivered short answers lacking conviction, and this conversation was the sign she wasn't being herself.

I leaned forward, hating the distance between us, but jerked back just in time—before I could do something stupid. Again. Like hugging her or comforting her. With my mouth. And my manhood. Buried deep inside her. Hammering the pain away. "We'll catch up later. Call me if you need anything."

"Sure. Thanks."

"Daddy, we're ready. Where are you?" Mikaella asked, her feet stomping down the stairs and closing in on us.

"I'm here." I gave Madison an apologetic smile as she closed the door in my face. And every door to my heart.

"Ready, Daddy," Justine said, running after her sister, dressed in a teal princess gown with colorful gems stitched to the bodice.

I lifted them both in my arms. "You girls look like queens. Let me grab my stuff, and we can go."

My attention stayed fixed on the closed door for what felt like infinite seconds.

"Can Maddie come with us? Her car is in the driveway. Daddy, have you seen her?" Mikaella asked. "Is she here? Maddie? *Maaaddie?*"

My heart bled in my chest cavity.

I had to grow a thick skin, and quick. "She isn't here. I think she left her car in the driveway last night. We'll call her later to know if she needs help to pick it up, okay?"

"Can we ask her to come with us?" Justine asked. "She loves *bracon*."

Mikaella folded her arms over her chest and pouted. "I want Maddie to come with us too. You're not *grinchy* when she's there. She can ride with us. Can we call her already?"

My heart leaped in my throat. "Another time, girls. Now let's go. I'm sure there will be a line to enter House of Pancakes, and I'm starving."

———

The week went by fast. Between rehearsals, radio interviews, and all the promotional appearances Riley had scheduled for my big return, I didn't have time to think about the other night. Until I came home, and Madison looked at me with those eyes of hers that could steal my breath away. And my heart. The ones that could turn me into a slave if she asked me to. The ones that reminded me of *the* kiss.

The ones that still displayed the sadness I'd pay big money to heal.

As long as I kept busy, I had no time to wonder about *what-ifs*, broken dreams, or impossible endings.

With her.

In all the time we spent around each other, we never spoke of that kiss again, both of us choosing to classify it in the *mistakes not to be revisited* file.

With each passing day, the weight of my loneliness sank in a little more every night when I went to bed. Alone.

Solitude had never felt this heavy before.

Then darkness settled around me, and I had to use all my inner strength to resist the object of my sinful temptation. Jerking myself off thinking about her was a feeble consolation prize, and felt all shades of wrong.

"Girls, tonight we're celebrating," I said as I joined them in the backyard where they were running after cottontails. Every now and then, the rabbits invaded our backyard to the girls' greatest pleasure.

"Why?" Mikaella asked, coming closer.

Justine was still chasing the poor animals around, chuckling and waving her arms.

"My album is done."

My daughter jumped into my arms. "Can we listen to it, Daddy?"

I shook my head. "We can play it, but it won't be the final version. Not yet at least. Now there will be people making it even better."

"Like music magicians?"

"Yeah, like that."

I caught a smile on Madison's lips when my focus landed on her. "Congrats, Sam. I can't wait to hear it too."

"Thanks," I said, bringing my attention back to my eldest daughter. "Let's dress nice and go out. To that restaurant you and Justine like so much with the aquarium wall and slushies."

My girl's eyes flared, and she wiggled in my arms until I set her down on her feet.

"Justine. Justine, Daddy said—"

"They're really proud of you, you know?" Madison added from beside me as my gaze followed the two bundles of joy dancing around, the cottontails now forgotten.

My heart filled to the brim with pride and love at their infectious display of happiness.

The girls came barreling toward us. "Can Maddie come?" Justine asked.

I shrugged, avoiding Madison's eyes. "Sure. If she wants to."

Justine hugged Madison's knees and looked up at her. "Please come with us." She made her sad puppy-dog face, which she'd mastered to perfection, eliciting a giggle from me. Mikaella joined in, and soon both my daughters were begging her to join us.

"I don't have anything good enough to wear, girls. I'm sure your daddy wants to celebrate with you two. We could bake a treat next time I'm here and celebrate together then."

Justine's lower lip shuddered. "Maddie, why don't you come to the *aquarellium* with us?"

"Please," Mikaella pleaded, now on her knees. "Say yes. Pretty please."

"Girls… I… Ohmygod, you're torturing me." Madison's amusement laced her voice.

My daughters looked at me with their big eyes, and I shook my head before kneeling down as well. With my hands folded in a prayer-like gesture under my chin, I batted my eyelashes at her. "Please."

Madison burst into a fit of laughter, wiping the tears pooling in the corners of her eyes.

It was the first time in a week that her smile seemed genuine. The sight warmed my heart.

"You guys are impossible. How can I resist? Can I go home to shower and change first?"

I jumped to my feet, her smile tugging at my heartstrings, unable to resist her pull. Why did I enjoy being tortured by her this much? Or was I just completely gone for her? Fuck, we'd agreed to keep our distance. Begging Madison to join us was far from being my smartest idea. I pinched the bridge of my nose and sighed.

I kept my focus on my daughters, trying to block out the woman standing next to me for a few seconds. "Girls, go on. Dress to impress, okay? But wash your hands first."

Once they disappeared inside, I spun to face the woman I'd longed to steal another kiss from and who was testing all my self-restraints.

"Sam, I won't come. This celebration is between your daughters and you. Just tell them I'm sick or something."

I lifted a finger to silence her protest, cutting her off before she could add anything else. "Stop. Don't. I told you already. You're part of this family now. The girls are right. It's a family celebration, so you're welcome to join us."

"But—"

"No buts. Not tonight. It's a big day for me. And we're friends, or I like to believe we are."

Madison cast a glance down and nodded. "Friends. Yeah, sure. I still have to go home to change."

I tipped her chin up with my finger and locked our eyes. "Go get ready, and we'll pick you up in about an hour. How does it sound?"

"Perfect," she said in a breathless whisper.

The four of us sat in a semicircle in a dark wooden booth at the back of the restaurant. Soft country music played from the speakers. Madison and I sat side by side, a girl on each side, giving them the end spots since they kept standing up to admire the twelve-foot-tall aquarium wall on our left. They were both dressed in matching peach-colored summer rompers and white sandals. The joy pouring out from them was contagious tonight.

They had chosen my outfit: black trousers and a raisin-colored long-sleeve button-up shirt, which I wore with the sleeves rolled up at my elbows. At first, I hesitated, thinking I might be overdressed, but right now, sitting next to Madison, I thanked my daughters mentally for convincing me to indulge—and to put aftershave after I'd first resisted.

From beside her, I did my best to be subtle, stealing quick sideways glances as I drank in the sight of her. Wearing a navy-blue belted dress with a layered hem, tied around her neck, she looked both sophisticated and sexy. It offered a full view of her delicate shoulders. When I picked her up earlier and saw she had forfeited heels tonight and chosen cowboy boots instead, a slice of my heart had bloomed. I had failed at reeling my smile in. We were so much more alike that it hurt to think I couldn't have her the way I dreamed of at night.

The loose, silky curls of her hair cascaded over her back, and all I wished for was to wrap them around my fingers.

Her pink-painted lips curved when her eyes found mine, and I was gone for her all over again.

The server returned to our table with a bottle of expensive wine and two glasses. My non-official date covered hers with a hand. "Not for me, thank you."

"You're not driving. We're here to celebrate, you sure?"

"Okay… Maybe just one. I won't let you drink by yourself."

We exchanged a glance, and the server filled half her glass.

I raised mine. "Cheers. To the album, the tour, and for everything you've done for the girls and me in the last few months. I wouldn't be here today without you. I don't tell you often enough, but I'm grateful."

Madison sucked in a small intake of air, and I felt hot all over. She blushed, the faint flush impossible to resist. "Sam, I'm just doing my job," she said, breaking the fragile silence that had settled and taken us hostage. "That's all."

I shook my head. "You're doing much more than that." She followed my gaze as it landed on the girls, laughing as they watched the fish. "You've brought us back from the dead. We've come alive since you walked into our home." I sipped my wine, letting the silence stretch between us.

"Do you…do you ever feel like everything around you is spinning at a dizzying speed and you can't stop the motion?" she asked after a long minute, the alcohol loosening her tongue and shattering the glass box she'd been hiding behind all week.

"Is this how you feel?"

Moisture welled up in her eyes. "Yes. No. I-I miss him. Growing up, I didn't have a lot of friends. I never had a best friend before Jacob. It was the first time I'd let someone else in completely, and I'm not sure how to deal with the loss. He's shut me out completely."

I placed my hand on hers and gave it a squeeze. "Losing someone you care about isn't easy. I'm the best example. It took me too fucking long to realize my wife's leaving was a blessing. I was so angry, so hurt, that I didn't take the time to connect with the real underlying emotions. In my opinion, getting closure is important. I never had that. Thus, I'll always wonder why she ran away. I'm okay with the fact, but a part of me would like to know the reason…if there's one. Or else I'll always wonder."

"I'm sorry she did that to you. You guys didn't deserve to be hurt like that."

"Nobody does. I'm sorry your friendship with Jacob blew up. I could tell you two liked each other very much."

"Well, it wasn't enough."

The girls sat back when the waiter brought our food, and I released Madison's hand.

"Thanks, Sam. For listening to me."

I returned the curl of her lips. Perhaps all wasn't lost, and Madison's and my friendship could survive the other night's mishap.

"Can I ask you for your input?" I asked when we got to our main course.

"Always," Madison said, her previous emotional over-load cleared now.

I transferred a few lobster ravioli to her plate when she shared pieces of her pork medallions with Justine after she refused to eat her chicken tenders because they were not shaped like dinosaurs.

"You don't have to," Madison said.

"You're kidding, right? Plus, you gotta try it."

She returned my easy smile. "Thanks." She took a bite, and I got hypnotized by the expressions crossing her face as she savored the flavors. A moan left her lips as her eyes closed in mouthgasm. "Okay, you're right. It's delicious." She took another bite, and I forced my focus to remain on my own plate. "What did you want to ask me?"

"Oh, yeah. I almost forgot." I turned my phone on and thumbed through the emails Riley had sent me earlier. "Album cover. I have four options to choose from. I have very distinct opinions about them and hesitate between two."

"You want my impression?" She rested a hand over her heart. "I'm touched."

"I always love having your input. You're straightforward. I respect that about you."

"Show me." I slid my device into her proffered palm.

"Shhh. Don't tell me anything." She placed a finger over her painted lips. "Don't influence me."

I rolled my lips over my teeth and focused my attention on my daughters instead.

"I'm ready," Madison announced after five long minutes, scooting closer to me and setting the phone on the table between us. "Option one. The design is nice. I love the color scheme. But we don't see you. I feel that with a comeback, your album cover should feature you front and center."

I nodded. So far it made sense.

"Option two. The close-up shot works. There's something in your eyes. It screams strength and vulnerability all at once. I love the black and white concept with a few strokes of color."

My pulse kicked up. It was like Madison had been reading my inner thoughts.

"Option three. The shot is nice. But somehow, with your back to the camera and that guitar strapped over your shoulder, it spells *goodbye* and not *watch out, I'm back*. And option four, I love the profile picture. I'm just not sure about the font choice, though. Overall, I believe number two represents who you are better. The last option misses the message your eyes convey." She met my gaze. "How did I do?"

I sat there, my jaw hanging open, speechless.

Madison wriggled in her seat. "So? Say something."

"First, you nailed it. I was hesitant between options two and four. Your thoughts mirror mine. One hundred percent. Second, thank you. It's now settled." I shot Riley my final choice and put my phone down.

"Do you like doing photoshoots?" Madison asked, resuming her meal.

"Not really, but it's part of the job. The first one I did, I was so shy, I looked frightened in all the pictures. It took another session to finally get me to relax and enjoy the process."

"I wish I would've been there to witness it. Sam Stevens, *The Legend*, afraid of a camera lens."

I joined in as her body vibrated with laughter. "Go on. Make fun of me."

Madison's thumb and forefinger almost met. "Just a tiny bit."

We finished dinner, the conversation flowing easily between us. I was relieved that the queasiness simmering between us over the past week had finally melted away.

Madison pushed her empty plate aside. "That was delicious," she announced after wiping her mouth with a black square napkin.

Justine moved to sit on her lap, and Madison leaned back to help her up.

"You're tired, sweetie?" My baby girl nodded as Madison wrapped one arm around her, the other one caressing her hair.

Justine buried her head deeper in her chest. The same exact spot where I'd dreamed so many times I could bury my face too.

Mikaella, on my right, busied herself with coloring books.

"I have to ask you a question," my date—or the woman I hoped could officially be my date—said, as I refilled both our wine glasses. "How did you know I was in the driveway the other night? I'm curious." She brought the Merlot to her lips.

"I was taking the trash out when I saw you."

"You were taking the trash out in the middle of the night?"

I shrugged. "I didn't wanna wake up the next morning with stuff all over the house and backyard, so I figured I'd clean everything before going to bed." I took a sip. "You're lucky I did."

A darker hue crept along her cheeks.

"Anyway, I couldn't sleep. I had a certain someone on my mind—"

"Can we go now?" Mikaella asked, the distraction more than welcome, cutting our discussion, and my confession, short. "I'm tired."

I lifted her up in my arms. "Sure, sweet pea. Let me pay the check, and we'll be out of here."

The server hadn't even returned with my credit card when her body grew heavier in my grip.

Madison and I walked outside and waited for the valet to bring the SUV, each of us carrying a sleeping child. "You sure you're all right?" I asked. "I can carry both."

"I'm fine." She returned my smile.

Tonight, she looked even sexier with my daughter deep asleep in her arms.

Reality hit me. It wouldn't be fair to her to date a single father of two.

She was young and had her whole future ahead of her. She didn't need reasons to settle down at her age. That was exactly what would happen if we went out together. She'd skip precious years of her life, forced to become a mother figure before she was even ready for it.

Some knots loosened in my upper back. I blew out a long breath.

Even though tonight I got a peek at what a relationship with her would look like, Madison could never be mine. It was about time I came to terms with the idea.

Thirty minutes later, I parked in front of the two-story powder-blue townhouse she lived in. During the entire ride, we barely said a word, too absorbed in our own thoughts.

"Thanks for tonight," she said, her eyes glistening in the dark. "I had a great time."

"Thank you for joining us." My tongue itched to say much more, but I remembered I had no right to steal her youth from her. No matter how attracted I was to her. A relationship between us could never happen. "I'll see you on Monday."

Something resembling hurt flashed in her gaze. "Yeah. Sure. See you Monday morning," she echoed, shutting the door behind her.

I watched her as she entered her house, and even after she disappeared inside, I stayed parked there, wishing she would walk back out, say *fuck it*, and drive with me into the sunset.

She's not yours. She'll never be. Get over her, Stevens, I said to myself as I drove away. *Time to move on.* For real this time around.

18

MADISON

I hugged the girls goodbye and left them to play in their castle while I joined Sam by the grill. He looked so damn handsome wearing a worn-out heather-gray tour shirt and black cargo shorts, his hair swept away from his forehead in a sexy I-don't-care kind of way that made my knees weak. I implored my heart to stay put as I inched closer. He offered me a beer, but I declined with a flick of my hand.

It'd been a week since the four of us went out to celebrate his album wrap-up, and we agreed to be friends. Yep, I'd been put in the infamous friend zone. The joke wasn't lost on me. Things between us had been sailing smoothly since. Agitation stirred in me every time we were close, and for that reason, without either of us saying a word, we had gotten good at keeping our distance whenever we were in the same space.

A few times, when he thought I wasn't aware, I caught Sam staring at me in a manner that should be forbidden, one that made me clench my thighs. Then he would look away, shaking his head, and the lust-filled moment would be broken. I knew because I did the same. I watched him from afar, recalling his callous fingers playing my body, the tenderness of his lips when they had feasted on mine. The memories of him always sent a new pool of heat billowing between my thighs. We were stuck in an impossible situation, and neither of us had any clue how to navigate the longing we felt but couldn't surrender to.

Then my brain would go back to Jacob. And the idea he wasn't in my life anymore transformed my lust into sadness. I missed him. A lot. Since the night I'd kissed Sam, I felt like a fraud and couldn't find it in me to call the one I used to consider my best friend. To check up on him. One night, I had sent him a text when I was feeling lost and vulnerable and cried myself to sleep at the idea our friendship was over—for real. He never replied. His cut was deeper than mine, so it'd take him much more time to be able to talk to me without shattering every time. I came to the conclusion that even though we both liked each other, the intensity of our feelings wasn't matching. I loved him, but I wasn't in love with him, like he was with me.

"You sure you don't wanna have dinner with us? There's plenty," Sam asked, his husky voice doing nasty things to my body without even touching it and setting every one of my nerve endings on fire.

These days, I was never in a hurry to go back home after work. Being alone, because Emily's and my schedule never matched, sent me into a spiral of sorrows. At the Stevenses', I had people who cared about me keeping me busy. Darkness stayed at bay while I was hanging out with them. So, even though I knew I shouldn't, I had accepted almost all their offers to stay over for dinner since the night we had celebrated the completion of his new album.

"Nah. I'm always sticking around. You guys deserve some family time. I should get going."

Sam's dark eyes bore into mine, and I sucked in a breath, looking at my feet, making a mental note to fix my nail polish sometime later. See? I could think about things other than my boss and my bruised heart when I put my mind to it.

"Are you still struggling?" he asked.

I nodded. In a moment of weakness, I had admitted to him I had a hard time fixing my heart after the loss of my best friend. "I'm getting there."

I spun around, but he gripped my wrist before I could step away. The way he always did that had been shattering my resistance from day one. A gasp parted my lips at the rough growl emanating from him, deep enough to rumble through me. Every particle filling the air smelled like him, a mix of musky and woodsy aftershave and something exclusively him. Gorgeous and forbidden. Sexy and dangerous.

"Wait—"

My eyes returned to his, but he added nothing else.

His throat worked, and I got hypnotized by the movement. A heat wave swirled through my body. "Are we okay? If there are remnants of weirdness between us, can we kill it now?" He paused. "For the girls' sake. And because I miss being friends with you."

Or because living on a bus for half a year together all the time will be impossible if we can't tame down the desire searing between us. We'll both be hormonal messes. Cranky. Unpredictable. Time-ticking lust bombs. And living in hell won't be good for anybody. But I added nothing, I stood there and nodded because I feared if I opened my mouth, I'd say or do something I'd regret—like begging him to give us a chance, or kissing him in broad daylight, healing both our hearts in the process.

Sam cleared his throat. "So?"

I came back to my senses, burying all the naughty images swimming inside my head and locking them away. In an *open at your own risk* drawer.

"Yeah, sure. No problem." I plastered a smile on my face. "I'm all good."

He winked, and I almost died right there but refrained myself just before I slipped. "Awesome, then you'll have dinner with us. Because that's what friends do. I would be a bad one if I sent you home to be all by yourself. You look off today. I'm volunteering to cheer you up."

I burst out laughing at the situation. Sam Stevens, the country music superstar, single father to his two adorable daughters, looked so cute right now and resembled a kid as he begged me with a boyish grin. How did I end up in this situation? It still made no sense at all. "God, you're killing me. Okay. Fine."

He raised his hands. "Ha. I knew you wouldn't be able to resist my cooking." His cheerfulness died, and a shadow crossed his eyes.

My gaze trained on his lips as he sipped his beer. No. Not going there. We could do this—meaning be professional in our interactions.

"Any city you're excited to visit during the tour?"

I thanked him mentally for the change of topic and forced a curve to my lips as if everything was fine. "Yeah. I've never been anywhere but Tennessee and Kentucky. I can't wait to go to LA, New York, and visit Texas."

"I'll get a lot of days off…for family time. One of the conditions when I agreed to move forward with Riley's big plan. I'll give you a tour of New York when we get there. I'm positive you'll love it. Let me know what would make you happy, and we'll book time for it."

"That's really generous of you. I'm looking forward

having my own personal tour guide. I'll let you know when I decide."

"Awesome," he said, his focus back on the grill.

"Huh, I'll go inside and make a salad if that's okay with you."

"Sure. Suit yourself. You can also relax and just keep me company here since your workday is over. After all, we just agreed we could act like two civilized human beings when around each other."

"I… We should see other people," I blurted out, before I could process the impact of what I'd just said.

Sam watched me with a surprised expression that didn't scream *I'm overjoyed with this idea*, and I brought my hands to my cheeks to ease the burn.

"That's what you really—"

A loud cry from the opposite side of the backyard startled us both and put an end to the awkward conversation. It seemed we were always interrupted whenever we tried to have a heart-to-heart discussion. We turned our heads in sync.

Justine came running, her sweet toddler's face morphed into a fearful expression. "Daddy, Daddy. Mika. She fell. Crack. She cracked her arm."

The kitchen tong in Sam's hand hit the ground as he sprinted in the direction of the castle.

Meeting a crying Justine halfway across the backyard, I scooped her up into my arms, with the sole objective of comforting her and easing her heart.

Mikaella's painful shrieks and Justine's fear-induced cries colored the silence.

"Shhh, I'm here. Everything's gonna be okay. You hear me? Your daddy and I will make sure Mika is safe and sound."

My lips lingered on the top of her head as I rubbed her back gently, my squeeze on her almost bone-crushing.

Sam entered my peripheral vision, his oldest daughter in his arms, looking like they'd just escaped a crumbling building together. Beads of sweat now grazed his angled eyebrows, and his lips formed a thin line. With Justine still in my arms, clinging to me with all her strength, I rushed to him.

"Daddy says I may have broken my wrist," Mikaella stated, her voice trembling and fat tears running down her reddened cheeks. She chose to let go this time and not shy away from the pain and allowed us to see the fragile side of her, the one she usually hid from everyone else, including her daddy. Most times, she concealed her emotions, choosing to act out when she was angry or sad instead of just crying it out. Holding back her tears until she was in bed, far from everyone else's attention.

"Good news is you'll have a super cool cast if it's broken," I said, trying to infuse her with some hope after I kissed her forehead. "And it could have been your leg. So, now you'll still be able to play outside and run."

"What's the bad news?" she asked with a wet frown.

"Being hurt is no fun, but you'll see, it will get better really fast." Flashbacks of my younger self wearing a cast years ago made their way to my conscious mind. "Huh, I broke my wrist when I was little. My sister drew on it to make it more pretty. Nowadays, you get to choose great colors. They're like a trendy fashion accessory in my opinion. Not fun, but necessary, so you better make the best of it. You'll be able to choose almost any color of the rainbow. Isn't it cool?"

"Thank you," Sam whispered, some of the wrinkles around his eyes vanishing.

At that moment, I wished I was the one erasing all of them by kissing his own pain and worries away, filling his heart with the love and hope he deserved

"Any color?" Mikaella asked.

"Yes. I'll call Emily, my sister. She's working at the hospital today. She'll meet with us."

Sam stopped me with a hand on my shoulder. "I'll go. You stay here. With Justine. If it's okay with you. Or I can take both girls if you wanna go home."

"Don't be silly. I either come with you or stay here with Justine, but no way am I leaving until I'm sure Mika is fine."

"Fine. I won't argue with you." His grip on me released suddenly as if he'd just realized he was touching me, and his arm fell at his side. He brought his focus to Mikaella, and the droop of his shoulders confirmed that he was worried about his child.

"Hey, listen to me," I said. "Everything will be all right. I promise. Mika is going to be in good hands. Ems is the best. I swear."

Sam's hand returned to my upper arm, and I enveloped it with mine to keep it there, knowing he needed the reassurance. "Thanks. I'll keep you posted." He let go of me and rubbed the skin between his eyebrows. "We'll get going."

I nodded and started to walk away when Mikaella's fingers fisted my shirt from behind. I whirled around to look at her. "What is it?"

"Maddie? Don't go home, okay?" she pleaded, holding her wrist against her chest, more tears building in her eyes. "Stay with us."

"I'm not going anywhere. I'll be here when you get back," I said. "Let me call my sister to make sure they're ready for you when you get to the ER." I kissed her fore-head, and she released me.

Sam nodded, and with Justine hooked to my neck, I made my way inside, searching for my phone.

———

With a sleeping Justine beside me, I scrolled through my phone, searching for the special video I had to edit and send over, the sound of her steady breathing the only noise in the room. She had fallen asleep in my arms, and I was still lying beside her in her bed, hesitant to move in case she woke up. Sam had texted me half an hour ago, confirming Mikaella had indeed fractured her wrist. Luck-ily, it was a clean break, nothing serious, and she would be out of her cast in about five weeks. The memories of my own broken arm from years ago twisted something in my stomach—something I couldn't quite pinpoint. A chill ran through me.

The chime of an incoming text message startled me. Sam had sent me a picture of Mikaella sporting a black splint on her left arm.

SAM

Still a teenager. No way is she gonna wear a colorful cast when they put it on in two days. *sigh*

The confession brought a smile to my lips.

ME

Black is badass. I love it *black heart emoji*

As I scrolled through my phone, searching for that video, my gaze rested on a picture of Jacob and me that we had taken when we went to a music festival downtown. With his arm around my shoulders, he looked at me as if I meant everything to him. Then I landed on a picture of us the night we had gone roller skating, dressed in flashy color outfits straight from the eighties.

My heart squeezed in my chest. Why had I told him about my crush on Sam that night? It destroyed us. We were happy. We fit together. I ruined everything by being too honest, my forbidden attraction for the man who had hired me not going anywhere.

I traced his smiling face with my fingertip. "I'm sorry. For everything. I love you. I still do. It wasn't fair to you that I also had feelings for someone else. I miss you. A lot."

A lump grew in my throat. An incoming message forced my mind back to the present.

EMILY

Met that boss of yours. Holy moly, Maddie.

He's one hands-on dad.

And he's hotter in person. Geez, girl. No wonder J got jealous. Sorry. Anyway, his little girl will be brand new in no time.

ME

Thanks, Ems. For taking care of her.

EMILY

That man spoke highly of you. He respects you. That much is clear. And the girl couldn't stop gushing about you either. They are good people. You're lucky to have them. I feel better knowing this since you'll be on the road with them for a long time.

A new picture came through. Mikaella eating a burger and fries, proudly showing her splinted wrist, and another one of Sam and her, flashing their pearly whites at the camera.

My finger traced the contours of his face next. His smile resembled a red moon, rare but something you never wanna miss when it shone in the sky—or on you.

"How will I survive six months of this?" I asked out loud to myself. Or maybe to a sleeping Justine. I buried my head in the pillow and closed my eyes as I abandoned my phone on the mattress next to me. The back of my eyes prickled, and I sealed my lids, preventing a trickle.

Just when I was about to fall asleep, a tiny hand caressed my cheek. "Maddie, look. They couldn't put a cast now. I have to wait for two days." Mikaella said. "Emily said I can even play in the fountains with it or go swimming. Are you awake?"

I peeled my eyelids open one by one, only to find her face about two inches from mine, her smile contagious, and her eyes illuminating the entire room.

I moved to a seated position and checked her bandaged arm. "Are you in pain?"

She shook her head. "No. Daddy got me a burger, then some medicine, and now I'm good. And Emily gave me a lollipop."

I pulled her into my arms and kissed her temple. "I'm glad you're okay. Wanna get into bed?"

"Can you read to me? Daddy said it's okay if you're the one who tucks me in tonight."

"It will be my pleasure. Let's get you changed first."

"Maddie, you said you broke your wrist too. How did you do it?"

I sighed. "I fell. I don't remember all the specifics, but I remembered wearing a cast."

Once Mikaella slept peacefully, I made my way downstairs.

Sam had set up the island with two plates of the chicken and rice I'd put in the refrigerator earlier after feeding Justine.

My heart lurched in my throat as I took in the *it's not supposed to look romantic* display.

"Hey you," he greeted me. "Hungry?"

"Starving."

"Good. I had no idea if you had eaten earlier."

I shrugged. "Couldn't. My stomach was tied in one giant knot."

We sat side by side and attacked our food in silence. "So," Sam started. "I met your sister."

I nodded, focused on my food instead of losing myself in his gaze if I risked a glance his way. "Mika told me she loved her."

"She's a super-doctor. Did and said all the right things to make her feel comfortable."

"I'll tell her. She'll be happy to hear that."

"Maddie, why did you lie to me?"

Why did my name have to sound so lustful when it came from his mouth? My body pulsed when he addressed me. Ribbons of sexual tension tied themselves around us.

I shook my head to escape his spell. His words finally made their way to my brain.

"I lied?" I pointed to my chest and gave him a quizzical glare.

Sam dropped his knife and fork with a soft thud on the countertop and turned until he faced me. "About your living situation." His harsh tone surprised me.

The accusation floated between us. Even though charged particles filled the void around us.

"I—" Why did I feel I needed to explain myself? Where and how I lived wasn't his problem.

He continued before I could tell him to mind his own

business. "You sleeping on a couch or an air mattress on your sister's bedroom floor is not okay. Am I not paying you enough to get your own place? You should have told me."

I buried my face in my hands, humiliation warming my skin. Tonight, I would kill my sister once she got home. She had no reason to tattle to my boss. This. Was. Not. Okay. Even though I knew she meant well.

"It's temporary. We're leaving soon. I didn't wanna rent a place and move in, only to move out right after. The new doctor, Emily's colleague, needed a place to stay. I offered my bedroom. It's no big deal."

"The guest bedroom. It's yours if you want it."

I averted my eyes and snorted. "Not sure you and I sleeping under the same roof is a good idea."

He rubbed the column of his throat and spoke in a whispered voice that rattled my core. "We'll be doing just that for six months. Better get used to it while we have enough room to breathe apart."

"I'm fine."

"Come on. Get rid of your pride. You don't have a bedroom, and I'm offering you one. What's the problem?"

I inhaled a jagged breath. "Stop. I said I'm fine. There're a lot of things you don't know about me. Stop trying to fix everything."

I pushed my plate away, not hungry anymore.

Sam's tone gentled, and his hand covered mine. "Hey, hey, it's not that. I'm just trying to help, not implying anything. The offer is there if you decide otherwise."

"Yeah, well… I'm in no rush to test the waters. Don't wanna compromise your tour. I'm dedicated to my job. I'll always do it the best I can. In the meantime, let's not rock the boat."

"If you change your mind—"

I moved to my feet. "I won't. Thanks for dinner, but I should go."

I grabbed both plates, but Sam stopped me, stealing the dishes from my hands. "Let me. You're not our maid, Maddie. You're the girls' nanny. And my friend. I can do this."

"I just wanna help."

He inhaled. "I know." He scratched his jaw. "Don't be mad at me. I'm sorry if I overstepped. I don't like the idea of you not having your own space."

My anger died down. "I overreacted."

"Wanna talk about what you said earlier? About us seeing other people? Is that what you really want?"

I pinched my lips together as I debated what to say. "Listen. I don't know why I said it. It's not my business what you do in your personal time. I was out of line. Forget it."

Sam's focus drifted back and forth between my face and the floor to finally settle on my eyes.

"Go home. It's late. I'll see you in the morning."

Without another look in his direction, I grabbed my purse and phone along with my pride and stormed out. I only halted when I reached the front door. With a roll of my shoulders back, I paused and turned around. "Night, Sam."

"Night, Maddie." Facing the kitchen sink, his hands were clamped to the countertop and his head bent down. Even without seeing his expression, I could tell our situation weighed heavy on him too.

The friend in me wanted to go to him, but the saner part of me knew leaving was the smart thing to do.

After one last look in his direction, I hurried outside, closed the door behind me, and let go of all the air I'd been holding in.

Phone in hand, I hovered my fingers over Jacob's contact. Right now, I missed him more than ever. More than I should. More than I was allowed to. If he asked me to drop out from the tour, would I be able to? A weight pressed against my ribcage. The answer hadn't changed. Unless Sam ordered me to, I would never be able to leave Justine and Mikaella.

A new realization sent a cold spur along my spine. Would I ever be able to walk away from Sam? Just the thought of not seeing him every day suffocated me. There, my body provided me with the answer to the question I feared the most.

In order to never be told to leave, I had only one choice. Let go of my infatuation.

Just then, I made a promise to myself. No more crushing on the man who possessed my heart without even trying to. From now on, I would stay away as much as possible and would move on when my time was up. I wouldn't let my emotions rule my life. I lost Jacob against my will, but I wouldn't let what happened with Sam wreck me even more. I'd been on my own all my life. I could still do this. Be happy by myself. I didn't need a man to make me feel good about myself or brighten my days. I was more than enough.

I put my phone back in my purse, started the car, and pulled away, feeling optimistic that I could really be the professional I'd told Sam I was.

That night, the nightmares I hadn't experienced in years woke me up. Sweat pearled on my forehead, and I sat up.

Air struggled to reach my lungs. Why was I feeling like someone was pursuing me? Dark shadows still lingered around me.

I couldn't recall what they were about, but they

brought up a wave of nausea. Hurrying to the bathroom, I emptied my stomach. Something about Mikaella's accident made me feel queasy. I returned to bed, hot tears burning the back of my eyes, as sleep claimed me, and I prayed for a restful night.

19

SAM

Rehearsal had ended early, and I came home to Madison folding laundry on the kitchen table. "Mind if I give you a hand?" I asked.

She shrugged. "Make yourself at home."

We exchanged timid smiles at the wit. Since we argued two days ago, things had been more strained than usual between us, and I hated that we had grown apart over a disagreement about her living situation.

"Can we talk?" I asked while I filled two glasses with lemonade and fixed a veggie platter with dip.

Madison nodded and followed me to the back deck, opening the door for me.

After I placed our snacks on the small table between us, Madison stretched on a lounge chair, and I handed her a glass.

I cleared my throat. "Listen, I wanna talk to you about moving in here," I said once I sat down.

She straightened up and turned toward me, ready to bolt. "Sam, I already told you I'll—"

I moved one hand up to silence her protests. "It's not

what you think. Before the tour, I'll be away often at night and sometimes for an entire set of nights because I have some warm-up shows scheduled after the album launch next weekend. I was thinking it'd be easier if you live here full time."

Her eyes rounded, and she sucked in a breath and stared at me as if I'd said something terrible.

"I-I'm not sure it's a good idea, you know, with everything."

I let out a heartfelt laugh. "At this point, I'm pretty sure we can sleep in the same house since we're leaving in just a few weeks. And, good news, our rooms aren't on the same floor. Safe distance."

She got flustered and glanced down. Pushing her hair over her shoulders, she shut her eyes, appearing to weigh the pros and cons. She scrunched up her face and lifted her fingers to massage her temples. I could see the gears of her brain working. How I wish she'd allow my input on the subject. It'd be easier if I could opine on whatever torture her mind.

When she re-opened her eyes, her gaze darted to mine. "You really think it's necessary?"

I swung my legs over the edge of the chair to face her. "Listen, I wouldn't ask if I didn't think it was the best idea for everyone involved. You included. We'll have sleepovers on the bus like we discussed. The girls will feel more at ease if they know that's how things are gonna be when we hit the road and get used to it. You'll still have your weekends off. I promise the girls and I will give you your space. I'll talk to them. We'll rework the schedule."

Madison pinched her lips and exhaled.

I gripped her wrist, rubbing the inside with my thumb, before she could find a reason to end this conversation.

"The night we talked about it… I-I didn't want to overstep. I'm sorry if I did. This tour will be a big adjustment for all of us, but mostly for the girls. If they're happy on the road and feel safe and secure, it will be easier for everyone. You and me, included."

She relaxed her stance. "Yeah, it's a lot of change for everyone." She paused. "Not that I'm not ready for this. I'll never be able to thank you enough for this opportunity. It's a *once in a lifetime* experience. I just don't want us to complicate things…you know."

"As your friend, I can assure you everything will be all right. Call it a gut feeling, but you and I, we're a great team. The girls are happier than they've been in years, and I am too. I get to do what I love, and it's all because you're doing an amazing job with them. And because being around you makes us wanna be better. There's this aura you project that's impossible to resist. Also, as I already told you, without you, this tour wouldn't be possible."

"Nah, you would have hired someone else."

"No. It had to be you. The girls love *you*, and they trust *you*. It's a match made in heaven as Riley once told me. I believe in destiny. This, us, is living proof. In many ways, you've become the heart of this family. I don't know how to explain it differently."

A pink flush bloomed on her cheeks. Madison always looked adorable when she was being shy. "Thanks."

We stayed like this for long minutes, basking in the enveloping silence.

"Do you trust me?" I asked.

"Yeah. I do." Her voice sounded like a whisper.

"Then everything will be all right."

———

"Will you be here when I wake up tomorrow morning?" Justine asked when I kissed the crown of her head. For the last twenty minutes, she'd been sitting on my bed while I got ready.

"Yes, baby. I'll be back later tonight."

"Daddy, you look pretty," she said with a snicker, cupping her mouth with both hands.

I curtsied. "Thank you very much, Princess Justine."

Her laughter doubled, then died down. "Daddy? What if Maddie leaves and you're not back yet?"

"Not a chance. She's living here now. Remember, we set up the guest bedroom last week, and she moved in this morning. She'll sleep downstairs, but she won't go to bed until I'm back. She promised. Don't worry, okay?"

Justine nodded, and I wiped the tears building in the corners of her eyes with my thumbs. I understood her fears. In the last two years, except for the night they spent at the hotel with my parents, we'd never spent a night apart. I just couldn't.

"Don't cry, baby. You'll be fine. You like Maddie, right?"

She bobbed her head faster. "I *lovvvve* her."

"See? Then it'll all work out. Kiss me one last time, because I really need to go. Uncle Riley is waiting for me."

"Love you, Daddy."

"Love you too, baby," I said, fastening my arms around my little girl's body and holding her close to my heart. "Let's go downstairs, okay?"

"Okay," she agreed as I picked her up.

We joined Mikaella and Madison in the dining room, working on a puzzle together.

"Hey, sweet pea. I'm leaving. Will you be okay?"

"Yeah. Fine. Bye."

She didn't even bother looking at me.

"Come on, girl. Can Daddy at least have a good luck hug?"

"I'll give you a good luck hug," my youngest daughter offered, securing her arms around my neck once again, then scrambling down.

Mikaella sighed and stood up to give me a half-hug. "Everybody will love your music, Daddy."

I leaned forward and kissed her cheek. "I love you."

"Me too. Can I go back to my puzzle now?"

So much for the display of enthusiasm.

I shook my head, unable to hide my smile. "Sure." I ruffled her hair as she sauntered away.

Madison moved to stand to follow me. "Sam, you'll be great. Go, do your thing. We'll be fine. I know it's a big deal tonight, so just focus on that."

"I usually come home no later than nine. Today, I'll be delayed. You sure you'll be okay?"

"Yes. Now go. Stop worrying. I've got everything under control. Riley doesn't seem like the type of guy who likes to wait." She pushed my shoulder so I'd get going.

I spun around and walked backward, lifting my hands in surrender in front of me. "Yeah, yeah. I'm going."

"Keep walking." The sparks in her eyes acted like an arrow to my heart.

Now that she'd moved in, even though I still believed it was for the best, we'd have to adjust to being around each other all the time, and also keep our relationship platonic and friendly.

The sight of Madison always brought me back to the night we'd crossed boundaries. The one I still dreamed about most nights when I lay in the darkness in the privacy of my own room.

The thought of having her so close and yet so far from me at the same time sent my heart into overdrive. It would kill me. Liar. The last thing I wanted was to die. There were so many pleasurable things I had yet to do to her. And it involved no murder. Just some weapons of choice, endless pleasure, cries of ecstasy, and breathless shouts of my name. *Keep dreaming, Stevens.*

It had taken a bit of convincing for Madison to agree to take over the guest bedroom, but a part of me relished knowing she was safe and sound, had her own space, and wouldn't have to sleep on an air mattress anymore. If Mikaella hadn't broken her wrist, I wouldn't have met Emily and learned about her living situation. Madison never mentioned she had forfeited her room so another doctor could move in with them. Her sister loved her, that much was clear, and I was happy she confided in me that night.

Anyway, if we could survive these remaining couple of weeks of living in close proximity, being all cramped up on a tour bus for six months wouldn't resemble torture anymore.

"You're right. As usual. I'll see you later."

I scanned the dining room one last time before leaving to attend my album launch party, my heart cartwheeling in my chest and my adrenaline at its peak. Something I never thought would happen again in this life.

———

"Glad you could make it," I told Carter as he met me in the backroom of Wild and Country, the bar Riley part-owned.

"You're kidding, right? Miss Sam Stevens's grand comeback? Never. I told you already. I'm too much of a fan when it comes to you."

I let out a chuckle. Carter Hills was the definition of a

country music superstar himself. He'd been at the top of the charts for a decade, first with his band, Carter Hills Band, then as a solo artist after they parted ways. He had stopped going on big world tours a while back, but still, every time he released a new song, it shot to the top and stayed there until the next one came out. He was the epitome of success in our business.

"Having jitters?"

"A little. It's weird being back. Feels like a dream. It's hard to explain."

"Yeah. Been there. After the band split, when I forfeited the idea of a solo career at first." He let out a breathy laugh. "You'll be all right. Ry can be pretty convincing when he puts his mind to something. Don't worry. Once you step on that stage again, it will feel like you never left," he said, clapping my shoulder. "The future is yours, Stevens. I've heard your new stuff. Some of it, at least. I'm telling you, *The Legend* is back."

"Thanks, man," I said as we both exited the room, and people rushed to pull me away.

Carter flashed me a knowing grin and shrugged before disappearing into the crowd.

Riley said a few words before I walked onstage, holding my guitar. The crowd cheered, and I blinked to keep my fizzy emotions at bay. I'd missed this so much. The music. The energy. The thrill. Every part of it.

The memory of Madison and me singing on a small stage a while back flashed before my eyes. I wished she could be here tonight to witness the fact that I was chasing my dreams once again.

For my own sake—and to keep my sanity intact—I blinked again and pushed the images of her away.

"Guys, thanks for coming tonight. It means a whole lot to me. For the longest time, I thought I'd never stand on a stage again. Thanks to Riley 'Stubborn' Burns—yeah, that should be his middle name—I'm back where I'm supposed to be. Thank you, man. For believing in me and saving me from myself. For being my friend when I got lost. And for kicking my ass when I was being ridiculous. Thanks for giving me the chance to show my kids to never settle for anything less than what they desire. I'll never be able to fully show you my appreciation, but I'll say this: You've made me believe in dreams again. You've made me believe in myself again." I scratched the skin between my eyebrows and cleared my throat as beads of emotion lodged in there. "*Echoes* is a collection of fourteen songs I wrote about the last two years of my life. All y'all, please be indulgent tonight. I'm kinda rusty," I added with a wink. Everyone laughed. And the tension in my upper back dissolved. I strapped the guitar around my neck and breathed out all my angst. "Here we go," I said, strumming the first chord of "Broken Heart."

Ecstasy coursed through my veins.

My heart bounced, lighter than it'd been in years.

Electricity tickled my spine.

I played for an hour, but it felt like ten minutes. I could've done this all night. Every night. Sing and play the guitar.

"Ohmygod, that was insane," Devon said when I met my friends near the crowded bar area some time later. "I can't believe I didn't remember how incredible you were onstage. Sam, you have a God-gifted talent. Yours was the first show I attended in my life years ago, and now I also got to witness your big return. Never hide your music for that long ever again."

I leaned forward to kiss her cheek. "Thanks, Dev. It means a lot to me."

I blew out a breath now that I was out of the spotlight

and slowly realizing what had happened tonight. The work from the last few months had paid off and the tour hadn't even started yet.

"How are you doing?" She squeezed my forearm, bringing my attention back to the present.

"Great. Much better."

"And with Maddie?" she asked with a quirked brow and a soft smile.

"What about Maddie?" I asked, my voice stilted and all my muscles strained.

"I just wanted to know if she's ready for the big tour."

I relaxed a little.

"Is there something I'm missing here?" she asked.

I tensed back. This wasn't the time or the place to lose it, so I forced a gulp of air in. "No. We're fine. She's fine. The girls love her. I'm glad she agreed to this," I said, gesturing to the space around with my hand.

"Great, then." She winked, and confusion stirred inside me.

What did she mean by that? A music producer neared us, and I pushed the awkwardness of our talk away. For now.

Aisha and Gavin congratulated me next. Then April. And a bunch of people from the industry I hadn't seen in ages.

I left around midnight, the longing to be on my own strong. Most of my friends were going to Carter's place in town for an after-launch party, but I had declined. I still required some time to adjust to this new pace of life. Baby steps here. After all, I had been hibernating for a long time.

I was confident I'd get there. Eventually.

All night, my thoughts had been drifting to my girls. I missed them tonight. I wished they were a little bit older and that I could have shared this moment, my big return to the music scene, with them. Then my thoughts traveled to Madison. Again. I was sure she would've liked it tonight too. Every time we met with my friends, she fit right in, and they all loved her. This was a more appropriate scene for a twenty-one-year-old than staying at home with young kids.

Since when did her presence in our lives become complicated instead of facilitating my existence? I was off my game on so many levels these days. I sighed and climbed into my SUV after saying my goodbyes.

And now, even the idea of going home felt conflicting. Could we really make it work—the two of us living under the same roof—or was I feeding myself lies to feel better about our situation? I would find out soon enough. I didn't have it in me to face the truth just yet, and still, I couldn't hide either. Was convincing her to move in really the right thing to do? My feelings and thoughts were tangled together, and nothing seemed straightforward anymore. I couldn't decide the right course of action. God, what had I gotten myself into? Had I complicated our situation even more by convincing her to come live with us?

20

MADISON

Sam had left earlier for his album launch party, and here I was, baking cookies with his children in his kitchen when all I yearned for was to be by his side. Like, *by his side*. I didn't care if he was rich and famous or poor and unknown, I loved how I felt beside him. As much as I told myself this was a dead end, I still couldn't put my feelings aside. Walk away from them. Forget about them.

The other night, he had sung us one of his old songs while we roasted s'mores over a campfire in the backyard, and the entire time, his gaze had rested on me as if he was delivering those lyrics straight to my soul—with a purpose.

Most days, the mutual decision not to be together still upset me. My head knew it was for the best, but it didn't change the fact I'd fallen in love with my boss.

Jacob was right. For a moment, I felt selfish for not choosing him. For not choosing the man who was allowed to love me back, without restraint, without holding anything back.

"You all right?" Mikaella asked.

The girls were perched on kitchen stools on either side

of me, perfecting their cookie decoration techniques with rainbow sprinkles and edible glitter.

"Yeah. Sure. Why?"

She snickered. "Because you're icing the countertop instead of the cookies."

"Oops. Got lost in my thoughts for a minute."

"You're funny," Justine said. "And your face is all red."

I blinked. *Yeah, having forbidden thoughts about your daddy can do that to me.*

Fantasizing about the girls' father while I was here caring for them was wrong.

Around seven-thirty, I put the girls to bed, and Justine fell into a deep slumber as I combed her hair with my fingers, humming one of Sam's songs.

"Do you know my mama?" Mikaella asked when I was about to tiptoe out of the room, thinking they were both deep asleep.

I froze in the doorway. The girl rarely opened up about her mother. With a step back, I returned to the bedroom and sat on the edge of her bed, taking her tiny hands between mine. "No, honey. I've never met her. I'm sure she's very beautiful."

She twisted her upper body to fish something out of her nightstand. A picture folded in two. She stared at it for a moment before handing it to me. It was a shot of her as a baby, nestled in her mother's arms, who smiled at the camera. I didn't have one of those. A wave of bittersweet regret swept through me. I owned no pictures of me as a baby. Or a toddler. Something my parents didn't think mattered when Emily and I were little. To them at least. But it did to me. I possessed too many from my older years, but none of the tiny version of me.

"I was right. She's pretty. You look very much like her."

Mikaella scooted closer and rested her head on my lap.

My fingers tangled in her curls. "It's okay to miss her, you know. My mama lives in another state, and I miss her too. I'm lucky I have my big sister around, though. She's my best friend."

"Did your mama leave you too?" she asked, her eyes clouded with an array of emotions.

A sensation I hadn't revisited in years paralyzed me. It froze my bones. Memories of my childhood resurfaced. For Mikaella's sake, I kept that part to myself. We were much more alike than I'd have ever thought. As if in some ways, these girls were living my own story, but with a different twist.

I decided to go with a distinct answer to the question she'd asked. "I moved away to attend college. I've always wanted to live in Nashville since I was little and we came to visit one day. I love everything about this city."

"My daddy used to sing in the bars downtown. He showed Justine and me around one time."

"I know. Your daddy is a great man. You're lucky to have him as a father."

"Maddie, do you think she misses us? My mama?"

My heart fragmented in my chest. I breathed out, searching for the right words. How many times did I ask myself the same question over the years? "I'm sure she does."

"So why did she leave us? Why didn't she take us with her?"

I wound my arms around her, wanting her to feel loved as she opened her wounded heart to me for the very first time. She rested her head against my chest, her tiny fingers entwined with mine.

"Sometimes people do things we don't always understand. I'm sure she had her reasons." *Or is it something we tell ourselves to lighten the pain? And to heal the scars of rejection?*

"Like she didn't love us?"

The vise around my heart clinched a bit tighter. With time, I'd come to the conclusion that people treating others badly was too often a reflection of their own fears. It wasn't about us, the ones left behind, even though we were the ones forgotten, ignored, or hurting.

"No. I bet there's a special place in her heart for you two." How many times had my parents repeated those same exact words to Emily and me growing up? Too many to count.

"And Daddy?"

I offered her a timid smile. "And your daddy too."

"Maddie? Do you think she'll come back to get us one day?"

"I don't know, honey. I hope she realizes how amazing, smart, and beautiful you and Justine are and comes visit… when she's ready."

"In my heart, I know she will. She has to. One day, she'll come back, and we'll be a family again. I'm sure Daddy misses her too."

The idea of Sam going back to the woman who had shattered his heart acted like a punch to the gut.

The clamp in my chest crushed me completely, and it pressed against my already bleeding heart, the wounds from my past hurting again.

"Can I tell you a secret?" she asked.

"Sure."

"I don't remember her a lot. That's why I keep this picture here. So I don't forget her face, because when I close my eyes, I can't see her face anymore. I tell my brain to make her appear, but it doesn't always listen to me. When I cry at night, it's because I'm not sure if I really miss her… And I wanna miss her. She's my mama. I should miss her. I should want her back and remember her face. Do you think there's something wrong with me?"

"Oh, Mika," I said, "She lives in your heart, and even if your brain can't recall her, your heart does. It forever will."

She tilted her head back to stare into my eyes. "But… Do you think it's the same for her? Like she can't remember us? Or what we look like? Do you think she has a picture of Justine and me by the side of her bed to make sure she remembers our faces?"

I dried the silent tears rolling down her cheeks, then the ones cascading down mine. "Mika, she's your mama. Even though she doesn't see you, she'll never forget you two. Of that, I'm certain. You'll always occupy a place in her heart too even if she's not around or able to visit."

"Do you miss your mama some days?"

"I do." I also wondered about the *what-ifs* sometimes, and would probably for the rest of my life. "It's okay to question things."

Mikaella and I hugged, the silence comfortably wrapping our confessions. We both injected love into each other. Our lives were much more similar than anyone could ever realize. We connected on a deeper level, and tonight had just proved it.

"It's late. You should get some sleep."

"Maddie?"

"Yes."

"Will you stay with me until I'm asleep?"

"Yes, Mika. I will."

I lay beside her.

"And Maddie? Don't leave us, okay? Stay. Forever. Please."

"I won't go away, honey. You two are stuck with me for a while." *Until the end of the tour at least,* I told myself. One day, I would have to go. I'd be the one leaving them behind. Tears coated the back of my eyes. I pressed them shut, keeping the painful sobs about to wreck my body locked inside. Someday I would abandon these little girls. And their father. Mikaella's breathing steadied, and her grip around my finger loosened. Before I burst into ugly cries, I hurried downstairs. In the garage, I rummaged through the boxes I'd stacked there earlier when I moved my stuff from my sister's house.

Before I could find what I was looking for, I dropped to the concrete floor and buried my face in my palms. My shoulders heaved as I wept. I should leave. I should leave now before I couldn't find the courage to leave at all before it was too late and we all ended up with broken hearts. I hiccupped. It was already too late. My heart belonged here, and I had no clue how to extirpate it from this house without ruining it for the rest of its existence.

Once I calmed down, I grabbed the novel written by one of my favorite authors and made my way back inside.

Making a glass of sweet tea, I sat down, desperate for any distraction.

At ten, my phone rang. I jumped at the noise and picked it up with trembling fingers when Jacob's face appeared on the screen.

A tightness squeezed my gut. My hands turned moist. I hadn't heard from him since the night I'd walked away from his car. Both times I had texted him, he never replied. I had stopped, choosing to respect his healing process.

I hesitated before answering, but my curiosity won the battle. Moving to my feet, I grabbed a blanket before curling back up in the comfortable chair in the den.

"Hey," I greeted.

"How are you?" The faint sound of his voice shook me up.

"Jake, I… We're… What's going on?"

My skin prickled. I missed him. The way he cared for me. His kisses. The glint in his eye when he was happy. Our discussions. The hours spent with him. Our friendship. Hearing his voice sent a rush of strange sensations through me, threatening to undo me even more than I already was.

"Maddie, come back. Come back to *meee*. I love you. I miss you so damn much. I tried. I really did. But I'm miserable when *youuu're* not in my life. Please—" His voice broke. Was he crying? "Come on. Say something. I should've never let *youuu* go."

"Are you drunk?"

"Fuck, Maddie. *Donnn't* start. I might have had one drink…or too many. Who cares? It's not…it's not the point."

"I was just asking. I miss you too," I said, fighting a new batch of tears.

"I'll come to get *youuu*. Tonight. Pack your stuff. We'll be happy together. I promise. *I'mmm* so in love with you that it hurts."

"Jake, you can't drive in this state."

Sobs broke free on the other end of the line. "Maddie, I'm a mess without *youuu*. What we had…what we had was real. Why did you choose him? Why did it have to be him? I love *youuu*, okay? From the moment I first saw you. It will always be you. *Cannn't* you see it? He'll never love you the way that I do."

"Jacob. Stop." I sucked in a hissing breath. "You were right. I love him. I'm not supposed to, and it's wrong, but I can't help it." I closed my eyes. Maybe this was the closure I required to move on. For some reason, that I refused to overanalyze, speaking the words out did not scare me as much as I thought it would. "You and I, we were good together. Our friendship was real. You made me happy. And I love you. You were my best friend. I probably will always feel something for you, but I'm not in love *with* you. That's the difference."

"How am I supposed to… How am I supposed to be okay without *youuu*?"

"You will be. We both will be. Give it more time."

He snorted. "Sorry I bothered you." He hesitated for a beat. "Are *youuu* with him right now?"

I shook my head even though he couldn't see me. "No. He has his album launch tonight. I'm watching the girls."

"Are you *fuckkking* him?"

I inhaled through my mouth. "We're not together. It's…it's complicated."

A thick silence enveloped us.

"Can I…huh…save your number?" Jacob asked in a croaky voice. "I'm not ready for a world *youuu're* not a part of."

"Yeah. I'll always be there for you. Perhaps time and space will make it easier. I miss you too. Every day. I'm sorry about everything."

Neither of us said anything.

"All I wish is for you to be *happpy*," he said after a long beat.

"I am. Or I will be… You take care of *you*, okay?"

He coughed. "Night, Maddie."

Messy emotions clogged my airways.

I pressed my palm against my chest.

Every fiber of my being hurt.

"Jacob, I want you to be happy too. Night," I said, hanging up.

Did everyone deliberately choose tonight to play with my heartstrings? First Mikaella, now him. My tears resumed, and I let them flow, hoping they would flush away my pain. I still loved him. Even though he wasn't the one. And I wasn't *in love* with him.

Mikaella's words replayed in my mind. *One day, she'll come back, and we'll be a family again. I'm sure Daddy misses her too.* Deep inside, maybe Sam shared his daughter's hopes and dreams. Maybe his nights too were haunted by the *what-ifs*, what could have been if his ex-wife hadn't walked away.

After my vision cleared and my emotions dissipated, I returned to the novel in my hand, the desire to evade my own life stronger than ever.

21

SAM

Lost in my thoughts, with the adrenaline still coursing through me, I pulled into my driveway and exhaled. It had yet to sink in that I had a new album out—that I was back onstage. I had actually done it. The oversized grin would stay anchored to my face for days, I could already tell. I had no idea how to erase it. Anyway, why would I want to get rid of it? Happiness suited me. I realized it when I'd looked in the mirror earlier.

I snickered to myself as I climbed out of my SUV.

The light in the hallway cast a golden glow in the mostly dark house as I entered from the garage door. There wasn't a sound inside. Something that almost never happened around here.

I tiptoed to the kitchen, then to the den, wondering if Madison was already asleep. I found her curled up in a pink fluffy blanket in her favorite chair, a novel in her hands and dark-framed glasses perched on her nose.

It was a new look on her, and she looked mesmerizing.

A lazy smile spread across my lips. I could watch her for hours, and the view would never get jaded.

As if she sensed she was being observed, she lifted her eyes from her book and met my gaze. "Oh, you're back. What time it is? I thought you'd be out all night."

I wrinkled my face. "Gotta re-learn how to do this. Late night. Crowded bars. How did it go?"

"Perfect. We had a great time. Sam, your daughters are wonderful. You're doing a fantastic job with them."

"Thanks," I said, pride slicing my words. Yeah, my kids were awesome. "Tired?"

Her eyes glistened in the dim light. "Not really. Mystery novels always keep me on edge. What about you?" Something sparkled in her eyes. Conflicted emotions passed through her sea-green irises.

The tip of my tongue burned to ask her if she was all right, but I had to continue minding my own business. Every time I got sucked into her life, I had a harder time walking away or staying indifferent afterward.

"No. I still have a performance high running through my bloodstream. I can't go to bed just yet. Champagne? Riley gifted me a bottle to celebrate the last time he came over, and tonight seems fitting. It's a big deal."

"I suppose it wouldn't be polite to refuse."

Madison jumped to her feet and neared me, discarding the blanket and her glasses. Dressed in an off-shoulder white cotton shirt and light-gray sweat shorts, she looked undeniably feminine, her presence exuding a newfound sensuousness. My eyes drank her in.

Tanned legs.

Perky breasts.

Long neck.

High cheekbones.

Slender chin.

Madison was not only amazing with children, but also had a warm laugh, a great personality, and was smart beyond words. On top of that, she was gorgeous. Many of the reasons why it was so hard for me to stay away. She possessed everything I was a sucker for. For a second, I remembered how it felt to kiss her. To touch her skin. To lose myself in the comfort she brought me. Even after all this time, the memory hadn't faded away. The replay of it had become my personal hell on Earth.

My eyes lingered on her chest for a split second, wondering if she was wearing a bra. I shook my head. *Repeat after me, Sam. The nanny is off-limits. The nanny is off-limits. The nanny is off-limits.*

She sat on a stool, and I snapped out of it.

With half a spin, I grabbed the bubbly alcohol from the fridge and two flutes. I popped the bottle open, and Madison clapped her hands before her.

"Ohmygod, you should be proud of yourself. I know the girls are. You've come a long way in the last few months. I've witnessed the change. You've earned the right to celebrate. Earlier, the girls and I baked congratulatory cookies. You'll get them in the morning."

I flashed her a smile as I poured two glasses and offered her one. We clinked our flutes.

"That's so nice of you, Maddie. I'm glad you're here. Really."

She mirrored my smile.

We sat beside each other at the kitchen island and drank in silence. I relaxed a tad, unbuttoning the top buttons of my shirt.

Madison cleared her throat. "Mika told me about her mama tonight. The parts she remembers at least."

I blinked, making sure I heard her right. My throat

closed. I took another sip, trying to drown the queasiness simmering inside me. "She did?"

My daughter had never talked to anyone about her mama leaving us. Up until now, she had never discussed Lisa with Madison, and barely with her therapist. She usually just made up stories in her mind that her mother was on a trip and would come back eventually.

Madison bowed her head. "She told me Lisa would be back one day. She really believes it. Since I didn't know all the details, I had no idea what to tell her."

"Lisa left when Mika was four." The words flew out of my mouth before I could lock them inside.

"You don't have to tell me," Madison said, interrupting me.

I chugged the rest of my champagne and poured myself another glass.

"Sorry I brought the topic up. I'm putting a dent in your celebration."

"It's fine. I have to tell you eventually anyway. Better now than later." I pushed my emotions away. The thought of Lisa, even after all this time, re-opened the wound I'd been trying to heal for a very long time. Not that I missed her. No, I'd realized much earlier that our relationship was a product of my imagination, and nothing about it had been real for a while. But the hurt she had caused our children, that was unforgivable. And that no matter however much I tried, I'd never be able to justify their mother's actions to them. "Mika saw her mama walking away that night. She was there when Lisa left without an explanation." My composure cracked. "She didn't even kiss her own kids goodbye. Mika stood there, and Lisa left without having second thoughts. My little girl should've never had to witness that. It's not fair to her." My voice broke on the last word.

Madison squeezed my hand, her warm touch sending waves of lust through me. Her skin on mine was enough to kill my demons and heal my insecurities. I was so damn screwed when it came to her. All the progress I had made in the last couple of weeks to grow a wall around my heart when she was involved was crumbling, brick by brick.

I craved her as much as I knew I had no right to yearn for her.

"Life, when I was super young, wasn't easy. For the first few years of my childhood, Emily and I…" Her lips quivered, and her eyes took on a glossy sheen, barely suppressing the tears building in them. Vulnerability swamped her face, and her gaze fleeted away before returning to mine. "We were…neglected."

I straightened, the confession surprising me. "What? What do you mean, *you were neglected?*"

Madison shook her head as if to erase a memory. "Let's just say our mother wasn't a fit parent. Neither was our father. And we suffered…a lot. Then it got better. It's all good now. We're super-knitted the four of us."

"I'm sorry. It's not what being a parent means. No kid should feel like a burden."

"There are a lot of unfit parents out there. Let's just say I have some experience with being left behind," she said. "I'm sorry Mika had to witness her mama quitting on you guys." She swallowed and averted her eyes.

I flipped my hand over and threaded our fingers, the simple gesture meaningful to me and meant to soothe the pain I saw in her gaze.

My breaths evened.

The storm in me lessened.

Knots around my heart slackened.

Madison freed her hand, and I felt the withdrawal of

her skin against mine. "Sorry. I didn't mean to overshare," she said, avoiding my eyes.

"It's okay. I'm aware you're just trying to be my friend." I swallowed the rock forming in my larynx. What was it about her touch that soothed me so much? Would any other woman's hands on me feel the same? I was so out of the game. "Did Justine give you any trouble at bedtime?" I asked, trying to put the weird moment behind us.

Madison's smile came back. It lightened her face, made her irises greener. "No. We listened to one of your new songs five times and sang along. Then she fell asleep within a minute. Mika and I talked for a bit, then she was out cold right after."

I tilted my head, meeting her eyes. "You sang one of my songs on your own?"

"Yeah. The girls and I often do that… Well, huh… sometimes…at bedtime."

A pink flush tinted her cheeks. I arched a brow, and Madison wrinkled her face.

I wished I could be the one erasing the crease etching her forehead with my lips. Instead, I ended up doing the same thing she had done a moment earlier—grabbing her hand in mine and giving it a squeeze. The warmth I'd felt rushed through me once again and twined around my vital organs. "Sorry," I said, pulling my hand back into my lap. "We should get some sleep. Devon and Riley will pick up the girls tomorrow morning, so you'll have the entire day to settle in."

"Okay. Great. Thanks." She busied herself, twirling the glass between her fingers.

I rose from my stool and turned around to look at the object of my forbidden attraction one last time. "Good night."

"Night, Sam."

An hour later, still wide awake, I lay in my bed, unable to chase sleep. My whole night replayed in my head. It had been surreal to be onstage again after a two-year hiatus. Every time the small crowd had cheered me on, it repaired the pieces of my heart and the shambles of my confidence back together.

I was born to be on a stage.

I was wrong when I'd pushed music away from my life for so long. Perhaps this break was all I needed to heal and get back to it with a stronger passion. My mind drifted to Madison sleeping downstairs. I shouldn't think about her. Not in that way. But somehow, I couldn't erase the images of her from my mind. The taste of her lips on mine. The feeling of the swell of her breasts under my palms. No matter how hard I tried to push it away, the memory always came back. In full force. Like a fucking boomerang.

Her legs, her ass in those shorts, her tits bouncing under her shirt when she laughed, her lips as she told me about her night. Having a woman too close to me when I'd been alone for two years was dangerous. Why didn't I figure this out sooner?

We already agreed we wouldn't go there. Why was my heart, and every cell of my body, not on board with the plan? Why was a piece of me still hoping things could be different between us?

The magnetism of Madison's smile always drew me in. Every time. From our first encounter. That night, in Riley's cousin's office, I hadn't been just mad because I thought she was too young to take care of my children. No, I'd freaked out at how much I was attracted to her. Big time. The moment I laid my eyes on her, it was like I was seeing a woman for the first time in forever. As if love had no bounds. No limits. As if she could shatter every wall I put around myself after Lisa quit on us only by smiling at me.

As if my entire body had recognized her as mine and she knew the secret combination to my happiness. The missing piece of the perfect puzzle that my heart was. The salvation of my soul.

After all this time, it still made no sense to me, but it did at the same time.

Madison was the means to my end, the treasure to my quest on this journey, and yet, I couldn't indulge in everything brewing between us. I was forced to keep her at a distance, to guard my heart against her. To push her away when all I yearned for was to love and protect her. With my whole being. Here, now, and for the rest of my life.

Or maybe my fantasies were doing all the talking.

My ignored-for-too-long hormones were acting out, demanding to be satiated.

As if he could read my mind, the lower part of me hardened in my boxer briefs.

Fucking traitor.

She's the nanny. She's the nanny. She's the nanny.

How many times would I have to repeat this until my penis got the message? Until he resigned and went back to its state of hibernation?

As the traitor he was, it pulsed and thickened instead of lying low.

With a sharp gulp of oxygen and promising myself to never go there ever again, I curled my fist around the hard part of me and pumped myself, enjoying the feeling and the anticipation of the high it would procure me.

The simple gesture didn't calm my screaming hormones. Instead, my dick pleaded for more, relishing the attention. Pushing all my troubling thoughts as far as possible, I worked myself faster. I couldn't stop. I would never be able to stop. I longed for more. A lot more. I wanted it all. The family, the love story, the career. The woman. Her lips, her ass, her tits, her mouth. Her heart.

Would she let me in if I knocked on her bedroom door? Inviting me in and pushing me onto her bed.

Would she kiss me back like she did that night? Like I was her only source of fresh air?

Would she take me into her mouth and make me forget that life before her had ever existed?

Would she let me taste her until all my senses were soothed? Devouring every morsel of her flesh until all that was left was the taste of her on my tongue?

Images of Madison in her red dress when I'd first met her swam in my head. Images of her curled in the chair tonight when I'd gotten home, sporting glasses, swirled around. The pink hue of her sinful lips. The crests of her hipbones. That little bracelet around her sexy ankle. When had I even become obsessed with ankles? The way she pushed her hair over her shoulder when we talked. Her enticing smile aimed at me—only me. The compassion in her eyes. The feel of her soft skin under the pads of my fingers when our hands joined. The way we connected, that appeared so easy, so natural. The sizzling chemistry we shared. Her ability to get me to open up about my past. And my fears. The glint in her gaze when she looked at me and thought I didn't notice. The smile she couldn't contain every time I showed joy and elation in her presence. Her laughter. Intoxicating and mesmerizing.

I stroked myself faster.

I felt the feather touch of her skin on mine again.

I heard the sound of her voice in my head. Her laughter. Her whispers.

No, I shouldn't think about her like that. She was living here. In my house. Taking care of my daughters.

She'd live on a tour bus with us. For months. I tried to put a stop to my imminent release but couldn't. The scent of her perfume filled my nostrils.

"Fuck," I grumbled.

I flipped the covers over, overheating in my bed.

The tip of my spine tingled.

This felt so good. Risky, but addictive.

My erection throbbed.

This was bad. But bad was hot. Bad was sexy. Bad was forbidden. Madison was forbidden. Our relationship was. Our friendship should be too. It put my sanity at risk.

Air rushed out of my mouth.

My toes curled.

I bit my biceps as I came, stronger than I had in a long time, swallowing the deep growls about to tumble out and fill the silence of the night.

My fantasies hadn't been this real in forever.

Breathless, I stayed there, my hand still around my grateful length, feeling the warmth of my release spilled across my stomach.

I inhaled. And exhaled. Trying to bring my pulse back to normal.

Impossible.

Madison occupied all my thoughts. Kissing her that night had been a rookie mistake. The flashbacks haunted my nights. Would I ever get relief from the ache?

My entire house smelled of her, her perfume permeating every corner. Right now, it was stronger. I could almost taste it. It enveloped me. It quieted the voices in my head.

I could feel her. In every room.

Her energy. Her cheerfulness.

I reclined, eyeing my mid-section covered with the aftermath of my orgasm.

A smile peeked out. Feeling alive had never felt so good. Almost too good. The real thing would ruin me. It would destroy me. In six months, I would be a free man.

Once I agreed with myself, and my traitorous dick, that this little mishap could never happen again, I cleaned myself up, rolled to my side, and closed my eyes, hoping sleep would come and turn my mind off for a few hours.

And deliver me from my own prison.

22

MADISON

While sipping champagne with Sam after his successful album launch, I was completely absorbed in the intimacy of the night—especially when he spoke about his ex-wife—and couldn't help reaching for his hand. How was I to know the sparks of our attraction would shoot right through me? A buzz arose where our skins touched, and my breath caught somewhere between my lungs and throat.

I hadn't planned on hinting at my childhood… It just came out in the heat of the moment. An invisible vise strangled my heart when I confided in him, and I prayed Sam wouldn't pry about my past any further. That's when *he* intertwined our fingers together, sending a bulk load of mixed signals to my body.

I pulled my hand away, unable to process how the minor gesture had such an impact on me.

After what felt like hours, Sam reached back for my hand. Of his own volition. Shooting addictive heat through my blood and more confusion into my mind, as if he couldn't *not* touch me. As if the small connection was meaningful to him too.

Right there, sitting beside him at his kitchen counter, I melted for him even more. And my stupid heart imagined scenarios that couldn't exist in real life, only in my mind.

Hours later, I was lying in bed, unable to rest my mind long enough for sleep to claim me. After an hour of tossing and turning, I got up and decided that sinking into a hot bath would help me relax. The scorching water did miracles to untie the knots in my back, but it did nothing to ease the one around my lower abdomen. Moving to my knees, I reached for the phone I'd placed on a folded towel on the floor and did something I'd sworn I'd never do. I put Sam's new album on, the one I bought the moment it got released. Setting my device back down, I immersed myself deeper in the water and closed my eyes, the sound of his voice erasing the remnant jitters waltzing within me.

How could a voice be powerful enough to appease my body, heart, and soul all at once? As if it connected us in a way no other words could express.

Rocked by every word he sang, I ventured one hand between my thighs, imagining those were his fingers. The ones I had never gotten to experience in the way I craved the most.

My breasts pushed out of the water, my back arching when I touched myself the way he would if he were here— with me. Not sleeping a flight of stairs above, unreachable.

I cursed at myself. Pressing on my clit with the heel of my hand, two of my fingers found their way to my throbbing center, and a crazed sensation zipped through me.

Sam's voice sang about love. And lust. My hand moved to the rhythm of his guitar, playing my own body like he played his instrument. With ease and abandon. With purpose and conviction.

My movements turned frantic. I increased the pace. My vision blurred. My breath spasmed with every exhale. My lower belly filled with pools of lava.

I pictured him in the country bar that night when he had sung on a stage for the first time in two years. Cooking on the grill, sending heated glances my way. His hands on mine when he had taught me to play the guitar. That irresistible grin that tugged at his lips whenever we argued, knowing he was right and I wasn't. The vulnerability he didn't hide when we had opened our hearts to each other, retelling the stories of our lives earlier tonight.

My head tilted back. My thighs spread apart giving me more space. I had no more conscious control over my body. It was only regulated by the pleasure building in its depths.

I strangled the edge of the tub with my free hand as the orgasm hit me. It rippled from so deep inside my core, that for an instant, I believed the ride would never come to a stop.

...Baby, I'm holding ya
Baby, you can count on me
I have your back, now and
forever...

The song ended, and tremors shook every fiber of my being as I landed back into my physical body.

I had touched myself dreaming about Sam in the past, but this, the images of him invading my head, the sound of his voice, the words he sang, it had never felt so real. He was with me, touching me, without even being here.

Breathless and relaxed, I toweled myself dry and ignored my reflection in the mirror. I wasn't ready to assess how pathetic I had become. Not even taking the time to put any clothes on, I slipped under the covers, chasing sleep.

A part of me still hoped Sam would walk in and relieve us both of the pent-up tension that was impossible to ignore whenever we stood close to each other, and touch me until his skin was branded on mine for the rest of my life.

Within a minute, I passed out, ready to continue the fantasy in my dreams, promising myself this would never happen again and knowing I would have a hard time resisting if temptation called my name again.

———

The next morning, I woke up early. I had my bedroom to set, some of my boxes to unpack, and my clothes to hang in the closet. I still wasn't sure why I had agreed to move into the Stevenses' home, other than it made sense to prepare the girls for their new adventure. No doubt, I would have to adjust too. When I'd lived on a yacht last year, it had taken my stomach two weeks to adjust to being on the ocean twenty-four-seven, the swell of the waves becoming more perceptible whenever I lay down at night.

The sound of little feet padding in my direction brought a curl to my lips. In no time, Mikaella and Justine stood in my doorway, wearing matching PJs and grins, fawning over every piece of clothing spread on my bed when I invited them in. None of the outfits were spectacular, but they ran their fingers over the material of the jeans, T-shirts, blouses, and summer dresses as if they were priceless pieces. Justine, spread on her front, took a whiff of one of my cardigans.

"Do you wear perfume?" Mikaella asked, now standing

next to me, her big sparkling eyes traveling over my few possessions.

"Sometimes."

"Can I try it?"

That was when I realized Mikaella never got the chance to do just that, wear her mother's perfume. Or try her heels and jewelry. Tiny needles pierced my heart as I watched her.

I neared her and tucked her hair behind her ear. "Absolutely. Let me find it first. I think it might be—"

Sam's voice reached us. "Girls, ready for breakfast?"

Justine jumped to her feet. "Maddie, come, come," she singsonged. She curled her fingers around my digit and pulled me after her, the sound of her laughter contagious.

I choked on a gulp of air when we stepped into the kitchen and I came face to face with Sam.

"Good morning," he whispered, his eyes locked on mine, an unreadable expression crossing his features.

"Morning." I coughed out the single word.

"Sleep well?" he asked with one tipped brow, a hint of a smile curving his lips.

"Mm-hmm."

Could he guess, just by staring at me, I had given myself an orgasm while my mind overflowed with images of him last night? While he sang to me? Oh. My. God. Was my face turning crimson? Were my eyes betraying me?

I swallowed, pretending to be immersed in something Mikaella said as I replied, "You?"

His throat worked, and he said nothing for a beat. "Yep." He pinched his brows together, shook his head, his smile still anchored to his mouth, and turned around, humming. A new buoyancy, I'd never noticed before, trailed behind him.

Something had happened. Sam Stevens wasn't the chirpiest guy on the planet. And now he looked rejuvenated. And in the best of moods I'd ever seen him.

I cleared my throat, wiped my moist palms on my jeans skirt, took a cleansing breath in, and offered, "Want me to make my special chocolate and strawberry waffle recipe?"

"Yes," the girls screamed at the same time.

Sam and I burst into a chuckle, and it filled the room with a lightness I couldn't resist.

Just like that, I became a full-time presence in their household, and for some reason, it felt strangely comfortable as if we'd all been living together forever.

23

SAM

Breakfast, the first one we shared with Madison, turned out to be much more of an enlivened experience than usual. The girls, in a cheery mood, couldn't stop chatting and laughing. At their request, as if she was a new shiny toy they had to carry around everywhere, Madison helped them get dressed before Riley and Devon picked them up and drove them to the zoo. I loved the idea of giving Madison some much-needed time and space to unpack and make herself at home, without my little chatterboxes asking hundreds of questions and creating additional cacophony to the task. We had almost two months left before leaving for the tour. The four of us living under the same roof was the final test to prove to me that we could do this—all of us, together.

"I'll be in my office if you need help with anything," I told Madison after I carried the rest of her boxes from the garage to her bedroom.

"Thanks. I should be fine." She offered me a warm smile. When she lifted her arms to pull her hair into a high ponytail, her shirt lifted from the front, giving me a peek of her toned midriff.

I swallowed hard and forced myself to look away.

After last night, I wasn't allowed to look at her in any way other than my daughters' nanny or the hired help. My dick and I had reached an agreement, and I was adamant about it, even though my body had hummed with bliss after I relieved some of the tension that had been crippling it. Now I felt like a new man. One who'd broken through some of the chains holding him in place.

I retreated to my office slash music studio before Madison could notice how I ogled her, and locked myself for hours, not risking a foot out, even to get lunch. Sure, last night had helped to get rid of the edginess, but I was a weak bastard when it came down to Madison Prescott. Truth be told, now that no children could walk in and break whatever moment we shared, I feared I couldn't be trusted to contain myself. Or that my willpower would snap if presented with an opportunity to kiss her sweet mouth without any lingering distractions.

When the doorbell rang around five, I put my guitar on its stand and rubbed my fists over my eyes, wiping out the exhaustion that weighed there. The front door opened before I had time to get to it. Two small tornados rushed in with blue cotton candy and sugary smiles.

"Daddy, I saw a monkey. And a giraffe. And a *pota-lalamus*. Uncle Riley told me we could go back again another time. With you and Maddie. Where's Maddie? Where's Maddie? Where's Maddie?" Justine hopped all around me, unable to stay put for more than a few seconds, her eyes round and glistening and her pigtails bouncing on either side of her head.

I looked behind me. No trace of Madison. I would've

thought she would come running at the commotion. She never resisted the lure of my daughters' innate enthusiasm.

I pinched my brows and shrugged. "In her room… huh…I think. Don't go in. Knock and wait—" My baby girl disappeared before I could finish giving her instructions.

Justine wasn't very good with personal boundaries. I'd have to tell Madison to lock her bedroom door when she didn't wish to be disturbed. Or maybe I could buy her a doorknob sign that said *Unavailable* or something funny to keep the girls out.

Mikaella inched closer. I lifted her up and dropped a kiss on the top of her head. "How is it going, sweet pea? Had a great day?"

My daughter sighed. "Yeah. I wanted to stay till late, but Uncle Riley said it was time to go, and if I stayed behind, I'd have to clean the elephants' cage." She scrunched up her adorable face. "Ugh, it's disgusting. Not cleaning elephant poop. It's huge and smelly. Yucky. Big no."

Riley, Devon, and I all started laughing when teen-Mikaella made a face that spelled *It's not funny Daddy*.

I swallowed my chuckle. "Sweet pea, you're right. I'm glad you decided to come home." I ruffled her hair, and she disappeared upstairs after saying goodbye to my friends.

"How did it g—?"

"Daddy. Come. Quick. Maddie is sick," Justine screamed from the other side of the house where the guest bedroom was.

My eyes traveled between Riley and Devon, and I lifted a finger. "Gimme a sec." I followed the sound of my daughter's voice that pleaded, "Hurry, Daddy."

"What's wrong, baby girl? I—" My words died on the tip of my tongue when I entered the room.

Madison lay on the tiled floor in the adjoining bathroom, her face ghostly white and her lips trembling.

I moved closer and crouched down beside her, combing the loose tendrils of her hair away from her face. "Hey, talk to me. What's going on?"

"I'm…I'm sick. I've been…I've been throwing up for the last hour." Her eyes were glossy and her hands shaky.

I felt her forehead with the back of my palm. "You're burning up. Why didn't you tell me?"

"You…you were busy. I-I didn't want to bother you. I thought it might just be indigestion."

"Want me to drive you to the clinic?"

She shook her head, and it took everything I had not to pull her into my arms and kiss her fever away. "Nah. It's probably a stomach bug…or…or the flu. I'll rest tonight. I-I should be fine by the morning."

"Your skin is gray," Justine said, framing her face with her little hands.

"She's right. You don't look so fine to me. Wait here. I'll bring you something for the fever."

Devon was standing outside the bedroom after I gave Madison the medicine. "Listen, Sam. Riley and I talked. We don't want the girls to catch something. If it's okay with you, we'll take them home with us tonight."

I sighed and nodded. Even if I knew she was right, I couldn't help my stomach from free-falling at the thought. My girls had only ever had a handful of sleepovers in their lives, and only with their grandparents. It wasn't exactly how I'd pictured their first real one to be. But honestly, what choice did I have? "You sure?"

"Affirmative."

I huffed. "Okay. Let me pack their stuff."

"I'll help you. Come on, sweetie," Devon said to Justine, tugging at her hand. "Let Maddie rest. Your daddy will take good care of her. Now we should get ready because Mika and you are having a sleepover at our place tonight. Isn't it exciting? I bet Hope will be ecstatic to have friends over."

Justine bounced on her feet, her smile growing larger by the second. She singsonged, *"Sleeporver. Sleeporver. Sleeporver."*

I shook my head with a grin. That girl.

I buckled Justine in her car seat, kissed both my daughters, and made them promise to be on their best behavior.

Mikaella stared at me, a wrinkle forming across her forehead. The tiny-teenager version of her had made a comeback. She waggled a finger before me. "You better not catch the flu, Daddy. It's gross when people vomit. Dis-gus-ting. Sabrina threw up in art class once, and it stank *soooo* bad."

I raised my hands. "Pinky swear. I'll do my best, sweet pea."

With my heart leaping in my throat at the idea my kids were experiencing a new milestone without me, I waved at the car pulling out of the driveway. My lips tilted up at the sight of Riley in daddy mode, driving Devon's SUV instead of his usual red sports car. Yeah, the family-man vibe kinda suited him. Once inside, I rushed to check on Madison.

Heaves rocked her body. She flushed the toilet, looking even paler than before. "My-my stomach didn't appreciate the medicine." A timid smile graced her lips, her eyes shadowed by dark circles. She rubbed her upper arms, chills shaking her body.

"Tell me what to do. I'd heat some soup, but I'm not sure you'll be able to keep it in."

Her teeth chattered.

"How about a blanket?"

She nodded. "Please. I'm *sooo* cold."

I returned to the room minutes later with a pile of blankets in my arms, helped her to bed, and wrapped one around her shoulders. "Better?"

"I'm sorry, Sam. I'm supposed to care for Justine and Mika, not the other way around."

"Get some rest and stop worrying. The girls left with Ry. Sleep. I'll check on you later." I half-closed her door so I could hear her if she needed me.

How could I have been so stupid, locking myself in my studio all day, to have missed Madison being sick? "See what you did?" I hissed at my dick. "All your fault. You can't behave, and now we're hiding from temptation. Nice job."

I fixed dinner, and for the first time in forever had to eat by myself. No sound filled the lonely silence. I was so used to living in squabbles and giggles that I had forgotten what quiet sounded like.

For a fleeting moment, I savored the calm. I knew the girls were safe, yet my insides still coiled at the thought of them being away.

Restless, I checked on Madison for the millionth time. The sight of her when I cracked open the door broke my heart. She was awake now, curled up on herself, knees drawn to her chest, shivering and her teeth chattering.

"Fuck. That bad, huh?"

She lifted her eyes, and her gaze pierced mine.

"Wanna take a bath? I know that's what I do when I'm not feeling well," I suggested, hands shoved into my pockets, not sure how to approach the situation…or her.

"Yes," she murmured. "Please. Can you—?"

I nodded. "Gimme a few minutes. I'll come get you when it's ready."

Hiding in the en-suite bathroom, I exhaled the tension swirling in me. I honestly had no clue what I was doing, and deep down I knew I wasn't the right person to help Madison. But who else would care for her when it was just the two of us left here?

Why didn't I insist Devon stay and help her out? That would have made much more sense. I sighed because I was an idiot, but not *that* much of an idiot. I would never risk Devon getting sick on my behalf just because I was too stubborn to keep my hormones in check.

I shook my head, chasing the dreadful thoughts away, and turned on the faucet. Once the bathtub was full and the water was slightly more than lukewarm, I went to get Madison, who hadn't moved from her position on the bed. "Still up for that bath?"

She nodded.

With careful steps, I helped her to the other room. I placed a clean towel by the bathtub. "You got everything you need?" I asked.

She whispered a low "Yes".

"Think you can manage on your own or do you need me to…you know…help you?" The words exited my mouth before I could analyze them, and I wanted to slap myself for being so absurd.

And now I was volunteering to help undress my children's nanny. Absolutely fucking great.

"I-I can manage. Thanks…for…huh…offering."

I rubbed my nape, keeping my focus on the water. "I'll be in the other room. Just call me if you want anything… or whatever… I'll be over there if you… Anyway, I'll let you do your thing now," I said, pointing behind me with my thumb. *Way to go, Sam. Real, smooth.*

After twenty minutes, I heard the distinctive sound of bathwater being drained and moved to my feet. Seconds later, Madison reappeared wearing only a purple terry cloth robe she adjusted at the waist.

"How are you feeling?" I asked, taking tentative steps in her direction.

"A bit better. But I'm still cold." As if summoned, chills traversed her, and she wrapped her arms around herself.

"I called our family doctor while you were in the tub. There's a stomach bug going around town. He said to call him back if the fever doesn't break within two days."

Madison returned to her previous position under the covers, and I tucked two more blankets around her.

"Want water?"

She nodded.

I left the room and came back seconds later with a full glass. She took small sips before discarding it on the bedside table.

Her teeth chattered.

I sat on the edge of her bed, and the voices in my head hollered that I'd regret what I was about to do. But damn it. Madison looked like shit, and if I could do anything to make her feel better, I wouldn't miss my chance. Ignoring the way my heart banged against my ribs, I raked my fingers through my hair and spoke the thing I feared I'd regret the moment the words escaped my mouth, "Scoot over. I'll warm you up." She shifted to her right, and I stretched my legs over the pile of covers. With one arm around her shoulders, I pulled her against me. My hand found her forehead. Warm as a furnace against me, her fever hadn't broken. "I got you," I whispered against her hair, my lips dying to kiss her right there.

Madison nestled in the crook of my arm, her head

resting against my chest, and her body grew heavier as she fell asleep.

A long while later, her chills abated, and her breathing evened out.

Half-seated, a pillow behind my back, I refused to move, not willing to wake her up.

The scent of her perfume permeated my nostrils. Citrus and Madison.

My eyelids fluttered, and my head hung lower. Before I realized it, I dozed off too.

"No, Mama, no."

Gut-wrenching sobs and a death grip on my upper arm jolted me awake. In the darkness, I had a hard time recalling where I was or if it had all been a dream or reality.

"No, please. No. Stop. It hurts."

The grip on my arm tightened, fingernails digging into my skin through my shirt.

Madison.

I cocked my head to watch her, the light from the hallway casting a soft glow on her tear-drenched face. With my thumb, I brushed away the wetness on her cheeks, noting that her fever had dropped a little. "Hey, it's okay. It's just a bad dream. You're safe. Nothing will happen to you."

Her glossy eyes captured mine, and for a second, I got lost in them. Her lips shuddered, and she blinked as if to reset her brain. "Thanks," she whispered, her voice rough.

"Still freezing?" I asked.

"*Yesss,*" she said, her voice carrying the remnants of fear.

"Want me to stay?"

"Please."

I reached for her hand, and she relaxed in my

embrace. With a quiet peace stirring in my core, we both drifted back to sleep.

The sound of my phone vibrating on the nightstand pulled me out of my slumber. It took me a moment to come back to a conscious state.

Still asleep beside me, Madison's head was pressed against my chest. I brushed my fingers across her forehead and realized her fever had dropped

I stretched my arm to grab my device and look at the time. *Nine o'clock.* My limbs felt so heavy that I would have sworn it was much later. Many notifications filled the screen. The first one was a text from Riley, sent over three hours ago. I clicked it open.

RILEY

We're fine.

Along was a picture showing him, Devon, and the girls at a pizza place, all grinning.

The latest one was of my girls deep asleep in his guest bedroom, Hope, their dog, squeezed between them.

RILEY

See? More than fine.

I smiled at this sight and typed back.

ME

Enjoy. They turn into monsters on day three.

RILEY

No, they're adorable.

ME

I know. Kiss them goodnight for me.

RILEY

Will do. I'll call you in the morning.

I placed my phone beside me and tilted my head back. Madison muttered something in her sleep, and I froze to avoid disturbing her rest. I held my breath, waiting awhile, wondering if the nightmares would make a comeback.

They didn't. She mumbled some more until she fell back into deep sleep.

Her company filled a void I never knew existed in my heart.

I missed that. Having a woman to cuddle. To care for. To love. Sure, I had my daughters to keep me fully busy and fill my heart with butterflies and magic, but I missed having a woman in my arms. In her sleep, Madison circled my waist with one arm like she could read my inner thoughts, and I was a goner.

A part of me yearned to stand and run away, to leave the room, but I couldn't because the rest of me longed for her comfort as much as she required mine.

Hating myself for not being strong enough to do the right thing, I removed the pillow behind my back and lowered myself onto the bed, and without giving my brain room to think, I closed my eyes and drifted back to sleep.

———

The early morning sun's rays filtered through the drapes and blinded me as I forced my eyes open. I fastened my arm around the woman splayed over me. Until my brain caught up and I remembered it wasn't just any woman, but Madison, my children's twenty-one-year-old nanny, wearing only a bathrobe.

Fuck.

The realization I'd slept in her bed, our bodies entangled, chased the last traces of sleep from me. I could feel the softness and warmth of her legs and stomach against my skin. What did I do? How could I have been so careless? This was a ginormous mistake. A big setback. Putting the tour at risk. If it went to hell, I'd never forgive myself. And Riley would kill me. My kids would never forgive me if Madison decided to leave us. They loved her. They needed her. I depended on her...and needed her too. Much more than she'd ever know.

Why was I acting like a hormonal teenager instead of a grown-up man around this woman?

Just as traitorous as usual, my morning wood stretched tall and proud, and her hand moved too close for comfort. My breath wheezed when I tried to squirm out of her hold. I failed. Her eyes sprang open, and I flinched internally at my predicament. I cursed all the saints I could remember the names of in my head.

Just when everything in my life almost made sense again, I screwed up the fragile balance by sleeping with the nanny. Well, not sleeping with her, per se, but beside her. As if that changed anything. We slept in the same fucking bed. In each other's embrace.

"Hey," I said, to break the awkward silence, running a hand over my face, unable to look at her just yet. "Listen... Huh... I'm sorry. I tried to warm you up, and I kinda fell asleep. This wasn't planned. Won't happen again." My body vibrated at the excitement of her not being in a hurry to escape my arms and the situation I'd put us in. It was like she belonged there.

The mishap woke up a thirst inside me.

For the first time since Lisa had left, I wondered when I'd let myself find love again. One day. Maybe when the girls would be old enough to understand and ready to welcome another woman into their lives.

Trying to conceal my more-than-obvious erection, I pulled the blanket over my lower body.

Madison detached from me and sat beside me, her hair disheveled, and her lips a dark shade of pink. The sight reminded me of that morning after we'd kissed, a lifetime ago.

I focused on her face. Sporting flushed cheeks and shiny eyes, I wondered if she was still feverish. "How are you this morning?" Small talk was something I didn't excel in. We had broken so many of our own rules yesterday. So many boundaries. So many everything. I had cared for Madison with the goodness of my heart, without any ulterior motives, but right now, in the light of a new day, our night together seemed to mean an awful lot more. No matter how hard we tried to stay apart, we always ended up entwined in each other. I'd be lying if I said waking up with her in my arms didn't feel incredible, and I hadn't slept this soundly in years.

"Better. I think." She nibbled on her lower lip, leaving tiny indentations I wished I could erase with a kiss.

"Good."

I stirred to rise when her hand reached for mine. "Thanks. You know…for making sure I didn't like…you know…be alone." She paused, her gaze trained on our joined hands. "And for warming me up."

I nodded. "I couldn't let you freeze to death. Ice blue isn't your color," I said in a teasing voice. I cocked my head to the side and ordered my entire body to stay put. "Now that you're doing better, I…I should go."

She nodded her agreement while fastening the tie of her robe around her waist and resting against the headboard.

"Listen, I know you told me once to never try to fix you or anything, and it's not what I did…or what I'm doing here. You were having nightmares last night, and they sounded kinda scary. I just… It would make me feel better if I knew they aren't memories. The other night, you mentioned being neglected as a child. Call it father's instinct...but I don't know… It sounded serious. Like you feared something—or someone."

Great, now I was rambling, trying not to sound like a patronizing idiot.

Madison cleared her throat. "I did? Oh, I'm so sorry. This is embarrassing… It used to be a daily occurrence when I was a kid. I haven't had those in years."

"Are you okay?"

She offered me a tiny curl of her lips. "Yeah, no need to worry. I'm fine. I've never been beaten up or anything. It's all in the past… Nothing to worry about."

"You'd tell me if it weren't the case?"

"Yes."

Without another word or look in her direction, I left her in the middle of the bed, closing the door behind me. Scratching my temple and pondering her words, I hurried to my bedroom upstairs.

24

MADISON

When I woke up, the scent of fever clung to me. My eyelids weighed tons, and I couldn't seem to open them. My body felt sluggish, my limbs unable to follow commands. Disjointed memories of the previous day overtook my mind. I recalled being sick and Justine screaming for Sam. And then, blackout. The fever had messed with my brain. I remembered feeling cold—teeth-chattering cold. I forced my mind to work so I could figure out if I had made a fool of myself. Or thrown up somewhere I shouldn't have. How did I even make it to my bed? I couldn't even twitch a muscle when I had laid down on the bathroom floor.

I swept my tongue across my upper teeth in a faint attempt to dissipate the bitter taste in my mouth.

A slight movement on my left startled me.

Oh no, had one of the girls joined me in bed in the middle of the night?

If so, we'd have to discuss it. Sam would never agree to this, and I wouldn't too. Talk about blurred lines. Also, the idea of them walking down the stairs in the dark was enough to send a wave of panic through me.

My heart banged in my chest at the thought of it.

The deep breaths couldn't belong to Mikaella or Justine.

Someone—a male someone—was lying beside me. Oh God… What did I do last night? Worse, I had no recollection of any of it.

My body recognized him before my mind had time to catch up.

His scent, a musky mix of woodsy aftershave and something exclusively him, filled my nose, and the realization hit me. I wasn't entangled with just anyone. I was entwined with Sam Stevens. My boss. And the man I was madly in love with, however much I tried to convince myself otherwise.

A nightmare. It all boiled down to this.

I messed up. *We* messed up. Something must have happened, because why else would we be sharing a bed?

I raked my brain, but I could only recall him talking about blankets. What did I miss? I sucked in a hefty dose of oxygen. *Think, Maddie.*

There must have been a logical explanation for this… huh…situation, for lack of a better word. No matter what, we were sharing a bed. A bed. My arm was around him, my legs tangled with his.

My breath hitched on its way out. Tremors rose in the depths of me—not the feverish kind this time.

My mouth filled with acid. Would I be sick again?

Could this be a hallucination? Perhaps my fever hadn't broken, and my brain was making up stories based on my fantasies. Perhaps I was still deep asleep and dreaming.

I inhaled, wishing I could wake up alone in my own

bed, and that all of this was just a figment of my imagination.

With renewed energy and motivation to learn the truth, I forced my eyes open, one at a time. Sam's gaze was locked on mine. My airways constricted and my chest tightened. None of it was a dream.

"Hey," he said, a tiny arc gracing his lips that depicted more anxiety than genuine happiness. His voice, sexy and rough from sleep, warmed my insides.

Feeling self-conscious, I secured the bathrobe tie around my waist. When did I even change into this? My brain was failing me. I couldn't seem to recall anything. Sam's gaze followed the movement of my fingers, and I wrapped the bedspread around me as he rambled.

After some forced small talk on his part, Sam's expression shifted from caring to worried. His next words shook me to my core. "Listen, I know you told me once to never try to fix you or anything, and it's not what I did…or what I'm doing here." He kept talking, but only every other word registered.

I wanted to disappear—this was so humiliating.

I hadn't had nightmares about my early childhood in years. These days, they manifested often. My boss had witnessed one of my *middle of the night* breakdowns. Was fever to blame, or were there similarities between my early years and his kids' reality? After all, he had confided in me about Justine's recurring nightmares.

When Sam exited my bedroom, after I reassured him I was doing just fine and he didn't have to make a big deal about my bad dreams, I resumed my breathing.

Once in the en-suite bathroom, alone, with my back leaning against the closed door, I exhaled, releasing all the agitation that churned within me.

Unwelcome heat crept along my cheeks. How could I

ever face my boss again after waking up in his arms, wearing nothing but a half-open robe? We'd agreed to stay apart. And now… Now, we'd woken up tangled up. In bed.

I undressed, praying the hot shower would quiet my racing thoughts before they erupted into a full-blown panic attack. The hot water soothed some of my frayed nerves and washed away most of the leftover traces of last night's fever.

Tiptoeing out of my room, dressed casually in a pair of lounge pants and a gray long-sleeved shirt, I approached the kitchen. Unsure about what to say, I rolled my bottom lip between my teeth, flicking my still-damp hair over my shoulder, trying to look unaffected. Sam's gaze found mine the instant I stepped into his peripheral vision. The intensity in his eyes pinned me to the spot, stealing the air from my lungs and the thoughts from my brain.

The words died on my tongue. Nerves gripped me. My heart shot up into my throat, and another wave of heat rolled over me. Was the fever coming back?

Even without being able to name it, I could tell something had shifted between Sam and me after waking up in his arms earlier.

The way our bodies fit together.

The zing of electricity that had sparked from him to me.

His tousled bed hair, lending him a boyish charm.

And his eyes—now I was certain—could read me, if I let him in.

"Feeling better? For real?" Sam asked as I poured myself a tall glass of orange juice and took a seat at the island.

"I think so."

"Hungry?"

"Famished. Something smells divine."

"Good. 'Cause I've made scrambled eggs. Want some?"

I nodded.

"Here," he said, pushing a plate in front of me. "I'm heading out to pick up the girls. Need anything before I go?"

I swallowed a mouthful of food. "No. All good."

"We are spending the day running errands. Just rest, okay?"

"You sure? I can take care of them if you have work to do. I'm not at the top of my game, but I'm feeling much better than I did yesterday, and I can deal with them."

"Nah. Take it easy."

I brought a forkful of eggs to my mouth but didn't take a bite. "About last night…huh…thank you. For everything." I paused and cringed. "Are we fine?"

Sam swiveled to face me. "I am if you are. It was a lack of judgment on my part. I'm sorry I put you in an embarrassing situation. Don't want you to think I-I took advantage. I shouldn't have—"

"You were there for me."

"Yeah…then… Okay. Yes. We're good."

Sam took off, leaving me all alone with my chaotic thoughts.

"What's wrong with you?" I chastised myself. "No matter how amazing the chemistry is between you two. Get. A. Grip. On. Yourself. Girl."

Caring and longing for someone were two very different things, and right now, thanks to yesterday's fever, I was mixing them both.

"Get your groove back on. You have a job to do." After I cleaned the kitchen, I wrapped myself in the pink fluffy blanket in the den and lay down on the couch, too weak to do anything but rest, as Sam had suggested.

I exhaled my annoyance.

Every time I tried to stay away from him and felt I was making progress, some incident pulled me right back to square one.

I breathed out the last remnants of mortification writhing in my lungs.

Adjusting myself, I sealed my eyelids and abandoned myself to sleep, praying it would make me forget all the awkwardness of the morning.

I sighed. All better now.

25

SAM

In a rush to leave and before the weirdness between Madison and me returned, I exited the kitchen, climbing into my SUV minutes later. Turning the key in the ignition, I savored the fleeting sense of freedom. If last night had taught me one thing, it was that this woman had the power to ruin me if I didn't keep myself in check.

Alone in my car on my way to pick up the girls, I got lost in my own mind. Images I tried to keep at bay flashed in rapid succession, my brain refusing to grant me the reprieve I begged for. Madison, with her hair loose on her back, still damp from her shower, and her cheeks now a healthier shade of pink. When she'd entered the kitchen earlier, while I was prepping breakfast. Her sea-green irises that had drawn me in, the moment she had neared me.

How we had stared at each other for a fat minute, neither of us strong enough to escape the magnetism we always fell under.

My heart thundered in my chest at the memory, the sight alone strong enough to unleash all the locked-up lust simmering inside me.

I coughed to loosen my throat and rolled my neck, my blood flowing to my groin instead of my brain.

"Daddy," Justine screamed, tackling my legs before I could lift her up as she opened the door at Riley's, a craftsman house he bought a few years back. My friend slash manager had the means to live in the most upper-class neighborhoods of Nashville, but after growing up in one of those mansions, he said he preferred living a much simpler life. Again, it suited him.

Hope came running too, and I squatted to pet her head while she licked my bare knee just beneath the hem of my khaki shorts.

Wrapping my baby in my arms, I kissed her cheek. "How was the sleepover? Did you girls have fun? Have you been nice?"

"Daddy, we're always nice." She giggled when I tickled her belly after I stood back up and kicked the door shut.

"Stop worrying, Stevens," Riley chimed in, handing me a mug of hot caffeine. "Hungry? We baked croissants."

"No. Just had breakfast before coming over." I entered the kitchen. "Hey, sweet pea," I said, nearing Mikaella and ruffling her hair.

"Daddy. I'm not ready to go. I wanna stay here with Devon. We have plans. Girls' plans."

I scratched my nape. "I understand, but I have a whole day planned for us too."

"Is Maddie coming?"

"Nah. She's gonna rest a little longer. She's already doing better, though."

Mikaella pouted and pressed her fists to her hips. "I like it most when Maddie is there with us."

Me too, Mika.

I pinched the bridge of my nose. The plan was to stay away from Madison all day—not to invite her to spend her day off with us. "How do you feel about the children's museum?"

Her eyes lit up. "For real?"

"Yes. But if you wanna go, you better finish your breakfast and get ready."

Riley snickered beside me as she attacked her food.

Devon joined us, and after kissing me on the cheek, she sat next to my daughter.

My friend motioned for me to follow him and led the way to his home office. "You good?" he asked.

"Yeah. Why?"

"Just wanted to check on you and make sure you were holding on. It's been an intense couple of months, and I don't want you to have a panic attack because you feel overwhelmed."

"Everything's great. I swear."

He frowned and studied me, searching my face for the answer to a silent question. "How is it going with Madison? Do you think it'll work out on the road for that long? I sensed some tension between the two of you the other day."

The tension wasn't between us. It was between my legs. All my egoistical dick's fault.

I blew out my discomfort. "All good. No tension. The girls love her. She's amazing with them, and I trust her, so that's all I'm asking for."

My friend clapped my shoulder and grinned. "Enjoy your free time then because your life is about to get a bit wild again." His cheerfulness vanished. "Stevens, I'm glad we're doing this together. I really am."

"Yeah, me too. Thanks for getting me out of my sad existence. I owe you one."

For the rest of the day, the girls and I visited the children's museum. It was enough distraction to keep my thoughts in line for a few hours.

On our way back to our car, both my daughters' hands rested in mine while Mikaella kicked pebbles and dust on my right, and Justine sang a cartoon theme song on my left.

The late afternoon sun shone through the buildings, warming my face. Birds chirped in the trees lining the sidewalk. My daughters had lasting smiles on their faces.

Life was great, and about to get even better.

We spoke about everything and anything when Justine asked, "Do you think Maddie is missing us?"

My throat worked at the mention of my forbidden crush. My daughter stopped in her tracks, trying to catch my gaze, her eyes shining with expectation.

"Yeah, I'm sure she is."

"Cool," she said, resuming her walk. As if her question hadn't just fucked with my mind and willpower to forget about the nanny for the time being. She continued, her happy demeanor never faltering. "Because I miss her too. I really don't like it when Mama's sick. It makes me sad."

My heart flipped in my chest. Beads of sweat popped on my nape. My mouth went dry, and black dots danced in front of my eyes.

Before I could object or come up with a reply, Mikaella jumped in. "Maddie is not your mama, loser. She's your nanny. You already have a mama. And you can't have two. It's the rule."

I let go of Mikaella's hand to drag a palm over my face before turning toward her once I regained some of my composure back. "Mika, you can't talk to your sister like that. It's not nice. What did I already tell you about using grown-up language?"

Justine's eyes filled with tears.

My eldest daughter's face was flushed with indignation. "I'm right. Maddie isn't her mama."

Awesome. Perfectly awesome.

"No. You liar. I don't have a mama, and I want one. And I choose Maddie to be *my* mama. No one else. She's nice. And kisses my booboos. And reads to me at night. And she thinks I'm a princess. Maddie is *my* mama." Sobs rocked my baby's body, and she hid her teary face against my leg.

I crouched down to draw her to my heart. The one about to escape my chest and leave me to deal with this mess all by myself.

Words jammed in my throat, while Mikaella continued her rant. "Your mama's name is Lisa. Not Maddie. You're so dumb, Justine. Stop being a baby. You cannot have two mommies. Just one. One. And you're not allowed to choose."

Her words shook me to my core, and I came back to my senses, holding my hands up to put a stop to the argument. "Girls, stop. Justine is allowed to wish she had a mama. It's perfectly normal. And Mika, you're right, Maddie is not your mama." How would I ever deal with this? It was bound to happen at some point. Madison and I had crossed lines. We had changed the rules. Even without realizing it, my daughters sensed it. I blamed myself for all of it. Even I had a hard time keeping up with the situation. For now, I wished the girls and I could have had this discussion later—much later. When they were old enough to get it. To understand the hues and implications.

Leading my daughters to the nearest bench, I sat with them on either side, my arms curled around their shoulders. "Listen. I know you have questions about Lisa. I do too. But I'm not sure I have the answers you're both looking for. Justine, Maddie is not your mama. She's a nice woman helping us out and taking care of you. She loves you two very much, but Mika is right."

"But I want Maddie to be *my* mama," she sniffled, pressing her runny nose against the sleeve of my T-shirt this time.

I tightened my arm around her. "I know you do." I inhaled a cleansing breath. "And Mika, no more calling your sister names. Enough with that. It's not how we speak to each other in this family. Justine is four. It's all confusing to her. Even I am confused sometimes. It's okay if you are too."

"What *confused* means?"

I let out a low snicker. "It's when you don't know something because it seems a bit complicated. And a lot of grown-up things are confusing."

"Can I call Maddie *Mama*?" Justine asked, her cheeks drenched with tears, but her eyes filled with hope.

"Let's call her Maddie, okay? Can you do that?"

My youngest daughter bobbed her head and moving to her knees, hooked her arms around my neck. "I love you, Daddy."

I pulled Mikaella closer. "I love you, girls. Now let's go home and make some mac and cheese and have a picnic in your castle. Sounds good?"

They both cheered up, and our discussion was probably not forgotten, but put aside for now. When Lisa left, she had put the burden of dealing with her departure on my shoulders. She fucking quit on us and didn't even have to pick up the broken pieces she'd scattered behind.

From that night, I'd dreaded the moment I would have to explain her actions to our children. No, *my* children. She had lost the privilege to call them hers when she forfeited her parental rights.

With my heart heavy in my chest, I made it home, exhausted by all the things I had no control over.

———

"Okay, girls. Today we're decorating the tour bus. I bought supplies to make it ours. Uncle Riley is freaking out at the idea we're painting it pink, but I'm sure it will grow on him."

They both chuckled.

Mikaella, Justine, Madison, and I were all dressed in old shorts and shirts, ready to tackle our pre-assigned tasks.

"Justine and Maddie, you're in charge of the bunk room. You're painting all four walls in the bubblegum pink we picked up earlier. Tomorrow, the artist I hired will come and paint the giant unicorn mural, so it must be done by tonight. Are you up to the challenge?"

They both nodded, their fists resting on their hips, paintbrushes hanging from their fingers.

"What about us, Daddy?" Mikaella asked.

"Sweet pea, you and I, we're doing some construction work."

"With the big saw?"

"Yes. With the big saw. And a hammer. And all kinds of power tools. Do you think you can help me with this task?"

She nodded. "Yes, Daddy."

"Great. Let's start. And grandma sewed matching comforters for your beds. She'll send them over."

"YAY." Both girls screamed at the same time.

Madison and I exchanged a glance. Things were better between us. Even after the night we'd spent wrapped up in each other in her bed. Following my conversation with my daughters that day, I had drilled into my head once and for all that Madison and I were better as friends, our relationship less confusing to all of us. The sexual tension between us had decreased from a wildfire to a blaze. Still scorching but easier to control. It seemed like Madison had come to the same conclusion because she didn't stare at me the same way anymore.

Things were great and going according to plan.

"Teams," I called out. "Ready, set, go."

Madison lifted Justine in her arms, and they hurried inside the bus. The bunk room wasn't big by all means, but with personal touches and love, it would be perfect for the girls.

"Okay, sweet pea," I squatted to level my eyes with hers, "you and I will put together the new doll house I bought, and then we'll build a small bookshelf to put in your room and a ladder so you can climb on and off the top bed. We wouldn't want you to break your other wrist, would we?" I could have bought all this, but I thought it would be more fun to do it ourselves. I wanted the girls to feel at home on the bus, and doing all the prep work with them sounded like a good idea.

She giggled, and it warmed my heart. "No, Daddy."

She had a few days left of her—against all odds—powder-blue cast, and since she was right-handed, the fracture had barely stopped her. Armed with multicolor glitter and paint brushes, Madison had embellished her cast, transforming it into a piece of art. My kid definitely had the most fashionable broken wrist in town.

"Where will Maddie live, Daddy? Is she going to stay in your room?"

A tingle I hadn't felt in a while shot up my spine. I pushed the pang of excitement down and brought all my attention back to my daughter. "No, sweet pea. Maddie will have her own bunk."

"Will she sleep on our bus?"

"Yes, she will. Don't worry about her, okay?"

Mikaella was busy applying a coat of white paint to our DIY bookshelf when Madison and Justine joined us, wide smiles on their lips and splatters of pink paint on their clothes and skin.

"We're done, Daddy. It looks beautiful. Come see," my daughter said tugging at my hand.

I followed her inside. "Wow, you did all this?"

She bobbed her head. "And we painted Maddie's bunk too. She agreed."

Could Madison ever refuse anything to my kids? A tiny smile tugged at my lips at the thought.

"It looks fierce, baby. I love it. Come on, Mika is almost done. Let's get you clean up before your nap."

The tour bus was parked in our driveway, an idea Riley had, so the girls could get used to it. We had even planned on spending a few nights on it so they'd get comfortable in their new environment before the big day. My friend was doing everything in his power to make this tour the easiest possible transition for the girls, and I would never be able to thank him enough.

After a quick shower, I tucked the girls in and met Madison on the back deck with a bowl of tortilla chips and two beers. She accepted the offered drink.

"How did Justine convince you to paint your bunk pink?" I asked.

She smiled, the sight contagious. "Oh, she didn't have to do much. The girls must have worked some magic on me. I can't resist their charm. Be honest. Have you seen them doing some voodoo lately? I suspect they are little witches in disguise. They're the cutest. Justine was so excited when she offered that I couldn't refuse."

We clinked our bottles. "Welcome to the club. I hope

I'll grow a spine by the time they turn sixteen, or I'll be in big trouble." I laughed, and she joined in.

"I can already see you getting gray hair just trying to keep up with them."

"It will be that frightful, huh?"

She bobbed her head. "Just wait and see."

The sound of her laughter warmed me up inside.

"I bet they'll team up against you. They remind me of Ems and me growing up. I'd want to be here to witness it with my own eyes. The Stevens girls are a handful when they put their minds to it. They follow in their daddy's footsteps. They're fearless…and own the biggest hearts."

As if she'd just heard her own words, and the meaning behind them, she turned her head, avoiding my eyes.

I was about to settle into my chair when I spotted a dab of pink paint below her earlobe. Wetting my thumb with my tongue, I rubbed the stain before I realized the intimacy of the gesture. Madison's breathing hitched, and I hissed a quivering gulp of air.

Her hand closed over mine, keeping it in place while she closed her eyes for the longest seconds of my life.

"Sorry, you had paint right there," I said, rambling the words out in order to explain my temporary lack of judgment.

She breathed out a whispered "Thanks."

If there were any lingering doubts in my mind, they weren't there anymore. I would die a starving man.

26

MADISON

T he voices coming from the house brought me out of my slumber.

I blinked, trying to reboot my brain and remember where I was.

How long had I been out? By the sun hanging low in the sky, I bet it was late afternoon.

Which meant…ugh…I had slept in bright sunlight for hours.

Sliding my sunglasses up onto my head, I raised my arms to inspect the damage. My green-army shorts and black tank top did nothing to cover my bare skin.

My stomach tightened. I looked like a freaking lobster.

The skin of my arms was devil red.

Another fuck-up to add to my already long list.

Since I'd moved into this house, nothing was going as planned. How could Sam trust me to take care of the girls if I couldn't even take care of myself? How could he see me as a grown woman if I wasn't even smart enough to use sunblock? Right now, I resembled a teenage girl on spring break who thought she was too cool for shade and sunscreen.

Today was my day off, and after Sam and the girls had left early this morning to spend the day at a family friend's farm, I'd decided to read on the back deck. Never did I think I'd fall asleep in the sun.

My hands flew to my cheeks, and the warmth of my skin told me everything I needed to know.

The back door slid open before I could cover up.

"Here, you are," Sam said in his rough southern drawl as he stepped outside.

Just the sound of his voice was enough to send a flight of butterflies to my belly. Damn it. *Get a grip on yourself, Maddie.* Could my resolve—not to lust after him and to keep my sanity—hold up when I needed it most?

I folded my legs and wrapped my arms around my bent knees, resting my chin on them as Sam took a seat in the lounge chair next to mine, stretching his long legs. At that moment, even his calves looked fabulous.

Stupid misplaced infatuation.

"The girls are looking for you. I told them it's your day off, but according to this"—his attention drifted to his watch—"we have about two minutes before they come barreling here." His eyes landed on mine for the first time, and I offered him a *I'm sorry* smile as his gaze trailed over the length of me, taking in the sunburn. "Shit, Maddie. Did you use sunscreen?"

I shook my head slowly, using all the strength I possessed to hold his gaze.

He swung his legs over the edge of the chair and leaned forward.

One of his hands landed on my knee, and the other cradled my face, his thumb tracing the ridge under my lips. His eyes translated every word his mouth refused to speak out loud. My fascination with him multiplied. Sam Stevens was made of so many layers, I had still to uncover them all. He jerked away the hand cupping my face, as if the warmth of my skin had burned his palm. In a slow movement, he leaned forward, his cheek barely grazing mine, his stubble rough against my sensitive flesh. Shivers zigzagged along my back.

I gasped.

He growled.

Could he hear my raging heartbeat?

I fisted his shirt, my head spinning, as the scent of him invaded my nose, my body requiring his sturdiness to avoid falling over the edge. Our breaths mingled.

Time slowed.

"I don't like you hurting," he whispered.

"I never meant to fall asleep."

The jolt of his touch on my knee went straight to my center, and I moved my leg to the side to escape it.

Sam lifted his palm and rubbed it on the fabric of his black athletic shorts after adjusting his white T-shirt. "Sorry." His Adam's apple bobbled, and he glared into the distance before bringing his eyes back to me. "You've got to treat those, or you'll be in a lot of pain over the next few days. Do you have any after-sun lotion or aloe?"

"No," I said. "I'll go buy some." My weak voice didn't sound like mine.

"Don't be silly. I'll go. Take a cold shower while I'm gone." He moved to his feet and half-spun around to study me, his fists clenched beside him. The muscle of his jaw flexed. His eyes darkened. "What were you thinking sleeping in direct sunlight?" His tone had turned harsh. Why was he even mad? First, I hadn't done it on purpose. I'd come out here to relax, not to get second-degree burns. Second, I'd hurt myself and no one else. "Anyway. Go shower. I'll be back." He yanked the door open, his stride long and heavy, his feet pounding on the hardwood floor. "Girls, get in the car. We're leaving." I heard some protests, but the door closed, and it drowned their words. I stood there, on the back deck, chills from my overdose of sun exposure running through me.

The front door slammed shut, and the house vibrated.

Why was Sam upset with me? We'd shared a moment. Again. He was genuinely concerned. I could tell. And then he turned ice-cold.

Feeling skittish, I rushed to my room, undressed, and locked myself in the bathroom, the cold jets of the shower cooling my cooked flesh. The water eased some of the burning sensations.

I got out, a towel wrapped around me, just in time to hear a knock on my bedroom door.

Justine stood on the other side, a tube in her hand.

"Hey, what do we have here?"

She handed me the lotion. "It's for you. Daddy said you gotta use this." She gasped. "Why is your skin red? Are you sick? Do you want soup? Daddy always makes me *chickling* soup when I'm sick."

A smile tugged at my lips. "Chicken soup, you mean."

"*Yesss. Chickling* soup. Mika's favorite. I'll ask Daddy to make it."

I shook my head. "No. Your offer sounds nice, but I'm okay." *And I wouldn't want to bother your father. He seems overly annoyed with me today.*

"Come with me," she said, pulling at my hand.

"Just a minute. I'll get dressed."

"No time. I wanna show you what Daddy got for you."

"For me?"

She nodded, her smile reaching both ears. "Yes. Come, it's a surprise."

With my other hand holding the towel firmly around my naked self, I followed her to the dining room.

On the wooden table, big enough to seat ten people, were a dozen different after-sun gels and creams.

"Whoa," I said, struggling to put my shock into words.

"Daddy said you can have them all because you have bad, bad, bad *sunbrunes*."

"Sunburns, sweetie."

She flipped her hand in the air like I was being silly.

I scanned the bottles, feeling a flush ascending my face. As if it could get any redder.

"I'll try this one," I said, picking an aloe-based gel.

"No. They're all yours. I chose the one in the pretty pink bottle. Because I like pink. And unicorns like pink too. What's your favorite color?"

I let out a snicker. "Pink is great. I love yellow too."

"Cool. Wanna play with me and Mika?"

"Sure. I'll meet you guys in about ten minutes."

"Mika is in the castle outside."

"I'll find you when I'm done here."

Justine traipsed away, a large smile brightening her face and her eyes full of sparks.

I started toward my bedroom when I noticed Sam frozen in the den's archway. Tight jaw. Flared nose. Dilated pupils. Firmed shoulders. He looked both intimidating and alluring. This version of him played with every thread of my control. He watched me. No, he undressed me with his eyes from afar. My towel could catch fire at any moment, so I tightened my grip around its edge. He said nothing and walked past me, leaving a whiff of his cologne in its wake, warning Justine not to climb on the kitchen stool by herself.

I had never felt more naked than I did right now.

In the bathroom, still shaky from the hot encounter

that had me squeezing my thighs together, I avoided looking at myself in the mirror as I applied one of the cooling gels to my sensitive flesh. Shivers moved from my head to my toes, the ache slowly settling in.

After I dressed in a loose cotton shirt and lounge pants, I gathered my clothes and towel and carried them to the laundry room at the end of the hallway.

I sucked in a quick breath, and my heart fluttered as I walked in.

Bare-chested and giving me a frontal row view of his muscled abs, Sam stood there, his black T-shirt hanging from one hand.

His expression darkened, a wrinkle forming across his forehead. From up close, he looked even more daunting due to his broodiness and the six inches he had over me, but also more handsome—and lethal—to me.

"Sorry," I said, glancing down, trying to get away from his spell. "I-I should have knocked. I didn't mean to… It wasn't… I was…"

I closed my eyes with a sigh and spun on the balls of my feet, ready to bolt. A powerful hand circled my wrist, holding me in place.

With a grimace, I tilted my head back.

Sam stared right at me. The strength of his gaze punctured holes through my blazing epidermis. "Stop apologizing, Maddie." His voice had roughened up. Again, why was my name so sexy every time it rolled off his tongue? "Justine dropped her juice all over me, and I had to change my shirt."

Could I conceal all the sensations dancing inside me if I tried hard enough?

Of their own accord, my eyes traveled down his corded forearms to the V leading into his pants. If I didn't get a grip on myself, I'd soon be drooling. I'd never ogled a man like this before, without an ounce of shame.

Whatever I told myself, I couldn't look elsewhere. My tongue darted out to lick my lips. The lines weren't blurry anymore, they had vanished.

"Are you okay?" Sam's voice brought me back to the present moment.

Was I still eating him up with my eyes while I was lost in my thoughts?

"I…I told Justine I'd play outside with her and Mika, but if it's fine with you, I'd take a nap instead. I-I feel lightheaded."

He talked gibberish.

"What?" I asked, blinking.

"Nothing."

"Are you sure?"

"Sure. I'll be out of town tomorrow. Hopefully, you'll feel better by morning. I'll come get you when dinner's ready."

We fixated on each other for another beat, way too long for my sanity, neither of us saying anything else.

Sam cleared his throat.

I blinked, trying to evade the enchantment.

"Thanks for…huh…the after-sun collection you got me. You didn't have… You didn't have to go into that much trouble. One would have been enough."

He cocked his head, looking so devastatingly handsome it almost hurt not to be able to do anything about it. "I had no idea what you usually use and what works. I didn't want to take any chances."

His tongue flicked across his full lower lip. Had he done it on purpose, or were my hormones out of control?

"Anyway, thanks. I'm sure my skin will get better soon."

Sam released his grip on my wrist, and I rushed to my

bedroom, closed the door, and leaned against it until my breaths evened out.

With a heavy sigh, I fell face first on the mattress, wishing I could go back two days in time.

Whatever I did to enrage him, this angry side of my boss had never looked so dangerous.

So intoxicating.

To me—and to my body.

27

SAM

The night had been a series of tossing and turning. Around two o'clock, still wide awake, I went downstairs. A golden glow illuminated the kitchen, making me curious. Instead of sauntering to my music studio like I'd meant to, I ended up staring at Madison's ass clothed in night shorts while she rummaged through the refrigerator, bent forward and offering me a perfect view.

As if she could sense me lurking behind in the shadows, she closed the door and whirled around until we faced each other, handing me a bottle of water. Her eyes bore into mine, and the air between us tightened.

Hair stood on end on my arms.

Invisible magnets pulled us forward. We both took a step toward each other. The semi-darkness did nothing to conceal the delicious curves of her body or the gleam in her eyes.

I uncapped the lid and downed the cold liquid in one gulp, my gaze never drifting from the woman standing before me. She followed each undulation of my throat, her facial expressions doing nothing to hide the thirst in her eyes, the desire overpowering. Madison Prescott was the reason behind my endless nights and of my mind going haywire. That no-sunscreen stunt she had pulled earlier had sent a pang of panic through me. Her flesh would hurt. She'd need care. And I wasn't allowed to be the one providing it.

Wrath boiled in my blood just thinking about it.

Tired and upset, I refused to be a gentleman and molded my hand to her waist, while I erased the gap keeping us apart. Her breath whistled on its way in. She parted her lips and splayed her palms across my heart, the pounding impossible for her to miss. I trailed the fingers of my other hand down the length of her bare arm. She shivered. My dick got harder. A moan crossed the cusp of her luscious mouth. A guttural groan left mine. I had turned into a starving animal that had been refused its favorite meal—and I was fucking famished.

Another step forward.

I backed her against the refrigerator.

I cupped her chin, leaning in so my mouth hovered near her ear.

Tremors worked through her.

Goose bumps blossomed under my fingers as my hand met the bare stretch of her stomach—the tiny strip her tank top couldn't conceal. The one about to drive me absolutely insane. Or push me past the line I'd been careful not to cross so far.

My thumb lingered over her juicy lips.

I pushed myself further into her space and smelled the faint perfume of the after-sun lotion she had put on.

In that instant, I hoped she could catch the scent of my rising desire, because I doubted it was concealed anymore.

"I'm fucking starving right now, Maddie. And I'm

fucking furious with you. It's not a good mix. I can't decide if I wanna punish you right here on this countertop or hold and kiss you until that sunburn heals."

With her devilish lips, she sucked my thumb into her mouth, the vision so hot my dick grew a couple of inches in my pants, begging to be freed. Madison twirled her tongue around the tip, nibbling he flesh with her teeth. Oh, how much would I pay to have her reward my hard-on in a similar fashion? Sweat crawled along my spine. She never looked away, even when a loud moan straight from the depths of her broke the tensed silence.

The rise and fall of her chest hastened.

"You're playing a very dangerous game," I said, barely holding it together, breathless and affected in a dozen different ways. I lacked the words to describe the overwhelming sensations pulsing within me.

Madison released my finger with one last swirl of her tongue, and I thought I would combust.

She edged away and escaped the cage of my arms. With her bottle in hand, she retreated to her bedroom without a word, pausing only once to glance at me over her shoulder.

The gears of my brain, already spinning at high speed, ground to a halt at the sight. Was it an invitation to follow her or a warning to stay away? I couldn't tell, my common sense long gone.

With that simple gesture, she had reversed the roles. She was now in charge. She was the hunter, and I was the prey, a role I had no idea how to navigate, or resist.

With my forehead pressed against the refrigerator door, I slid a hand under the waistband of my pants to offer my dick the attention he was throbbing for. I couldn't think clearly anymore. What was I supposed to do?

I shut my eyes and cursed at myself.

I'd almost bent Madison over the island and got my way with her. Picturing myself ramming into her with abandon so we could move forward once and for all, and I would stop imagining the taste and feel of her every time I found myself alone with nothing but my thoughts to keep me company.

My heart pumped too much blood.

Each inhale burned the lining of my throat. I was done lying to myself and becoming more miserable with every passing day.

Minutes ago, Madison had showed me just how much she lusted for me too, not hiding behind pretenses and fake excuses this time. She'd flashed her desire right into my face, without even breaking eye contact. Fuck, that was hot. She was far braver than I was. And a lot bolder.

It was a very dangerous game she had started, probably aware I'd have a hard time resisting. And that I would never leave unfinished.

Desperate to put to rest our suffering, I padded toward her bedroom.

My fist floated inches from the door, ready to knock and kill that arousal paralyzing both of us, when I heard a muffled cry coming from inside the room. Pressing my ear to the wooden panel, I listened, unsure if I'd imagined it. Another cry, more audible this time, resonated from the other side. Oh, geez, I would die tonight. That was how I'd leave the Earth. With her gasps echoing in my mind. And my erection standing tall and proud, stiff as a flagpole.

My hand returned to my crotch, my dick relishing the idea the woman we were both obsessed with was pleasuring herself after a heated encounter with us.

"Fuck," I muttered through clenched teeth as I rubbed myself to the sounds of her shallow whimpers.

This was wrong. I had become a man I didn't recognize. I couldn't ever name all the ways my actions were wicked.

Madison's eyes, when she'd glanced at me over her shoulder minutes ago, weren't issuing an invitation or a warning, but a challenge. A dare. I'd walked straight into her trap. I had struck the match and set myself on fire.

She had won—big time—and by doing so, she owned me a lot more.

Feeling like a voyeur, or whatever listening to things I shouldn't through a closed door made me, I let go of my erection. A low curse passed my lips. I braced my shoulders, walked away, and locked myself in my music studio, desperate to find another outlet to the blaze searing within me. Since jerking off thinking about the nanny had revealed itself to be a fucking mistake in the past, I used music as my escape this time.

Much better. And much safer.

No way I was risking my sanity, or my dick—or any other part of my body—to release the tension coiling inside me.

I went back to bed around four and slept for about—I picked up my phone on the nightstand to check the time— an hour. I blinked. Could it really only be five in the morning? I was screwed. I was so screwed, I didn't even have words to describe how lame I'd become lately. My middle-of-the-night lack of judgment had proved it.

Restless, I swung my legs over the edge of the bed. No need to prolong the inevitable any longer. Getting up now would give me more time to jumpstart my day and prep breakfast. Or maybe I could go for a run. Clear my head. Get rid of the angst or whatever cocktail was simmering inside me even hours later. It'd been a long time since I'd jogged around the neighborhood to release crippling tension in me. Yeah, I should put on my runners and exercise until both my body and my brain surrendered.

With my fingers, I rubbed the sleep off my eyes and got up.

The first pink and orange streaks over my backyard treetops greeted me as I drew back the drapes, filling me with hope for the new day.

Tonight, I had a concert scheduled in Charlotte and another one in Atlanta tomorrow. The first few to warm up, test the set list, and make some tweaks before leaving for the tour.

Jitters had taken over my stomach since yesterday, at the realization that it was real and there was no turning back.

The thought of leaving the girls for two days and being back onstage for a full concert rattled my nerves—one part of me anxious, the other brimming with a thrill nothing else could match.

Dressed in cotton pants, a gray Henley, and a Carter Hills Band vintage black hoodie, I tiptoed down the hallway and checked on the girls as I passed their room. They were both deep asleep, tucked under their comforters, looking peaceful, the sound of their steady breathing enough to calm me down, or at least ease a little of the tension still gripping me.

In the kitchen, I made myself a coffee, cursing at the coffeemaker when it made grumbling sounds—something I'd been doing a lot since my little escapade downstairs in the middle of the night. I had to keep quiet. Madison waking up right now and being all adorable and sexy at this early hour would do me no good in my present state of mind, especially now that I felt vulnerable and angsty, and my testosterone had been spiking a little too much these past few days.

Asking her to move in had been both the stupidest and smartest decision I'd made since she entered our lives.

Last night's events replayed in my head, and to be honest, I had almost given in without a second thought. What Madison had done was hot as hell and had completely unraveled my composure on a whole new level. She hadn't been ashamed, and she had shown me exactly what I was missing with that little session she'd indulged in behind closed doors afterward. It would forever be etched in my memory. Her cries. Her moans. My blood bubbled like lava at the reminder.

The sane part of me wished we'd met under different circumstances so we could figure out our relationship—and the arousal reverberating between us. If she weren't working for me, this impossible-to-ignore craving between us wouldn't feel so inappropriate, would it? If that were the case, would I still feel like being with her meant stealing her youth? Yes, her age would stay the same. She was barely in her twenties. I could never ask her to skip a decade of experiences and fun times to play mommy to my daughters. Everything about the idea of being together felt wrong, even though, deep down, it felt awfully right. This was an impossible situation, one my hormones, my heart, and my head couldn't settle on. A part of me wanted to fuck her out of my system, another craved to make her mine and hold on to her, and the third knew both of the others were wrong.

With a coffee mug in my hand, I grabbed a stack of documents Riley had asked me to read, that I'd discarded on the counter yesterday, and made my way to the back deck. An hour or two of peace, witnessing the awakening of a new day should ease my annoyed self. It usually did the trick.

Just when I was about to take a sip, I halted, stumbling

over my own feet, the scorching liquid almost spilling all over me when I lowered the mug in a jerky movement.

Every lingering residue of sleep left me.

My heart bounced in my throat.

I exhaled, trying to dull the new surge of fire coursing in my veins. The tension between my legs. The thunderous hammering of my heart.

Was life playing with my flimsy willpower on purpose? Was it all a test?

Despite myself, my eyes were drawn to her sculpted thighs and plump ass in those purple spandex leggings, the toned skin of her midsection, the curves of her waist, the swell of her boobs peeking from the top of the sports bra.

Bent over on the mat spread across the deck, her hands and feet planted as her hips lifted toward the sky, Madison looked breathtaking in the morning light—and sexy. And too dangerous to be in this house. In my house. Around my sex-deprived self.

My sleep-deprived brain couldn't deal with so much exposed flesh and temptations at this early hour in the morning.

Oblivious to the fact that I was watching her through the glass pane, she switched from one yoga pose to another. Her face, arms, and feet—still red from the sunburn— already looked better than they had yesterday.

Deep breath in. Deep breath out. I would rupture at the seams, and nobody was prepared for the devastation that would ensue.

My dick sprang wood. No blood irrigated my brain anymore. Many forbidden thoughts tempted me, no matter how hard I tried to lock them away. I was dizzy, barely able to stand on my own two feet.

Once I regained some composure and adjusted the

crotch of my pants, I pushed some of my annoyance down and yanked the back door open.

The desire coursing through me turned to wrath. Yeah, this was the only way I could make this work. Be angry instead of a lustful mess.

All the images haunting me came back with a vengeance. Pushing Madison against the wall and punishing her with my cock for looking so young and innocent—and too fucking appealing—and finishing what we'd started mere hours ago.

My anger escalated. The images intensified instead of receding. My imagination ran wild.

If I had my way with her, I would ram into her from behind, spread her legs with my knee to get the perfect angle, and then I'd lower her to *her* knees and let her suck every last drop of cum from me until we both got it out of our systems and we rode a wave of bliss neither of us was ready to come down from.

I'd seen it in her eyes when she bumped into me in the laundry room yesterday, and again during our encounter against the refrigerator door. She was lusting for me as much as I was craving her. Yesterday, she couldn't run away fast enough from me after she bumped into me while I was bare-chested, panting, after ogling me like she was starving. Then she had closed her eyes—yep, she shut them —too weak to face me, with unmasked arousal straining her features. And then later, she had fucking sucked my thumb as if it were my dick. She knew what she was doing when she did it. She was aware it would mess with every string of my composure. She couldn't hide the glint in her eyes when she'd aimed her challenge-filled stare at me over her shoulder. Gone was the nice woman I had gotten to know in that instant. Madison had become a temptress testing my limits. And she won. She mastered that little game between us.

I had to take back the control, or it would end badly. For the both of us. We had said we wouldn't cross the set boundaries, and I was adamant about keeping my end of the deal.

As I got closer to her, my annoyance increased a couple of notches. I couldn't contain it. I had to explode, one way or another, no matter the form. So, I chose the less damaging for both of us.

Now on all fours, one leg bent at a ninety-degree angle behind her, and one stretched fully in a straight line, show-casing the curve of her ass, Madison turned her head to face me as I stepped next to her.

"What are you doing up at this hour?" I asked, my voice laced with fury I couldn't pinpoint the source of, other than my raging hard-on. She blinked, and I lowered my voice, my words still clipped. "It's too early to be doing…to be doing whatever you're doing dressed like this."

I gestured to the length of her, and she sat on her ankles, her eyes wide and full of questions. "It's my morning routine. I get up at five, three times a week."

The pink flush on her face turned a shade darker.

I put my mug and papers down, and tugging at the back of my hoodie, I pulled it over my head and threw it at her. "Wear this."

Madison's lips parted, and she murdered me with her gaze. "Are you serious?"

I crossed my arms over my chest and tipped my chin up. "Do I look like I'm joking? You can't wear these clothes. It's just…well…inappropriate."

"Pardon me?" She scowled at me, no other sound coming from her.

We both engaged in a staring contest, neither of us ready to back down—to accept defeat.

After a moment, with a glower that turned her eyes into weapons, she slid her arms into the sleeves and stood to her feet, her eyes still zeroed in on me. Too big on her, my hoodie ended just above her knees.

Something in me clamped tight.

She was supposed to look less tempting wearing more clothes. Instead, she looked even more attractive with my hoodie on.

This. Wasn't. Supposed. To. Happen.

Her long dark ponytail swept over her shoulders.

The muscle of my jaw ticked, and I clenched it until my teeth hurt.

"Happy now?" She folded her arms across her chest, mimicking my stance. "When I signed up for this job, I don't recall the contract saying anything about being treated like a child or getting a second father figure in the process."

My irritation toward her seared. She hadn't gone there, had she?

My lips pursed, but I couldn't find the words to express my ire or my thirst because, at this point, there were hard to untangle, both heating up my blood and other parts of my body and taking over me.

"Stop being a brat. I'm not your father. These thoughts I have about you are not father-daughter like, I swear. You should be aware by now."

Madison yelped, her lips parting, so ready to be kissed. Or fucked.

No, man. Stop. Enough.

She stared at me, her pink lips pursed, ready to speak.

There. Better.

"Then stop acting like you are." Her tone imitated mine now. Edgy and full of sass behind the laced-with-hunger annoyance. "You're not allowed to dictate how I should dress. And you have no right to barge out here and get mad at me when I'm off the clock. When I agreed to move in here, you promised I'd have my own space. Right now, your acting out is in contradiction to your own words. You've asked me if I trusted you before. I did. I still do. But this… this invasion of my private time is unacceptable." She ended her rant with a tip of her chin, defiant and even more alluring as she didn't back down from the fight *I* started.

My anger reached new heights.

Madison took a stand before me, and I fought with myself not to shut her up with a kiss—or a swirl of my tongue all over her soft flesh. The apex of her thighs. Or those perky nipples that were pointing at me through the fabric of her bra minutes ago.

"Commenting on my appearance is a new low for you. Better think about it twice next time before chastising me with undeserved criticism."

"Well, if you wear such little clothing in September, what do you even wear in July?" She opened her mouth, but I continued. "Don't answer. I don't wanna know. Anyway, I…I already do. Gosh, Maddie, you can't parade in spandex and think I'd be cool with that. It's distracting. *You're* distracting. Not that you can't wear what pleases you, I agree…but…" I shook my head in defeat. "No but… This whole situation is unbearable." I closed my eyes and exhaled the air screwing with all my brain cells. "Now get dressed before you catch a cold."

A cold? Was I being stupid on purpose? Damn it. A cold. Now I really sounded like a dumb teenager's father. The urge to facepalm myself itched my arm. Instead, I stood my ground in front of the woman wrecking my world.

Right about now, I had no clue how to control this hormonal storm invading me, and I readied myself for the disaster waiting to happen. When had I transformed into this pathetic version of myself?

I used to be fun. And I loved to party and have a good time. Drink, dance all night, make love under the stars, come up with new and exciting plans, be optimistic, and dream big.

Fucking Lisa.

How long was I going to blame her for everything bad happening in my life? How long could I fault myself because she had abandoned me? My forbidden crush on Madison had nothing to do with my ex-wife. Except for the fact that I wouldn't be standing here in this aroused state I could do nothing about if she hadn't walked out on us.

Would we still be happily married if she hadn't left, though? No.

Because the attraction I'd felt for Lisa never even neared the one I felt for the girl standing in front of me. One day, it would have caught up with us. She had just accelerated the process—in the most heartless and worst possible manner.

This one, right here, was on me.

The impulsive side of me had just confirmed to my kids' nanny, in not so many words, all about the nasty things I wished to do to her. Not only had I spoken them, but I had thought them too. Been thinking them for months.

A feeling I'd never experienced before adhered to my heart. It made me feel small. Without another glance at her, I pivoted around and vanished inside, leaving a flabbergasted Madison behind.

Now I would have to burn my hoodie because I bet the scent of her would forever cling to the fibers.

At seven, I woke the girls up, looking forward to the distraction they'd bring.

I lifted them both in my arms and carried them downstairs, pretending to be a big bad wolf about to take them to my secret lair.

"Did you make breakfast?" Mikaella asked, her eyes half-mast from sleep and her curls tangled into a nest at the back of her head.

"It smells *gooood*," Justine sang, looping her arms around my neck and kissing my cheek.

"I did." I plopped them onto stools around the kitchen island.

"Where's Maddie?" Mikaella asked.

"I'll get her," Justine said, climbing off her seat and running toward the guest bedroom before I could call out her name.

"Wait for me," Mikaella said, running after her sister.

With my elbows on the countertop, I rubbed my palms over my face in defeat.

After I'd argued with Madison about her poor choice of clothes earlier, she returned to her bedroom and hadn't yet come out. I already feared she would parade in a tiny bikini just to disturb my mind even more—and to prove a point. That she was unattainable, to someone like me—especially to someone like me. A single dad with young children trying to resuscitate his dead music career with an attempt to tour the country. Not the perfect match for a beautiful, barely adult woman with dreams of her own and her whole life in front of her.

With my newfound caveman attitude and Madison moving in, my stupidity level around her had multiplied by ten. I had lost my mind, and I kept rolling, piling up mishaps. Starting with kissing her, sleeping in her bed, and spilling my dirty thoughts.

Everything she did or said pushed a button inside me. It messed with me. She wasn't the problem, though. None of it was her fault. I blamed the tour. It got me anxious. It would all go back to normal once I found my footing again. Or maybe I could blame Riley. For putting all these silly ideas in my head and placing Madison on my path.

Two minutes later, the girls returned, tugging at Madison's hands.

"Sit beside me," Justine said.

"No. Maddie is sitting next to me," Mikaella argued.

A wide smile lightened up Madison's face. "I'll sit in the middle. That way, you'll both be by my side."

Justine hopped around with a contagious grin.

"Who's gonna sit next to me then?" I asked, arching one brow, my eyes traveling between my daughters.

"Me." My baby girl raised her hand. "I'll sit beside you too, Daddy."

I moved one seat to my left to let the three of them sit beside one another.

The conversation flew easily, but an invisible wall had risen around Madison and me.

She had changed into dark jeans and a white tank top. Madison wearing something of mine earlier had mattered to me, and I kinda missed the vision of her dressed in my hoodie. I wouldn't object if it were all she ever wore from now on. My thoughts were conflicted. Desire tangling with reality had become a big web around my sanity I had no clue how to escape. With a heavy sigh, I made conversation with my children instead of entertaining the images playing in my head.

"Girls, Daddy is going away for two nights… Just like we discussed. Maddie will stay here with you."

"Is she gonna sleep in your bed?" Mikaella asked.

My eyebrows shot to my hairline. "What? No. She'll sleep in her own room."

"But I'm scared. I want Maddie to sleep upstairs. Next to our room," Justine said, her lips quivering, the corners of her eyes filling with tears. "What if I have a *nightlemare?*"

"Nightmare, baby," I said. "It's gonna be okay. Maddie will hear you if you wake up in the middle of the night. I found the baby monitors in a box in the garage. We'll set them up. Together."

Tears drenched my little girl's face. "No. I want Mama to sleep upstairs. With us."

Air frizzled in the kitchen.

The room fell silent.

We could only hear Justine's sobs. And my deafening heartbeats.

I closed my eyes, trying to come out with a smart reply. We already had this conversation, Justine and I, and I believed she understood.

"She's not your mama, dummy," Mikaella said, igniting the already explosive situation.

"Mika. Where did you learn all these words from? For the umpteenth time, be nice to your sister. And stop using this language."

"Whatever. Justine always wants Maddie to be her mama. It's stupid." She lowered her head. "We have a mama. Her name is Lisa."

I cursed a couple more saints under my breath. At this pace, by the end of the tour, I'd know all their names.

Why did Justine have to open that door right now? This morning, of all days?

Before a well-scripted answer could pass my lips, Madison jumped in.

The first few words left her mouth and carried away

the fears swirling inside me. "Sweetie, I can't sleep in your Daddy's room because I have my own room. And Mika is right. I'm not your mama. I'm sorry yours isn't here, but I can't be her. I can be your nanny, your teacher, and your friend. I can play many roles, but not your mama's, okay? Do you understand?"

Justine threw a fit, kicking her stool and thumping her tiny fists on the counter. I'd never seen her acting out like this.

My damaged heart plummeted down my chest at a dizzying pace.

"I don't want Lisa. She's not my mama. I don't love her. She's mean. I want Maddie. I love Maddie. Maddie is *my* mama. Just Maddie."

I sprang to my feet and wrapped my arms around my daughter. "Shhh, baby. Shhh, it's okay. It's okay to be upset. Shhh." I pulled her against my heart as it fractured into more pieces inside my chest. My face rested against her head, her body shaking in my embrace.

Sitting on the floor, I rocked her back and forth, wishing I possessed special powers to repair my child's wounds.

One look at my watch told me I had one hour left before Riley picked me up.

With my thumb, I wiped the tears cascading down her cheeks. "It's okay. You're allowed to be upset. I was too for a moment. Fine, lots of moments. But it'll be all right. I promise."

I rocked my baby until the fight left her, not turning in Madison's direction the entire time, avoiding the look in her eyes. Or maybe because, in that instant, I wished she was the one healing my bruised organ.

Once the air cleared, I tried again. "Let's go and set those monitors up and see how they work." With Justine in my arms and Mikaella attached to my hand, we grabbed the devices from the garage.

For the next half-hour, the girls and I talked to one another from across the house after we plugged them in. Once they were appeased, I gathered my suitcase and guitar and everything I needed for the next two days.

"Here," I said, placing the keys to my SUV in Madison's hand.

Her eyes rounded. "Why? I already own a car."

"Yeah, but I'll be more at ease if you use mine. Anyway, the girls' car seats are in there. Take it. I don't know why I didn't think of buying you a new one, to begin with."

She closed her fist around my keyset. "It's not necessary, but it's nice of you. Thanks," she said in a strangled voice that peppered goose bumps down my back.

A strand of hair fell across her forehead, and I fought with myself the urge to push it away. Restlessness clamped my shoulders as we stood closer than we had in a long time —if you didn't count last night's refrigerator clusterfuck.

After a second, she brushed the tendril away herself.

"If you need anything, call me, okay?"

"We'll be fine, Sam. I've spent the last few months caring for Mika and Justine. I know everything there is to know. Don't worry. Do what you have to do, and don't let your mind run wild."

"Listen, about earlier"—I had no idea how to deal with the whole mama-thing situation Justine had thrown at us, as if Madison required more reasons to bail on me— "thanks for jumping in. I've been having this conversation with Justine a few times already, but for some reason, she has decided that my explanations aren't satisfying enough. I'll talk to her again when I get back."

The same strand of hair that Madison had pushed

away seconds ago, fell over her eyes once more. This time I didn't think before I combed it aside, shaping my palm to her cheek.

Electricity, powerful and sizzling, traveled from her visage to my hand. Hair stood on end on my arms. I breathed, but my airways had gone on strike.

The temperature of the room skyrocketed.

Our gazes melded together, and everything around me stopped. She pressed her cheek into my palm.

With a strangled voice, I added, "I'm sorry. For this morning. I was out of line. And an idiot."

"Which part?" she asked.

I licked my lips to return moisture to my mouth. "All of it."

Justine ran our way and snaked herself around my leg, interrupting us. This kid had a skewered sense of timing. "Daddy," she singsonged.

I released Madison's face and dropped my hand at my side to pet her hair, and the suffocating tightness between Madison and me evaporated.

I swallowed hard.

"Come here, baby," I said, lifting her up and perching her on my shoulders. "Uncle Riley will be here soon. Let's wait for him outside." I angled my body to face the woman it hurt to leave behind.

We locked eyes. There were so many truths I hoped I could tell her.

Instead, I said, "Call me. For whatever reason. I'll be back in two days."

"Don't worry."

She waved at me, avoiding my stare as I walked away, a rock replacing my dying heart and my heels heavy as concrete.

28

MADISON

Sam had left about four hours ago, and already I was a living bundle of nerves. It didn't help that he called twice to make sure I had no questions or missed anything. Both times, I'd heard the anxiety lacing his voice, and it had sent a fresh batch of jitters to my stomach. I knew tonight was a big deal for him. Even bigger than his album launch. And even though my place was here, taking care of Justine and Mikaella, a big part of me wished I could stand tall by his side. Holding his hand and whispering in his ear that I believed in him and everything would be all right. That he got this. But all those scenarios were just fragments of my overactive imagination.

The girls and I had prepared a surprise for him. Something I'd planned with Riley to ensure the first show after his long hiatus would be epic. To make it super special. Unforgettable.

Now that the girls were napping, I busied myself with folding laundry and sorting tiny pairs of socks. When that didn't work to distract me, I sat with a novel on the back deck, away from any direct sunlight, and lost myself in the pages.

The rest of the day passed in a blur.

We called Sam on video chat after dinner, and I put the girls to bed soon after since they kept arguing about anything and everything. They too could sense the anticipation permeating the air.

Sitting in my favorite chair in the den with the novel I'd started earlier, I tried to keep myself busy and prevent my thoughts from wandering to uncharted territory—Sam's territory. Unable to get engrossed in the story this time, I opened the messaging app on my phone, a tug-of-war rising inside me over whether or not I should wish him good luck for his big show.

Even after convincing myself it was cringe-worthy, I still did it.

ME

Enjoy tonight.

He answered seconds later. A part of me wished he was wrestling with the same question on his end—whether or not to contact me.

SAM

Thank you. How are the girls? I felt the excitement earlier when we talked.

ME

Deep asleep.

Couldn't stay put for more than a minute.

They asked me to tell you they were proud of you.

...

For what it's worth, I am too. It's something amazing you're teaching them. To get back out there. Even if they don't realize it yet.

SAM

Thanks.

I hate being far away from them, though. It's hard. And it's just been a few hours.

ME

They're happier when you ARE happy. Want my honest opinion?

I sank lower in my seat, loving how easily our conversation flowed, now that we didn't have to face each other—or deal with the burning desire that could mess it all up.

SAM

Please. Enlighten me.

ME

You're a great dad. You're allowed to put your needs and dreams first sometimes. Don't feel bad for doing this. I promise you everything is under control. Just enjoy your night.

SAM

...

Thanks, Maddie. I needed to hear that. Gotta get ready. Riley is knocking on my door.

Talk to you later.

ME

Night.

Miss you, I added in my head.

I reread our exchange a few times before putting my

phone away. Not really tired, but no longer feeling like playing detective for some fictional characters, I locked myself in my bedroom. For the first time, since I'd started working here, I cried myself to sleep, feeling lonelier than I'd had in a long time.

I shed sad tears for something I could never have.

And happy tears for the man I loved who faced his fears and mental blocks to pursue his dreams.

29

SAM

I stepped out of the green room, my face set and my back firm. This was it, the moment when everything in my life would finally fall into place—or at least, I hoped it would.

Riley met me backstage. "Ready, Stevens?"

In the last hour, the jitters that had plagued me all day had turned into excitement.

"Yeah," I said, pulling him into a hug. "I can't believe I went through with your crazy idea, man, but I'm glad I did. Right about now, it seems right."

"Don't thank me yet. Just do your thing. Mika and Justine will be proud. I know I am."

I blinked my emotions away. "Thanks for believing in me. And thanks for kicking my ass. I needed this. Someone to believe in me again when I didn't. I'm not sure I would've gone through with it if you hadn't been the one pushing me." I coughed to release the emotional rock lodged in my throat.

"Anytime."

From our spot by the side of the stage, we watched the

crowd of expectant fans. I shook my legs, stretched my arms, and cracked my neck. This was the moment I'd been dreaming about for a long time and thought would never happen again.

I blew out a long breath. "It's a full house." All my cells vibrated with a renewed zest I wasn't used to experiencing anymore.

"Make the most of it. For the next two hours, forget everything else."

I nodded and pulled my friend into one more hug. "I'm thankful you brought me back."

Riley clapped my shoulder. "Go shine out there. And have fun. You deserve it."

With my confidence back, I walked onstage, my heart so full I thought it would rupture my chest. The cheers and applauses of the crowd packed more tears into my eyes.

I raised a hand in the air, waving at all those people who came to see *me*, letting their energy course through me. The grin on my lips matched the dampness of my eyes, both mirroring the emotions surging inside me. *God, I've missed this.*

With a tilt of my head, I grinned at my manager who stared at me with overflowing pride.

"Hey, folks." The cries of the crowd intensified. My grin widened. Wolf-whistles. Applauses. People screaming my name. "Thanks for being here tonight. It's been a while." More whistles. "I can't believe I'm standing here right now. It's a dream come true to be back after over two years. I'll play some of my old stuff and new material from my just-released album tonight. The last two years have been rocky, but I've made it through. None of this would have been possible without Riley Burns, one of my best friends, and the guy behind all this. Without him, I would still be living a life that's not mine, thinking I shouldn't play music ever again. Once again, Ry, thank you."

I saluted him before strumming the first chords of "No Matter What." The crowd sang along with me. They knew every word. This song was probably the one playing the most on the radio even after all these years. Six years ago, it won the *Song of the Year* category at the most prestigious country music award show. I'd written it the day Mikaella was born.

Seated on a lone stool in the middle of the stage, I played acoustic versions of "Small Town" and "All Those Who Came Around." Flashlights from cell phones became tiny pinpoint stars in the darkness, thousands of glittering beams aimed at me.

I closed the concert with "You're My Whole World," an emotionally charged ballad I'd written to my daughters a few weeks back. In the studio version, we could hear their voices and laughter in the background.

My fingers strummed the first chord of the chorus when an unexpected "I love you, Daddy"— Justine's voice —filled the stadium, and a clip of me running around with my girls played on the giant screen behind me. Emotions I couldn't contain or define jammed in my throat. Then "Daddy, you're the best," out of Mikaella's mouth, played from the speakers.

My heart bounced in my chest.

Hot tears ran down my cheeks.

I let them roll. Up until then, I had ignored the healing power they carried.

I inhaled, closing my eyes to steady my voice and everything that screamed to be let out inside me, and after some of my composure returned, I sang with all my heart until my voice broke on the last note.

Cheers and screams mixed with my own pulse

pounding in my head, deafening me in the best possible way.

"Thank you, Charlotte," I said as I walked offstage, my face drenched with all the fervor this night had brought.

Riley pulled me into his arms the moment I walked backstage. "Stevens, that was sick. Incredible. You did it. For some reason, you're even better than you were when you left. That confidence. You owned the stadium. You delivered one hell of a performance. And it's your first show. Imagine after fifty." He paused and pointed behind me with a finger. "Listen to the crowd. They never lie. It's insane. All for you, man. Bask in the recognition."

The rush of the moment warmed my blood.

My body hummed with delight.

He led me further away, but I stopped and pivoted to face him. "Did you do this? The girls?"

We both smiled.

"Yeah, we did. A while back. I'm astounded they haven't said anything to you. We wanted to surprise you."

"That was incredible. You nailed it. I thought I would collapse on the stage. How did you make it happen?"

"Maddie. It was actually her idea. She's the one who captured the video and made the montage."

"She did?"

"Yeah. All her. She respects you very much. Now go change. We have a VIP party to attend."

Still high on adrenaline, I entered the VIP section of the bar. I had no idea how I'd survived two years without music in my life. Tonight, I felt ten years younger, and every layer of pain around my heart had faded away. They didn't exist anymore.

Nothing could temper my ecstasy.

Now that the addiction had set in, every bit of me itched to go on tour. To be onstage most nights. To fill stadiums with screaming fans.

To be where I belonged.

The security guard at the top of the stairs stepped aside to let us in.

I froze as I entered the dimly lit room. So many people were there.

Carter and April, Dahlia Ellis—Carter's ex-bandmate and best friend—and her husband Nick were chatting with Devon in one corner. Dylan Daughtry and Trevor McLachlan, two country stars I considered close friends, were talking with Aisha and her husband Gavin by the bar. Dozens of other people from the industry were scattered all across the room.

"What are you guys doing here?" I asked as I stepped closer to my friends and hugged them, happiness waltzing through me.

"We wouldn't have missed your big comeback for anything, man. You were great up there. It suited you. As if you've done it before."

I elbowed Carter in the ribs as he let out a warm chuckle after his quip.

"Ohmygod, the last song was so emotional. Did you know about the video?" April asked. "You looked to be in total shock."

"Because I was. I had no idea."

"Well, I was a crying mess. That was beautiful," Dahlia chimed in.

"Thanks," I croaked out, another surge of emotions building in my throat. "How have you been, Dah? It's been a long time."

"Great. I'm glad I didn't miss your big return. Next

time you guys are spending time together, we'll try to be there. I'm sorry we missed your birthday."

"It's okay. I know how crazy life can get. I'm happy you came tonight. It's good seeing you. Gimme half an hour. I'll say hello to everybody and be back so we can catch up," I said, leaving them as Riley joined us.

Four hours later, I entered my hotel suite and perused the empty space around me. A set of leather couches, a small kitchen with a dining table by the floor-to-ceiling windows overlooking the city, a bar along the wall leading to what I assumed were the bedroom and bathroom. With its ten-foot-high ceilings, wooden-planked floor, and dark-colored artworks decorating the walls, the sumptuous suite —too big for one man—lacked some liveliness. Every-thing was immaculate, a contrast to my home where toys, glitter, and princess outfits brought a touch of life to every room. Here, the reality of my loneliness weighed heavier than ever before. In the last two years, I'd never been away from home. Somehow, I doubted I would ever get used to the pristine and superficial decor of hotel rooms again.

Being here felt wrong. My children were with a nanny instead of their parents. Their mother should have been the one caring for them. Kissing them goodnight, and tucking them into their beds.

Adrenaline still ran high in my bloodstream, not letting me close my eyes and surrender myself to sleep. I craved a diversion. Something to keep my mind busy.

Music was my drug of choice.

I doubted any junkie could go to bed after shooting their best stuff up their arm.

Dressed in a pair of washout jeans and a long-sleeved black cotton shirt, I made my way to the hotel bar. I looked at the time. Twenty minutes until last call.

I sat on a stool by the bar and ordered a whiskey. "Make it a double," I told the bartender.

I fidgeted with the paper coaster as he poured the drink before me. I chugged half of it in one gulp, relishing the burning sensation down my throat.

Some of my nerves settled. A sense of calmness washed through me.

I closed my eyes and listened to the mellow song playing in the almost-empty bar as I nursed the rest of my drink. Slower this time.

The alcohol relaxed me.

I could breathe easier.

My thoughts moved far away from the two little girls waiting for me at home.

With a wave of my hand, I addressed the bartender, now busy drying glasses with a white cloth. "Hit me again."

"You want company?" a woman, about my age, dressed in a short cobalt dress asked as she took the stool next to mine.

"I'm fine," I said, keeping my gaze low.

"You sure? You look lonely." We exchanged small smiles. "Here for business?"

I cringed at the interruption but answered anyway. "Sorta. What about you?"

"My sister's wedding. She's the worst. I was supposed to stay at her place tonight, but she went all bridezilla at her maid of honor. Got the hell out of there before it was my turn." She let out a laugh that warmed my insides.

I raised my glass. "Cheers to getting away. Crazy brides-to-be are the worst."

The woman brought her wineglass to her lips and pushed her long blonde hair over her shoulder before holding out a hand. "I'm Lucy, by the way."

"Sam," I said, shaking her hand.

"Do this often? Come to the hotel bar and drink by yourself?

I shook my head, mirroring her smile. "Not in a long time."

"Closing in five minutes," the bartender said, picking up my empty tumbler.

"Already? I thought I had more time. Can I get another one?" Lucy slid her credit card across the counter. "Pour Sam one too and put his tab on my card, please."

"You don't have to do this, but thanks," I said with a nod.

"It's my pleasure. You want to finish your drink upstairs?" She arched a perfectly plucked brow, her chin pointing at my glass.

Could losing myself in a beautiful woman cure me of my nanny obsession?

Lucy squeezed my forearm, her touch comforting. "No pressure. We can just talk. I'm not tired, and I could use some friendly conversation. I flew from Europe, and let me tell you jet lag is a real thing."

"Conversation. Yeah, I can do that."

She fetched her purse. "Follow me then." We both grabbed our drinks and walked to the elevator in easy silence. I cast a discreet glance toward the lobby. No doubt Brent, the security detail shadowing me tonight, was some-where around. I caught sight of him as I stepped into the car, and he joined us just in time, before the door closed.

"Which room are you in?" I asked, for Brent's sake, and to prevent him from following me.

"Fifteen-o-seven. Why?"

I shrugged. "No reason. Was wondering if we were on the same floor."

My bodyguard gave me a subtle nod once the elevator

car stopped. Before we could even shut the door behind us, he'd be standing by Lucy's room.

———

Lucy's hand landed on my thigh as she sat beside me on the mattress. Her touch warmed me up and sent a foreign buzz through me. My brain swam in a whiskey bliss, just enough that every tingle running through me electrified my body. Her floral scent, mixed with the wafts of red wine, spiraled around me. Her teeth left indents on her lower lip, and I leaned closer, ready to leave my own.

She locked her fingers behind my neck, and pulling me closer, she brushed her lips against mine. I sucked in a breath, contradictory thoughts battling inside me. Right then, I decided to turn off all the warning signals screaming inside my head.

Lucy lowered her fingers to my belt buckle. I tried to relax. To enjoy the present. To let go. But no matter how hard I wanted to relax and surrender myself to her touch, everything about this moment felt wrong. As if I was a guy cheating on the most precious person in his life. And truth be told, I'd never been the *fuck random chick on the road* kind of rock star. All my life, I'd been in steady and lasting relationships. I wasn't interested in those games. Up until now, I'd only slept with women I had genuine feelings for.

Lucy moaned against my mouth as she unzipped me, and I pushed back. She searched my eyes, lust filling hers. Something I couldn't share, however much I tried to convince myself. Even my body wasn't into it.

Before her hands could reach the waistband of my boxer briefs, I jumped to my feet. "I'm…I'm sorry," I said, scratching the top of my head.

"It's not you, it's me? That's what you're about to say, right?"

I swallowed my uneasiness. "Yeah… There's someone else. I've been trying to move on, to forget about her, but I see her everywhere, even in my dreams."

"Lucky girl."

I let out a half-snort. "Let's just say it's complicated."

Lucy patted the comforter beside her. "Wanna talk about it?" I eyed the empty spot I'd vacated seconds ago. "I'm not gonna jump your bones. I promise. At the bar, I said we could talk. So here I am, inviting you to confide in me."

I zipped and buttoned my pants and sat next to her after buckling my belt. I had no one else to talk to about this. If I went to Riley, he would freak out. Devon would worry about me and the girls. Carter would tell me, "I told you so." And none of my other friends knew Madison, so they wouldn't be of any help. Perhaps opening up to a stranger would be best after all.

"Okay, let's see. Where should I begin?"

The woman offered me a lopsided smile. "The beginning?"

"Well, my wife divorced me two years ago. She packed her bags and left one night. No explanations other than she hated being a mother to our daughters. So, the girls and I have been alone all this time… Well, until my best friend persuaded me to hire a nanny so I'd be able to go back to work and live again…"

And just like that, I told a stranger all about my relationship with Madison without giving her too many details, just the main facts.

A weight left my back as I spoke the words out. "I'm unable *not* to think about her. All the time. And we're about to live in close quarters for six months in a RV because I have to go on the road for work, and I'm barely holding it together as it is." The RV was close enough to a tour bus, I figured. I wouldn't reveal too much about myself, keeping it vague in case she hadn't recognized me.

Her hand enveloped mine in a comforting gesture. "Sam, does she love you back?"

My head cocked in her direction at the L-word. "I'm not…huh…it's not… No one said anything about love. It-it's just a crush, but for some reason, it won't go away. Even after all this time. Even after I've told her she was too young for me. She doesn't deserve to be tied down with two kids at her age. That would be incredibly selfish to ask that much of her."

She shook her head. "Sam, did you ask her what she desires? You can't make assumptions and decisions for her. She's an adult. She deserves to make her *own* choices, to decide what's good for *her*. Whether it's you and your daughters or something else, that's not your call to make. It's hers. I'm pretty certain, with everything you've told me, that she's strong enough to deal with whatever she chooses. But either way, you gotta respect her voice. It would be a shame to deprive your daughters, and you, of this amazing woman because you can't accept where her heart stands, don't you think?"

I pressed my clammy hands onto my thighs. "But what if…what if she misses out on her youth because she dates me? What if it all goes to shit and my girls lose the only woman who has ever truly loved them?"

"What if it's the best thing for all of you? Aren't you curious to find out? Are you willing to miss out on the opportunity just because you're afraid of hypothetical situations that haven't even occurred yet?"

I shook my head, keeping my chin down. "Guess not."

"So, what are you doing here then? Why are you here

with me instead of there with her? Why aren't you opening your heart to her and seeing what she thinks? Where it'll take you?"

I fought my breathing to return to normal—and the words to stay put.

My gaze met Lucy's and she nodded, waiting for me to speak the truth.

Time halted for endless minutes.

My heart drummed in my chest, unable to stay still.

"So?" she pushed.

"Because…because I'm scared. I-I'm fucking scared. Happy now? The last time I trusted someone with my heart, she walked away. She fucking left and never explained anything to me. How can I be sure that this time with Maddie, it won't be a re-run of the same saga? How can I be sure I'm not putting my heart at risk again? That I'm not the problem? That my love isn't defective?"

Lucy smiled. "You can't be. You are not the problem. Love is like that. It *is* messy. And complicated. But it is also beautiful."

Her words thrived in the space between us.

"It's late. I should let you get some sleep." I stood up, and she walked me to the door. "Thank you," I said, dropping a kiss on her cheek. "It doesn't seem much right now, but you've helped me figure things out. I'm sorry I couldn't go through with whatever we were doing earlier."

She rested her hand on mine. "I'm happy I could help. For what it's worth, and I know we've just met, I can tell you're one of the good ones. That girl is lucky to have you by her side. She'd be a fool not to trust you with her heart."

I opened the door.

"Good night, Sam."

"Night, Lucy."

30

MADISON

I woke up to the chime of my phone. My eyes stung from the tears I'd cried earlier. In a short span of time, I had lost my best friend and fallen in love, hard, with my boss, a man with whom I had no chance of a future. The harsh truth hit me like a freight train. And stomped on my broken heart. A new notification came through. I patted the bed around me, looking for my device. With a deep inhale, I checked the screen, not sure I was ready in case it was Sam. Texting with him, even over silly subjects, would only magnify the reality I'd forever be his friend.

Nothing more.

I relaxed my shoulders at the name flashing on my screen.

RILEY

Click the link below. It was a hit. You're a genius. You should be proud of yourself. I know I am. It was even more emotional than we thought it would be. Check his reaction. It's priceless. I filmed it for you.

Great job, Madison.

Don't have too many awesome ideas, or I'll
have to hire you full-time, working for me.
Just kidding. I recognize talent, and you're
exceptional at what you do. Working with
kids is your calling.

[link]

Tears burned the back of my eyes the instant they landed on Sam onstage, hearing his daughters' voices just as he strummed the first chord of his latest song's chorus. The one he wrote for them. He looked around as if searching for them, then found the video playing on the screen behind him. The same video I had shot of the girls running around in the backyard last summer, their faces split with huge grins, and laughter in the air. Pure happiness. Raw moments between a devoted father and his adoring daughters.

I cupped my overexcited heart with a hand as I watched the video for a second and a third time.

Even on the tiny screen, Sam looked handsome. This video, filmed by Riley or someone on his team from backstage, showed a side of Sam that none of the other clips I'd seen online revealed. A lightness. A sense of belonging. Of calm. Something that wasn't visible in his earlier career days.

ME

Thank you for sending it to me. It means a
lot. I'm glad it was a success.

An emotion I couldn't name wrapped tightly around my heart, and I sealed my eyelids, wishing sleep would claim me again so I could be free from the agony swarming within me.

By the morning, my good spirits had returned, and the girls and I spent the day making craft projects in the den, the rain outside taming their bubbling excitement.

It was almost two at night when cries woke me up this time.

"Monster. Monster. The monster is here."

I bolted up the stairs two at a time, panic rising in me when I heard Justine screaming in her sleep. It was the last night before Sam returned home. We had chatted with him earlier, and he'd told the girls he would be here after breakfast the following day. I adjusted my tank top and night shorts before pushing the door open and tiptoeing into the room. A nightlight cast a soft glow around the space. The sight of Justine, her face and neckline soaked in tears, broke my heart.

"Hey, sweetie. It was just a bad dream." I pulled her into my embrace as I squatted before her, dabbing her tears with my fingertips, and sprinkling kisses along her hairline. "I'm here. It's okay now. You're safe. I've got you."

Nightmares.

Growing up, they had been a nightly occurrence. Until they appeared further and further apart and stopped. Now that they had made a comeback, I prayed they would leave me alone soon enough.

"I'm here, and I'll chase all the monsters away."

She heaved and hiccupped, never loosening her white-knuckled grip on me.

"Want me to lie down beside you until you fall asleep?"

"*Yesss.*" Her voice shook with the remnants of her nightmare.

"Then scoot over. Let's cuddle."

We settled ourselves under the covers. I kept my arms around her, and she pressed her face into my chest.

"Sing Daddy's song."

"You want me to sing it to you or play it on my phone."

"Sing."

I coughed to loosen my voice, and the lyrics spilled from my lips. Each girl had a few favorite songs from their daddy's repertoire and without asking, I knew which one would soothe her better. Justine's eyes fluttered close, and before I was even done, she had fallen back asleep, her tiny fingers fastened around mine. A spark shone in me. I had become someone else's safe harbor. The small gesture confirmed I hadn't landed in the Stevenses' lives by chance. I was always meant to be here and help them heal. The same way people had done for me all those years ago.

I combed Justine's hair with my fingers, singing the last verse of Sam's song.

Once I was sure she was back in dreamland, I made my way downstairs toward my bedroom.

In the dark, humming the song I'd just sung, I didn't notice the silhouette lurking near my door. I bumped into a human wall and almost crash-landed on my ass if it weren't for his strong arms circling my waist just in time.

My pulse went ballistic.

"You?" I asked once the shock subsided and my vocal cords regained their function. "What are you doing here? You scared the shit out of me. I thought… I thought you said—"

He ran a hand through his hair, and my eyes followed the gesture, mesmerized. "What you did minutes ago was hot."

My eyebrows furrowed. What was he talking about? "Almost falling?" I risked.

He shook his head, and my throat worked hard to catch up with my overzealous breathing.

"What then?"

His stare moved down to his hands still holding me in place. I drew in a shaky breath. Heat vibrated through me where our bodies connected. Would it be strange to wish his hands could stay anchored to me longer?

"Maddie, you sang *my* song." Sam's voice sounded rougher than usual, and I wondered if it was due to him belting out lyrics two nights in a row or if my presence affected him with an intensity I'd never truly realized before.

"You…huh…you heard that?"

He bowed his head, now standing so close my lips could skim his if we just tilted our heads little to the right.

"I heard from the second verse. Goose bumps spread on my arms. I'll say it again, even though I already know it —you have a great voice, Madison."

He took his time pronouncing my name, rolling it on his tongue like a prayer.

My heart, my composure, my head, they all spun at a vertiginous speed.

We fixated on each other.

"Sam, what are you doing here? You said you were coming back tomorrow."

He cast a glance at his watch. "It's already tomorrow, isn't it?"

I dissolved at his proximity.

"Being alone in a hotel room sucks. I missed you guys. And there was something I kinda had to do."

Blood couldn't reach my brain anymore because I saw stars. Now, I had no more doubt. This husky tone was Sam's turned-on voice.

"What?" I swallowed—or tried to—in vain.

"Thank you. For what you did. Also, I gotta tell you something else since I had a lot of time to think."

"You gotta? You had?"

He bobbed his head.

I swallowed my angst. "What about?"

"Us."

Like two poles attracted to each other, the space separating us shrank.

His smoldering gaze nailed me to the floor, and I got sucked into the vortex of everything that Sam Stevens was. He hadn't even touched me yet, and already he possessed me in the most intimate ways.

My jaw went slack as I watched him.

Mischief and hunger crossed his eyes, all directed at me.

Only one question echoed in my head. Would I survive the night?

31

SAM

"I gotta say, that video, with the girls and me… Wow. Riley told me it was your idea. Maddie… It's the most amazing thing anyone has done for me in a very long time. It touched me…in a way I'll never be able to fully explain."

I wished nothing more than a chance to swim in the pool of her irises as Madison watched me with something akin to adoration. Was it? I watched her a little longer, taking in the trembling of her lips, the spark in her eyes, the quick, uneven breaths. Those signs didn't lie. Yeah, this girl was as gone for me as I was for her.

"It was nothing, I…I just thought you'd like it. Have a piece of them with you. Every night."

"Maddie, it was not nothing. It was everything." I paused, my eyelids heavy, the moment hanging between us. "Both nights I was away, I wished for one thing…and one thing only."

Her tongue teased the edge of her lip as she waited for me to go on. The small movement felt like a quiet invitation.

"*You.* I wished I could share those moments with *you.*"

She blinked twice. "You did?"

"For an instant, I tried to forget you. To convince myself I was too old, too damaged, and my life was too complicated for you."

The column of her throat rippled. "How did it turn out?"

"Bad. Super bad. I'm desperate. I wanna know if it's all in my head. The connection we share. The lust. The desire. The chemistry. The easiness. Tell me I'm wrong, and I'll never bother you ever again. Tell me it's all in my mind and that I'm an old man and you feel nothing for me. Tell me to leave you alone and to move on."

Her eyes darkened. Her pupils dilated, almost wiping out the color of her irises.

Desire flooded us, thick and unrelenting. It clung to our skin, saturating the air between us. I could feel it in every one of my cells, wrapping around me. Making me its prisoner.

Madison shook her head. "No, I won't. I-I shouldn't think about you like that, but I can't help myself. You're *always* on my mind. My days get better the second you look at me...or smile at me. Or when you enter a room. I'm sorry. That's not... That's not why you hired me. Every day, it gets harder to keep the longing that consumes me locked inside."

I exhaled my relief. "All I want is to kiss you, but I can't. God knows I crave it… I crave you. Every part of me aches to. But we can't cross that line. If we do, we'll never be able to work together afterward, and we're leaving for almost six months on a tour bus."

"I...I agree." Her low murmur only fed the inferno that burned between us.

Lust and craving—they were tearing at my sanity. Soon enough, I'd lose my mind.

Madison twisted a strand of her hair around her finger, and I was dying to do it myself. I wanted to touch her, to feel her heart beating against mine. Her heat all around me. Engulfing me. Possessing me.

I forced out the words that made the most sense. "I-I'm sorry. I need you… The girls need you. I can't…I can't risk everything. They've lost too much already. I can't be the one who chases you away from their lives if getting together messes everything up."

Instead of pulling back, we collided.

I cradled her face with both hands, and I lost myself in her eyes.

Her lips called me in.

Her breast molded to my chest as I pulled her closer, my fingertips digging into the crests of her hips.

"Sam, I—"

"I know, babe." I closed my eyes. "Just bear with me here." I couldn't look at her anymore. The temptation to eat her up staggered my being.

Madison's hand froze over the bulge in my pants, and I forgot how to breathe as fireworks exploded inside me.

How could just her caress feel so right?

The shackles of my constraints crumbled. I stopped overthinking the meaning of our magnetism and chose to be its willing participant—to surrender myself to the electrifying pull simmering between us. My reasons deserted me, and I ceded to the lure of her heart-shaped mouth. Backing her up against the wall, I dug my fingers into her plump ass and lifted her until she could lock her legs around me, her center rubbing against my painful erection.

Madison's tongue swept over mine. She stole every speck of air from my lungs.

I could die now, and I'd die a very happy man.

"Sam," she purred in a way that left me in pieces, then stitched me back together. "I never wanna stop."

I kneaded her breast over her top with one hand, and she deepened the kiss. "Me neither. Never. I'm so gone for you." Every trace of common sense I once had evaporate.

Flames licked my insides.

"Keep doing what you're doing because it feels too damn good," she muttered against my lips.

Her words acted like a magical spell, and my dick throbbed in my pants, desperate for the attention of the woman rocking my world. Every inch of her.

Her fingers traveled under the fabric of my shirt, and I tensed, every part of me alert and ready to be cherished. It'd been so long. How could I have spent all this time without this? Affection and sex. Someone to love. To share my life with.

My chest muscles tensed under the pads of her fingers, each touch bewitching.

A carnal thirst rose in me, and my lips found hers. I peeled her tank top over her head and cupped her naked breasts with my palms. I flew to heaven right there. I died and came back to life. "You're beautiful," I said, between pants. "So fucking beautiful."

"I'm all yours. I want you… All of you. Claim me."

Her words broke years of restraint. They brought me back to my essence. To me. The one person I had neglected over the last two years.

I pushed her hair away from her face as I lost myself in the depths of her eyes. Into the promises that shone right through them. In the simple but powerful gesture, Madison bared her soul to me, not hiding anything from me. All the answers I was looking for lay right there, ready for me to hold on to and never let go.

My heart vibrated against my ribcage.

The vision of her, exposed and vulnerable, but taking what could be rightfully hers stole my breath away.

My mouth returned to assault her with a passionate kiss. I couldn't breathe on my own. Madison possessed the only viable air my body required to survive.

We kissed until it shut all the voices in my head. Until only *us* mattered. Until I surrendered myself to the animalistic desire coursing through my bloodstream, and nothing could stop me anymore.

After she got rid of my shirt, she took my hand in hers and pushed it past the elastic waistband of her night shorts, her eyes pleading with me. As if it already had memorized the path before, my fingers followed the moisture trail leading to her wet heat. Her breath hissed out when I slid one finger inside, then a second. She bit her bottom lip as I glided my digits back and forth, yelps spilling from deep within her. A melody to my soul.

She rode my hand and looked both magnificent and incredible as she did.

Fucking mine.

Our hastened breaths mingled. My head spun, the oxygen molecules around us getting scarce. The temperature of the room reached dangerous heights as we combusted together.

We were humming the same chorus.

We were singing the same lyrics.

Madison Prescott was the music in my life. More real than any note on a sheet of paper could ever be. More than any chords from my guitar.

She rolled her hips over my hand, chasing a release. She dug her nails into my nape, anchoring herself to me. I slid my digits in and out faster and captured each of her whimpers with my lips. I tangled my fingers in her hair, guiding her head so I could steal every breath. She traced the seam of my mouth with her tongue. My balls tightened, and I clenched the muscles of my ass, doing all I could to prevent myself from shooting my load. Madison was my downfall. I had become a bomb, ticking and ready to explode.

Her moans filled the silence of the night.

My pace turned frantic. Goose bumps tickled my spine. A heady heat surged through me.

"Sam." She whispered my name like a prayer.

I played with her swollen bundle of nerves with the pad of my thumb and lowered my other hand, my fingertips digging into her soft ass cheek to lift her up and hold her closer to me.

Her head tilted back. I watched her, relishing the lust drawn on her features and the blush coloring her cheeks.

My mouth devoured hers, our tongues famished for each other. My teeth and lips feasted on her slender neck.

Her grip on me tightened, and she shut her eyes. I accelerated the rhythm of my fingers. Her body clenched around my digits as she surfed the first wave of pleasure. I fastened my arms around her, holding her against me, wishing she could decode the thrumming of my heart and grasp the depth of my feelings. I couldn't speak them aloud —not now, at least.

Not before the tour was over and we could give our relationship a real chance.

My fears lingered on the outskirts of my mind, ready to make a comeback and screw with my head.

I lowered Madison back to her feet, helping her with her balance. We fixated on each other. If I indulged us, there would be no going back.

"Sam, I need you. Inside me," she said with a trembling voice.

It brought me back to the present. To us. It killed the apprehension lurking at its source. Before I could react, she plunged her hand into my pants and boxer briefs and fisted my steeled length, shaping her hand around it. Taking ownership of the part of me that already belonged to her —no matter what lies I told to convince myself otherwise.

A relieved puff of air escaped her lips. A guttural growl rumbled from mine.

I had no more doubts.

Madison owned me. Body and soul. And I wished nothing more than to be hers. Here, now, and forever.

"Fuck, I don't have a condom," I said, breathless and barely able to speak coherent words as she worked my rock-hard manhood like nobody else had done in years. Like only she could. Scorching heat clung to my vertebrae. My breathing hitched. How could I be so stupid? I hadn't worn or bought a piece of rubber in almost ten years. That was a rookie mistake. A faux pas. I was in such a hurry to get here tonight that I'd convinced Riley to drive me straight home after my show, not thinking clearly. The adrenaline of giving a concert always got me horny. For the length of the entire show, Madison had been the only person I wished I could live that moment with. I pictured her standing on the side of the stage so often that I started believing she was there with me after the fifth song. In my head, I dedicated each one to her. Only her.

I raked my fingers through my locks. "Babe, I'm sorry."

"Sam, I never had sex without one, and it's been a long while since the last time."

I blinked. "I believed—" I didn't want to voice those thoughts out loud. I didn't want the idea of her with another man to spoil the moment.

"No." She shook her head, pursing her lips. "I…

couldn't." Two words. Two words that wrecked me and spread a wave of euphoria and something else I couldn't quite name through my being. We eye-fucked each other for far too long, air still rushing to get in and out of our lungs. "I'm on the pill." She studied my reaction. "I'm okay with it…with you. Unless you wanna stop." She looked vulnerable right now, offering herself to the greedy man in me without a second thought.

"You sure?" I smoothed the length of her bottom lip with my thumb.

"Only with you," she murmured, her eyes pulling me into a new trance.

My lips returned to hers. Hungry. I ate her mouth as if it were my last meal. Our tongues tangoed with each other. I cupped one naked breast, rolling the hard tip between my fingers. A scorching rampage stirred within me. How could kissing and touching her feel so damn right? The clouds of my conscience parted. Light came back into my life, brighter and more blinding than ever before.

Her hands returned to my crotch, pumping me until my knees weakened.

I leaned forward to lick her diamond-hard rosy nipples and played them with my teeth while Madison's hand worked me in long and tantalizing strokes.

"Only with you," she repeated, bewitching me with her hooded eyelids, flushed cheeks, and swollen lips. Looking perfect. All my doing.

With an exhale, I ordered, "Turn around."

This wasn't delicate. This was desperate. A yearning I couldn't contain anymore. One I knew I might regret later but couldn't stop. Couldn't deny myself any longer.

Yanking her tiny shorts and cotton panties down her legs, I held her arms over her head with one hand while positioning her pelvis with the other. With my knee, I pushed her legs further apart. Her face pressed against the wall, and the sparks that flashed my way when our gazes met over her shoulder got me harder—as if it could even be possible. My fingers returned to her folds, coating them with her arousal. Urging her down with a palm between her shoulder blades until her ass pointed up, I lined my dick with her opening. Chills ran along my back. My teeth dug into my tongue, forcing me to focus and not let go too soon. Inch by inch, I pushed into her tight channel. Madison welcomed all of me with one push, her ass flush with my lower abdomen.

"Ohmyfuckinggod," I mumbled. Bending my upper body to mold to her back, I caught a fistful of her hair, searching for her mouth.

We breathed out together. Embedded inside her walls, unable to move, too many overwhelming sensations coursing through me, I devoured her in a manner I couldn't prevent myself anymore.

My fingers tangled in her hair.

Slowly, I got into a rhythm. My hand holding her arms above her head grounded me to this instant.

I accelerated the movements, unable to go slow anymore. Too engrossed in this woman to deprive us of this. The connection. The ecstasy.

Thrusting into her, my hips moved with purpose.

Madison cried out my name, and I swallowed the whimpers tumbling from her lips.

"You're perfect. So perfect," I said, breathless, getting her hair away from her nape so I could feast on the flesh there.

My growls became her moans.

My body ended where hers began.

I pounded into Madison again and again. My brain

blanked out, my body only driven by the sounds passing through her luscious lips.

I let go of her hair, withdrew from her warmth, and flipped her until her back hit the wall. We stared at each other, panting, no word strong enough to express the intensity of the moment.

"Oh, Sam," she moaned as I lifted her up, spearing her with my dick, and rammed into her with abandon. Her grip around my neck tightened. I sank into her, using my arms to glide her up and down my shaft.

We were catching fire together.

The chains I had fastened around my unavailable heart loosened.

Madison cried out my name again, and I hammered into her like it was my sole mission in life. The reason for my existence. My purpose.

My fingers wrapped around her neck of their own volition, and I pressed my forehead to hers as I caught my breath. Our lips reconnected. I'd never get enough.

One of my palms returned to her breast, and I kneaded it while my tongue cherished her other nipple.

My hand traced down her body, halting at the junction of her thighs. As I pushed into her deeper, my fingers rubbed her clit, eliciting muffled cries from her.

Madison moaned. Her back hit the wall with every roll of my hips.

A loud groan exited my mouth. I was combusting inside out.

I clasped her chin between my fingers, holding her in place, and lost myself in her eyes as she surfed her climax.

She vibrated against me, and we never broke eye contact.

My own release was held by a flimsy thread. I was so close, but I dreaded the instant it would all be over.

My movements were less precise as I fought with my orgasm.

I tried, I really did, but I couldn't prevent myself anymore.

When I lowered Madison to her feet, I pulled out. She wrapped her fist tight around me, milking my cock to the last drop.

Gravity left me.

I nibbled her bare shoulder with my teeth, grounding me to this world. She cried out, and I soothed the sting with my tongue and more kisses. I surrendered myself to her, my eyes closing, desperate to remember the bliss. More jolts traversed my body. Panting, I tried to suck in a breath. A million sensations filled me. Colored dots danced in my vision.

Once I came down from the high, I opened my eyes.

My release adorned Madison's bare stomach, and both our gazes landed there.

I rested my hand on the side of her face as I pressed my forehead against hers, the two of us panting for air.

I'd never experienced anything like this before. A sense of belonging, of being home. A perception I had found my place in this world. More than any concert could ever provide me.

My mouth descended on her reddened lips, and I took my time kissing her, aware it would be the last time. No way would I let myself go there ever again—for the time being—no matter how incredible it felt. Not before we finished touring together. Because if I messed up, it would affect my kids and everything we all had been working for.

"You know it can't happen again," Madison said as if she could read my mind—and my worst fears. "Not for the next six months at least."

I bobbed my head.

"Then kiss me one last time."

Without another word, I molded my lips to the woman's who owned my heart a lot more each day. The one who was quickly becoming the center of my universe. And my dreams.

She grinned at me as I stepped back. The lightness in my chest was something new to me, and I relished the feeling and the freedom it provided.

I balled the fabric of my T-shirt and wiped all traces of me from her belly.

Madison watched me with eyes beaming with adoration. "Thanks," she said once I finished.

My forehead returned to hers, and our fingers intertwined. "Tell me to walk away," I asked.

She shook her head, a soft laugh breaking the wheezing of our breathing.

"I'm not strong enough to resist you, Maddie. I don't have it in me to stay away from you. You gotta be the bigger person here and order me to go. To leave you alone. It's been too long since the last time I've felt something for someone else. And right now, I'm feeling lots of things for you. And my mind is spinning with a whole lot more dirty things I wish I could do to you after what we've just done."

My eyes followed the length of her, lingering for a moment over her chest, her breasts rising and falling with every intake of air. I closed my eyes, doing my best not to touch them again, to remember how they fit into my hands. Not to let my dick rule my common sense and love her with infinite passion this time around. Sure, we got rid of the built-up tension that had been intoxicating our relationship since day one, but I wanted to cherish her with passion now. But if we continued what we'd started, I'd never be able to stop or be reasonable.

Her eyes glistened with bliss, and she chewed on her

lips. I ran my thumb across their fullness, relishing the aftermath quakes of her body under my touch.

"You'll be the end of me. We must come up with rules on the road, or I'll get you naked every chance I get. And fair warning. The adrenaline coursing through my bloodstream after playing concerts makes me horny."

"I can stay in the crew bus. It's no big deal."

"No." I clutched her upper arms. My throat worked. Electricity darted between us. "I want you on *our* bus. On *my* bus. That's where you belong. I don't consider you staff, Maddie. You're much more than that. You're much more to me. You should know that by now. You're family. Whether we want it or not, we're tied together by some invisible thread neither of us can escape. And in all honesty, I could never envision going on this tour if you weren't there—beside me. Loving my daughters as your own. Sharing our lives… *My* life. I trust you. I need *you*. The girls do too. You'll stay with us. End of discussion."

Madison nodded, her irises drawing me in, threatening to swallow me whole and make me hers now and forever.

"What if it doesn't work?" Her voice had lost her previous amusement.

"Babe, we'll make it work. Don't worry. I'm just… We'll find a way to be around each other without complicating everything until we can be together for real. As I said, we'll set rules. Trust me, okay?"

"Yeah," she said, her voice low and tantalizing as it blanketed us with promises we had no idea how to keep. "Rules…right." Moisture clouded her eyes, and I almost threw all my own words out of the window right there and promised her everything she was silently begging for.

I couldn't look away. Madison's energy always captured me, and I liked every minute of it. I felt alive. I felt like a man again, not just a father, but a complex being with desire and a dick useful for more than just taking a leak.

"Walk away now," I urged. "Or I'll lock us in my room, and I'll never let you out. I'm a starving man, and you woke up the beast in me, babe. My blood boils, and my dick stirs when you're around."

"Sam, I'm not sure I can…"

I placed a finger against her lips. She kissed my digit, and the simple touch awoke new sensations inside me.

"Believe me, I'm dying to touch you, all of you, again. To savor your flesh. Every corner of it. To hold you in my arms while I sleep, to kiss you every second of every day." I shut my eyes. The smell of her washed over me, and I wondered if she could spray it over my pillow. Just for tonight. I shook my head again, flushing away my silly thoughts.

My mouth returned to hers, and our bodies blended together. Less desperate this time around, but our hands still in discovery mode.

"You smell divine." One kiss on her shoulder. "Your skin is velvet." A kiss on her collarbone. "I could eat you up for the rest of my life."

I sucked on a pebbled nipple while she massaged my scalp with her fingers. Her whimpers increased when I played her with my teeth. She ground her hips against mine, and I held her still. My entire self hated me as I leaned back. I noticed the gloss in her eyes. The love marks on her neck. The rosiness of her puckered peaks. Dropping to my knees, I laved her soaked center with one flick of my tongue.

Madison gasped.

"Now I can't wait for the tour to be over," I said. "You'll think about me every time you touch yourself. And the taste of you will linger on my tongue."

"Leave now, or it'll be me who locks you up in my bedroom. You're not allowed to tease me this good. It's unfair that I'll have to wait half a year for the real thing." A contagious grin stretched across her face.

I kissed the apex of her thighs and made my way up to her sticky abdomen, the moist valley of her breasts, her scruff-marked jawline, and her cherry lips. All traces of me, I had branded onto her.

"Yes, it is unfair," I confirmed.

Madison crashed her lips on mine. My head spun at a dizzying pace. Her touch jolted my heart back to life. Fireworks, butterflies, sparks, all that shit filled my stomach. I clutched her waist, pulling her closer to me, wanting to feel every inch of her pressed against every inch of me one last time.

Before I could deepen the kiss, she leaned back. "Sam, be honest. Every time we touch, your heart rate picks up." She positioned a hand over my chest. "Don't go to bed thinking it was a mistake, okay? I feel it too." She grabbed my hand and splayed it over her left breast. "See?" We stared at each other for a few beats. After a minute, she pushed me away, using both hands. "Go. Now."

"Good night, Maddie," I said, kissing her one last time, branding my mouth to hers.

With my heart swelling in my chest, so full it could burst at any second, I turned on my heel, leaving her behind, and climbed the stairs leading to my room.

"Night, Sam," Madison whispered in the dark before turning the light off. Her bedroom door clicked as she closed it behind her, the sound sinking my spirit.

How would I ever be able to resist her now that I had tasted what should be mine?

32

MADISON

"Do we have everything ready for tonight?" Sam asked, listing the items he had noted on his phone. "Bouncing house. *Check.* Endless supply of hot dogs. *Check.* Ice cream. *Check.* Music. *Check.* Decorations. *Check.* Makeup for the kids. *Check.* Drinks for the adults. *Check.* We're good to go." He put his phone away, pushing the buggy toward the checkout counter, Justine and Mikaella standing at the far end, giggling.

He brushed his fingers along my lower back as I helped him place everything on the conveyor belt, and I shivered under his gentle touch. We were leaving in a week, and since the night we had sex, despite our best resolve, we couldn't keep our hands to ourselves for long periods. Not completely at least. A touch here. A caress there. A kiss on my temple. Grazing of our fingers. Those were insignificant details for any onlooker, but to me, they meant a lot.

Each time we faced each other, my body hummed, begging to be abandoned to his expert hands. This dance had become our reality, and our nightmare, tied together with a giant bow of blazing lust.

Tonight, we were having that party Sam had talked about when I first started working at his house. The one to celebrate us going on tour. Friends of the girls were coming over. Some of Sam's friends and neighbors, Emily, my sister, and her friends too. People we loved and would miss while we were away.

Back home, I put excited little girls down for a nap before helping Sam to finish the last details. We had made plans to sleep on the bus tonight. For the second night in a row. Last night was a bit chaotic. The girls stayed awake past their bedtime, unable to calm down, and I barely slept in my bunk. Just the thought of Sam lying behind the wall had my body and mind going haywire. How many times had I pictured myself joining him in his room or woken up with a start, thinking the noise I'd heard belonged to him as he climbed into my bed?

As the party raged outside and the guys ran the grill, I retreated inside, making sure nobody missed anything.

Devon came to me after a moment. "I was wondering where you went. How are you doing?" she asked, bringing her drink to her mouth. "Is everything all right?"

I pasted a smile onto my lips. "Sure. I just felt like escaping the madness for a few minutes."

She leaned against the countertop next to me, her eyes following my line of sight through the window. "Have you talked about it?" she asked after a beat.

"About what?" I asked, unable to grasp where our conversation was heading.

"Those feelings you two have for each other."

I coughed behind my fist and sipped my drink, trying hard to look unaffected. "Not sure what you're talking about."

With her eyes still trained outside, she continued, "It's

easy to see, Maddie. Only fools wouldn't be able to grasp the intensity of your chemistry."

As if he sensed my eyes on him, Sam's gaze found mine through the glass, and he aimed that irresistible smile in my direction—the one I couldn't resist—and waved.

A lone tear leaked from my eye, and I wiped it off. "It doesn't matter. We won't be doing anything about it." I shrugged.

"Why not?" Devon asked, her attention now locked on me.

"Because… The girls. The tour. The risks. The complications. Nothing plays in our favor. We'll wait until after the tour and see. Anyway, I'm on his payroll. I'm just an employee, so it would be weird."

Devon gripped my upper arms and turned me so we faced each other. "You're not. You're the woman who stands beside him as he tries to give his dreams another shot. You're the woman his kids are head over heels in love with. And he is too, in case you were wondering. Sam can't stop talking about you when you're not around. Maddie this. Maddie that. He adores you. You changed him…for the better."

"It's the music."

"Nah. It is, in part, but it's mainly due to you. You put his heart back in his chest."

"Does Riley know?"

She shook her head. "I think he suspects something but has never said anything about it. Right now, he's so wrapped up in the tour that I'm not sure he grasps anything beyond it."

"Please don't tell him, okay? I'm not ready for the truth to be revealed. Like I said, the tour is the priority. And the girls. Nothing should come between any of these."

"I'll never tell a soul. But promise me that when it

gets too much and you need to vent, you'll come to me, okay? I'm having my first tour bus experience too, so we'll have each other to lean on. I wasn't sure at first when Riley proposed we join you guys for a few months, but I think the change of air will do us all some good. Life has been intense since we've met. We both need a breather in our daily lives. And I can work remotely, so why not?"

She squeezed my arm one last time before leaving me alone with our shared confessions.

Seconds later, Emily walked in. "There you are," my sister said. "That man of yours told me I'd find you here."

I pressed a hand over her mouth. "Shhh, Ems. He's not my man."

She burst out laughing. "Yeah, right. That's why he's not making conversation with anyone, too busy stalking you from his spot in the backyard. When Becks and I arrived, he made a joke about where my sexy baby sister was, and Sam almost jumped him. Told him to grant you the respect you deserve."

I blinked.

"See? I'm sure you two are banging. I'm just surprised you haven't said anything about it."

Warmth pooled in my cheeks at the way she studied my reaction. "We are not. It's complicated. We'll go on tour and discuss whatever this is afterward if there are still feelings involved. The timing sucks."

I downed most of my drink in one gulp. First Devon, now my sister.

"So, there are feelings involved?" she asked in her *big sister knows it all* tone.

"I didn't mean feelings, I meant attraction. Lots of it. It's distracting."

"Distracting. Nice choice of word." She smirked, and

the urge to rip it off her face with my nails tickled my fingertips.

I offered her a pointed look instead. "Fine. I have feelings. Happy now? Nothing says he mirrored them, though." I sighed. "It was supposed to be a short-term crush, not a *full blown scorching head over heels* firework."

"Ha, I knew it." Her smirk vanished.

Our eyes drifted to Sam through the window. As if he could tell I was staring, his eyes found mine again, and we both froze, transported into a world where no one else mattered but us.

"See?" my sister whispered. "It's not just you. He's infatuated with you too. What's meant to be will be. Don't overthink it. Just see where it takes you."

I bowed my head and sighed. "That's the plan."

"Maddie, one thing, though. Whatever goes down between you two, just make sure you're not pushing your own dreams away in the process, okay?"

"I'm not. I'm exactly where I wanna be. This tour, the chance to go on a new adventure, has my blood pumping. That's what makes me feel alive."

"After that. If you two are together… How will you fit your lifestyle with being a mother? Because no matter what you tell yourself, that's ultimately what you'll become. A mama to those kids. Are you ready for what it implies?"

"To be honest, that's the part that scares me the least, Ems. We are already bound. I love them so much. But you're right… After the tour, I don't wanna work a nine-to-five job or get a permanent teaching position. Or be someone else's trophy wife. I guess we'll see how the next six months go, and I'll reevaluate my career choices from there. Lots of things can happen in half a year. I'm confident it will turn out okay."

My sister pulled me into her arms. "Now I'll have to

serve Sam Stevens my big-sister *I'm watching you* and *don't mess with my little sister* warnings. I'm already excited." She rubbed her hands together, mischief flashing in her eyes. "You think Mika and Justine will one day be as close as we are? That their tragedy will bring them closer? Like it did to us?"

"Yep. They already are." I paused to drink a glass of water and cool down my conflicted emotions because the mere thought or talk about Sam got me unnerved.

"Have you told him? About our past?"

I shook my head. "Not yet. I opened up to Jacob. It was the first time I trusted someone enough to be honest about everything, and it didn't prevent him from walking away. Next time I'll tell someone I love about my history, I'll make sure we're meant to have a long-lasting relationship. I've learned my lesson. It hurts too much when someone I care about breaks my heart."

"Love. You deserve it. Never settle for anything less."

I looked away, the tumult inside me messing with my composure.

"Maddie, about our story… I understand. I have a hard time telling it too. It's okay. Don't rush anything. I'm not a relationship expert, but if Sam Stevens is the one, you'll know. Yeah, I believe he'll respect you enough to wait until you're ready to share. Don't stress over it."

"Thank you, Ems. For always having my back. Even when you were just a kid. I wasn't your responsibility, but you always made sure I was safe and sound and nobody could hurt me. That I had food to eat. You sacrificed a lot for me. And you saved my life."

"Anytime. I would do it all over again if we were faced with the same situation. You're not only my little sister, Maddie, but also my best friend. I'll always have your back."

"We turned out pretty good, considering the shitty hand we were dealt with. It made us stronger. In retrospect, I'm not sure I'd change our past because we wouldn't be standing here today if our stories had been different."

"It feels like a lifetime ago. Are you happy?" she asked.

"I am. The reality of the tour gets me giddy, and along with that, all aspects of my life are finally clicking into place."

"Big sister's warning. Follow your heart, okay? It's usually pretty perceptive and rarely wrong."

I nodded, and my sister wrapped her arms around me.

"Everything will be fine, Maddie. I have a great feeling about this. I love you."

———

"I heard my girls have rehearsed a song, and they asked if they could sing it today," Sam announced in front of the people crowded in his backyard.

His eyes searched mine when he said *my girls*. Effervescent feelings soared inside me.

"Yeah, they're following in my footsteps. I had no idea, I swear. It was a surprise to me too." His proud grin illuminated his face. "Please give my daughters the applause they deserve."

Justine, Mikaella, and I took the stage, aka the back deck. Jitters worked inside me. How could Sam do this for a living? Entertain a crowd. The girls looked to be in their element, though. They inherited their father's performing genes, both of them confident and strong-headed, even at their young age.

"The girls and I have worked hard to be ready for

tonight. Sam, this one is for you," I said, my voice quivering. I held my breath.

He watched me with sizzling intensity and tipped his head. I dissolved there, unable to look elsewhere. The connection we shared broke only when our gazes drifted to the girls, now standing in front of me.

Aisha Jones, whom I'd asked earlier if she could accompany the girls with her guitar, strummed the first chord of "Summer Night."

Justine and Mikaella started singing like we'd practiced, standing tall in the middle of the makeshift stage, holding each other's hands.

One Friday afternoon, that
    summer
The wind was blowing my hair
Convertible, country music, a
    picnic in a basket
And the girls in the backseat
The kids asked for waterfalls
    and sunshine
I asked for fresh air and a sign
    everything would be all
    right
We drove for hours, lost in our
    world...

Sam's eyes darted to me, and he mouthed a *Wow* and a heartfelt *Thank you.*

I placed my hands on my chest and mirrored his elated expression. I'd never be able to lie to myself. Emily was right. I loved him—more than logic could explain. Even after all this time, the night we'd gotten drunk in that bar, lost in each other, still haunted my dreams. The dance we'd shared under the girls' watchful eyes still sent jitters through my heart when I let myself relive the moment. And the night when we'd finally given in to temptation still haunted my days at the mere thought of it. No matter however much I tried to block the memories, they came back with a vengeance, pulsing through me until I combusted.

Aisha stepped forward and joined the girls in the chorus, her voice low, making sure not to steal the spotlight.

> **…Sunset, laughter, memories in bulk**
> **This is how happiness should be (yeah, it should)**
> **As long as those smiles on their faces never falter**
> **As long as those magical summer nights never get old**
> **Just grab my hands, babies, and hold tight**
> **And together, let's forget about everything else for a little longer…**

Riley walked to me and nudged my arm. "Maddie, what you're doing for those kids is priceless. You are a blessing in their lives."

I squeezed my eyes shut to control the dampness forming behind my eyelids.

We returned our focus to the girls, so adorably dressed in matching ruffled denim dresses and teal cowboy boots.

The song ended, and Sam rushed to them, hugging his daughters and praising their performance.

From a safe distance, I melted at the scene, feelings of glee shooting through me.

Sam steered his face my way, and a spark I'd never noticed before flashed in his irises. A sparkle intended for me. Only me.

Right there, I had the certitude that if given a chance, we'd make it work because we were two parts of the same soul, always drawn together and finding comfort in each other's presence.

———

Sitting outside the bus hours later, around the portable fire pit he'd bought earlier, Sam and I enjoyed the silence of the night. The party had been a success, and the last guests had left over an hour ago. The girls were fast asleep in their beds inside, the day having drained all the energy from them.

"You rarely talk about your dreams," Sam said, uncapping a bottle of beer, his profile illuminated by the dancing flames. "Want one?"

I shook my head. I was satisfied with water at this late hour, my head still spinning from all the sangria I'd had earlier.

"What do you want?" he asked.

I frowned. "What do you mean?"

"In life. Career-wise. Family-wise. Passion-wise. In general."

I wiped the condensation off the glass in my hand. "It's funny you ask. My sister told me today to never put my own dreams on the back burner for someone else."

Sam let out a throaty groan, and my gaze drifted to the

rippling of his throat. "Are you? Putting your dreams on hold?"

I said *No* with a shake of my head, unable to stop smiling. "Nah. I'm exactly where I wanna be. The tour, this opportunity, it's what I like. I can't say it's what I'll always want, but for now, I'm perfectly happy where I am. Thank you for taking me with you. I've never said it. But I'm thankful. Every day."

His piercing eyes studied me. "What about the rest? Where do you see yourself five years from now? Still traveling the world or doing something else?"

"I will still work with children. That, I wouldn't trade for anything else. And I hope to be settled down. Maybe have kids of my own, a husband, be happy, and aim for new dreams. I know most people my age would cringe thinking about it and just wanna have fun, party, get high, and surf life, but I've never been like anyone else. I march to the rhythm of my own drums. Whatever it means."

"I think too many people in their twenties miss opportunities because they're trying to do it all without getting attached to anyone or anything. I'm not saying it's bad, but when I was your age, I had a plan. I stuck to it, and it worked out. So, I feel you."

I pinched my lips together, things I had meant to ask him burning the tip of my tongue. I breathed in a mix of air and courage and spoke. "Hypothetically, could you see yourself going the distance with me? I mean if it could work out between us, or are you always gonna see me as a kid? Someone not old enough to be with you… Someone too inexperienced to share your life…and your world."

He said nothing for a long while. I squirmed in my chair after I put my glass down on the ground and hid my hands in the sleeves of the hoodie he had lent me earlier. The one that smelled of him. Woodsy aftershave and clean man. The moonlight shone on him, and it distracted me, as I couldn't detach my eyes from his angular face sporting a happy grin most of the time nowadays. A part of me believed I was the reason—or at least, a big part of it.

A wave of discomfort washed through me. The longer it took him to reply, the worse the scenarios my mind fabricated became.

"Maddie."

I held my breath and stayed silent.

"I tried. I really did. To come up with tons of reasons why you and I wouldn't work out in the long run. Age mattered at first. Or maybe it was just an excuse to find… well, an excuse to keep you at arm's length. And for the record, I don't see you as a kid. That's another thing I tried to convince myself of. It didn't work either. You're a kickass woman. All grown-up. You're smart, funny, distractingly beautiful, sassy, and you have me wrapped around your little finger." He let out a warm chuckle. "I can see the appeal because it seems to work great with the girls. Anyway, there's nothing I wouldn't do for you, and we're not even an item. So, conclude whatever you want and scratch the word hypothetically from your vocabulary. I don't do hypothetical stuff when it comes to you. To answer your question, yes, I can see myself going the distance with you. Have babies, share our lives, grow old together. If that's what you wish too."

Was the blood pooling in my cheeks visible in the inky night?

"You'd have more kids if I asked you to? Hypothetically. Sorry, not hypothetically…"

We exchanged smiles laden with heavy, unsaid promises.

"I would if it were something you envision too…with me. We never know how the future will turn out to be, but so far, you and I, we make a great team. We connect on a level I had no clue existed before we met. We understand each other without words, and there's the pull. It's hard to resist. Also, I can picture us in a couple of years. You with a huge belly. Someday. And a little Maddie running around. No pressure, though. I have my arms full right now."

We both snickered. And my frantic pulse found its rhythm back.

Sam cleared his throat. "Before she quit on us, Lisa suffered two miscarriages."

"I'm sorry. I had no idea." I paused, surprised by his confession. "Do you think it broke up your marriage?" I asked.

"No. Life has a way. As if it knew we weren't destined to be together much longer. So, somehow, it prevented more children from being hurt by their mother's abandonment." He laughed as he said, "Took me hours of family therapy to acknowledge the fact. And to accept it."

"I'm glad it worked out in the end. Do you think the girls are better off without her?"

"At first, I didn't. Now I know they are. No questions asked. I can see how wrong our relationship was and how it would have affected them in many other ways growing up if she had stayed. Looking back, I'm not sure we even loved each other. We came together very young and got lost in the excitement of my career. It was fun… Until it wasn't. She was toxic to our family because it was never about our kids and always about her. She would often use headaches as an excuse to avoid interacting with them. She was lethal with me too. When she would make unreasonable demands and get angry when I couldn't meet her unattainable standards. It took another dozen hours of therapy to grasp that piece of info."

We watched each other, both of us assessing the latest confessions we'd shared. Something potent simmered between us. It charged the air with more lust particles and a meaningful amount of trust and respect. For being able to open our hearts with no limitations. For being able to tell our truths as they were.

"Why did you walk out on me that day? At the agency?" I asked. The question had been nagging me since the day we had met, and the intimacy we shared right now felt like a good moment to clear the air once and for all.

"Because"—Sam rubbed his nape—"at first, I felt contradictory emotions toward you. And I had a fucking hard-on. You woke up something in me, something strong, and I panicked because I couldn't picture myself spending six months in close proximity to you. Some fifty-year-old woman wouldn't have threatened my sanity. And my libido. But you did. From the get-go. And it freaked me out."

I relaxed my stance. "What changed your mind?"

"Riley. He said to give you a chance. To dream again. And that in order to do so, I needed you by my side."

My skin heated up at his words.

"Let's just say he wasn't wrong. And not just on the nanny part of the deal."

Neither of us said anything else for a long time, everything we'd confessed becoming more pieces of string binding us together.

"Can I ask you something?" Sam asked, sipping his beer. "Why did Emily threaten to ruin me if I messed with her little sister, aka you? What did you tell her?" He arched a brow, and I could tell he wasn't mad I confided in my sister, but rather curious.

"She said you were acting like a possessive creep out there when Becks made a joke about me. And she came to the conclusion our relationship wasn't just..huh…business. Or platonic. I confirmed nothing, but she knows me. She's good at reading people. Don't worry…you're not special. She gives the same speech to any guy getting too close to me."

Sam arched his brow higher, amusement playing on his features now. "So, I'm not special?"

I snorted. "Just a teeny tiny bit," I said, bringing my thumb and forefinger together. My teasing faded. "We leave in a week. Does the reality of kicking off the tour make you anxious?"

He held his hand out, palm facing up. Without thinking, I slid mine into it and relished the way our fingers threaded.

"Truth?" he asked.

I nodded.

"Every tour. Every album. Every concert is stressful. You never know how it'll turn out. How the crowd will react. But it's also addictive. And this time, I have you… and the girls. So, I'm calmer than I've ever been. Even if I fail or it doesn't work out, I know I will have tried. Now I understand that my life doesn't begin or end on a stage. There are people counting on me. People I care about. In the equation, they are much more valuable than any song I'll ever write or any crowd I'll ever entertain."

My heart bloomed in my chest. Even without saying it in words, Sam had just declared me as an important part of his life.

"We should get some sleep because you look very hot right now with the moon shining on you. And that curve of your lips is hard to resist," he said with a glint in his eye.

I loved how we had come to terms with our attraction and could now talk about it openly, without having to keep everything under wraps anymore.

"Are you sure we'll be able to behave once we're on that bus seven days a week for months?"

Sam grinned, the tilt of his lips giving him a boyish, mischievous allure. "No. But we'll try."

"I should get to bed then because I've had a few drinks tonight. My control is flimsy right now, and I can't promise to be on my best behavior."

Never letting go of my hand, he turned the fire off and led me inside our home for the next six months.

His lips descended on the side of my face.

He kissed my cheek, and my knees buckled as his hand found my waist and held me in place. "Again, thank you for today. The song, the girls. It was amazing. I'm still at a loss for words, which says a lot. Now I'll have to watch them closely, or Riley will try to sign them."

"They were badass up there, right? It looked like they'd been doing this multiple times in the past. A natural talent they've inherited from you."

"Pride isn't strong enough to describe how I felt. For now, I'll stick to thank you. Thank you, Madison Prescott, for coaching my kids to sing one of the songs that means the most to me. And for making us ridiculously happy." His lips brushed mine in a featherlight kiss. "Night, Maddie."

I sucked in a breath imprinted with the scent of him. "Night, Sam."

Lying in bed, unable to catch some sleep, my mind raced as I thought about my day, my conversations with Devon, Emily, and Sam. Everything he had said. All he'd confessed. My pulse went ballistic as I replayed his words —all perfect to me.

The expression in his eyes when the girls had taken the stage. It would forever live within me. The exhilaration. The pride. Because I felt important to him. Cherished. Unique.

On my tiptoes, I escaped the confinement of my room and approached his bedroom. He had a queen-sized bed and a dresser, and a private bathroom, while the girls and I shared ours. Not that it mattered, though. A shower was just that, a shower. And fancy wasn't in my vocabulary. My living quarters, which were exclusively mine, were more than enough.

I inhaled a cleansing breath and knocked on his door.

"Come on in." His voice resonated from the other side of the panel.

I walked into the dark room, careful not to bump into anything.

"Hey you," Sam greeted me when I reached his bed after he turned the bedside lamp on. "Can't sleep?"

"Nope. You?"

"Same." He flipped the covers over and invited me in.

I hesitated for a moment, but he reached forward and tugged at my hand, and I surrendered.

"I was about to come get you."

"You were?" I turned to my side, and his arms pulled me closer to his chest.

"After everything we shared tonight, it felt wrong to put that much distance between us. And I wanted to make sure I didn't scare you with my honesty."

"Why?"

"Because I talked of babies. And the future. And I don't know... I feel it's best to know from the get-go we expect the same things from a relationship, but sometimes it can come out as a bit intense. Just so you now, I'll never put pressure on you, Maddie. I just wanted to clear the air. Make it obvious in case it wasn't before."

"Can I sleep here? For a few minutes? With you?"

My boldness impressed me, and my heart flipped in my chest as I waited for his answer.

Sam nuzzled my neck from behind, his unconcealed manhood pressing between my ass cheeks. "If it were just me, you'd sleep here forever. If it were just the two of us, there would be no questions asked, no self-denial, no walls to erect around us. I wouldn't waste another second being without you. Not being buried inside you. Kissing you and loving you."

A batch of happy tears lodged in my eyes. "What would you do to me if it were just us?"

His breathing quickened, and my body throbbed at the first words that passed the rim of his lips. "First, I would get rid of all these clothes between us. Then, I would take my sweet time, exploring each inch of your body. With my hands. With my teeth. With my tongue. With my cock. Once I'd know it so well I could draw it from just memory, I would taste you. All of you. Until you climaxed on my tongue and you saw nothing else but faraway galaxies when you closed your eyes. Until my name became the sole word in your vocabulary. Then I would kiss you. So you could taste yourself on my lips and see why you're driving me so crazy. Finally, I would push myself deep inside you. Until our bodies and souls bonded together and there was no telling us apart. I'd play your body the same way I play my guitar, with dedication and confidence and in perfect harmony. And then we'd come together in a bliss neither of us could escape from, our souls forever connected. Then I would start all over again because I would never be satiated."

I hadn't even realized Sam's hand had plunged between my thighs, too entranced by his words while he recited how he'd pleasure my body if given the chance.

He shoved my panties to the side, tracing the seam of my arousal with a rough finger.

I swallowed, new sensations surging through me. "I

thought we said we'd wait?" I whispered, my body responding to his touch like he knew it inside and out already.

I rolled my hips over his hand.

Fireworks exploded in my belly.

I moaned, and Sam growled behind me, his lips busy sampling the skin of my shoulder, his teeth nibbling my flesh, and his tongue soothing the pain.

"I won't be able to sleep until I know you're fully taken care of."

"What about you?" I croaked out, breathless, whimpers exiting my mouth.

"I'll wait, babe. Let's say kissing and you coming apart in my arms aren't things I can forfeit anymore. These are both allowed. I've just changed the rules."

His fingers accelerated their pace, pressing inside me as the heel of his hand brushed my clit with every stroke.

"But..." I couldn't think clearly anymore. My vision blurred. "Y-you." I could barely keep it together. "I wanna please you too. Touch you." The sensations inside me exploded. With my hand blanketing his, I made sure he never went off rhythm as I chased the orgasm about to rip me apart. "Please."

Sam laughed behind me. "Are you begging me to end you or to make me come?"

"I..." I breathed faster. "You." Why was I unable to form a complete sentence? "Me. This." My toes curled. My head tilted back. "Both. Ohmygod, Sam." His fingers pinched one of my hard nipples over the fabric of my shirt, and I came undone, turning my head and crying my release into my pillow.

"Stay," he whispered against my skin.

With my hand still enveloping his, I kept them between my legs, not in a rush for him to withdraw his intoxicating fingers from my body. No doubt I'd feel empty without them inside me once we broke apart. "I don't wanna leave. What are we gonna do?" I asked, breathless.

"I'm done being afraid." Sam flipped me to my other side and tilted my head back to meet his eyes. "I was thinking…" He rolled his jaw back and forth, and I was mesmerized by the action. "I'm done here."

A chill traced my spine, and I steeled against him.

His hands froze on my scalp. "I've thought about it. We have no idea what life will throw at us. Why should we wait to be together? I'm dying to do all those things I promised earlier. My bed feels empty each night you're not in it. We could make it a permanent thing… You sleeping here. What do you think?"

I blinked. My pulse kicked up. "You-you wanna make it official? Us? You and me?"

He shrugged, and his lips turned into the most bewitching smile, all aimed at me. "Not at first. Because we gotta ease the girls into the idea. Justine would be okay with it, but Mika… She'll react. And I can't prevent it or guess how it'll go. Thus, we better go slow and show her it's better for everybody. And that you're taking the place that is rightfully yours."

"You sure?"

"One hundred percent. And perhaps we could wait a bit to tell Riley. Until he knows it's serious and we're not trying to mess up the tour. He put a lot of work into this, and I don't want him stressing over the repercussions of our relationship."

"Sam? You really wanna be with me? No more restrictions?"

He shook his head. "Been thinking. A lot. Lying here in the dark. I'm done not living my life the way I intend it to be. If it goes south, let's promise each other, here and now, the girls will always be the priority."

"I swear." It was impossible to contain all the euphoria spreading inside me. The emotions I read in Sam's gaze—commitment, devotion, trust, and a whole lot of lust—played with every string of my heart. A dreadful thought arose in me, spoiling the moment. "Sam, there's something, though. I can't be paid to be your girlfriend. It's wrong. On all counts."

He smiled at me. "You're not. I'm paying you to care for my kids. I'm paying the nanny and teacher in you. It's just business. When you're not teaching them or watching over them, you're mine. And no one is paying you to be with me. Okay?"

Twinkles of mischief flashed in his eyes, appearing for the very first time. I relished how they were directed at me. As if he couldn't refrain from the dirty thoughts swimming in his head anymore.

"Wanna continue what we've started?" I asked.

"Nah. Tonight, I wanna hold you in my arms. And feel your heartbeat. We have our entire lives in front of us."

Time slowed down.

My pulse evened out.

His breathing steadied.

And before either of us realized it, we fell asleep in each other's arms. For the very first time.

Safe and content.

And closer than we'd ever been before.

33

SAM

Waking up to an empty bed, I sighed and scanned my surroundings, wishing Madison could still be in my arms this morning. My bed felt oddly cold without her in it. My palm lingered on the pillow next to mine. The one she'd cried into when she'd come last night. Having her here, in my arms, felt so natural. It was like she'd been always sleeping beside me. For a second, I wondered if she had switched bedrooms in the middle of the night, fearing my kids would catch us, because I had no recollection of her leaving my side.

Refreshed, in a better mood than I'd been in a long time, and ready to kick off the tour, I showered and exited the silent bus on my tiptoes, not wanting to wake up the three girls still asleep inside, the ones who owned all of my heart. The rain outside did nothing to deter my cheerfulness as I sauntered to the house.

In the kitchen, I found a note Madison had left on the counter, and it eased my mind to know she hadn't left my side out of fear or because she had second thoughts about us.

Gone to get donuts.
Be back soon.
Last night meant a lot.
x

A traitorous grin formed on my lips. After fighting my own desires for a long time and keeping Madison at a distance, I had no more fear where she was concerned. I meant everything I'd said to her yesterday. Every word. My life had a new meaning, a new direction, and I loved every minute of it. It had just taken me a moment to acknowledge the fact that she made me a better man and to stop the self-inflicted torture of keeping her at arm's length.

A wave of thrilling happiness I had never experienced before washed over me, and my heart soared at the realization I might have found my person—when I least expected it.

The doorbell disrupted my thoughts, and I welcomed Riley in.

"Hey, man." I glanced at my watch. "What are you doing here at this hour?"

"We have some last-minute details to go over. Sorry I didn't call ahead. I was in the neighborhood and decided to stop by. Is it a good time?" He surveyed the silent room around us. "Where's everyone? No morning greeting from the two little superstars?"

"They're still asleep. Enjoy the quiet while it lasts. Coffee?"

"Yes."

I was about to sit when the front door opened and shut. Seconds later, I got cornered by a cheerful Justine wearing a bright orange dress with blue butterfly wings strapped on her back and a plastic crown perched on the top of her head. I forgot Madison had helped them choose outfits yesterday.

"*Daddyyyy*." She sprinted into my arms and I lifted her up.

"What's up, Princess? Sleep well?"

She squeezed my face with her tiny hands. "*Yesss.* Love the big bus."

"Where's your sister?"

"Coming. Where's Maddie? I can't find her anywhere. *Maddddddie?*" she hollered.

"Out. She should be back soon."

"Breakfast?" I asked at the same time Mikaella walked in, her hair a curly mess. I fought a smile. "Morning, sweet pea. Hungry?"

She growled something I interpreted as a *yes*.

"Mika," Justine said, rushing to her sister and hugging her as if they hadn't seen each other in months, not just mere minutes ago.

My heart vibrated with a new layer of excitement at the journey we all were about to embark on together.

Once the girls were settled with waffles in front of the TV in the den, I focused my attention on my friend. "Sorry. Where were we? Oh yes, last-minute details. I'm all ears now."

"Where's Maddie?" he asked. "You never said. I thought she would attend our meetings because there's a thing or two we gotta figure out with her. Logistically speaking, it would be better if she were here."

My phone went off in my back pocket, and thinking it might be her, I brought it to my ear and raised a finger toward Riley, as if to say, *Just a sec.* "Hey, where are you? Everything all right?"

"Mr. Stevens? Mr. Sam Stevens?"

I made a throat-clearing noise and straightened at the

sound of my name, spoken in a voice far too serious for this early hour. Just the caller's tone sent chills down my spine. I could already tell it wasn't a courtesy call. My blood iced in my veins. Goose bumps spread across my body.

My airways constricted, but I succeeded in letting a low "Speaking" cross my lips, bracing myself for whatever news this person would deliver.

My heart pounded in my skull. I tried to swallow, but my throat tightened, making it nearly impossible.

Riley's phone buzzed, and he frowned at the screen before bringing the device to his ear, a somber expression taking over his face.

The voice on the other end of the phone kept talking, but it sounded miles away. I could barely make out the words.

My heart felt like it had been punctured, and I feared I would bleed out on my kitchen floor.

34

MADISON

I *can't see. I have gone blind. No, not blind. I can't open my eyes. My skull feels as if it has burst into two. Pain. So much pain. More than I can bear. I can't feel the rest of my body. Why is my pulse racing? What is happening to me? I can't breathe. Sam. I need Sam. Where is he?*

Darkness pulled me under.

I pried my heavy eyelids open to a blur of light and shadow. I blinked, trying to dissipate the fog, but it wouldn't clear. How much time had passed? Had it been hours? Or days? The pounding of my heart reverberated against the walls of my skull. An iron taste lingered in my mouth. *Blood.* Why was I bleeding? Nausea swirled in my stomach at the stench permeating the air. I rubbed my temple, trying to soothe the pain all over my head and neck. Nothing worked. A tear flowed down my cheek. Dark spots appeared in front of my eyes.

Where am I? Where is Sam? I want Sam.

My eyelids weighed a ton. No matter how hard I tried, I couldn't keep them open. A curtain of darkness descended, swallowing me whole.

Another wave of nausea hit me. Stronger than before. The ringing in my ears wouldn't go away. Excruciating pain held me captive as if a dozen trucks were running over me. I couldn't seem to move my left leg. Panic crept in. I tried to wiggle my toes, but only the ones on my right foot responded to my silent command. Something held me in place. I tried to move my hand, to feel around me, but a sharp pain shot through my ribs and stopped me.

I am feeling cold. So, so cold. Why am I freezing?

Shivers started deep in my core and raced up and down my body in multiple ripples. Sweat drenched my clothes. Or was it blood?

Sam, please save me.

My stomach churned. My heart felt like it was going to burst out of me.

A scream built inside me. Why did my entire being hurt so bad? It was as if I were trapped in hell.

Shadows closed in around me. I wanted to sleep.

Sam, are you there…? Can anyone hear me? Ems? I should call my sister. She would come get me.

A sharp pain radiated through my body, and I wailed in agony.

I lost the battle against the exhaustion taking over me.

An alarm rang in the distance.

Then nothing.

Only darkness and silence.

35

SAM

"Accident."

"Madison Prescott."

"Surgery."

"Car crash."

I blinked. The words didn't register. I must have heard them wrong.

My entire body hurt.

What was going on?

My children, now standing beside me, tugged at my shirt.

"Daddy, why are you screaming?" Justine asked, her eyes full of questions, her brow creased with fear.

Was I screaming? In what parallel universe had I landed?

"Daddy?" Mikaella echoed, her voice quivering. "Daddy? Why are you crying? There are tears on your cheeks."

Tears? I brought a hand to my eyes. They were damp. What was going on with me? Was I going nuts? Was this how it felt to lose your mind?

With a step back to escape the little hands pulling at my clothes, I surveyed the space around me, not registering anything.

Riley tore the phone from my grasp and spoke to the stranger, whose name or role I didn't know.

The buzzing in my ear blocked all other sounds.

Tears burned at the back of my eyes, then spilled down my cheeks. I could feel them now. Shards of glass lined my throat.

After what appeared to be hours, Riley led me to the couch and forced me to sit down. "Stevens?" I watched him but couldn't see him.

I blinked. My focus refused to come back.

"STEVENS?" he repeated, louder this time.

That did the trick because I snapped out of it. "Wh… what?" My voice came out gravelly and weak.

"I called Devon. She's on her way. We'll go as soon as she gets here."

I blinked again. Nothing he said added up.

"Sam," he ordered, sternly this time. "Listen to me."

My friend wasn't the type to get angry, so when he spoke to me in that tone, I had no choice but to listen to him. "Madison had an accident. She's at the hospital. Her sister Emily called me. She'll meet us there. I won't lie to you. It…it sounds bad. They reached out to her, but she's in Atlanta for a medical conference. She needs you to go there until she gets back. Can you do that?"

I nodded, still unsure I was hearing him right.

"Wh…huh…what? How?"

Devon joined us and exchanged words with Riley, but nothing registered with me. She rested her hand on my shoulder in a comforting gesture before taking a seat opposite us.

"Okay," Riley continued, "I had June on the phone

moments ago. You know, my assistant. Sam, are you even listening? She'll take over, so I can go with you. She's already made a few phone calls." He rubbed his eyebrows, averting his eyes for a second. He inhaled before bringing his attention back to me. "A guy ran a red light and crashed into the side of Maddie's car at full speed. She got stuck inside. They had to use the jaws of life to extricate her. We gotta go. Now."

He helped me to my feet.

"Is Maddie okay?" Mikaella asked nearing us, and I hated the idea she'd witnessed this. My daughter was seeing another moment of pain. She was growing up too soon. At first, it was her mother abandoning us. Now Madison was hurt, and her father was in shock. I needed to pull myself together. For her.

Before I could do that, Devon kneeled before her. "We don't know yet, sweetie. Your daddy and Uncle Riley will go find out. You and Justine will stay with me."

"Is she going to die?" Mikaella asked, despair swimming in her glossy eyes.

"Let's pray for her, okay? I'm sure she'll be able to hear us," Devon continued. She swallowed, and her eyes met mine for a fleeting second.

Mikaella turned to me, fat tears streaming down her cheeks. "Daddy, do something," she pleaded. "When I'm scared, Maddie always holds my hand. Hold her hand, okay, Daddy? Make her better. Bring her back."

I lifted my daughter in my arms. "I swear I'll do my best, sweet pea. Stay with Devon and your sister. Be a good girl."

I kissed the top of her head and hugged both my kids, reassuring them, before Riley led me away to his car.

For the entire ride, I watched the scenery pass by through the passenger window, unable to make sense of

the turmoil raging inside my head. Riley spent the entire
time on the phone, barking orders to one and all,
discussing press releases and deadlines with June, and
calling the hospital to have them ready to meet with us.

"Hang in there, Stevens." His words reached my ears,
then dissipated into thin air.

He clapped my shoulder a few times and said something to me, but I couldn't hear it. In a state of numbness,
I looked at him without computing any word he said. I had
no emotions, no fears, no nothing. The whole scene felt like
a dream. And none of it seemed real.

Riley stopped the car in front of a door in the base-
ment where no one could spot me. For now, I required a
little privacy, and I was grateful to my friend for having set
this up. Brent, my head of security, met us there, and we
followed him and a nurse through a series of corridors up
to an elevator. On the sixth floor, we were brought to a
room where the medical team was waiting for us. I registered only white walls and recessed lighting as we walked
toward them. Frigid and cold.

A doctor wearing green scrubs held out his hand. "Mr.
Stevens, Mr. Burns, I'm Doctor Bera, the head of surgery,
and these are Doctor Connor, the head of orthopedics,
and Doctor Patel, the head of plastic surgery."

The roaring of my heart rang in my ears.

Plastic surgery? My stomach churned. I felt lightheaded.
Bile rose in my throat. With a step back in an attempt to
capture some air to breathe on my own, I closed my eyes
to avoid fainting. I joined my hands together in prayer over
my mouth while I made every effort to stay in the
moment, to silence the scenarios my mind wanted to
conjure.

Plastic surgery? It crushed my heart just thinking about it.
Fuck, how bad was it? Would Madison even survive? I

licked my lips, inhaled, and raked my fingers through my hair, trying to keep my cool.

"How is Madison?" Riley asked, and I thanked him mentally for taking over, as all my words were locked in my throat.

"Ms. Prescott suffered injuries all over her abdomen and leg, with metal fragments lodged in the left side of her ribs, pelvis, and thighs. We managed to remove them. In the impact, she banged her head. There's no fracture of the skull or brain edema at the moment. We are monitoring her closely, but we're not overly concerned. Her brain activity is normal, and there is no active bleeding. What we're worried about is her left leg. The bones are crushed, and she's lost a lot of blood. She will be in surgery for some time as we are trying to salvage her limb. But it is touch and go. We are doing our best, but we cannot be certain yet whether she will need an amputation. With an injury this extensive, we also have to closely monitor for infection and sepsis."

My tongue untied, and words finally passed my lips. "Is she—? Will she—?" Even if I tried, I couldn't voice those possibilities.

"At this point, we have no way of knowing how it will turn out. She needs surgical debridement of her limb and stabilization of her multiple fractures with rods and screws. Her young age plays in her favor, though. Still, if she survives the rounds of surgeries, she'll have a difficult and painful recovery in front of her. Therapy will be an extensive and long process. Tough on her and on all of you."

A wave of shock nearly knocked me off my feet. I clenched my fists at my sides and dug my heels into the linoleum, struggling not to crumble as pain coursed through my body.

"Can I...can I see her?" I asked.

"No. Not right now. Sorry."

"Just once. I need to see her once."

"Please let us do our job. I know how hard it must be for you, but you have to trust us. We're doing our best to save her. We'll keep you updated. Our staff set up this room for you, so you don't have to sit in the common waiting area. We're aware if the news leaks out, the media and some unwelcome fans may invade the hospital, and nobody wishes for that outcome. Again, if you need anything, let us know." The same nurse who was with us earlier entered the room. "Mr. Johnson will take over from here."

After the medical team left, silence filled the room as we tried to absorb the weight of their words. Seconds later, Riley was on the phone, slipping back into manager mode and informing June of the latest development in case she had to answer any questions. Then he asked her to be ready to cancel my shows and all engagements for the first two weeks of the tour. He called someone else, but by then, I had tuned out his voice.

Time idled.

My brain went blank.

Nothing else mattered anymore.

The arms on the clock, fixed on the opposite wall, moved at a sluggish speed. Seconds felt like hours. And hours like years.

All this time, I sat in a chair, leaning forward with my elbows resting on my knees and my face buried in my hands. I turned down every attempt my friend made to talk, and every cup of cheap hospital coffee Brent brought me.

The morning passed in a blur.

The sun wasn't at its zenith anymore when a familiar figure entered the small room.

"Sam."

Emily hurried into my arms when I moved to stand up. We hugged for the longest time. "Any development?" she asked when we broke apart. I took in her swollen eyes and reddened cheeks.

I shook my head. "The doctors said something about metal fragments in her body. Left leg being crushed. She's lost a lot of blood."

Riley jumped in. "She'd been in surgery for hours. I would have flown in another surgeon, but it turns out Dr. Bera and his team are the best in their field. Madison is lucky they're the ones in charge. We're still waiting for an update. When we talked earlier, they said they were trying to salvage her leg."

Emily spoke again. "Yes, Dr. Bera is indeed a very good surgeon. I've assisted him a few times, and I can vouch for him. I'll get updated on Maddie's situation. You all stay here. I'll be back as soon as I have more news for you." As she spoke, the concerned sister vanished, leaving only the doctor. I bet it helped her cope with the trauma. Maybe seeing it through the eyes of a doctor made this surreal reality easier to bear. She squared her shoulders and let out a long, deliberate breath before leaving us.

Without another word, Riley, Brent, and I all sat down, with our silence for company. Only the ordinary hum of the hospital and the rush of our breaths echoed through those bleak walls.

The wait became untenable. I watched my phone screen every couple of minutes as if Madison would text me any second to tell me it was all a prank. Unable to stay still any longer, I jumped to my feet and paced the room. With my fingers laced behind my neck, I inhaled through my nose, praying for the coils tightening my stomach to loosen.

After what felt like forever, Emily walked in, followed by Dr. Bera and his team.

Riley joined me in the middle of the room. I held my breath, balling my hands into fists, bracing myself for the updates about Madison's condition.

Emily stood next to me, clasping my hand in hers. I was grateful because at this moment, I needed every bit of support I could get.

"So?" I asked, in a breathless voice.

36

SAM

Seated in an armchair, I held the hand of a heavily sedated Madison, just as Mikaella advised me to. Since I couldn't pull her into my arms, it was the only thing I could do, other than speak to her, that would let her know I was here by her side and would never go away.

"Hey, it's me," I said.

Her visage was bruised and swollen. She had stitches on her cheek, a bandage over her forehead, IV lines attached to her arms, a neck line for life-saving drugs, and a tracheal tube down her throat connected to a ventilator. The rest of her body was wrapped in dressings under the hospital covers. She looked nothing like the woman I'd kissed goodnight almost twenty-four hours ago. Since she was placed in isolation to prevent infection, I had to be suited up—gown, cap, mask, gloves—before I could meet her.

The constant beeping sounds of the machines regulating all her vitals reverberated through the room.

A tear trailed down my face. "I'm...I'm so sorry...for

everything. You shouldn't be lying here." I used my sleeve to rub my watery eyes. "The doctors said the next few days are critical. They can't tell me your prognosis until then. I am shaken up, Maddie. I need you. You-you have to fight this. Do you hear me? You gotta come back to me." I raked my fingers through my hair. "I don't wanna lie to you. It is…it is bad…huh…pretty bad. You have been banged up inside out. Don't worry about your head, okay? It is fine. Your left leg suffered the brunt of the injury. Nobody knows the outcome yet. You were in surgery for almost sixteen hours." I paused, collecting fragments of courage within me, steeling myself to continue speaking. "The surgeon said there were some moments when the blood loss was massive, but you did good. I swear. You didn't allow yourself to be sucked in. I'm so proud of you. You are strength and courage, Maddie, and right now, I am learning so much from you."

My voice stuttered to a stop as I tried to swallow the giant lump in my throat.

"Maddie, I gotta tell you something. I…I am done hiding my feelings from myself and from you. You see… I love you. I've been afraid to voice them out loud for the longest time. Afraid if I did, my happiness could be stolen from me. I realize now it never mattered." I snorted. "I-I didn't even say the L-word out loud, and you still got hurt. My heart almost got ripped out of my chest no matter what. I should have told you when I had…when I had the chance… I'm so sorry you never heard those words from me before now." I tightened my squeeze on her fingers and took a deep breath in to calm the storm raging in me. "Madison Prescott, I love you. I'll tell you that every day for the rest of my life if you come back to me…to us. I will make your happiness my life's mission."

I leaned forward, hoping my words carried to her ears.

"You gotta be strong, okay?" I stared at her as if the intensity of it could reach a place deep inside her, and I addressed the flame, I knew she possessed, to fight for her life. "You better fight this and win. I know you'll get through this because you're strong and stubborn, and you never back down when you know you can do something. I won't let you give up. You have my word on that." I huffed. "You're not alone. You have me. Just get better, okay?" A soft laugh left my pinched lips. "If you could see how badass you look right now. Like you got knocked out in the ring. Don't worry, your face…it'll all heal."

I pressed my forehead to our joined hands, hoping I could send all the healing power I could muster through this small contact. I closed my eyes, trying to quiet the wild beating of my heart, and prayed like never before.

Then I opened my eyes. "Emily has been taking care of you. We're all waiting for you to get well. I'm right here. I'm not going anywhere."

The automatic doors of the ICU slid open, startling me. I straightened in my chair, wiping away the tears that soaked my face.

"How are you holding on, Mr. Stevens?" Mara, the nurse in charge of Madison asked, wearing an isolation gown identical to mine, observing the data displayed on the monitors and noting them on a tablet.

"Same."

"Let's talk outside, okay?"

I nodded and followed her after I whispered one last *I love you* to Madison.

Mara and I both removed our masks, and I let the heaviness of the situation register. Away from Madison, I didn't have to pretend to be stronger than I really was.

"Any updates?" I asked, pushing my hands into my pockets, not knowing what to do with them.

"Ms. Prescott's vitals are stable. The next forty-eight to seventy-two hours are critical. She's not out of the woods yet, but she's in good hands. She's strong. We're hopeful."

I bowed my head.

Emily joined us and moved to stand up beside me, gripping my arm fiercely. "How is she holding up?" she asked the nurse.

"Your sister is a fighter." Mara addressed both of us. "We'll continue to monitor Ms. Prescott closely. Don't hesitate if you have questions. I'll give you two some time before I come back to check on her in a little while."

The door closed behind her, and Emily pivoted to face me.

"Sam, you look like hell," she said, the corner of her lips lifting up. The expression in her eyes betrayed her worries.

"Yeah, well, I have no idea what I'm doing. Beside her, I can't seem to stop talking. Filling the silence and masking the beeping of the machines. I'm a mess."

"Even if she can't speak, Maddie knows you're here. I know how hard it must be for you," she said, squeezing my arm. "Hold on, okay? Keep talking to her."

I inhaled, averted my eyes for a beat, and returned my attention to her. "Last night…after everyone left…we made the choice…we've decided to be together. To give our relationship a try. Not to hide from our feelings any longer." I let the words settle in. "Ems, I love her, and I never told her. For the longest time, I was being a chickenshit, keeping her at a distance, convincing myself she was better off without me. And now I'm afraid I'll never get a chance to tell her how much she means to me."

The tears I swallowed felt like tiny needles when they ran down the fragile, raw lining of my throat.

Emily wrapped her arms around my shoulders this

time, and I held her there. In the simple gesture, we brought each other comfort. Strength to go through the reality that was hitting us. In that instant, she reminded me so much of her younger sister, her heart bleeding for those she loved. Like Madison, I could recognize the strength emanating from her, and for a moment, I wished it would rub off on me. One thing was clear, though. The Prescott sisters were angels on this Earth, and I was thankful for their presence in my life.

"And you, how are you holding up?" I asked once we broke apart.

She sighed. "Inside, I'm freaking out. But the doctor in me is trying to see the situation from a medical perspective. I've never faced this kind of challenge before." We both remained silent for a long while, watching Madison through the glass door. "I spoke to my parents. They're arriving tomorrow."

"Ask Riley for June's contact. If you need anything, she'll take care of it. She always does."

Emily returned her attention to me. "Sam, you're one of the good ones. Maddie is lucky to have you in her life. For the longest time, I feared she wouldn't find her place in this world. She never had a lot of friends growing up, always preferring to be on her own... Unable to let people fully in. Then she started traveling, looking for something she thought she couldn't find here. A purpose. She's the best person I know, and my gut tells me everything she's been searching for was right under her nose the entire time."

I dragged my hand through my hair, unable to avert my eyes from the pallid figure on the bed.

"Thanks to you and your children, she's thriving. I haven't seen her this happy in...forever. She has never seemed as at ease anywhere than around you guys. I'm thankful to you for all of it. We've been through a lot together, and I'm happy she's loved the way she should be. Even more with the current turn of events."

A fresh batch of tears welled up in my eyes. "Ems, be honest with me. I know how strong she is, but do you think she will fight back? Or if she makes it through, do you think this," I pointed to the monitors, "will change her forever?"

"Maddie went through some hard times when we were little. If she survived those years, I have no doubt she can survive this ordeal. She's a fighter...always has been...or else, she wouldn't be here."

My attention drifted back to her, and I tried to read between the lines to grasp the words she didn't speak out loud. "What do you mean?"

Her eyes dimmed, and an expression I could not decipher filled her eyes. "If she hasn't told you yet, it means she's not ready. The time will come. I have no doubt. And, to be honest with you, I would rather she tell you herself."

I nodded. "Should I worry? She once said she'd been neglected when she was a little girl."

"Sam, give her some time. It's hard for her to open up about her struggles. She'll do so when she's ready. But don't worry. The past will never come back to mess with her."

I cast my eyes on Madison's figure and watched each wave on the ECG to make sure she was still alive and with me.

My eyes burned. The tears and exhaustion had taken their toll on my body and mind in the last few hours.

"Sam, you should get some sleep," Emily said after her while. "I can take over. I'm used to staying alert and awake all night. And Mara is a good friend of mine. I'll be the first to know if anything changes. I won't leave her side, I promise."

"What if she wakes up while I'm gone?"

She shook her head. "She won't. The medication will keep her sedated and on the ventilator until she shows signs of healing. If there's any change, I'll call you. Your kids need you. Your little girls must be scared. They need their daddy."

"Yeah… I talked to them earlier. Explained as much as I could." My voice cracked. "I have no idea how to face them without being able to answer all their questions because I lack the answers."

"Be honest. That's what matters. Right now, all we can do is pray. And hope for the best."

I hung my head low and stepped forward to hug her one last time. "I'll be here first thing in the morning," I said.

"Just rest for now. Want me to write you a prescription to help you sleep?"

"No. I refuse to numb myself. Thanks, though."

After I followed protocol and put on another set of sanitized clothes, I returned to Madison's side. Bending over the bed, I grazed the small patch of skin with no bandage on her forehead with my fingertip. "Get better. I love you and will be back in the morning. Emily will stay with you tonight." My lips curled into a tentative smile. "Don't give her trouble, okay? Good night."

―――――

I crashed on my bed as soon as my feet landed on my bedroom floor without even undressing. Devon had called earlier to tell me she'd keep the girls overnight. She'd taken them home after dinner. The gears of my brain worked at a dizzying speed. How did I go from hopeful to this version of despair within a day? I had no clue how to stay positive while facing this type of tragedy. Madison, my heart, the tour, my children. They had formed one big chaotic mess I wasn't ready to analyze. My insecurities clung to me like a second skin.

Madison must have been terrified, even if she couldn't show it. In the state she was in, how much could she understand about her situation? Could she tell that her life was hanging by a flimsy thread?

My stomach churned at the idea she was aware of the reality that had hit her.

I wondered if she could tell or if the medication prevented her brain from forming thoughts. There were so many questions swirling in my head for which I had no answer.

Then it hit me. That the next few hours could change the course of her life. Forever.

My eyes stung, and I squeezed them shut, pressing my fists against them to ease the pain. The one reminding me I was alive—and that I had to stand up for those I loved.

Unable to sort out my own thoughts, I abandoned myself to sleep, praying I would wake up and this shit show would turn out to be a very horrible dream.

The subdued voices of my daughters woke me up the next day.

"Justine, walk on your tiptoes," Mikaella whispered. "Don't wake Daddy up."

"Okay," my baby whisper-shouted. "Can I kiss him good morning?"

My eldest daughter sighed. "Sure. Uncle Riley said not to wake him up. That he didn't sleep for long and needed his rest. Hurry."

"Do you think he's still sad?" Justine asked.

"Yes, Justine. Devon explained it to us. Maddie got hurt, and Daddy is taking care of her."

"Will she go to heaven?"

I heard Mikaella's loud swallow. "I don't know."

Their conversation roused me from my sleep. I blinked, trying to make sense of everything that had happened the previous day. A stone was crushing my chest, preventing air from fully reaching my lungs. According to my daughter's discussion, none of it was a dream.

Trying to evade my gloomy thoughts and needing some love, I sprang to a ninety-degree position, and my girls came running into my arms.

"Daddy," they screamed.

This morning, I hugged them a little tighter than usual. "I love you," I said in a gruff voice that betrayed all the tears I had cried in the last twenty-four hours. "I missed you two."

"Where's Maddie?" Mikaella asked.

"Is she okay?" Justine asked next. "Can we see her?"

I sat them on my bed and inhaled through my mouth to dissipate the wave of nausea swirling in my empty stomach. "Let's see. Maddie had an accident yesterday morning. She got hurt a lot. The doctors did their best to repair her broken bones and heal her wounds. Now she's asleep because it will help her get better. She gotta rest a lot."

"Is she going to wear a *clast* like Mika?" Justine asked.

"Cast. And yes, I think she will."

"When will she come back home?" Mikaella asked next.

I rolled my shoulders back, trying to project a bit of confidence, even though my tone betrayed my agitation. "I don't know. Her sister is with her. And her parents will get here later today. I may have to spend a little time there too later."

"Can we see her?" Justine asked. "We drew butterflies and kittens yesterday. And made a card. For her."

"Not today. She's in a special room at the hospital, and people can't really visit her for now. Once she gets better, I think she would very much like to see you two. Even if she's still asleep." I paused and reached for my babies' hands. "Maddie will need all of us to be strong for her. She will need us to air blow kisses her way because kisses make everything better, right?"

"Like when you kiss my booboos?" Justine asked.

"Same." I mirrored her tentative smile. "Okay, you two. Hug me once more." We stayed in one another's arms for a long beat. "Hey, how did you get here on your own? Last I heard, you were sleeping over at Uncle Riley and Devon's."

Mikaella pushed back. "Uncle Riley is on the phone downstairs. He drove us here to get clean clothes, because last night we forgot to take any, while he's dealing with someone named June. Devon had to work, so he's watching us. He said you two gotta talk while we play outside. And if we're nice, he'll order pizza and slushies for lunch. We wanted to see you first. Are you mad?"

"Me? Never. I missed you too much. I'll never be mad at you two for wanting to see me."

"Can we eat bunny pancakes?" Justine asked.

"Sure. I'll walk you back downstairs, shower, call Emily, and get to it afterward. Do we have a deal?"

"Yes," they both cheered.

Once I locked my bedroom door to make sure the girls wouldn't enter and eavesdrop on my conversation, I called Madison's sister.

I firmed my back, trying to inject some courage into myself.

"Sam," Emily greeted me. "Did you get any sleep?"

How could she worry about me when her sister was confined to a hospital bed?

"Yeah, I think I did. How is she? Any development?"

"Same. Which isn't bad news per se. As I told you yesterday, it means she's holding on, and right now that's what we wish for."

"You should get some sleep," I said. "You've been up all night. I'll take over."

"I was waiting for you to be back. I have a few of my own patients to see this morning, so don't stress over it."

I sucked in a breath. "Listen, I promised my kids we'd make pancakes. I'll try to swing by right after."

"Sam, you're already doing a lot. Don't blame yourself for being a father first. I'm aware of how much you love my sister. I could tell two days ago. She argued there was nothing going on between you two, but I knew better. And I know her. Which means, your daughters should always come first. That's what she'd want."

I blew out a long breath. "You're probably right. Thank you. For everything."

We hung up, and I squeezed my eyelids shut, trying to keep the fresh tears at bay.

———

It was almost eleven o'clock that morning when I finally made it to the hospital. After breakfast, I'd met up with Riley while the girls busied themselves in their castle. We had agreed he'd ask Janice to send help. Someone to watch over the girls while I found my bearings in this new reality. The idea of trusting someone else with my daughters was a big stretch for me, but what other choice did I have? I had to compromise to make it all work.

Riley and Devon were already doing much more than

they should, but last night, I'd come to the conclusion that I couldn't do everything on my own. I would exhaust myself, and my children and Madison both required the best of me.

After much consideration, I refused to postpone the tour. We all had worked so hard to get here. Canceling shows would mean failing all those people. The girls, Madison, and me included. Pacing my house for hours every day wouldn't help the situation. It wouldn't heal the woman I love faster, nor would it make me keep the promises I had made to my daughters. On my drive to the hospital, I'd called June, trying to work out a flight schedule in between engagements so I'd be in Nashville as often as possible. She was mainly Carter's assistant, but she had agreed to be mine too until I found my own. My trust in strangers wasn't fully back yet, but I was getting there.

The hallways of the intensive care unit were silent as I sauntered toward room fifteen-zero-three. With every step, I could feel the fragility of life clinging to the walls. Dr. Bera was already in the room when I entered, dressed in a disposable gown to reduce the risk of infection for vulnerable patients such as Madison.

I held my breath at his sight. "Any good news?" I asked.

"Mr. Stevens. Hi. Right now, we're monitoring Ms. Prescott closely for any sign of infection. As we told you, with the extensive repair we did to her leg, post-operative sepsis is a real threat. We've started her on broad-spectrum antibiotics. Her vitals are good. Her blood pressure is a bit high, which is not surprising after what she has gone through. Nothing to worry about for now, but we're keeping an eye on it just in case."

I nodded and secured my hands in my pockets because I had no idea what to do with myself. "Will she——?" A new lump formed in my throat. "When will we know she's out of the woods?"

"It's a bit too early to tell. So far, she's hanging in there. The next few days will let us know more. We can't assess the damage to her leg. We'll have to wait and see. The scar across her pelvic bone might become puckered and not very pleasant to look at. The other scars down her leg may lighten over time but won't completely go away. Plastic surgery can be an option later on. She's lucky to be alive, so in the bigger scheme of things, the scars aren't what concern us the most. As long as the wounds don't get infected."

"What about her spine?"

"Her spine is fine, not damaged in the accident. Her leg is still our major concern since we had to repair bones, muscles, nerves, and restore blood supply."

I nodded and couldn't think of any other questions to ask, my brain going blank.

Dr. Bera checked Madison's pupils with a penlight. I hated the idea I had to stand on the sidelines, but there was nothing I could do to make her situation better.

"If you have any questions, ring me. Try not to worry."

It was almost one in the afternoon when I finally found myself alone with Madison in her hospital room.

"Hey, it's just the two of us now. You can't wake up just yet... Listen, it's best if you stay sedated for a little longer. The girls asked questions this morning. I had no idea what to tell them because I don't know a lot myself. They miss you. We all do. They wanted to come visit. When you are out of the ICU, I'll bring them over. I know you'd enjoy having them around."

The beeping of the monitors filled the thick silence.

"I did something. I-I asked for help...to take care of Mika and Justine while you're here so you can heal without stressing about anything. Devon has work. And your sister too. I can't be with them while being by your side or onstage. Janice will send another nanny. I'm not replacing you, I swear. It's just for now. Until we figure it all out and you get back on your feet. It's a big step for me, asking people to help me out. I thought you'd be proud of me." I exhaled. "The girls were kinda excited at the idea you'd wear a cast too. They're already planning on adding glitter to it. I also packed you a bag with some of your stuff for when you get your own room. That fluffy blanket you always wrapped around yourself and a stuffed koala the girls asked me to bring for you. I have no idea if you can hear me. I…I hope you can. That you can tell you're not alone." I pushed a tendril of her hair back, trying to busy myself with something. "You're beautiful. And strong. In a day or two, we should know more. I promise to keep you updated on everything going on."

A nurse walked in, drew some blood, and left after noting data on her tablet.

"I'm still here," I said. "I made bunny pancakes this morning at Justine's request. They weren't as fabulous as yours, but for once, she didn't seem too concerned. I'll try my hands at brownies later. The recipe you always bake. When the hospital called me, I thought you were gone…"

With my thumbs, I massaged her palm.

"I've decided something else. I'll continue with the tour. It was a hard decision to make. I could hear your voice in my head, pleading me to go. It's not the same knowing you won't be there with us, though, and that I have to do this without you by my side. I was really looking forward to sharing this experience together—" My voice cracked, and I paused, trying to regain some control. "We're working on a schedule so I can be here as much as possible. I'm not leaving you, okay?"

I drew patterns on her palm with my fingertips.

"I wish things were different… The plan wasn't to watch you fight for your life." I tipped my head back and closed my eyes, struggling with the emotional overload about to crash through me. "The plan was to do this together. All those silly rules about staying apart… We're both aware it would have failed. Big time. I don't know about you, but when you asked me the other night if I could see myself going the distance with you, it lit up a spark inside me. I never want it to die. I have no idea how you did it, Maddie, but you stole my heart—every piece of it. This journey we're on… I'm done pretending we shouldn't give it everything we've got."

I watched her, once again wondering if she could hear my words.

Her face missed the usual curl of her lips and the glint in her irises.

It missed the look she would give me when she thought I wasn't looking and the cheerful grin she always displayed when she was with the girls.

The automatic doors slid open, drawing my attention. Emily walked in followed by a middle-aged couple I assumed to be her parents. A mask of distress painted the woman's gaze. She blinked her red-rimmed eyes as she neared her youngest daughter. On my feet, I went to meet her husband.

"Sam, these are my parents, Evangeline and Rupert." The woman joined us. "Mom, Dad, this is Sam Stevens." She hesitated for a split second, and I offered her a tiny nod. "Maddie's boyfriend."

"Mr. and Mrs. Prescott, it's nice to finally meet you. I wish it was under better circumstances, though. Maddie speaks about you two all the time."

The woman patted her eyes with a tissue before pulling

me into her arms. "Mr. Stevens, we heard so much about you too."

"Please call me Sam."

"Sam," she continued. "You and your precious daughters make my little girl happy. And I'll forever be grateful you were put on her road."

I swallowed around the rock-hard lump in my throat. "I'm the one who should thank you. Your daughter is one of the best things that has happened to me in a long time. She's the most loving and generous person I know. You should be proud."

Madison's mother hugged me once again. "Thank you for loving our precious child."

When she pulled back, Mr. Prescott wrapped his arms around me. "Thank you for making sure she gets the best care. It means a lot to us."

"It's the least I can do," I said. I spun to face Emily. "Ems, I'll give you some space and go back to my babies. Call me if anything changes, okay?"

"Yes. And Sam, thank you for spending the day. I'm aware you're dealing with a tight schedule."

"There's no place else I'd rather be."

I walked to Madison and leaned in to whisper, "Heal my love. I'll be here tomorrow."

As I made my exit, I called out, "Night," waving my hand over my shoulder.

37

SAM

"Wanna hear the song I came up with on my way here? It's not done, but it sounds good. I'm sure you'll enjoy it. I wrote it for you," I said as I sat in the chair next to the bed.

It'd been three days since the accident. Madison was still hooked up to the ventilator because she had to undergo another round of surgery on her leg—less extensive this time—later today. Her doctor had explained the nerve damage would be mind-numbing for quite some time and they preferred to keep her asleep for as long as possible to avoid her suffering because, once awake, the painkillers wouldn't do a good job of masking the pain. After the full repair her leg had undergone, they were hopeful for her recovery. Madison's life wasn't in danger anymore, and I held onto this piece of information to get through my days. Late last night, they'd moved her from the isolation ICU to a regular ICU room, one with a large window spread on one wall because I knew that was what she'd wish for. To see the daylight when she'd wake up. Because the sky always dazzled her.

Nights and days.

I sang the melody to a song I'd only rehearsed in my head so far.

Once I got to the chorus and last verse, I took a deep inhale to be able to deliver the words that meant so much to me, and I hoped she could hear, even in her sleep.

> **…Come back to me, come**
>   **back to me**
> **I'm half the man I should be**
> **When you're not here**
> **The sky is darker**
> **The colors faded**
> **And my heart is lost**
> **Come back to me, come back**
>   **to me**
> **Here and now, I don't wanna**
>   **live without you**
>
> **There's something I gotta tell**
>   **you (yes, there's something**
>   **I gotta tell you)**
> **There's something I can't keep**
>   **to myself anymore (no,**
>   **baby, I gotta tell you)**
> **I'm in love with you.**

I cleared my throat and breathed out. "What do you think? I won't perform it on tour. I'll record it, but it'll be yours. I called it 'Maddie.' It's yours," I repeated, about to break down. "And so is my heart."

Tears rushed to my eyes. For the longest time, I let them flow. Once I regained enough composure, I sang to the woman my heart belonged to. All the songs she loved.

Including the one we danced to, that time in my kitchen. I had no clue if she could hear my love through the lyrics, but I hoped she did. Because it prevented darkness from enveloping me and my brain from going crazy.

"Nurses should be here soon," I told her. "To prep you for surgery. I'll be here waiting for you when you get back. I know we're asking a lot from you these days. The girls are making you *Get Well* cards every day. I swear you'll have the biggest collection when you get out of here. Justine demanded we find you a prince who could kiss you to help you wake up." I smiled at the memory of my baby girl speaking the words. "I told her I'll see what I can do. I wish I could heal you with just one kiss, Maddie."

Madison's parents joined me, cutting short my confessions.

"Mr. Stevens," her father greeted me.

I moved to my feet. "Please, call me Sam."

Mrs. Prescott neared her daughter and whispered words of love to her.

"When are they coming to get her?" Mr. Prescott asked.

"They should be here any minute. The doctor said it would last two hours if everything goes as planned. Just a few more repairs they hadn't tackled after the accident. Nothing major." I paused, my eyebrows knitting together in confusion. "Huh, have you seen Emily? She hasn't been here at all today."

"She's in surgery. She'll try to come by later."

I nodded. "Gimme a minute, and I'm out of here. You deserve some time with your daughter."

I neared Madison and kissed her forehead. "I'll leave you with your parents for now. I'll see you later. Be strong out there. I love you."

I started to walk to the door when Mrs. Prescott

stopped me. "Sam, our daughter is lucky to have you in her life."

I darted my tongue out to moisten my lips. "I'm the lucky one. She makes everything better. Even my music."

"Did you sing to her?"

"Yes. Thought she'd like it. When I'm here, I ramble all the time. I'm sure she prefers music."

"She does enjoy it. I can tell. Call it a mother's instinct. My daughter is a big fan of yours."

————

I woke up with a strained neck and a hand shaking me out of my slumber. "Stevens, we gotta get going. Did you spend the night here?"

I forced my eyelids open and used my sleeve to rub the sleep away from my features.

"What time is it?" I said, stretching my neck from side to side to relieve the tension there.

"Eight. We said we'd get going at seven-thirty. We drove to your place, but Doris said you hadn't come home last night."

Today was day one of the tour. And day seven since the accident. The excitement from yesterday, when the girls couldn't stay still for more than ten seconds, died the moment I stepped into the frigid hospital room. It drained all the cheer from me, leaving my heart heavy and cold.

For most of the night, I'd sung to Madison, hoping she could hear me again, and that it would make up for the days I wouldn't be able to visit her. I sang until my voice quivered. Until my insides clenched so tight, it hurt to even breathe.

"You look like a mess, man. I'm glad we hired drivers. No way would I let you drive yourself."

My grip around Madison's hand tightened.

"Have you told her you love her yet?" my friend asked.

My eyes snapped in his direction. "What are you talking about?" I asked, doing my best to prevent my face from betraying my feelings.

He snickered. "Did you forget I was there the day you two met at the nanny agency? Sparks ignited between you guys the moment you stared at each other for the first time. I'm not stupid. I knew back then that's why you panicked and ran away. It had nothing to do with Madison's age."

I offered him a sharp look.

"Okay, maybe you freaked out because you realized she was younger than you. Or that she was younger than you expected her to be. But I witnessed it. The attraction. The magnetism. You can fight it all you want, but it's there. It's all around you two when you're in the same room. It's dazzling. No wonder Jacob let her go after the barbecue on your birthday." He paused. "The other night, while the girls sang at that party, I thought you'd eat her up every time you glanced in her direction. I felt like a voyeur, watching two people making love, and you were both dressed and standing thirty feet apart."

"You're talking shit," I blurted out.

The smirk on Riley's face turned devilish. "You wish."

"Whatever. We were supposed to keep it low-key. We failed. I've been alone for so long… She's the one, man. I'm fucking gone for her. Now I can't imagine walking away from her when she needs me the most."

"I gotta say you're much happier when Madison is around than when she's not. It's obvious to everyone already. You're a grumpy asshole when you're by yourself. Now I understand so many things. *So many things*," he repeated, stretching each word. "Eye-fucking each other is almost a full-time job for both of you."

"And I thought I was being subtle." I rolled my eyes and sighed.

"Think again."

He shook his head, and I punched his arm unable to hide the waves of joy filling me whenever the topic of Madison was evoked. "I'm just trying to do the right thing the right way. And now, I'm torn about leaving her. It's hard, man."

"Madison would want you to go on with the tour. I don't even have doubts about it. I talked to her sister, and she confirmed it too. She'll be proud of you, Stevens. For not walking away when things got tough. It's a great love lesson. And for what it's worth, I'm proud of you too. Music will do you good. It always does. Trust me, we'll make it work."

"You really believe it?"

"I'm convinced. And when have I ever been wrong?" He winked, and I winced at his confident poise.

Riley exited the room, and my heart banged in my chest when I returned my focus to the person I couldn't leave behind without pieces of me staying with her.

"As you might have heard, today is the day. The one you circled on that calendar you and the girls fixed to the kitchen wall at the beginning of the summer. For a long time, it appeared so far away in time, but now that it's here, I can't seem to find the courage in me to leave. The girls are beyond thrilled. In a way, I am too. But I'm also sad. It's a weird combination." I molded our hands together. "It's so fucking hard, you know. I'm excited to go back there, but it feels wrong since you lie silent here."

For a long beat, I watched her chest rising and falling, the soft lines of her profile, the shape of her lips, her smooth eyelids. I wish they would open right about now so I could lose myself in the sea-green pool of her eyes.

"I love you, Maddie. I'll come back between my shows. I'm not leaving you behind. You have family around. You're not alone. And I'll come visit. Just get better, okay? That's all I'm asking."

Whatever lesson life was trying to teach me right now, I could really do without it. I already had my share of lessons. I could skip a few.

A knock on the door cut short my drowning thoughts.

"Hey, Sam," Emily said as she entered the room. "I saw Riley in the hallway. It's time for you to go."

I nodded, my throat so tight no word could pass the rim of my lips.

As she did every time she was around, Emily checked all vitals and the readings on the monitors. "Go. She is in good hands. I'll never let anything bad happen to her. I'll call you every day to keep you updated like we've discussed. I promise."

I bent over a still Madison and kissed her forehead. "I love you. I'll be back in three days."

Without looking back, I walked away. Because if I did, I would never go on with this tour.

———

It had been thirteen days since Madison's accident. And as much as I could, I split my time between my music, my children, and the women I loved. Doris, the new nanny, was the antipode of Madison—stricter, more somber, and less energetic—but so far, she got along with my girls. That was all I could ask for right now.

Armed with my guitar case, I followed Brent through the basement-level maze toward the elevator. I knew the route by heart by now, but he still made sure, every time, I wasn't hunted down whenever I visited Madison.

Her parents had gone back home two nights ago. The day before I left on tour, we had lunch together. They formed a quick bond with whom I hoped one day they'd consider to be their own granddaughters. The girls couldn't stop bragging about Madison the entire time. Justine sat on Mrs. Prescott's lap all through dinner after showing her around the house and parading in every princess gown she owned. I could tell the woman relished the distraction. Just like her daughters, she had love in buckets pouring out from her.

"How is it going today, Mr. Stevens?" Mara, the nurse caring for Madison, welcomed me as I passed before the nurse station, carrying my guitar case. "We missed you around here."

"As best as I can in the circumstances." I placed a box of pastry in her hands. "For you guys. As a thank you for watching over her."

"Thank you," she called after me. "Your lady is lucky to have private concerts every time you're in town. I know a lot of staff members who are jealous they missed the one you gave here the other night. It was very generous of you and your team to organize this little gathering. We're all grateful." I mirrored her smile. "Go ahead, I'll come see you in fifteen minutes."

"Hey, Maddie. How are you?" I asked after I kissed her forehead and sat in the chair by the bed. "The girls are asking about you twenty times a day. We miss you so much. Our new home on wheels feels empty without you. I played a concert in Arkansas last night and flew back as soon as I could. I boarded a jet at eight this morning, once the girls and Doris were set for the day. I'm flying back later this afternoon because I have a show tonight in Dallas at seven. Somehow, I'm glad I refused Riley's offer to cancel the tour. Honestly, I didn't think I had it in me to go back up there without you around, but I did it. I faced my fears. And I have faith it will all work out in the end. I'm doing what I know you'd want me to do if you were awake. To keep living. And thriving. Until you're ready to join us."

If music left my life too right now, I'd go nuts. Yeah, I'd been there before. A guy angry at the world. I wished to never be that version of me ever again.

"Ready for your stop on the Sam Stevens's US tour? You get all the free spots on my schedule."

Just like every time I was by her side, I played Madison her song as an opening act.

> **…There's something I gotta**
> **tell you (yes, there's some-**
> **thing I gotta tell you)**
> **There's something I can't keep**
> **to myself anymore (no,**
> **baby, I gotta tell you)**
> **I'm in love with you.**

I was about to continue with "Snowed In" when Doctor Bera walked in.

"Mr. Stevens." I rose to my feet to shake his hand. "As we discussed yesterday on the phone, we've been tapering the medication since this morning. You should expect her to wake up soon."

"Oh, it's that fast?"

"Yes. Patients usually wake up within three to four hours after being taken off the ventilator."

I rubbed the column of my throat to erase the dryness there. "Will she be okay?"

"We're watching her closely and monitoring her vitals all through the process. She's in good hands."

He checked her reflexes and wrote something down before promising to come back later.

I grabbed Madison's hand and squeezed it between mine. "Babe, you're going to wake up. Listen, I need you to be brave when you do. Your life is safe now. You might hurt some." I kissed her knuckles. "I wish I could take away your pain. No matter what, I'll be by your side. Emily says you're a fighter, and it is so true. I have seen it these past few days. I just want you to know I miss you. And I love you. We'll get through this, you hear me? Whatever challenge life throws at us, we've proved we are a great team so far, you and I, so make sure you remember this."

Playing my guitar, I sang for the woman who held my heart.

"If I grab something to eat real quick, will you wait for me? To wake up?" I asked when I took a break around one in the afternoon. "I don't want you to open your eyes and be all alone. Emily is in surgery all day, so it's just you and me now."

I skimmed the back of her hand when I felt a barely perceptible twitch of her fingers. I blinked, certain I had conjured the movement. Just in case it wasn't my imagination playing tricks on me, I rested my gaze on her hand for a tad longer.

It took about a minute for Madison's fingers to spasm again, and only about twenty seconds for a third spasm.

Springing to my feet, but never releasing her hand, I pressed the emergency button attached to the railing of the bed. My pulse went haywire. A new form of energy arose in me. I hesitated between jumping around, pumping my fist, and screaming my excitement at the top of my lungs. Then I remembered just in time that this was the ICU, not the place to be loud.

Within seconds, Mara walked into the room. "Mr. Stevens, how can I help you?"

I sucked a cleansing breath in to calm the jitters filling my stomach. "She moved. Her fingers. I think she's waking up," I said, the words tumbling out of my mouth. I zoomed in on Madison's face. The bruises were mostly faded, and the bandage on her forehead had been removed days ago. Even the laceration on her cheek looked better. "Maddie, do it again. Please. Move. Do it for me." I lifted her hand and kissed her knuckles one by one. This time, her eyelids fluttered. Like the wings of a butterfly. "See?" I asked the nurse. "I told you. Did you see it? Please tell me I'm not going crazy. Is she waking up?"

"Yes. She is." She pushed a button, commanding a blood pressure reading and checking other waveforms on the machine, before saying, "I'll get the medical team. Wait here. We'll be right back."

"Okay." I talked to Madison, my voice strained with new emotions, hope and fear mixing together in nerve-wracking anticipation. "Babe, you gotta do it again. Moving, I mean. Your fingers. Or your eyelids. Even your toes." I leaned over the bed, waiting for another sign.

Madison's eyelids fluttered faster this time, until they finally opened and locked onto me.

My voice got stuck down my throat.

My eyes filled with hot tears.

My heart flipped in my chest.

I stood there, barely able to take a full breath in, readying myself for her next action.

We stared at each other, taking in our expressions, as if we were seeing the other for the first time.

At the sight of her, awake, a million different feelings surged through me.

Dr. Bera and his team entered the room, and I was asked to step back while they examined her. I let go of her hand reluctantly. It broke my heart to sever the only connection we shared.

Standing in one corner of the room, I was transfixed by all the commotion surrounding me. Buttons were pressed, and orders were given. The beeping sounds of the machines stuffed the silence in-between the chatter. The doctor nodded, and the nurse asked Madison to take a deep breath, then removed the tracheal tube, a harsh cough escaping her lips.

Her eyes perused the room, and when they landed on mine again, they stole my breath away. *Sam*, she mouthed this time.

"I'm here. I'm right here," I said, unable to hide the turmoil invading me. My feet brought me next to her of their own volition. My fingers laced through hers before I could even comprehend what I was doing, and my lips connected with her forehead. "You're awake. I'm not going anywhere."

Her glossy eyes stayed glued to mine. The doctor asked her questions, and the entire time, Madison watched me watching her, and it slid the bruised part of my heart that belonged to her to its rightful position.

The doctor touched my shoulder to catch my attention. "She'll be in and out of it for a few hours. Don't worry. It's normal. We'll come down later to get her to perform some tests. So far, everything looks promising."

"Even her leg?"

"Even her leg. Don't hesitate to call us."

They all exited the room.

Madison had fallen back asleep. For the next hour, I watched her, counting her breaths and staring at the monitor to make sure her heart was still strong and her oxygen levels were high enough. Just in case the doctors had missed something.

"I love you," I repeated over and over. "I can't believe you're awake. God, I've missed you so much."

She squeezed my hand back, and for the first time in almost two weeks, hope fully returned to my heart.

38

SAM

“What do you mean she should stay in Nashville?” I asked Riley when he joined me later that day, fury bleeding from me as I spoke the words. “She just fucking woke up. What is it supposed to mean? Why would I leave her behind?”

He rested his hand on my shoulder, forcing me to take a full breath in and calm down.

Madison was out of it. She’d been all day. That was the only reason I had agreed to leave her room, and I couldn’t wait to get back to her side.

“I’m about to break at the seams here, and you wanna remove me from the only person keeping me sane. Tell me how being away from her is logical, especially when she is awake now. I’m listening.”

I sat down in a chair, trying to give him the benefit of the doubt. My friend had never screwed me over, and I couldn’t believe he’d do it this time. He knew what was at stake. Not only the tour, but also my heart. And my fucking sanity.

Restless, I fisted my hands and rested them on my thighs. "Talk."

"If you wanna help Maddie, you gotta be at the top of your game. In every area of your life. Right now, you're exhausting yourself. The doctors said her recovery would be long and painful. You can't bring her on the bus. She requires constant medical care, along with daily physiotherapy, to relearn how to walk. And above all, she needs stability. And to keep her stress levels as low as possible. How do you picture the next few weeks? Tell me. Because I've been trying to come up with a plan, but I can't. Nothing makes sense except for keeping her here, where she has all she needs. And before you tell me, flying in and out every day or two is also not realistic, Sam. You've been doing it for two weeks, and already you look drained. How can you keep doing that for eight, ten, or fifteen additional weeks without collapsing?"

I stayed silent, doing my best not to bark at him. His words weren't farfetched. It didn't mean I had to agree, though.

"Mika and Justine need you too. Right now, they are spending more time with Doris than with their own father. When you agreed to this tour, it was the one thing you were adamant about. To make them the priority."

Riley pulled a chair and sat before me, elbows propped up on his knees, leaning forward.

"I know it will break your heart, but Madison won't be on her own. Emily, her parents, and friends can visit her if she stays in Nashville. If we move her around, she'll be alone when you're busy. It's not good for her recovery to feel like a burden. How will she be able to move around the bus in a wheelchair? Before you argue, I'm not saying you're not doing all you can to make it easy on her, but she'll be better here. In Tennessee. You can fly in once a week to visit."

"Ry, I wanna watch over her myself. To make sure nothing bad happens ever again. How can I make sure she's safe if she's not around me?"

"Stevens, if you had been in that car with her, would you have been able to prevent that jerk from running the red light?"

"No."

"And she would have been under your watch the entire time. It just took a split second for her accident to occur. Whether she's with you or not, you don't possess the power to prevent destiny."

I ran a hand over my short stubble.

I hated the fact that everything my friend said sounded accurate. In my head, I had pictured Madison coming back with us, with medical professionals caring for her when I couldn't. This scenario would appease me the most. But would it be what was best for her?

"Ry, what you're asking from me is hard. It goes against everything I wish for." I paused, casting a glance down while I rubbed the sole of my shoe against the tiled floor. "I'll talk to her. See what she thinks."

"I already made all the arrangements. If she agrees, she could be moved to your home in about a week. Her doctor said she'll be discharged by then. Emily is on board already. It's for the best."

I got to my feet and kicked the chair next to mine. "Nothing goes as planned. It's all a big giant fuck-up."

Riley pulled me into a hug. "Life happens. It wasn't part of the plan, but we're all doing our best to accommo-date you and your family. Trust me, okay?"

I nodded as we broke apart and shoved my hands into my pockets.

Without another word, I spun around, got the hell out of the room, and exited the building, desperate for some fresh air to settle my mind.

And assess my options.

———

"Hey you," I whispered when I walked back into the hospital room an hour later.

Madison's breathing was soft and steady, and I listened to it for a while before taking a seat beside her bed.

When I touched her hand, her eyes wavered open, and she offered me a weak curl of her lips.

"Sam," she whispered.

I leaned forward, my lips connecting with her cheek.

"What's going on?" she asked. "Why am I here?"

Tears filled her eyes, and I used the pad of my finger to dry them.

"Two weeks ago, you got into an accident. It was bad. The doctors weren't sure you'd make it."

"Two weeks?" She winced. "You sure?"

"Yeah. I'm sorry. You were put under sedation."

She swallowed a sob. "How bad? No rainbows. Be honest with me." Her voice had lost all her usual spirit and sounded so slurred I had to make an extra effort to understand her words.

"Your left leg. It got crushed. They did extensive reconstruction work to fix the damage, but it will be a long recovery. You could have lost your limb. There're scars across your pelvic bone and down your left thigh and leg. They might require plastic surgery in the future. We gotta wait and see."

Madison lifted her arm, her hand seeking mine. I

knitted our fingers and brought our joined hands by her side, squeezing hers a little more than usual.

"Will I—?" More tears escaped from her eyes. "Will I ever walk again?"

I bobbed my head. "Yes. Your spine is fine. With time and physical therapy, your leg should be fully functioning again."

A heart-wrenching sob punctured the silence.

I let her cry. My own eyes were watery at the sight of her distress. I combed her hair back with my free hand, resting my head on her shoulder while we navigated this new reality together.

"And the girls? Who's watching them?"

I swallowed the bile rising at the back of my throat. "A woman Janice sent over. Her name is Doris."

She bowed her head. "Is she…is she nice?"

"Yeah. She doesn't teach math while baking and doesn't throw dance parties, or know the steps to a line-dance, but other than that, the kids like her. They miss you, though. They ask about you all the time."

"When can I see them? I need a hug. Or two hugs." A little smile peeked through her sadness.

"Soon." I gathered some courage from deep within me to speak the next few words. "We gotta talk about something," I began. "I'm touring Texas right now. I fly here every couple of days, but I talked to Riley. And he talked to Emily. And we think it would be better if you stay in Nashville. For now. Here, you have your sister, who happens to be a surgeon, and your parents live a few hours' drive away. Bringing you on a bus right now doesn't make sense. We have to discuss logistics."

"You want me to stay here?"

I looked away, putting order into my messy thoughts. "It would be for the best. If it were realistic, you'd be on the bus with me, and I would hire a nurse to care for you when I'm unavailable. But the truth is, you need physical therapy and a schedule. A wheelchair. And lots of rest. And I can't provide that. Not short-term at least. Not until you are a bit stronger. If you agree you'd be better here, Emily could move in with you at home. You wouldn't have to leave the house."

She nodded, not saying anything.

I tightened my grip on her hand. "I'm sorry. If you don't wanna go ahead with this plan, we'll figure something out. I might just require a little more time to make it happen."

Madison swallowed and looked away, and a tidal wave of sadness and guilt enveloped me.

"I love you, Maddie. I love you so fucking much. And the thought of losing you almost killed me. You came this close. I…I was so helpless."

"You love me?" Her glossy gaze locked on mine.

"Like crazy. I'm sorry I didn't tell you sooner. I thought I would never get to tell you… That you were gone. I decided it was time to be honest with myself. And with you. About us."

"Sam, I love you so much. Before meeting you, I had no idea I could love someone this much."

I pressed my forehead against hers, and we stayed immobile for a long time.

"My home is you and Mikaella and Justine. That's the only place I wanna be. Where I belong." She paused. "Since I can't wait to be with you and I need to heal for it to happen, I-I'll stay in Nashville. It's not like I have a lot of options…"

A part of me wished she had disagreed, that she had gotten mad and forced me to bring her along with me.

I buried my face in the crook of my elbow, calming the

conflicted storm raging in my core. I couldn't let her see how much the idea troubled me.

I firmed my back, trying to project confidence. "Fine. I'll tell Riley to set it all up."

"Can I ask you a question, though?" The vulnerability in her voice rattled every cell in me.

I nodded.

"Did my parents visit since the accident, or is my brain playing tricks on me?"

"You remember?"

"It's like I dreamed of it. It's hard to explain."

"They did. Do you recall anything else?" I asked, holding my breath for whatever she was about to say.

"A song. It's not one of yours even though it sounded like it. I heard it all the time. It spoke about the sky and colors and love. It was beautiful."

My breathing hitched. "Babe, it was…me. I sang to you every day I was here after you were moved out of isolation and into a single-patient ICU room. Your song. It's called 'Maddie.' I can't believe you heard it." I leaned in to drop a kiss on her cheek. "Wanna hear it?"

Her eyes shone, bringing some color to her face. For a fleeting second, Madison looked like herself, glee radiating from her.

With my guitar in my hands, I sang the melody, watching the array of emotions painting her features. From elation to joy to pride. And love.

**…There's something I gotta
tell you (yes, there's something I gotta tell you)
There's something I can't keep
to myself anymore (no,
baby, I gotta tell you)**

I'm in love with you

"Sam... It's beautiful. That's the one. The one I held on to. When everything was dark. When I had no idea how to find my way back."

Sobs shook her body. Her shoulders heaved. She hid her face with her hands.

The high-pitched sound escaping Madison's lips shattered my heart.

Balancing myself beside her on the bed, I wrapped my arms around the love of my life. She relaxed against me, accepting the comfort I brought her. Never loosening my grip around her body, I rocked her until sleep claimed her once again, my lips lingering on the top of her head.

At some point, I must have fallen asleep because a nurse touched my arm, and my eyes sprang open. Confused by her sudden appearance, I blinked to reboot my sluggish brain.

"Mr. Stevens. We need to perform some tests and change her dressing. Can you be back in thirty minutes?"

I untangled myself from a still-sleepy Madison and kissed her cheek. "I'll be right back. I love you. Don't go anywhere."

A soft tilt of her lips told me she'd heard my words. "I love you too," she murmured.

I found Riley still seated in the office the hospital had let him use and informed him Madison had agreed to stay in Nashville. For the time being.

For the rest of the day, I remained by her side while she drifted in and out of sleep.

Around six, I gathered my stuff. I was supposed to fly back two hours ago, but I had rescheduled my flight after Madison woke up. Now I would need to get to the venue right after I landed. I had missed sound check and hoped I could still be able to deliver a great performance, even though my heart was stuck in a hospital room in Tennessee.

"Maddie, I gotta go, or I'll be late," I whispered in her ear. "I'll be back in four days because I have three back-to-back shows."

She cracked her eyelids open, and her sea-green irises swallowed me whole. Her throat worked. "Sam, don't come back." Her voice sounded so weak.

My hair stood on end on my arms. "Why?"

"The girls. They need their daddy. You can't spend all your free time here. They'll resent us. They will want to be with you. That was the plan…for the tour. To make them a priority."

"But—"

"No buts. We agreed on this. Listen to me. I want this. For you to thrive. And be a father. I'm not going anywhere anyway. Please don't come back. Not for the next week at least."

I pulled her into a hug. "I'm not sure I can stay away that long."

"You must. It's a dare. Don't deceive me."

"Will you call me if you feel down? Or change your mind? Or if you just wanna hear my voice or your song?"

"Yes. Now go. I'm glad you didn't cancel the tour. I would have been very angry if you had."

I locked my emotions inside. "I know."

After I kissed her one last time, I neared the door, my heart sinking to my heels as I padded away.

"Hey, Sam?"

I pivoted to face her.

"Don't fall in love with the nanny, okay?" She winked, and I burst into a mix of giggles and tears.

With the back of my hand, I wiped my damp cheeks

and returned to her side. "Never." I closed my eyes and kissed her lips. "I love you. Only you."

"I love you. Thank you for everything you are doing for me." Her voice trembled. "I'm sorry I can't be there to cheer you on."

With her hand hooked around my nape, as if she feared I'd disappear before she was ready to say goodbye, Madison held me against her, returning the kiss. Together, we let the sadness wash away, bringing each other the comfort we both needed so badly.

39

MADISON

It had been six days since I'd moved back into Sam's house, and into my old room. I was wearing one of his sweaters while lying on my side. My entire body hurt. Radiating pain crippled my left half. Every time I shifted position by myself, my eyes watered, and I had to grit my teeth until the wave of agony subsided. Even my arm muscles had weakened since the accident. June, Riley's assistant, had come over to set up the house so I would have everything I needed. Sam had hired a nurse to live here with me full-time, and Emily had taken over the third bedroom upstairs.

I wasn't alone, but in a sense, it felt as if I was.

Unable to bathe or go to the bathroom by myself, I was dependent on so many people. For someone who wasn't used to having people hovering over her, it was a tough pill to swallow. The permanent state of pain I was in added to the embarrassment. I felt like I was losing my mind. Anger simmered just below the surface, and every time things didn't go my way, I wanted to hit something—or someone.

Since waking up after the accident, I had spent most

nights crying in agony. The doctors weren't kidding when they said the painkillers would only partially work. The rest of my atrophied leg would demand grueling physiotherapy. Muscle spasms ran down my leg, paralyzing me and making it hard to breathe.

Due to the cast covering my flesh, I could not massage my thigh, the half that had required the most work, and had to ride the excruciating pain. Not knowing what the scars looked like got me anxious. And being unable to comfort my own leg was hard enough.

A part of me wished Sam would be by my side, reassuring me and murmuring in my ear I'd get through this. That his strong arms would wrap around me in a tight hug, his love soothing every ache.

The rest of me thanked the tour for his absence. I didn't relish the idea of him seeing me like this: a victim of circumstances, glued to a bed all day with no choice but to wait it out.

With every passing hour, my positivity drained away bit by bit. Each time I woke with a start and screamed in agony, I felt myself slipping further and further from who I once was.

A new bout of excruciating pain coursed through my body, and I had to clutch my pillow with a death grip to ride it out. I lashed every curse into the soft cotton until it released me. Scorching tears prickled the back of my eyes. My pulse hastened, and I could barely suck in any oxygen through my clenched teeth while I waited for the tremors to subside, aware they'd be back soon, ready to haunt my days. This happened every few hours, a relentless, vicious cycle.

Yesterday, Sam came to visit me and left within a few hours. He had spent every minute by my side, lying beside me and shielding my body from the outside world as he held me against his heart the entire time. I fought with myself the entire time to pretend his presence didn't affect me. Now that he was gone, I struggled not to miss him. I still hadn't seen the girls. When I told Sam, I had changed my mind and wasn't ready to face them yet, hurt flashed in his eyes. He said nothing, just nodded with quiet resolve.

Deep down, I knew that if they made the trip to see me, I would be heartbroken once they left. Even my soul would have a hard time letting them go. For now, I'd chosen to keep them at a distance. We video chatted twice, and it was about all I could manage for the time being.

Jeremiah, the nurse on duty, peeked his head through the ajar door. "Madison, dear, there's someone to see you."

I wiped my runny eyes with my sleeve.

Before I could refuse, the door opened, and Jacob stood there.

I gulped a big intake of air. "You? No. *No, no, no.* You can't be here. Why are you even here? You…you should go. I'm not in the mood to see you right now."

Images of our last time together flashed through my mind.

"Maddie—"

"Jake, what do you…what do you want?" I tried to push myself up to roll onto my side and winced.

Soon, Jacob had his hands around me, helping me shift position. "Hold on to me. Let me help you," he said. Just the sound of his voice created a tsunami inside me.

"Thank you," I mumbled. "Why are you here? Who told you?"

He glanced away for a second, discomfort written all across his face. "I ran into Becks two days ago. He…he thought I knew. I called Emily, and she told me what happened. I'm sorry, Maddie. I know how much this tour meant to you. It hurts me to see you in pain." He took a seat in the chair next to the bed. "Wanna tell me what's going on in that head of yours?"

Averting my eyes, I refused to talk for the longest time.

"Maddie. Don't keep it all inside."

"Why should I tell you shit? You flushed me from your life, remember? You kicked me out of your car in the middle of the night."

"That's not how it went down," he argued.

"You didn't want me there. Same result. You pushed me out of your life."

"Maddie—"

"Don't Maddie me. We haven't talked in months unless you count that phone call where you asked me to drop everything and run back to you. You were my best friend, Jake. My closest friend. I confided secrets in you I've never told anyone else. I thought you had my back. And because I couldn't return your feelings, you acted like I never mattered to you. You broke my heart. Big time. And now that I'm confined to a bed, you swish back into my life and act like we're fine. News flash, we're not." I paused. "Nothing goes the way it should. It's all a big clusterfuck."

He hung his head low and said nothing. After a moment, he hunched forward, and I could tell I'd hurt his feelings.

"I don't want to be angry with you." My voice had lost its previous edge. "But I'm not sure how to be friends with you anymore… Or if we can salvage what we once were." A yawn escaped me as I shifted on my pillow, my eyelids feeling like they weighed tons.

Jacob stood to pull a blanket over me—the same one Sam had brought to the hospital, noticing it was my favorite. Without a word, he sat back.

"Sam and I, we-we're together," I said, unable to keep my eyes open, the painkillers finally doing their job.

"I figured. We'll talk later. Don't worry. Now sleep, okay? Rest will help you heal faster. I'm staying right here. I promise. I'll watch over you. Let me do this. I need to do this. Please."

I sighed. "Fine."

I heard the distinct sound of Jacob swallowing, but he said nothing as I surrendered myself to sleep.

Hours later, I woke up to find him reading beside me.

I blinked, trying to make sense of the scene.

"You're real?" I asked. "I thought it was all a dream. What are you reading?"

He shrugged. "Something I picked up on my way over here. Thought I could read to you, and you might…huh… like it. Change your mind and stuff."

I said nothing for a while.

"Unless you want me to go," he finally said.

Was the silence stretching between us as uncomfortable for him as it was for me?

"You can stay. Only if you get me tacos."

"Tacos?"

"Yep. I want fun food. And chocolate chip cookies. If you can make it happen, you don't have to leave just yet. Chocolate is—"

"Good for the soul," he continued. "I know." A large grin illuminated his face. For an instant, my best friend was back. Gone was the tension in his demeanor. He jumped to his feet. "Mission accepted. Be right back."

Once he exited the room, I bit my tongue as debilitating pain spread through my lower self. I clung to the mattress with all my strength, praying it would recede quickly.

"How am I supposed to live like this?" I asked through my tears, to everyone and no one. "It doesn't get better."

The excruciating agony seemed to worsen every day—or was it my tolerance for pain that was waning?

Once the bone-deep ache released me from its claws, I grabbed the empty glass of water I kept on the nightstand and hurled it at the wall with all my might. I fixed my gaze on the shattered glass shards scattered across the wooden floor, and they reminded me of my body. For a moment, I wondered if I would ever feel whole again, or if, like the slivers of glass, I would remain forever broken—pieces of me lost for eternity.

Jacob came back twenty minutes later. I could hear his footsteps approaching on the other side of my bedroom door. I straightened my posture, wiping away all traces of sadness from my face with a corner of the blanket. Seeing the smile tugging at his lips, I knew Jeremiah hadn't exposed my earlier meltdown to the guy who used to be my best friend.

He insisted that we ate in the kitchen, so after helping me sit in the wheelchair I kept by my bed, Jacob and I settled ourselves in front of a Mexican buffet. For the first time in weeks, my mouth watered at the sight of food, and some of my appetite returned.

For the next two weeks, Jacob visited me every day after work. Slowly, we were learning how to be in each other's lives again. I doubted we'd ever be best friends in the long run, but for the time being, I cherished our moments together and his company. It felt like it could heal the wound we never had a chance to fix.

Tonight, we were in the den, admiring the fireplace as I sat in my favorite chair, a blanket tight around my legs while Jacob read me chapters of the novel we'd begun three days ago. After a few days, I'd come to enjoy our daily reading sessions, a simple pleasure I had not enough energy to indulge in by myself.

A loud yawn escaped my mouth, and without missing a beat, he helped me to my bed. Knowing my routine by heart, he handed me two painkiller pills and a glass of water from the bedside table.

"Do you need anything else before I go?"

"Nope. All good."

With a heavy gaze, he scanned my bedroom, searching for his next words. "Maddie, I gotta tell you something… We've always been honest with each other. The truth is... I'm still not over you, and I don't know if I'll ever be," he whispered. "The time we've been spending together, it means something more to me."

"I know. But you gotta move on," I whispered back.

He bowed his head, his eyes slowly drifting to my face. "Do you regret it? I mean…huh…choosing him?"

"No." Tremolos shook my voice as anguish clouded his face.

"I was hoping you'd say yes." He offered me a sad smile.

"You've been coming here every day. Perhaps we should take a break. Not that I won't miss you, but I don't want you to expect something from me that won't happen. The last thing I desire is to break your heart all over again. I can't be anything else than your friend."

"You'll get back on your feet. I know you'll thrive. I'm just sad I won't be by your side when it happens." He squeezed my hand with his, injecting me with tiny doses of courage.

"Again…I'm sorry. For everything," I murmured.

Jacob let go of me. "Our moments together are always too short. We always run out of time." Hurt filled his words, and it bled on me. "You should call him. He misses you. How can he not? If I were him and you were keeping me at a distance, I'd go nuts. It's been almost ten days since you last answered his call."

I looked away. Over the past two weeks, I'd refused every attempt Sam made to visit me and always pretended to be too tired whenever he called. He had to focus on his daughters and the tour. Not me. I had become the unforeseen variable, throwing off the careful balance of his life.

The well of darkness surrounding me was tightening its grip, and I refused to let Sam become one of its collateral victims.

"Maddie, I know you. I'm aware you've been pushing him away, thinking you're doing the right thing. What if it's not what you both need? What if it makes the two of you miserable instead? Have you thought about it?"

We both stayed silent for a while.

"You should rest," Jacob said, breaking the awkward silence. "I'll make sure the pantry is stuffed with cookies and brownies before I leave."

I returned my attention to him. "You don't have to."

He shrugged. "That's what friends are for."

"If I go to sleep, will you be there when I wake up?"

"It's better if I'm not," he said after a stretch of silence.

Tears pooled in my eyes. "Jake, you're going to be okay. I swear. You'll find the one. You're a special kind of someone. Any girl would be lucky to call you hers."

"Anyone but you…" A smile appeared at the corners of his mouth. "Sorry. I know you mean well. You own the biggest heart in the world, Maddie. Now rest. You need that sleep. Whatever happens between us, I meant everything I said. I want nothing more than for you to get better and to go back out there and catch up with the tour."

"Jacob… Thank you for being my friend. I'm sorry you had to put your life on hold to be by my side. I'll never be able to tell you how much your taking care of me has meant." Hot tears rolled down my cheeks, and I covered his hand with mine—the only comfort I could offer after he'd lifted my spirits and cared for me in the most selfless way, making me his priority over what his heart truly desired.

He drew in a shaky breath. "Today is the last day I see you, right? It's goodbye." He could still read me after all this time.

"Yes. It's for the best. I'll miss you." My emotions swallowed my words. "I'll forever cherish the memories of us."

"You really love him?"

I wiped my teary face with my free hand. "I do. I'm happy. For a long time, you were my entire world. I would never lie to you."

"Goodbye, Maddie. And for the record, you were the best friend I've ever had too."

He moved to kiss my forehead, and I let sleep claim me so I wouldn't have to witness him leaving and breaking my heart all over again.

40

SAM

Frustration poured out from every inch of me as I exited the stage. I almost threw my guitar after the third song, unable to get in the mood to perform and belt my heart out to the screaming crowd. Usually, I could slip into my performer mindset even when my personal life was a mess or I just wasn't feeling it. But tonight? Impossible. Too many things weighed on me, and made it hard for my mind to rest.

Every conversation I'd had with Madison lately left me seething. She was pushing me away, thinking it was what was best for me. And the tour. And the whole fucking world. Breaking news, it wasn't.

She was slipping away—I could tell. The realization had shattered the last flecks of hope left in me.

Before walking onstage tonight, I'd called her, and she refused to talk to me. Again. The last time we had a real conversation, she made me promise not to visit her for at least a month. A whole fucking month. I was going insane. Her sister kept updating me every day, but it wasn't the same as being there and seeing for myself how she was really doing. Being there to kiss it better on the days she felt like there'd never be light at the end of the dark tunnel she was trapped in.

Yesterday, Emily had confided that her sister's mood swings were getting harder to handle. They'd started around the same time she began distancing herself from me. I knew Jacob had been visiting her for a while, reading to her after dinner. Then, one day, he stopped coming over, and that too coincided with Madison's new bout of fussiness. And here I was, playing music instead of being there to comfort her. What a joke.

In about three weeks, I'd have a stretch of four days off, and I'd planned to fly to Nashville with the girls to spend a couple of days at home…with her. I was done being on the sidelines, feeling helpless, and watching my heart crash and burn without doing anything about it.

If we were in the same room, Madison would have no choice but to hear me out. I'd given her enough time and space. It was time to face the music—and everything that came with being in a relationship with me. I took care of the people I loved. No exceptions.

Enough was enough.

My own temper agreed with me. And my daughters probably did too. Mikaella told me this morning I was back to being *grinchy* and that she missed her cheery daddy.

Justine had called me a *mad, mad, mad daddy* last week after I'd broken a glass and was tempted to storm out.

When I got home, I would take Madison on a date and shower her with love, hoping she'd reconsider keeping me at a distance. That she would open her heart to me. She was struggling, bottling everything up, and being angry at everyone wouldn't fix a thing. I knew, I had been that guy. She had saved me, and now it was my turn to save her from her demons, and, in the process, reclaim my own inner peace. I didn't like the angry version of myself. Nah, I much preferred my in-love persona.

When I'd confided in Riley, he told me to be patient. Well, my patience came with an expiration date. The more space Madison put between us, the more restless I became.

That had to stop. Right about now.

Storming off the stage, I handed my guitar to a technician, chugged down a bottle of water, and wiped my forehead with a towel. People came to shake my hands and congratulated me, but I blocked the noise. I didn't deserve the recognition. Or the accolades. I didn't deliver what the crowd expected of me tonight. I was haunted. Angry. And sad. And it showed. The critics would agree. They would call me a fucking mess, and I wouldn't be able to get mad at them because it was the truth. I hadn't only failed my fans tonight, I had failed myself too.

"What was that?" Riley asked, cornering me as I stalked toward the green room, ripping my shirt open, my flesh on fire and my throat dry.

His presence cut short my spiraling train of thought, keeping me from blowing a gasket out loud.

I waved my hand, dismissing him. "Not now." My tone was clipped and my words rugged.

"Stevens. Stop." It wasn't a demand but an order.

I kept walking.

"Right now, it's not your manager talking, but your friend. Even though the manager in me should have a talk with his artist right the fuck now."

I swiveled around. "What? You wanna tell me I was a mess up there? I'm aware. No need to remind me."

He placed a hand on my shoulder, and I jerked away. "Talk to me."

"No." I clenched and unclenched my hands at my sides. "What's the point?" Fury blurred my vision. Black dots danced before my eyes. "She's too far away. It weighs on me, man. I'm trying here. Real fucking hard. She refuses to let me fly down to see her. The kids are asking for her too. What if she has changed her mind? What if she has no intention of ever letting me in again? What if the accident fucked us up?"

"Stevens." Riley's annoyance had decreased a notch. "It's just a minor setback. You two will be fine. Give her more time to heal. The accident didn't just crush her leg, it crushed her spirits too."

"I sound like a jerk. I know I do, but I can't help it," I said. "I'm back to my broody ways. My kids are sad too. We're all missing her. She makes us better. She makes *me* better. She makes the entire fucking world better."

"Sam, you don't have a show tomorrow. Let's go out."

"Not in the mood," I barked.

"It wasn't a request." Those words shut me up.

We went back to the buses, and after I showered and drowned some of my rage away, my friend joined me. His feet hadn't even touched the floor before Riley slid a whiskey bottle into my hand. "Nick's private label. He and Dahlia gifted it to me on my birthday. Great stuff. The girls are asleep on my bus. Let's drink this, then go out and get shitfaced. Like old times. It's been a while, and I could use the stress release too."

I nodded. What else could I do? I had run out of options. "Devon is okay with that?"

"Yes," my friend said. "She's happy to have the girls over. She's the one who spoke to Doris this morning and offered to take over for the entire day. They had a spa day, did the school stuff Maddie had put on the schedule, and made their own pizzas for dinner. They're more than fine."

"You two should be parents. It suits you both."

He snickered. "Yeah. Maybe. We've talked about it.

Your kids are growing on us, man. We'll see. I want to propose first. If I'm doing this, I'm doing it right."

"You're lucky. Dev is perfect for you."

I didn't miss the irony of my own words as I spoke them out loud. My eyes took in the label. "Whiskey and Country? I sense a pattern here," I teased.

Riley shrugged. "It fits them. You gotta meet Nick one day. He's a nice man. Reminds me of you. A lot. Minus the grumpiness."

I gave him a sharp look. "Thanks… I guess."

Bringing the bottle to my lips, I let the liquid slide down my throat, relishing the burn. It made me feel alive. I had no idea when I'd last been drunk. Yeah, it was measured in years, not days.

I drained more of the whiskey in one gulp, ready to visit Drunktown.

"Hey, leave some for me, would you?"

"I need it more than you do, man. And you were right, it's pretty good stuff. I had no idea Dahlia and Nick were in the whiskey business. You should sell it at Wild and Country. Exclusively."

Riley stole the bottle from my grip. "Yeah. Well, for now, it's just a small production. If they wanna expand, I'll be more than happy to talk business with them. Anyway, Tucker has already set his mind on convincing them to turn their hobby into something bigger. The guy is relentless, and Nick is his childhood best friend. We'll see how it goes. About the bottle… I brought it, and it was *my* gift, so I'm entitled to at least half of it."

I shook my head. "Don't come crying tomorrow when you have a massive hangover."

"Don't be a pussy. Just drink. The sooner you get wasted, the sooner I might be able to drill some sense into your stubborn brain."

I scrunched up my face and took the bottle back, nursing it as if it were a newborn. "I'll be too drunk later to tell you this, but thank you, man. Again, thanks for getting me out of my stalled life. I'm thankful for all this," I said, using the bottle to point around me. "And for always having my back. And caring for my girls."

"You're worth it, Stevens. You're a good man. And a good father. Just a shitty lover," he added with a wink.

"Yeah. Stop talking. Let's get drunk."

I woke up to the sound of chatter. Little girls' chatter. When had they come back here? Who was watching them? Then Devon's laughter filled the silence. My head thundered. I hid my head under my pillow, trying to muffle the sound. In vain. Once I regained consciousness, the voices of my little ones warmed my heart.

"Girls, be quiet. Your daddy and Riley had a rough night. They need their beauty sleep. I'm sorry we can't go play outside. It's raining. Let's hope freshly brewed coffee and bacon, eggs, and grit will wake them up from their slumber."

"Can we make hot *crotchcolate* too?" Justine asked.

"With marshmallows," Mikaella chimed in.

Devon chuckled. "Sure. Let's get to work."

I alternated between consciousness and sleep for what seemed like ten seconds when Devon's voice resonated through my skull again. "Girls, it's time. Let's wake up the beasts."

Seconds later, prickly fingers pried my eyelids open. "Daddy." I pretended to be deep asleep and snored. "Do you think he's dead?" Justine asked, strands of her hair sweeping my face and tickling my nostrils.

"No," Mikaella replied. "I think he's *grinchy*."

"*Grinchily?*"

"*Grinch-y*. Like in the Christmas movie."

"His skin isn't green," Justine remarked.

"Mm-hmm. It doesn't matter. He's still *grinchy*. It's because he misses Maddie."

My heart pinched in my chest.

"You think?"

"Yes. She's away and hurt, and now he's not happy. Let's bring her back," Mikaella suggested.

"How?" Justine asked.

"Let's get his phone like we did last time. We call her and tell her Daddy is sick…or dead. She'll freak out and run back here. I miss her too. Do you miss her?"

"Yes. She always plays with us and bakes the *most* better bunny pancakes." Justine paused. "Do you think she'll come back?"

"Yes. She loves us too much."

"I want a hug."

"Me too," Mikaella agreed.

"And a dance *partly*."

"We're calling her," Mikaella concluded.

I could picture my baby girl bobbing her head, quickly.

Listening to their thinking process and their plotting fascinated me.

"Do you know where his phone is?" Justine whisper-shout.

"Let's check his pants pockets."

Perhaps I should let my daughters call Madison and use their charm to persuade her to let us come see her.

Before they could empty my pockets, I wrapped my arms around their bodies and unleashed the tickle monster. The happy melodies of their laughter eased all my worries.

No matter what, we'd be okay because we had one another.

"*Daddddyyy*, stop," Mikaella giggled.

Justine hiccupped, unable to get a word out.

"*Grinchy* bear is up now, little creatures. I wonder what he'll have for breakfast. Little girls sound like a fancy meal I could indulge in." I rested my back against the headboard and released them. "Run before I catch you. Run."

Once they gave Riley, who was deep asleep in Madison's bunk room, the same treatment, the five of us had breakfast, the girls talking a mile a minute, as if they could feel I enjoyed their conversation filling the silence and preventing my brain from going rogue.

One of my conditions to go on this tour was to take days off from driving around and just be with my children. All these little moments—like having breakfast together without being rushed—mattered the most, because one day they would be the memories we'd look back on from this adventure. The concerts were mine, but our family time was ours.

The food and the painkillers I'd swallowed after I'd woken up helped to dissolve the rest of my hangover. Letting the hot stream of water from the shower loosen the tension in my back, I prayed it would chase my leftover grogginess away.

With red-rimmed eyes and dark circles around them, I grimaced when I saw my reflection in the mirror.

My last memory of the previous night was of Riley falling face first on the couch, snoring like an old pickup truck in desperate need of a new muffler. But between the moment we started drinking and then, I couldn't remember much. After I'd convinced him to use the bunk bed nobody used anymore, I had sauntered to my bedroom, my brain turned off, swimming in gallons of amber liquor.

"Ready?" I asked, my voice still croaky as I joined the girls and my friends in the small living room section of our bus after I dropped a kiss on my daughters' foreheads. "What are you guys doing?"

"Arts. We're making a *trapbook*," Justine said. "For Maddie. Because she misses all the cities we visit. And we did the numbers caterpillar with Devon after we woke up. It's Maddie who made them."

"You mean a scrapbook," I corrected my daughter. "It's a wonderful idea. Are you gonna put pictures of me in there?"

"Only if you're not *grinchily* anymore," Justine exclaimed.

"*Grinch-y*," Mikaella replied. "And only if you smile."

"I'll think about it then," I said with a wink that made both of them laugh.

My daughters, as usual, pushed my gloomy thoughts away.

Devon and Riley left to enjoy their day off, and I lifted Justine up when she raised her arms. Today, it'd be just the three of us.

"When is Maddie going to come back?" Mikaella asked.

I shrugged. "No idea. But I have a plan. Let me just put it into motion to see if it could work. Do you trust me?"

She bobbed her head.

"Are you ready to go to the fair?" I asked them. "I've heard they're only in town for the weekend."

"*Yesss*." Their screams of joy sent a warm feeling through my chest.

"Daddy, can we eat *colton* candy at the fair?" my baby girl asked. "Lots of *colton* candy."

"You want lots of cotton candy? What about your teeth?"

She bobbed her head fast, her eyes sparkling. "Yes. I want a big, big *colton* candy. Pink. Maddie says it's okay if we brush our teeth after."

Her genuine delight healed a part of my heart, while the remembrance of the woman I loved cracked a layer.

Justine's tiny hands wrapped around my neck, then she wriggled until I put her down on her feet. "Come on, Daddy. Don't make us late."

MADISON

"Ems, I'm not wearing that," I said, pushing away the knitted dress she was handing me. "No way. I'm perfectly fine in my PJs."

"No, you're not. We're going to get that cast removed, and then we're celebrating, you and I."

I shook my head a couple of times. "All good here. Not going anywhere. Forget it. There's nothing to celebrate, anyway."

"You need to get out of this house at some point."

I folded my arms over my chest. "I don't. I'm good. Just leave me alone, Ems."

I clamped my teeth together as the lightning of agony spread through my left leg. A stabbing sensation so strong a wave of nausea hit me. Using both hands, I pressed hard against my cast, aching to tear it off.

Emily sat beside me. "Breathe."

My jaw tightened, and tears filled my eyes. "It's like it's getting worse each day."

"Post-surgical neuropathic pain is real. But it's a good sign. It can take a few months to resolve." She touched my toes one by one, asking me questions. "I'm not worried. Given the repair your leg has undergone, this is all normal. With the supplements you're taking and the daily physical therapy sessions you are doing to strengthen your muscles, especially of the other leg, it'll help with the healing. And to relieve some of the nerve pain. You're lucky Sam arranged twenty-four-seven in-house care for you. It makes the whole appointment thing so much easier since you don't have to leave the place." Her voice softened. "But I hear you, okay? Give it more time."

"Time? Time?" I repeated. "It's been over two months. My heart almost jumps out of my chest every time the pain hits. I wish they had cut my leg when given the choice. At least I wouldn't have to endure the distress that comes with it being patched up."

My sister's eyes snapped to mine. "Maddie, you don't mean it. You're just hurting. Anyone in your situation would be."

"Easy for you to say. It's not *your* leg. *Your* body. *Your* life."

"No, it's not," she said. "But I've seen enough cases similar to yours to know what it implies."

I huffed, ire swirling inside me at a dizzying speed. "Again, it's not you who's glued to a bed all day."

She pointed to the discarded wheelchair in the corner of the room. The one I refused to use. "Maddie, you *are* choosing to stay in your room. You *are* choosing to forget you have options. I agree they're not the ones you'd normally aim for, but lashing out at the world won't help. You can do better than that. Where's the girl who survived neglect growing up? Where's the one who's always chasing her dreams?"

"She's dead. All I'm reduced to is a cripple, unsure if I'll ever get full use of my leg again, all because some idiot ran a red light. Why do I have to be the victim of *his* bad judgment?"

Emily shook her head. "Again, you're the girl choosing to position herself as a victim. It's so out of character for you."

I looked away, refusing to acknowledge her words.

After a long beat, I spoke up. "Maybe I'm just exhausted. Maybe it's all asking too much of me. What if I'm tired of always fighting for my life?"

My sister wound her arms around me. I steeled against her, but she didn't let go, and I relaxed after a full minute.

She caressed my hair and leaned back. "Maddie, you're doing a lot better. What angers you, aside from being injured, can be boiled down to two things."

"What?"

"Missing your man and the tour. You two were just beginning to acknowledge what you were to each other. Those first moments got lost in the chaos of the accident. They'll return…when the timing is right. You should call him."

I whipped my head around to look at her. "I was about to go on a once-in-a-lifetime experience, and it got stolen from me. I'm missing it all. I thought my life was finally making sense and *pouf!* All gone. I've missed two months, Ems. Two months I'll never get back."

"Why won't you allow them to visit you? You're both miserable. Sam loves you, Maddie. He's really trying to give you your space like you've begged him to and to just focus on the girls, but it's been hard on him too. Every time I call to update him, he sounds a little angrier."

"He can't fly here every time he has a day off. I'm not the priority here. The girls are. And that's what matters."

"Maddie, you matter too. To all of us, you do. Stop convincing yourself otherwise. Stop putting yourself last.

It's okay to wanna be a priority too. Nothing wrong with that."

I cocked my head to avoid her piercing gaze. "There's so much rage boiling inside me. I'm restless. All I wish for is to regain full use of my legs…and my independence. To do what pleases me without having to ask others for help. It's heavy, feeling incapacitated." I paused. Some of my wrath melted away as I spoke the words that were poisoning me. "Ems, I'm tired of being angry, you know? I want my life back. I want it all back. The same exact way it was."

"The girls called this morning…while you were asleep. You should at least video chat with them. And let them visit, Maddie. It would be beneficial to all of you. They don't understand why they can't see you or why you keep them at arm's length."

I parted my lips to argue, but my sister kept going.

"I understand your point of view. But try to understand theirs. They are just little kids. It's stressful for them. When you got injured, their lives changed overnight too. What they had known for months was taken away from them without any explanation or heads-up."

Her hand reached for mine.

"All those years ago, when I got you out of that hell, you asked for *them*. Even though deep down you knew *their* actions were hurting you, the kid in you couldn't imagine a life without *them*. You told me once you would have a hard time walking away from Mikaella and Justine after the tour because they had already been deceived before by an adult who was supposed to love them before. And now, you got taken away from them too. The least you can do is not break that bond you guys share and reassure them you're still part of their lives. If that's what you wish too… Deep down, I'm pretty sure it is. You guys are all hurting. Why not rely on one another to go through this episode instead of doing it all on your own?"

"But—"

"No buts, Maddie. I'm trying here. I really am. At one point you'll have to snap out of it and just take the control of your life back."

"I've been on bed rest for weeks. I don't want to suck them into my darkness. Some days, I feel like I'm stuck under piles of bricks. My entire body hurts. I wake up at night in sweat because the pain paralyzes me. How am I supposed to feel like myself? And as if that's not bad enough, I'm scarred all over my lower half. I know it will look like I've been cut open. Oh wait, I was."

My sister didn't let go of me as she watched me while delivering the next few words. "You could be stuck in a wheelchair for the rest of your life. Or missing both legs. Would you rather be unable to walk ever again?"

"Yeah, okay, I sound ungrateful. Sorry to be a pain in your life."

"You're not. I love you, but enough is enough. Let's eat out tonight. Trust me, it will uplift your mood."

I remained silent.

"Let's get you changed first."

"Ems, I'm not going," I said with a pout. "I'm entitled to one more day of self-loathing."

"Guess you'll wear that cast until you turn fifty then. Or maybe it will disintegrate in a few years if we're lucky."

I poked my tongue out at her, and she just shrugged.

"I'm not supposed to celebrate being handicapped," I said after a long pause. "It's wrong."

"We're celebrating your cast being removed. Come on. Help me out here, Maddie. Getting rid of this smelly thing"—she pointed to the cast on my leg—"is one more step toward healing. You should be proud. Not see red."

"I-I'm just not ready… To see…to see how bad it looks underneath," I finally admitted.

She signed. "There will be scars, sure, but perhaps you imagine it worse than it is in reality. I'm not saying it will be all pretty and perfectly healed, but I'm sure you'd be surprised at how much better it looks than what you've pictured in your mind."

"Sliced flesh is a sight I can't miss. You're right. Go, me."

"Keep going. Be dramatic, Maddie," my sister added. "Let me know when that dress is on, and I'll do your hair and makeup. You'll see. It'll make you feel beautiful. It's good for the spirits."

She exited the room without another glance at me.

Once she closed the door behind her, I exhaled, letting go of my annoyance. "Fine," I hollered after a minute.

Emily opened the door, grinning like a fool. "I knew you wouldn't be able to resist. I'll get my makeup bag and be back." She tossed a cookie onto the bed. "Get your chocolate fix."

I exhaled. Fishing my phone out, I watched the screen for a long time before I gathered enough courage to make the call.

"Maddie," he exclaimed when he answered after the second ring. "Everything all right?"

"Riley, I want back in. I need to get on that tour bus. Can you make that happen? I'm going nuts being stuck here. I'm driving my sister insane. My mood is all over the place. I know I need physical therapy, so maybe not this week…but as soon as it's physically possible, take me back, okay? I'll lose my mind if I spend too much time away. I miss them. I miss him. I can't heal if my heart is broken."

"Maddie, I'll see what I can do. Have you talked to him lately?"

"Last week. It was tense. He doesn't agree with me about not wanting him to visit. It's…it's for the best… I'm doing it for him."

"He loves you. You gotta let him help you," he said. "He worries a lot and feels helpless right now."

"He's already done more than enough. All the care… It's more than I could have ever expected. Every time he leaves, I end up crying myself to sleep for days afterward. How is it beneficial for anyone? We're all suffering."

"I hear you. Can we talk later? I have a meeting in five. I'll call you after dinner, okay? We'll figure something out."

"Yeah, I gotta go too. Bye."

———

"That splint looks badass on you," my sister said after we exited the doctor's office. "The X-rays look better than I expected. I'm impressed by the healing so far. It's all promising."

She pushed the wheelchair while I scrutinized the new apparatus around my leg. All I could see were the scars decorating my flesh that I would have to learn to accept. I still had a hard time with the one on my left hip. The leg ones were longer, but at least they were not as awful in appearance.

"Ems, I'm not feeling good enough to go out. My head spins. I wanna go to bed—"

Pain radiated down my limb, stealing my thoughts in the process. My entire body became taut as I prayed for the blades of fire shredding my muscles to dissipate.

Cold shivers lined my back, and I nipped at my bottom lip to refrain from crying.

"Ems. Raincheck, okay? Can you drive me home?"

My sister engaged the brake of the wheelchair, circled it, then gave me a pointed glance. "How bad? On a scale of one to ten?"

A moan escaped my lips as I squirmed in my seat. "A hundred."

"Fuck."

She loosened the straps of the splint and pressed firmly on the muscles in spasm. Each movement of her fingertips sent a lightning bolt of agony through me. She kept the rhythm going, massaging the flesh in circular movements until they slowly relaxed, one fiber at a time. A sigh left me as my whole body collapsed and I sank into the chair. I could breathe at last. I wiped the moisture building in my eyes with my fingertips. "I seem to be wrecking all our plans."

"Hey, it's okay. You come first. We can go out some other time."

"I acted like a brat earlier. I really wanted us to have dinner somewhere. We dressed up. Sorry, Ems."

Emily cupped my cheek, wiping my tears away. "We can still have fun. Let's grab takeout on our way back. Then we can watch a movie. I really wanna spend my night with you. Just us sisters. Okay?"

"O…kay. Thank you."

42

MADISON

I adjusted the crutches under my arms for the umpteenth time, my flesh raw where they dug into my ribcage. I maneuvered as best I could, pinching my lips together, as if that could stop me from falling flat on my face. Claudia, the physical therapist who'd started coming over ten days ago, stayed close but didn't intervene. I cursed under my breath as I lost my balance and had to grip the rail.

My foot pressed into the ground, and a sharp pain shot through me. The orthopedist, who had removed the cast, had instructed me to start putting a little weight on my leg and walk short distances every day. Easier said than done since it freaking hurt to do so. After the surgery I'd undergone, he confirmed it would take a while before I could walk on my own two feet again.

Being on bed rest had been hard on me. Even though the nurse, who'd been by my side since I came to live at Sam's, made sure I exercised every day so my other limbs wouldn't atrophy, I still had lost some muscle mass. And most of my patience, and whatever faith I had left that things would turn out okay.

My eyes brimmed with tears at the intensity of the pain, and I cursed some more before capitulating and sitting on a chair, ready to throw a fit. Sure, I could walk around just fine with crutches. But using them while putting weight on my bad leg wasn't as easy as it looked.

"It's not getting better," I spoke through clenched teeth. "I've been practicing for days, and I'm still unable to walk more than half a dozen steps without nausea hitting me because it hurts. Stupid accident. Stupid leg. Stupid crutches."

"Are you done complaining?" Claudia asked with a raised brow as she neared me. "You can go back to the wheelchair if you prefer. Would you? But I don't see it helping you get back on that tour bus if you do."

I offered her a pointed look before murdering her with my gaze. Yeah, she had teamed up with my sister to make my life an even bigger living hell than it already was.

"Claudia, you're supposed to root for me," I said with a deep exhale. "Not turn into a boot camp instructor."

"Maddie, I am rooting for you. If I don't push you, who will? You seem to have lost faith in yourself. Good news, I haven't. So, get up. The break is over. Show me what you can do. No excuses this time. We're not done for the day until you walk across the house in one go."

I grumbled something under my breath, got up, and executed myself. It took me four attempts to succeed.

Once I did, pride sizzled inside me. Pearls of sweat lined my forehead. The temperature in the room felt ten degrees warmer.

After the third try, I almost announced I was done, but now I was glad I had persevered.

Claudia high-fived me. "See? I knew you had it in you.

Now you gotta walk back there. I'm not gonna carry you around." She sauntered toward the kitchen, leaving me behind in the den.

With the crutches under my arms to help with the balance and remove some weight from my leg when it got too much, I gathered what little energy I had left and joined her where she rewarded me with a cupcake and a glass of lemonade. Yep, my sister was behind the bribing for sure.

"See? It wasn't too hard, was it? I knew you could do it. Practice till the next session. I'll be able to tell if you slack off."

Once Claudia left, I took a nap.

I woke up when my phone went off. I looked at the screen, and sighed, wishing it was Riley. Since we talked ten days ago, I hadn't heard back from him, and I wondered what was taking him so long to reach out.

Many times a day, I was tempted to call him, but I was choosing to exert some patience and give him more time. Maybe my request was not an easy one, and he needed longer to figure things out.

Emily picked me up at five. I had agreed to a redo of the dinner date I'd bailed on the day my cast was removed.

"Where are you taking me?" I asked as I hauled myself into her car without any help, panting as if I had run two miles, while she stowed the crutches on the backseat. "After what Claudia put me through today, I could use a drink. If Dr. Prescott agrees."

"One, since you're still taking meds. And we're having Thai tonight. That place we haven't been to in forever. Speaking of Claudia, how did your physical therapy session go?" she asked after I buckled my seatbelt and relaxed against the seat.

"Why did you recommend her to me? She's a sadist.

I'm telling you. She gets high on the idea of putting people through the wringer. There's nothing sweet or gentle about her."

I caught the grin forming on my sister's lips. "I knew you two would get along just fine. You may hate her, but look at you, you're done feeling sorry for yourself."

I quirked one eyebrow.

"Okay, not done, but you're getting there. Hate is a form of passion, Maddie. And being passionate is good. It's getting you somewhere."

I shook my head. "I guess. Anyway, thanks to your barbarian of a friend, I can maneuver around the house with the crutches. And walk a short distance using both legs. I'm getting stronger." I sighed. "One day at a time."

"That's the spirit."

We were finishing our plates when Riley Burns walked in and sat across the table, propping his elbows on the table and watching me with his I-mean-business stare.

I blinked and wiped my mouth with a napkin. "Huh, hi. What are you doing here?"

"Taking you back home, Maddie. "Isn't that why you called me the other day?"

I swallowed hard. My pulse went ballistic. "Is this a joke, or is it for real? Because if it's a prank, I'm not sure I'm mentally strong enough to deal with it."

Emily reached for my hands across the table and gave them a squeeze. "If it's what you still desire, it's now a viable option. We've been working together"—she motioned to herself and Riley with her fingers—"on a plan to get you there since you left the hospital after the accident. We were just waiting to see what the orthopedist would say and get Claudia's insight about your physical therapy needs."

"Are you two serious? The last time I talked to Sam, he said nothing."

The two people opposite me exchanged a glance. "It's because we haven't told him yet."

"What? Why?"

"Let's just say, if your doctor or physical therapist hadn't agreed, or if you hadn't shown such progress, this wouldn't be possible. We just wanted to make sure you two wouldn't have to live on false hopes," my sister said.

"When?" That was the only thing I could ask right now as excitement bubbled up inside me and chased away any other thoughts.

"Tonight. If you're ready to go."

"But—"

"Your suitcase is in the trunk of my car," Riley said. "I picked it up as soon as Emily texted me after you left the house earlier."

"I'm going home?" I asked, just to make sure it wasn't all a dream.

Moving to stand, I used the table to support some of my weight and reached the opposite side to pull my sister into a hug.

A surge of emotion filled me, and I could barely get a word out. "Thank…thank you," I croaked through the thickness of my throat. "I love you."

She tightened her grip around me. "Go get him back, Maddie. You deserve your happily-ever-after. And you're doing so much better. I'm proud of you. I know it'll be tough for quite some time, but you're getting there. I have faith in you. I've always had."

I leaned back, drying my tears, then hugged Riley.

"We missed you, Maddie. I'm glad you're healing. I know a few people who can't wait to have you back."

I let out a teary giggle. "Is this a dream?"

He shook his head. "It's all real."

For the first time in weeks, I could contemplate letting the ones I loved back into my life. I still had a long recovery ahead of me, but with Sam, Mikaella, and Justine around, every challenge appeared easier—and possible.

———

"What's the plan?" I asked Riley once the private jet reached its full altitude.

"Wait a sec. I almost forgot." He fished his phone from his pocket, tapped the screen a few times, and handed me the device.

My eyes stayed glued to the screen.

My grip on the phone tightened.

I pressed play on the video.

It had been filmed from the side of the stage.

Sam filled the screen, bent over a piano—I had no idea he could play—and the first note of a song I'd never heard before reached my ears, tearing my heart apart. It wasn't just the lyrics. It was the melody. The melancholy in his voice. The raw emotions etched in his eyes. His stance, more fragile and less assured than usual.

A hot tear escaped my eye and trailed down my chin. I caught it with the back of my hand.

Goose bumps spread all over my arms and the nape of my neck.

My throat constricted, affecting my breathing, as my emotions lodged there.

"Is it—?" I asked, unable to complete the question. The song wasn't the same one he'd sung to me at the hospital. I'd never heard it before.

"It's yours. I had no idea he had written it, and I bet he has written a few. It's his way of coping with the hardships of life. He played it last night…out of the blue. As an encore. Said he felt closer to you… That he wished his words could reach you somehow. To help him hold on to the specks of hope that you'd let him back into your life."

"It's beautiful. Listen… I-I didn't mean to push him away. I just wanted to ease things for him…"

"I'm aware."

I couldn't move my focus away from the screen, immersed in Sam's performance. In who he was. In the man hurting and pouring his heart to me into a song.

The song ended, and I was a sobbing mess.

Riley made a box of tissues and a glass of water appear, and I thanked him.

His lips stretched into a smile while he tapped something on his phone before bringing his attention back to me. "I was thinking. Only if you're up to it… You could surprise him at his show tonight. We'll miss the beginning, but we should be there for at least the second half. It's just an idea."

Warmth swirled inside me at the thought of seeing the man I loved again, knowing I would never have to leave his side afterward.

"I love it. Let's do this."

"Welcome back, Madison."

———

From where I stood, away from the stage, I let out a long breath, waiting for Riley's direction. A few feet away, Sam was belting his heart out to the crowd, and I could hear him, even though I couldn't see him. Just the sound of his voice was powerful enough to stir flutters in me and warm my skin.

Sadness laced his voice. His tone didn't carry the same

potency, the same mesmerizing pull as the night he'd sung in that bar.

He sounded…lonesome. That was the only adjective I thought was fitting to describe Sam Stevens at this moment.

His performance lacked the contagious joy and energy he usually carried onstage. Sure, he was still an incredible artist and musician, but I knew him well enough to notice the difference.

A vise closed around my heart at the realization he was hurting because of me. Because he thought I was abandoning him too. Because the moment we chose to be together, everything went sideways.

Even though his vocals were filled with heartache, steeped in every word leaving his mouth, my love for him only deepened because he was himself—the one who never shied away from his emotions. That was what made his music so unique. So relatable. So intoxicating. And right then, I understood why he had been named *The Legend* of country music years ago. Yes, Sam Stevens was truly a legend in his own way. But right now, he was a lonesome heart alone on a stage, trying to mend the broken pieces of himself through his art.

I was staring at my phone for the umpteenth time when Riley's text message came through.

RILEY

A guy named Rocky will come get you. Stay on the side where he directs you. There will be a stool so you don't fatigue yourself. I made sure he'll play your song again as the encore. That's your cue. Like you asked. I'll be cheering you on from offstage.

ME

Thank you. You're like our fairy love godmother.

Or godfather, I guess.

RILEY

Not sure Sam would agree with this term of endearment.

ME

It fits. What can I say?

RILEY

Go surprise your man. We're babysitting tonight. Devon's orders.

ME

I'll owe you one the day you have kids of your own.

RILEY

We have a deal.

I followed Rocky, maneuvering my crutches the best I could, and took my place next to the stage, just behind the thick black velvet curtain, out of Sam's sight. For the first time, I was grateful for Claudia's tough love in getting me ready for this day. Without her, I would probably still be in bed, alone with my dark thoughts and sinking hopes.

Sam sang four more songs, and the crowd exploded in cheers and applauded, begging for an extended performance.

My heart jackhammered in my chest. All my senses were attuned to the man singing his heart out. Just being in his vicinity again was enough to make me forget about the pain numbing the left side of my body. Why had I kept him at arm's length for so long? I needed him as much as he needed me. We were two halves of the same whole.

Two souls needing each other to reach our full potential. Two hearts carved from the same flesh.

I loved him beneath the broodiness and all the walls he'd built around himself when I first got to know him. I fell for him the moment I discovered how generous and beautiful the heart he hid inside truly was. Even when I tried to convince myself my feelings weren't reciprocated, I still loved him. Simple as that. What I felt for him could only be defined as a *one of a kind*, I *possess no words to describe it* kind of love. One that lived under your skin. That rattled your soul. That called to you in the middle of the night, waking you with a start because you thought you'd lost it. One that left you breathless. The intensity of my feelings for him was still disconcerting and foreign. Being here right now forced me to face the truth: how much I'd missed him, and how much of a fool I'd been for thinking he was better off without me.

I froze when Sam walked offstage, watching him through the crack between the curtains. He handed his guitar to Rocky, uncapped a bottle of water, and drank it in one gulp. After wiping the sweat from his face with a towel, he took his place behind the piano. He glanced around, as if searching for something he couldn't find. Could he feel my presence just mere feet away?

Riveted by the sight of him, I couldn't look away. I was bewildered, entranced, unable to tear my eyes from him.

Now that I could watch him—really watch him—I couldn't hide away or pretend anymore. The hurt radiating from him hit me straight in the chest, heavy as a boulder, pressing on my ribs, suffocating my breath.

Sam cleared his throat, and I blinked.

A force, strong and electric, pushed me forward. Toward him.

He scanned the stage, a frown creasing his forehead, as

if he could sense my presence but couldn't bring himself to believe I was here.

With a roll of his shoulders, he shook his head and scratched his temple.

I linked my hands together under my chin.

Every second I waited felt like a lifetime.

The butterflies in my belly whirled at a dizzying speed.

The lights turned off, replaced by a single spotlight aimed at him.

Placing his fingers over the keys, Sam took a big inhale while I held my breath not to miss a word.

I've been turned to stone
    long ago
I can't feel the sun warming
    my skin
I can't feel the raindrops on
    my face
I'm numb. So numb.
My heart is locked up in a cage
No one is allowed inside...

On my crutches, I stood and followed the sound of his voice. The pull he possessed on me. The galvanic lure I had no idea how to escape.

Sam had written me another song. One he had agreed to share with the world. An emotional ballad that appealed to every particle of my being. To both my heart and my soul.

He launched the chorus, and I melted some more. Exiting the dark corner where I'd been hiding, I faced him, my lungs shaky with the air I was still holding in.

> **...The sight of you jolts my**
> **heart back to life**
> **Your smile thaws every layer**
> **of ice I hide behind**
> **Your touch soothes my**
> **sorrows**
> **It heals my pain**
> **Your lips taste like freedom**
> **Your skin feels like passion...**

Our eyes connected.

My breath itched on its way in.

Halting by the side of the stage and supporting my weight on the crutches under my armpits, I pressed my hands over my chest to calm my overzealous heart.

Sam blinked. And blinked again. His fingers played the keys with renewed determination, as if they were in control. His shoulders relaxed, and fire returned to his gaze. The one burning for me. The one directed at me.

A lazy curl grazed the lips I couldn't wait to kiss.

His eyes stayed locked on mine as he poured his heart out in front of a roaring stadium full of fans. Cell phone lights brightened the dark amphitheater. Shiny stars, the witnesses to our love story unfolding before them.

> **...Let me shine in your light**
> **Let me breathe in your air**
> **With you, I'm alive again**
> **With you, I'm myself again...**

With careful movements, I neared the center of the stage, unable to stay put. Sam's magnetism couldn't be avoided anymore.

He mouthed, *You're back?*

I bobbed my head , my lips stretched so big, they would stay fixed into a grin for the rest of my life.

A hint of a smile lifted the corner of his mouth. *For good?*

I bobbed my head faster.

With a jerk of his head, he gestured for me to join him.

I frowned, not sure if I understood right.

I perused the area around me and caught Riley's eyes. He nodded, letting me know it was fine.

My gaze returned to Sam, waiting for me, scooting to the left on the bench, engrossed in his music—and me—all at the same time.

Rolling my lips over my teeth, to prevent them from trembling, I tried to ignore the fact that tens of thousands of eyes were fixed on me. I blocked the wolf-whistles and "Oohs" and "Aahs" as I took the spot next to my man. While he sang the last verse, my love for him blossomed to a whole new level.

...And kiss me
I crave the kiss of an angel
Of an angel
A kiss from my angel

His band took over. Sam, abandoning his instrument, turned toward me and crashed his lips on mine, not giving me a second to catch my breath.

"I love you, Maddie," he whispered against my mouth. "I'm fucking gone for you. I'm not letting you go. Never again."

"I never meant to hurt your feelings. I just knew what this tour meant to you and your team and didn't want to interfere with it. I was wrong because I hurt you in the process. And I also hurt myself. I love you so much. And I missed you. Being away from you has been one of the hardest things I've ever done."

"I was a fucking mess without you."

I kissed him back, desperate for his love.

He detached his mouth from mine, faced the microphone, and hollered to his screaming fans, "My woman is back."

A nervous laugh escaped me, and I placed my hand over my mouth. "Ohmygod, you didn't just do that," I said. Laughter, shyness, and elation all blended inside me.

"Oh, babe, I'll shout it out to anyone who's willing to listen for the rest of my life. I can't believe you're here."

I straightened and circled my arms around his neck, molding my body to his and claiming his lips.

"Get a room," someone yelled from the crowd.

"We will," Sam muttered against my mouth. "And nobody is allowed to disturb us for the next twenty-four hours."

"Thank you, all y'all. Good night, Denver," he said to his fans, crushing me gently against him, the rhythm of his heart syncing with mine.

The curtains closed, and Sam lifted me in his arms, honeymoon style, our mouths hungry, and our hands busy.

"My crutches," I said, breathless.

"Someone will get them." A smirk formed on his lips. "God, how I wish I could fuck you in my dressing room right now."

"I don't know how we'll manage that," I said, my voice husky, casting a glance down at my left leg. "Though, I love the aftershow horny side of you."

"Maddie, I love you so much. I wanna make love to you. I never got a chance to show you just how much. We'll find a way."

Palpitations stirred within me, and my lips found their

way back to his. "You and me." Kiss. "Riley is babysitting." Kiss. "Let's get out of here." Kiss.

"You won't sleep alone tonight," Sam said, shielding me with his body as he carried me offstage. Once we distanced ourselves enough from everyone else, he stopped, searched my eyes, and asked, "How are you doing? Be honest with me." His serious tone killed some of the sexual tension bouncing between us.

"I'm a work in progress. The pain is unbearable at times. And I'm still not accustomed to it. Not sure I ever will be. It's paralyzing when it diffuses through my leg. I can walk a few steps on my own with the crutches now. Also, my mood fluctuates…a lot. I get mad easily when it becomes too much, and the pain doesn't fade away. Fair warning."

His lips reached for mine. "I can't take your pain away, but I'll do my best to do everything in my power to make things easy for you. Let's say my mood has been shifting a lot too lately." He breathed out. "I'm so relieved you're here. You have no idea."

"I wouldn't wish to be anywhere else."

"Welcome home, Maddie."

43

SAM

Holding Madison high in my arms, her mouth attached to mine, we maneuvered to shut the bus door after climbing inside. "I've missed you so much," I said, feasting on her lips. "I can't believe it's been over a month since I last saw you and held you in my arms."

Blistering desire unleashed inside me, and I believed I'd combust.

Madison unbuttoned my shirt with her small fingers, but unable to be patient, I sat her on the bed and ripped it open, buttons flying. Her eyes traveled over my blazing skin, her throat rippling and her face illuminating.

"Loving what you see?" I asked, unable to resist, relishing the blush on her cheeks.

"A lot. It's better than in my dreams."

"You dreamed about me?" I asked, arousal tinting my words.

"All the time," she admitted. "I was about to go crazy. Countless times, I woke up with a start in the middle of the night, thinking you were asleep beside me, only to realize none of it was real. I wore your clothes, trying to have a piece of you with me. When I couldn't sleep, I imagined your arms around me, rocking me until I found some comfort."

"Do you think…we…huh…can go ahead?" I asked, not sure how to bury myself deep inside her without hurting her injured leg in the process.

She worried her lip, studying me. "I want to. As long as the pain isn't too intense, I think we can manage. I'll tell you if we gotta stop."

Sitting down beside her, I peeled her sweater over her head in a slow, tantalizing movement that sent shivers through her.

We'd never made love before, and the realization got me both excited and nervous. The good kind of nervous.

Holding my face still between her palms, she sucked in a deep breath before talking. "The scar across my hip…it-it's ugly." She pinched her lips together. "It's not…I'm no… Let's just say I'm glad my left leg is covered right now."

"Maddie, everything about you is beautiful and endearing. The scar is just that, a scar. It's not a testament to who you are as a person. It doesn't define you."

Never detaching my eyes from her, I unclasped her bra and let the lacy fabric fall next to us. Trying to lengthen the pleasure when all I craved was to bury myself inside her, I leaned forward, my mouth finding her erect nipples. Madison let out a sharp yelp that vibrated through me and got me harder for her. I shaped my palm to one of her breasts and kneaded the softness of her flesh.

With the pad of my thumb, I traced the red line marking her abdomen. "All I see when I look at it is strength. And vulnerability. And life. Because you could have died. This is proof you survived an experience that could have ended in tragedy. It shows me how brave you are… How resilient…”

“You mean it?” she asked in a low voice.

“Yes. Every word.”

She tugged at my hair with her fingers, their tips digging into my scalp and sending tingles down my spine.

With my hand locked around her nape, I kissed her senseless. Our tongues tangled in a choreography of a dance we hadn’t rehearsed often enough. Madison pulled my lower lip between her teeth, and I groaned, deepening the kiss when she released it. Our hands ventured all over each other, desperate to touch every inch of bare skin.

“Can I taste you?” I asked as we broke apart to catch some fresh air.

“I never…Nobody ever…”

“Relax, I’ll make you feel good. I promise.” I helped her to her back and kneeled on the floor.

“Sam?” I twisted my neck to meet her eyes. “Don’t get repelled by my choice of underwear. Emily ordered those.” She grimaced while I peppered kisses around her navel and along the scar across her hipbone. She tensed for a second before letting go as my tongue drew patterns over her bare skin.

“Maddie, you should know by now nothing that you say or do can turn me off. Much less a pair of… God, how does this thing work?”

She stifled her laughter with a hand pressed against her mouth. “Way to kill the mood, huh?”

I watched her laughing, and it eased the wounds of my heart her absence had caused.

“There’s a Velcro on the left side. Sorry, it’s anti-climactic.”

I slid them off delicately. “No, I think it’s clever. It serves its purpose.” I threw the piece of white cotton behind me. "No need to worry. They'll not be needed anytime soon."

Now that I got rid of the last piece of clothing shielding her, I returned to my exploration. Still on my knees, I kissed my way down her stomach.

The air charged around us, and my pulse kicked up.

Madison trembled underneath my touch when my lips brushed the soft flesh of her clit. Using my tongue, I licked the seam between her thighs, and her hips lifted off the bed. "Oh, Sam."

I stopped, making sure her cries were from pleasure and not from pain.

"Why did you stop?" she asked, lifting her head from the mattress and searching my gaze.

That was all it took to unlock the side of me I'd been restraining for two years. I devoured Madison with my teeth, my tongue, and my lips. I sucked on the mound between her legs until a series of moans tumbled out of her mouth and she begged me for more. Sliding one finger, then another in, I glided them back and forth, spreading her arousal over her folds and bringing her closer to the edge. My tongue toyed with her at the same time, until an orgasm built inside her, and she clenched around my digits, surrendering her pleasure to my greedy self.

Still not satisfied, I stood at the foot of the bed and hovered over her, caging her naked body between my arms.

We had sex before, but this…this felt like the first time. The one that mattered the most. The beginning of something erotic. Beautiful and exciting. The beginning of us.

"Can we keep going?" I asked.

She nodded.

My dick stood tall between us, and with steady movements, she unbuttoned my jeans and freed it from the confinement of my boxer briefs.

She worked my length, and shivers spread through me. With half-masted eyelids, pleasure ignited deep inside me at the sight of her hand around the hardest part of me.

Taking my wallet out of my back pocket, she picked up one of the condoms, ripped the foil, and sheathed me with dedicated gentleness.

Our eyes fused together. Hers sparked with a lust I'd never witnessed before that cast a spell on me.

Careful to avoid touching her splinted leg, I eased inside her, inch by inch, watching the elation displayed on her visage the entire time I pushed my engorged self inside her walls. Madison gasped as I filled her to the brim, and we connected deeper than ever before.

Every cell in me shook with anticipation, as if I were floating, about to rip at the seams.

The sensations swirling inside me stole my breath away.

Madison shifted on the bed, as if adjusting to the feel of us. Nothing had ever felt this good. Nothing compared to the feel of her flesh against mine.

A string of whimpers passed her quivering lips as I thrust into her. She closed her eyes and tilted her head back, breathing out. Perfection. It was a privilege only I possessed to capture the essence of her in that moment.

Her hips rolled against mine in an enticing wave, sending high-voltage electricity up my spine.

I slowed down, making sure nothing I did could cause her any pain.

Madison's eyes snapped open and fixated on me. Her pupils were dilated, her cheeks a light shade of pink, and her lips parted on a half-cry. She looked at me with a mix of adoration and reverence.

Right then, I had the certitude we belonged together. That she was the one for me—the only one.

With one hand, she gripped my hipbone, pulling me to her and encouraging me to keep going.

Our bodies fused in a primal way that shattered all my inhibitions—and all my doubts—as I rammed into her, unable to prevent myself, now that I'd experienced how perfect we could be.

"I missed you," Madison whispered as I kissed along the length of her collarbone before moving to her jaw and her lips.

I pushed a wild strand of her hair away from her forehead when she stilled underneath me. A soft gasp passed her lips.

I propped myself up, using my arms. "What's wrong? Are you okay?"

She closed her eyes for the longest second, her teeth pressed into her bottom lip, trying to mask the pain. "A spasm. They come and go."

"We'll stop," I said, about to withdraw from the depths of her.

She held on to me, preventing me from sliding out. "Don't. Stay there. Gimme a moment."

"I can—"

She silenced me with one finger. "I've been waiting for months for this. Don't you dare stop now."

I blinked, at a loss for words, seeing the determination and strength painting her features.

"Kiss me," she pleaded.

I obliged. Nothing tasted as good and looked as incredible as Madison Prescott naked with my dick embedded inside her.

Her right leg closed around me, erasing the space between us, and giving me permission to resume my pounding. We found our rhythm back. Pleasure built deep in my core, ready to be unleashed, unable to be contained anymore.

"Fuck, I won't last long," I mumbled. "Oh God, you feel great."

Madison's hand flattened on my chest while I increased the tempo. My hands rested on her hips while I tried not to explode and to savor every second. Watching me through hooded eyelids, she abandoned herself to the passion pulsing between us.

Her whimpers, our rushed panting, and the smacking of our flesh filled the silence.

I molded my hands to her waist and traced the scar on her hip with my fingertip. She shuddered under me, and the sensation rippled through my soul. I couldn't *not* touch her, fearing if I broke the connection, she would vanish.

"Sam, I love you."

I got lost in the woman who owned every bit of my heart, admiring her beauty. The devotion in her eyes. The curve of her lips. The halo of her hair. Everything that made her, *her*.

"Sam—" The plea in her voice, the sound of my name spoken in a breathless murmur, sent a discharge through me.

"I'm right here, babe. I'm right here with you."

I pounded into her with abandon. I bent over to suck on her nipples, to nibble the skin of her breasts, to lick the column of her throat. To cherish every inch of her and then surrender myself to her entirely, with all that I had left.

Madison wound her hands around my neck, keeping me close to her. Her eyes never left mine. She was mine. All mine. And right now, I had the assurance.

The clouds above us parted.

My thrusts accelerated. I had to brand her. To soak into her.

We moved in unison, enraptured and insatiable.

Her breaths quickened. Every inch of her took me hostage.

Her lips quivered. "Sam—"

When her body clenched around mine, I pounded faster, not missing a beat.

She held me against her, never breaking eye contact.

She cupped my cheek with her hand, and I locked my teeth around her thumb. She gasped. And I lost all sense of gravity.

I plunged into her with a rhythmic jerk of my hips. My fingers would leave bruises on her porcelain skin.

Madison purred. She cried out my name. She reached her high and surfed the waves. The entire time, my eyes were trained on her. She was magnificent. A gem I found when I wasn't searching. A precious gift who had driven away the darkness of my life. The part of my soul I'd been desperate to find. To reunite with.

The sight of her, spread naked on the bed, putting all her trust in me, unraveling me from the inside out, was my undoing.

I resumed my thrusts, my sole mission to go over the edge and take her with me. I pushed into her. Again. And again.

"Oh, Sam. Yes."

Madison's walls strangled my erection, and I surrendered. I committed everything I was to this woman. Drunk on her, I shot my load in powerful jolts, anchored where I was born to be.

Our fingers intertwined, and I guided our joined hands above her head, pressing them into the mattress.

My mouth descended on her, tasting her lips, my

tongue sweeping hers with reverence. Only then did I relax, knowing I hadn't dreamed the last few hours of my life. My muse, my love, was back. She'd rocked my world in a way only she could, taking what we already had to a whole new level—and cementing what we'd forever be.

———

Madison and I fed each other French fries we had ordered in, still naked, lying on our sides on the bed. She had propped her injured leg on a pillow, gently massaging the top of her thigh every few minutes. We were waiting for the painkillers to kick in. After tonight's concert, Riley had made it back to the buses before us and had dropped Madison's luggage, crutches, and medication before we arrived. I was thankful he always had my back—and best interests—at heart.

My fingers left shivers in their wake, trailing up and down her arm. "You sure you're okay?" I asked, unable to mask the worry lacing my voice.

Madison smiled at me and nodded, but I could tell her limb was bothering her.

"I'm ordering you to rest. This was enough exercise for the day."

She watched me but added nothing for a beat. "It's just... I-I didn't wanna miss another opportunity with you. The accident made me think... Well, that's all I could do when stuck to that bed. Life is unpredictable. Not missing out is something I'll value more from now on." She reached for my hand. "Sam, I'm sorry...for pushing you away. You've been nothing but amazing to me. It was inconsiderate of me."

I swallowed. "I thought I'd lose my mind. It just... It

felt like I was being left behind again… I hate fighting with you."

We remained silent, lost in each other for a long minute.

I traced the length of the scar across her hip with the tip of my finger. "Does it hurt?"

"It's not as sharp as the pain in my leg. It's more of a tingling sensation that comes and goes. If my leg wasn't hurting so much, maybe I'd consider this pain worse. Does it make sense?"

"Yeah. About your leg… I know the recovery is going to be long, but we'll get you the best specialists and physical therapists to look after you on the road. This is not a topic open for discussion, so don't try to get out of it."

"Sam, Riley and Ems took care of everything. They're the masterminds behind my being here. They have set up appointments all over the country to fit your schedule. Doris will stay for a while until I can get back to my feet and follow the girls around. If it weren't for your friend and my sister, I would still be miserable in Nashville while you're here. We'd *still* be apart."

I blinked. "They are? Wait, Ry said nothing about bringing you back. He never even mentioned anything."

"Emily neither. I learned coming to you was an option one hour before getting on that plane." Madison watched me, sucking in a breath. "Are…are we okay?"

"We are. Or we will be."

"How are the girls?"

"They miss you. But I missed you more." I couldn't hide the smile in my words.

"Whoa, that's a big claim to make," she said, a grin anchored to her face.

"My kids love you, but I'm *in love* with you. It means a whole lot fucking more."

"I love you too."

"You have no idea the impact of those four words on me right now. When I got that call… I…I thought I'd lost you."

"Never. And Sam?"

"Yes, babe?"

"I'm relieved to be home. You're my home. The three of you are."

"That's all I'm asking for. Your love. And to build something together," I confessed.

Tears glistened in her eyes, and a comfortable silence settled between us.

I brushed her cheek with a knuckle, smoothed the length of her lips, and pushed her hair back.

A quick shower later, I returned to bed. Sleep claimed Madison as we held onto each other under the covers, never breaking apart. I shaped my front to her back, and wrapped my arms around her waist, where her hands rested on mine. The sound of her breathing acted like a balm to my heart.

I listened to the steady rhythm, fearing if I joined her in sleep, I'd miss out on something. Her words from earlier replayed in my head.

Life is unpredictable. Not missing out is something I'll value more from now on.

I agreed.

My lips found her nape, and I kissed the soft skin there. Madison pushed herself against me and muttered something. I cherished the bare skin of her shoulder and the side of her neck with my lips.

A muffled purr escaped her, and I wished I could record the sound.

Lyrics that mirrored my feelings played in my head.

**There's no more clouds shad-
     owing us from above
Nothing stands in our way
     anymore
I'm a country boy
And you're an angel
Please shower me with your
     light
Please let me love you tonight**

Softly, I recited part of the chorus of the song I'd written for her months ago—the night she returned to my house after forgetting her purse. The song I never thought I would perform because I believed an *us* wasn't possible back then.

Life proved me wrong.

The past few months had taught me some invaluable lessons. Never again would I take anything for granted. We had both been hurt, but now I truly understood how precious our love was.

Sleep claimed me too, and for the first time in weeks, I wasn't afraid anymore.

44

MADISON

My eyelids opened, and I blinked to adjust to the semi-darkness around me. For a beat, I wondered I was lying. Sam muttered in his sleep, and his arms fastened around my waist, pulling me closer. I smiled, relieved my being here with him wasn't a dream but a reality.

I tilted my head to kiss his lips.

In the last twenty-four hours, I'd gone from despising my physical therapist to going back into the arms of the man I loved.

Sam splayed a palm across my stomach, preventing me from escaping his embrace.

"I need to use the bathroom," I whispered against his lips. "You gotta let me go."

Before I could register his movements, he was standing up and turning on the light on his side of the bed. After he put a pair of boxer briefs on, he held out his hand for me to grab. "Come on. Let me help you."

Pushing with my hands, I moved into a seating position. Sam slipped one of his T-shirts over my head, steadying me as I stood, his other hand anchored to my hipbone.

I tucked the crutches under my armpits and made my way to the en-suite bathroom. The bus's open layout made it easy to navigate with the crutches without bumping into everything each time I moved. At the front, a small living area with two couches and a TV mounted on the wall opened into a combined kitchen and dining space with a four-seat table. A narrow hallway led to the back, where two cozy bunk rooms were located—one of which had been my old living quarter—and a compact two-piece bathroom. Beyond them was the master bedroom, modestly decorated with a queen-size bed squeezed between two small nightstands and a dresser beneath a square window. The en-suite wasn't large by any means, but it had a decent-sized shower and a vanity with counter space. Our room at the back gave us the privacy we needed, and its small size meant I could always rely on the walls or furniture for balance if necessary.

Sam turned on the light and stood close behind me.

"I can do this on my own," I said. "While we're both up, I might give the shower a try if you don't mind."

"I can help," he offered.

I sighed, trying to refuse while not offending him. He just stood too close for comfort. I dropped a crutch, the narrow space making it hard to maneuver both of them, and a curse slipped from my lips.

Sam's hands steadied me rom behind.

I flinched and pulled away from his touch. "I said, I can do this," I repeated with a tone harsh enough to surprise even me.

He backed up a step, his arms lifted in surrender. "Fine."

I shut my eyes to calm down and opened them again.

"I-I'm sorry. I didn't mean to say it like that. Let me… Just let me do this. For now I can manage, but I'll need your help to shower, though."

He turned around and pressed a shoulder against the doorframe to give me a little privacy.

Clean and wearing his shirt, I returned to bed. I searched his eyes. "Earlier…I didn't mean to snap at you. I know you're trying to be there for me. It'll take a few days for us to adapt to this," I said, pointing to my leg. "Don't give up on me, okay? Ems said I was hard to live with. Don't lose hope. I'll try to be better."

Sam pulled me against him. "We'll find our normal. It's a lot of changes for both of us. A relationship, your accident, living in cramped quarters, being apart for so long, the girls. I don't wanna rush things, but I'm not waiting anymore. You're too important to me. I almost missed my chance once. Never again."

I claimed his lips—slow and torturous—unable to resist him when he spoke with that kind of honesty.

Pushing myself up, I removed the shirt covering my bare skin. Sam's irises darkened when they roamed all over my blazing flesh.

"You sure you're up to it?" he asked in his husky voice that always melted every cell in me.

I nodded. "Yes. I want you. I've missed you too much. We have two months to make up for." I dived my hand into his boxer briefs, and I pumped his hardening erection, relishing every groan his lips couldn't contain.

"Maddie—"

"I love you. And you know how much I love dessert. And treats." I wriggled my eyebrows. "The thing is… I can't reach down on my own. Would you feed me *your* treat?" I batted my eyelashes. "Please."

Sam's fingers lowered between my thighs and coated

with my arousal, they played with my clit. I dug my nails into his biceps, pleasure clinging to me in waves as I rocked my hips over his greedy fingers.

"Oh, it feels good," I cried, barely holding it together.

He leaned back to remove the last piece of clothing between us and balanced over me, feasting on my mouth as if he feared I could disappear. Sliding down the bed and pressing hot kisses in his wake, my man licked a trail down to my throbbing center. "Sam," I pleaded, "I said *I* wanted dessert."

"I'm hungry too." Our eyes connected, his so dark I could barely make out the color in the early morning light.

"Feed me first. I *dare* you."

His gaze lit up at the challenge. I loved this playful side of him, knowing he would never back down from a dare I threw his way.

Kneeling beside my head, he leaned forward and returned his fingers between my thighs as whimpers of pleasure tumbled out. I enveloped his hand with mine to set the pace. My lips parted on a cry, and Sam used it as an invitation to guide his erection inside my mouth. I blinked and relaxed my jaw when he slipped himself further in. I secured one hand behind his ass cheek and steered the movements of his hips as he fucked my mouth. With hollow cheeks, I sucked him harder. He continued his assault on my sex with his fingers. Stars blinded me. I hesitated between closing my eyes and letting the pleasure consume me or keeping my gaze locked on him, watching him unravel—because of me.

Hushed gasps left me.

"Do you like being fed my dick, Maddie?" he asked.

I nodded, molding my lips to him.

Unable to resist giving in to the tension building in him

any longer, Sam moved his hips with controlled urgency, and I relished the throaty growls he let out.

"Are you satiated yet?" he asked, his voice laced with repressed desire.

I shook my head.

Sam pulled away, and I tried to draw him back into my mouth.

"What do you want, Maddie?"

"You," I cried out as he dragged a first orgasm out of me with his fingers. I screamed my release, my walls engulfing his digits deeper and holding them there. I tried to fist the hard part of him, but Sam backed further away from my grip.

The flames rising in his eyes ignited my core. Plunging forward, he sucked on my lower lip, his teeth tugging, and his tongue licking every corner of my mouth.

Hovering over me, he lowered onto the bed until he could nestle himself between my legs, laving my center and tasting my arousal. I purred as he accelerated the pace of his tongue, the sweet torture of my demise.

His fingers returned to between my legs, moving in and out at a quick tempo. Before I could come undone, he kneeled, and pushed inside me. We trembled together when he thrust deeper, taking my breath away.

"You good?" I nodded. "Don't worry, I'll pull out."

He grabbed my shoulder with one of his hands, keeping me in place, and covered my mouth with the other, shoving a finger between my lips.

"Suck it, Maddie. While I fuck you."

He pounded into me faster at a slight angle—making sure to avoid brushing my left leg—while fingering my mouth.

I moaned louder and pushed myself against him, increasing the contact of our bodies. Wrapping one arm around my waist, Sam rocked his hips in quick succession. Every cell in me quaked and vibrated with bliss.

His tongue circled one of my puckered nipples, and he teased the flesh with his teeth, forcing me to arch my back when addictive sensations invaded me.

When he lifted his head, our eyes met. The vision of him, covered in sweat and loving every inch of my body—even the parts I could barely look at myself—intensified my feelings for him.

Sam moved his free hand to my other breast, massaging the flesh and twisting the tip between his fingers. I yelped, the flimsy line between pain and pleasure highly addictive. He leaned over me, one arm hooked around my neck to kiss me. "I'm done punishing you for keeping me at arm's length, Maddie." His breath was warm against my skin, sending a shiver through me. "I'm done marking you. Now I wanna make love to you."

Sliding out of me, he kept his weight on his arms as he looked into my eyes. And my soul. The glint in his eyes brightened the room.

Panting, we eye-fucked each other, neither of us breaking the contact.

"I love you," I whispered, hoping he could read the honesty in my words.

My heart did a complete rotation in my chest when he replied, "I love you, Madison Prescott."

"Show me."

"If you let me, I'll show you for the rest of our lives," he said.

Sam pulled me to him, and we combusted together. There was no more urgency. Just two people, devoted to each other, coming together. Fusing together.

My mouth devoured his. His tongue flicked around

mine. I caressed the side of his face, wanting to immerse myself in his love until my heart only belonged to him.

Forever.

While we lost ourselves in an Earth-shattering kiss, he removed the elastic band from my hair, letting the wavy strands fall around my face.

Leaning back, he admired me, a twinkle in his eyes. "You're beautiful. Everything about you is." His mouth returned to mine.

My lips teased his, molding them as I savored their taste.

I glided my fingers over his arm. The contours of his ribcage.

He skimmed the dips of my waist. The bone of my hips.

Hoisting my good leg around his middle and clamping my thigh, Sam entered me, neither of us in a hurry for this moment to end.

We kissed, our hands insatiable in their mission to touch each other everywhere.

Sam plunged in and out of me at a slow, riveting pace. He combed a strand of hair away from my forehead, and I got mesmerized by his gaze. By the depth of his soul.

I had the certitude, right there, that Sam Stevens didn't appear in my life by mistake. We were destined to meet. To fall together.

His mouth descended to my neck, nibbling and licking my salty flesh.

My hand curled around his biceps, keeping him as close to me as possible.

We rocked in sync, about to go over the edge, to reach a new high together.

Our movements hastened. They became more urgent. Less delicate.

When I went rigid in his embrace, my back arching, and my moans intensifying, Sam leaned back, looking at me with reverence. Then he pounded into me with no more restraint.

Once I came, he tried to move out, but I held him in place. "Come with me," I said.

"Are you sure?"

I nodded. "Let go. I want you to."

Grinding against him, I rolled my hips until his words failed him.

My teeth left indents in the bare skin of his shoulder when he collapsed over me at the same time he went over the edge, still buried inside me.

Tremors shook my being. Heat spread through me, followed by a calming sensation I could easily get addicted to. I had found my other half. The missing part of my soul.

"Maddie." Sam spoke my name between harsh breaths. His full lips seduced mine in a lazy kiss. "I… We…"

"Whatever we just did, you've branded yourself to me, Sam Stevens, and now I'll never be the same. Only you can fill me the way you do. You're stuck with me now."

"Maddie. I don't have any intention of ever letting you go. Never again. I was miserable. Cranky and a whole lot fucking sad."

For a long time, neither of us dared to break the spell, lost in our love bubble.

"We'll have to tell the girls," I murmured against his chest once we climbed down from the rush and cuddled after cleaning up.

He held me against him, his heart rate reverberating through me. "Yes, but for a little bit longer, you're mine. Only mine. I'm not sharing you with anybody else. Once we return to the real world, I'll have to share you with them, and I'm not ready. Let's be selfish for a few more hours."

I felt his smile against the skin of my nape.

"Sam, I love being yours."

With a finger under my chin, he tilted my head in his direction. "I love being yours too. You belong with the three of us. Never doubt it, okay? Even if Mika—or even Justine—says something or they act out, you're mine. Even if I sometimes act like a grumpy old man, promise me you'll stick with me….with us. No matter what. I need you in my corner, Maddie. I won't survive another heartbreak. It may take the girls a little time to adjust, but they'll come around. They'll see how happier I am now that you're back in my life."

I traced the lines of his face with a feather touch. "We're in this together. I'm up for the challenge."

Sam shifted position, and an expression I'd never seen before painted his face. "Maddie, we'll be a family. The four of us. Don't you think playing mommy to my girls will make you run for your life someday? I know it's not fair, but I come as a package of three. I'll have to split my time between all of you guys. You're the only woman who's been in their lives since Lisa left. Sometimes, it won't be easy. Aren't you scared it's gonna be too much at some point?"

I placed a finger over his lips. "Sam, I've been around you guys for months. I know exactly what I'm getting into. I'm not only in love with you. I'm in love with them too. With all of you. The only thing I fear is that Justine and Mika think I'm overstepping into their lives and stealing their daddy from them. I don't want them to resent me. Ever. For the rest, I've never been so sure about anything else in my entire life."

"We'll talk to them today. Together. Okay?"

I nodded, and he tucked a tendril of my hair behind my ear.

"And I'll ask Riley to add babysitting hours to my contract. He's the one who pushed us together—not once, but twice—so it's only fair he volunteers some of his time to make sure our relationship starts on strong foundations."

My chuckle reverberated across the room. "I agree. We can't let your daughters walk in on us when I give you head in the shower or late at night. And they can't be there when you fuck me on the couch or against the wall…" I paused as I registered what I'd just said. "Not now…one day. When…huh…when it's possible."

"You dirty girl. I love you. Let's get some sleep because soon we'll have a lot of questions to answer and a lot of explanations to give."

———

I woke up to muscle spasms in my left thigh. Shedding tears in my pillow and gritting my teeth, I rode the waves of pain for a few minutes, praying the entire time it wouldn't wake up Sam. After how perfect our reunion had been, I wasn't ready for him to see me like this. Broken. And hurting. I anticipated the look of helplessness in his eyes and could do without it for a bit longer. When the pain released its death grip on me, I sat on the side of the mattress, stretched my legs, and checked my phone. Almost ten o'clock. Our love session in the early morning felt like a lifetime ago. My gaze lingered on the man snoring beside me, and I fought with myself, struggling not to touch his skin or kiss his lips.

Hopping on my good leg and fetching my crutches, I made my way to our small kitchen after I slid on the T-shirt Sam had lent me earlier.

My stomach grumbled, and I decided to surprise him with breakfast in bed. Maneuvering the crutches and the egg carton didn't go as planned when I lost my footing and dropped half of it on the floor. A new zing of pain traversed my left side. Silencing the curses teetering on the edge of my lips, I pivoted to grab paper towels—only to knock over the glass of water I had set on the counter earlier. My crutches ended in the mess of water and egg yolks at my feet, and I clamped the countertop with both hands to prevent my own fall.

Hot tears welled up in my eyes, and I used my shoulder to wipe them off.

My earlier confidence shattered.

Sliding to the ground, I studied the state of the kitchen floor, my shoulders heaving with suppressed sobs.

My tears multiplied, and I choked on them as I hollered Sam's name. A mixture of fury and despair boiled in my veins, and it drained the sound of my voice.

How had I become so dependent on everyone else?

From where I sat, I could hear the steady rhythm of his snoring. I called his name again. Once more, my voice died as it left my mouth when I hiccupped. I had no more fight left in me. I had to go. To leave. To relieve the people I love from the burden I had become.

My heart fractured in my chest.

How would I ever be able to say goodbye?

45

SAM

I woke up to the sound of pots and pans slamming. It took me a beat to patch together last night's events. Without even trying, my lips drew into a smile I had no intention to conceal.

"Babe, come back to bed," I called out, braced on one elbow, desperate to catch sight of Madison from the comfort of my bed. "We can tackle breakfast later. I wanna cuddle. And do more dirty things to you."

Her figure appeared in the doorway, but instead of a grin shaping her lips, a deep wrinkle marred her forehead.

"Hey, what's wrong?" I asked, taken aback by the fury I could read in her expression. "Come here."

She eyed me, her crutches resting against her ribcage, helping her to keep her balance.

"I'm just done with all this." She pointed around with her hand. "It's not working. I've tried, but it's not."

Her words made no sense. What happened to the comfort and elation we had experienced earlier?

I jumped to my feet, slid into a pair of sweatpants, and neared her. "Hey, hey. Talk to me." I closed both hands on her upper arms, but she yanked free from my touch. I blinked, unsure if I was awake after all. "I don't understand. This morning you were happy. What changed?"

"Sam, I'll never be okay again. Can't you see that? I can't even pour myself a glass of water or cook breakfast without being clumsy and pain paralyzing me. I'm not useful. Now there's an egg and water mess all over the kitchen floor, and I'm one slip away from breaking my other leg. Congrats on getting a crippled girlfriend. By being here, I'll just complicate your life. I won't even be able to watch over the girls on my own. How pathetic have I become? Please don't answer. You should send me back home."

"Home? I thought you said last night your home was wherever I was."

She blinked, and the intensity in her eyes magnified instead of vanishing.

I spoke before she could say something else she didn't mean. "Stop with the bullshit. Sure, we gotta find our footing. You've never lived on a bus before, let alone with crutches. It's not the most practical place to call home in your situation, I agree, but we'll figure it out. Together."

I stepped forward, but Madison blocked me with a crutch. "Don't. Don't come closer. Can't you see it? We shouldn't be together. It doesn't make any sense. I realize it now. Perhaps the accident was life trying to teach me something. To prevent us from getting too deep before it was too late. Whatever the reason, I can't stay here. I'm suffocating. I long for air. And a fucking break."

"Maddie. No. Listen to me." My tone sounded harsh, but I didn't care. She had to hear me out.

She raised one arm and let it fall beside her. "Not now." Her eyes brimmed with tears.

I felt helpless as I watched her. Broken. No matter how

wonderful last night—and earlier—had been, reality hit me in the morning light. The situation we were in couldn't be ignored. I could tell the accident had changed her. Some part of me prayed it hadn't changed us too.

Madison pivoted to leave the bedroom when she tripped over her own feet.

I rushed to her and circled her waist with an arm before she could crash face first. I lowered myself to sit on the floor, bringing her with me.

Sitting on my lap, crying as she struggled to escape, her body shook with desperation. I held her tighter, unwilling to let go, even as she fought against me.

"Let me go," she shrieked. "Just let me go." Her punches hit me square in the chest. "Send me back. Send me so I'm not a deadweight in your life."

Her voice cracked.

Sobs rocked her body.

"Maddie. Stop with the nonsense. You belong here. Unless going back to Nashville is really what you desire. Be honest with yourself…and me. If the words you spoke when you arrived last night were true, then you'll stay with us, and we'll find a way to make it work. Together. I'm not giving up on us—on you—and neither should you."

She turned her face away, making sure I wouldn't be able to read the expression spreading across her tear-streaked face.

Her body got rigid against mine. I could feel her drifting away.

I continued, hoping my words would reach her heart and make her reconsider fleeing. "You said yourself you were miserable on your own. Now that I got you back and we finally have a real chance to be together, when I'm ready to go all in, you wanna ditch me? You wanna ditch *us*? I understand your anger. I do. Remember, I was angry for a long time myself. I kinda get how you feel. One thing I can tell you is that it will all get better. Maybe not today or in a week… Maybe not next month… But one day, you'll wake up, and the pain will have faded. You'll wake up from the nightmare you think defines your life right now and find yourself stronger. You'll see how far you've come—and how much you've overcome—and realize that failure was never an option, and healing was always meant to happen."

She relaxed a bit against me, so I kept going.

"When you're upset or feel like you can't put in the effort anymore because it's just too much, don't keep it all inside. Don't let the hard times overshadow the good ones. Believe me, even the challenges we think we'll lose are worth fighting for in the end. I'm the perfect example… If I had thrown my life away two years ago when I was bathing in permanent darkness, I wouldn't be here today, and I wouldn't have found you. You can be mad as you want, but you gotta open up to me when it gets too tough. It's the only way this is going to work."

She snorted, but there was no conviction behind it.

"If you want to go back to Nashville, I won't stop you. But if there's even the tiniest part of you that believes we're meant to be together, that your place is here, on this tour, with us, then let that part speak up." I paused, letting my words sink in—both into her heart and the analytical part of her mind. "Whatever you decide, talk to me. I'm right here, and I'm not going anywhere. If you choose to leave, I think I deserve an explanation. It can't be just because you dropped a couple of eggs. Don't bull-shit me."

Madison ignored me for the longest time, her shoulders heaving, until the fight left her, and she sank into me.

I combed her hair back with my fingers. "Maddie. No

one said it would be easy, but it will be all worth it," I repeated. "I swear."

She sniffled, still not looking at me.

"When you came into my life, I was mad most of the time. With your selfless heart and contagious optimism, you pierced through my stony heart. Your kindness seeped through the cracks, and it healed my broken self. You never faltered when I was being a jerk and held your head up and argued when I was being wrong. This time around, you are the one who requires someone in your corner. To help you get back out there. And thrive. And kick asses. Because the Madison Prescott I know wouldn't let some bump in the road set her back. She'd get up and wrestle the shit out of her misfortune."

When she spoke, her voice had lost all conviction—and warmth. "Sam, I'm just tired of the fight. Of the pain. I've been fighting all my life. From the day I was born. I struggled a lot growing up. Nightmares. Making friends. I can't do this anymore. It's asking too much of me."

"Maddie, what happened to you? I'm not a pushy guy, but I gotta know. Please confide in me."

She buried her face in her hands.

I said nothing, wishing she'd let the walls come down around her once and for all.

Swallowing the pebbles growing down my throat and disrupting my normal breathing, I asked, unable to hide the alarm rising in my voice, "Did someone hurt you?"

Her gaze returned to mine, and she shook her head. "No. Not like that. I swear."

Relief washed over me. "Then what?"

Madison inhaled and wiped the traces of her meltdown with the hem of the T-shirt she was wearing. "Remember that time I told you I'd been neglected?"

"Yes. I met your parents when you were in the hospital.

We even had lunch together one day. They're nice people, and they love you. That much was evident. I can't imagine them being careless with you as a child."

"Sam… Emily and I were…were adopted. When we were five and three. Our biological parents didn't care for us. I-I spent days in my dirty diaper when I was a baby. I only learned about it because it was written in our file, and our real parents, the ones who raised and loved us, told us much later. The ones who conceived us forgot to feed us or would disappear for a day or two, chasing their next high…or their youth. I don't know. Ems took care of me. She was just a baby herself, but she made sure I had food to eat and rocked me to sleep every night. She protected me. Sacrificed her own needs to fulfill mine."

She fidgeted with her hands, keeping her gaze down.

I remained silent so as not to disturb the story of her childhood.

"One day, I fell and broke my wrist. She…huh…she dressed me up in dirty clothes because that was all we had, and we walked a mile to get to the next house. Our neighbors had never heard of us. We lived in a rural area, and we hadn't ventured outside before that day. Our parents never took us anywhere with them. The neighbor called the cops, and paramedics to care for my arm, then fed us, and cleaned us up. One day, in therapy, they showed us pictures she had taken that day. It was terrible. We were skin and bones, with disheveled hair and ghostly complexion. Not what kids that age should've looked like."

I turned her hand over and threaded our fingers.

"The first family who fostered us—it was a temporary placement—forced me to sleep on the floor after I peed the bed twice. They said they were paid to foster a kid, not a dog. Ems says I was crying all the time, and they wouldn't let her comfort me. After a few weeks, they removed us from that horrible family. But then they failed to find someone who could take us both in, so Emily and I got separated. I don't have very clear memories of that time, but I still can feel the fear twisting my insides when I think about those years. I was all alone and scared. Emily had learned to fend for herself, but I hadn't. I was just a baby... Eventually, I ended up with a nice lady, but no matter how much she tried, I wouldn't let her in. I stopped eating. I wouldn't communicate with her. Emily's and my language skills were so far behind, I had no idea how to express my feelings. I missed my sister, and they wouldn't let me see her."

She closed her eyes, then opened them and continued.

"My adoptive mother...she heard some of the ladies working in the foster care system one day talking about the feral sisters who were raised like animals and had to be separated, and they worried the younger one would never heal from the psychological trauma she'd experienced in her short life. My dad and she had already discussed fostering or adopting children. The idea of siblings enticed them. Ems and I were the perfect match. They found us and brought us home. From the day we met, I've felt a pull toward them. They saved us. They...they saved my life."

I tightened my squeeze on her hand. This was so much worse than any scenario I had pictured in my head. Wrath simmered in me, directed at the people and the system who had failed Emily and Madison at such a young age. But then Madison offered me a small tip of her lips, and my rage evaporated. She was here. With me. None of those people could ever hurt her again.

"My trauma isn't the same as Justine and Mika's, but I can relate to them...even though it sounds crazy."

I resumed my breathing, the knots around my stomach loosening.

"Somehow, I know I haven't landed into your lives by chance. I've cared for a lot of kids in the past, but I never bonded with them as much as I bonded with your daughters. Like we can understand one another. Like we connect on a deeper level. When we were kids, it took years of therapy for Emily and me to come to terms with what we went through. That's why we were so resilient at such a young age—we fought to survive and made a promise to ourselves early on in life that we wouldn't settle for less than we deserved, and we would reach for our goals. Our parents decided to homeschool us because, for a long time, the idea of being sent to a classroom full of students, too many people cramped together, was a trigger for my anxiety. It turned out to be the best decision for us. We healed. We got stronger. I'm not mad at my biological parents. They had us when they were still kids themselves… It didn't excuse their behavior, but I guess they didn't know any better. Thanks to them, we grew up with the parents we were always meant to be with and who couldn't have children of their own. The ones who love us unconditionally."

Madison closed her hand over our joined fingers, and I traced the side of her cheek with my knuckles.

"Maddie, I don't know what to say. It…fuck, it breaks my heart. For the younger version of you. For your sister. I'm so sorry you had to go through this. Wow, I'm speechless right now, and that says a lot… Your story is tragic but beautiful at the same time. How can it be both?"

"I could say the same for you guys. If Lisa hadn't left, we wouldn't be here right now, having this conversation. As I said once before, I believe, you and I, we were meant to meet."

"No," I said. "You and I, we were meant not to only meet, but also to love each other."

"Sam—"

"No, let me finish. I love you. And I know for a fact you love me too. I saw it in your eyes last night. Deny it all you want, but I don't believe the lies you're feeding yourself this morning."

"But—"

I cradled her face and claimed her mouth. Madison stiffened against me, but soon relaxed and kissed me back.

My lips molded to hers in a breathless kiss. She clutched my forearm as our tongues danced together. Shivers traveled through me. She purred against my mouth, deepening our connection, her other arm locking around my neck.

"Do I need more arguments to prove my point?" I asked, pulling back for a split second.

She shook her head.

"Babe, I promise, here and now, you'll never feel like a burden and be alone ever again. You have my word. You've found your place in this world. We'll find all the help you need and get through this. You and me, together."

Her lips returned to mine, cementing the invisible link tying us together.

46

MADISON

Sam's hand wound around my waist as I knocked on Riley and Devon's tour bus door. His lips brushed that spot behind my ear, and I shivered.

"Ready?" he asked. "Let the fun and thousand questions begin." I heard amusement in his voice. We had decided to tell the girls together, hoping it would make answering all their questions a little easier.

After my meltdown earlier, Sam and I had a long and emotional conversation. One where I cried. A lot. Every word he said to comfort me soothed the fears that had tightened my insides. Sam made me believe we could defeat the circumstances that were forcing us to adapt to our new reality. That our love was strong enough to overcome what I had perceived as impossible.

Confiding in him about the doubts weighing on me lifted a burden I hadn't realized was so heavy. I realized that the pressure I'd been putting on myself to rush back to my normal life before my body had time to heal wasn't just unhealthy—it was foolish. I needed time.

I still had a long road to recovery ahead of me, but this

time, I had chosen to let him in entirely. My gut told me it was the right choice, and somehow, I felt a quiet ease settle over me once I accepted it.

After I told the man I loved about my childhood, the burden of the secrets I'd been carrying for so long evaporated. It felt right to be completely honest with him, and I realized I should have opened up a long time ago. Even though I'd had my reasons for withholding that piece of information in the past, I knew I had to lay everything out in the open if we were ever going to move forward as a couple.

Mikaella and Justine's screams of joy hit me before the door was fully open. All my cells transformed into particles of glee. Yeah, I was exactly where I was supposed to be. Their contagious enthusiasm, even before they saw me, confirmed every word Sam had spoken to me earlier. For now, I was choosing happiness over despondency. Sam and I had promised each other we'd revisit this discussion later once the emotions of my comeback had settled.

The girls barreled out the door, down the steps, and straight into my arms. Standing with the help of the crutches, I lost my balance, but Sam caught me before I hit the ground. He steadied me, keeping his hand on my waist as I leaned forward to level my face with his daughters'.

"Maddie," Mikaella and Justine both cheered, their arms wrapped so tightly around my neck, I thought I might choke.

From the corner of my eye, I spotted my man beside me, his eyes filled with tears, watching us as if he had just won the lottery.

I wriggled a hand to the side and laced our fingers. The smile he aimed at me shook me to the core. Drying his eyes, he mouthed, *I love you.*

Justine grabbed my face between her hands and offered

me a pointed look. "Why was it so *loooong*, Maddie? I missed *youuuu*."

Sam helped me to a folding chair, and I sank into the seat, appreciating the rest. The girls eyed my splinted leg and moved closer, careful not to bump into it.

With both arms now free, I fastened my grip around them. "Oh girls, I missed you two so much. I can't wait to hear about all you did while I was away."

Justine placed a wet kiss on my cheek and nestled her head in the crook of my neck.

"Are you in pain?" Mikaella asked.

I grimaced. "Yes. Sometimes. But being with you makes it all better."

"Are you staying with us forever?" she asked.

I nodded, my gaze steady on hers so she could see the honesty in them. "I am. As long as you guys have me, I'm not going anywhere."

Even though I'd tried to convince myself otherwise earlier, and I was sure I would try to leave again from time to time whenever I felt dejected, I knew my place was beside them.

Having them in my arms, I had no more doubts.

"Did Daddy kiss your booboo?" Justine asked.

I heard laughter around me. Adult laughter.

"Yes. He did."

"Did he make it all go away?"

"Not totally, but he's working on it."

"Listen, girls," Sam said, sitting in a chair next to me. "There's something we gotta talk about. The four of us."

That brought their full attention to him.

"Madison and I, we are lovers. It means she is my girlfriend."

We had already decided the terms sounded juvenile, but we hoped it would resonate with them.

A spark of joy ignited in me as he confirmed the status of our relationship in front of everyone.

Mikaella's eyes ping-ponged between us, her features hardening.

"Are you my mama now?" Justine asked, her tone full of expectations before we could clear the air.

Mikaella backed away from me, incomprehension filling her golden eyes. "Daddy, because of you, Maddie will leave. She already left once." Fury distorted her face. "I don't want another mama," she screamed. "And I don't want Maddie gone. You're mean, Daddy. You're not nice. I hate you. I hate all of you."

Before we could react, she went to our bus and sat on the step, ignoring us.

Sam started to stand, cursing under his breath.

"How can she still blame me for her mother leaving? Lisa abandoned them. She quit on them. Without ever reaching out or explaining herself. How can I be the one responsible for her actions? How am I the mean one?"

I reached for his elbow before he could go after his daughter.

"Maddie, I gotta fix this." He dragged a hand over his face.

"Sam, if you're serious about us having a future together, about all you've said earlier, you'll let me talk to her. She's mad at you right now, not that it's justified, but I wanna do this. I'm as deep into this as you are. Trust me."

Before he could argue, I placed Justine in his arms, kissed her cheek, and managing the crutches, joined Mikaella.

Her shoulders heaved with heartbreaking sobs.

"May I hold you?" I asked once I took my place beside her, resting my crutches next to me.

She nodded, and I wrapped one arm around her

shoulders to pull her closer, until she sank into my embrace, her small body quivering.

"It's okay to be confused," I said. "It's a lot to take in. Do you wanna talk about it?"

"O…kay."

Over the months I'd known her, Mikaella, the angry little girl I had met the first day, had ceded her place to a more trusting and blooming version of herself.

Watching her, I gulped a big dose of air, forcing my racing heart to stay put. "Are you and I okay?"

She nodded, staring at the space in front of her, not sparing me a glance.

"Are you mad at your daddy?"

She nodded again.

My insides clenched as I prayed to find the right words to get through to her.

"You know your daddy loves you, right?"

She shrugged.

"He does. He loves you so much. You and Justine are the most precious people in his life. I swear."

She remained silent.

"Adults like your daddy and I are looking to be loved too. Your daddy knows you and Justine love him very much, but he also needs another adult's love. Someone to be his special friend. Like you and Justine are. You see, like Riley and Devon. They are each other's special friends. And once upon a time, your mama and your daddy were too." I inhaled. "When your mama left, it broke your daddy's heart. Remember when he was grumpy and barely smiled before?"

Another nod—all the encouragement I needed to continue.

"Well, it was your daddy being sad…in his heart.

Because he didn't have a grown-up special friend anymore. Someone to reassure him when he was afraid or be by his side when he was having a bad day. Daddies can be scared and have broken hearts too. When I started coming to your house to take care of you and Justine, your daddy was often angry, and it broke my heart. One day, we became friends. Really good friends. We started laughing together, and then, not so long ago, your daddy and I realized we could be each other's special friends, so that when we were together, we didn't feel alone anymore. And we made each other happy."

Mikaella stayed immobile beside me.

"When adults become special friends, they kiss each other. Because we can't go on play dates. Duh, we're too old for the slide or trampoline. Instead, we hold hands. And we have sleepovers. And when we both are so happy that we are always laughing and kissing, we know we have found a very special friend, and we should hold on to them because they make our hearts jump in our chests and send butterflies to our bellies."

Mikaella said nothing, so I kept going.

"Your daddy and I discovered we're very good at being special friends. I'm not your mama, and I will never be unless one day it's you who's asking me to be. Your daddy and I are great together. You wanna know why? He holds my hand when I'm afraid and smiles at me when he's happy. When I'm sad, he pulls me into his arms to comfort me, and when I go to bed, he kisses me goodnight. Remember when I told you that before being your nanny, I traveled the world with other families? Well, I didn't know it back then, but I was searching for my own special friend too." I sighed and dropped my shoulders. "Can I tell you a secret?"

Mikaella nodded.

"I never really felt at home anywhere and didn't have a lot of friends growing up. I thought traveling would help me find where I belong… It turns out that since the day I met you guys, I don't feel lost anymore. I know where my home is. It's with the three of you. It's wherever you guys are. I don't ever wanna go away anymore. Not if you guys aren't around because I'm scared I will get lost again."

"Were you sad when you were hurt and all by yourself?"

"Yes. And I was angry too because I missed you all so much and had no idea when I'd be back."

Mikaella turned her head my way, watching me with interest now. "Daddy and you are special friends? Like Jacob and you were?"

I sighed. "Jacob and I were good friends, but I'll tell you another secret." I lowered my voice to a whisper. "I thought for a moment he could be my special friend, but it turns out your daddy is. A lot, lot, a whole lot more. He is my *true* special friend. And I am his."

"What will happen now? Are you gonna leave us? Because Lisa did." Her eyes, still brimming with unshed tears, studied me closely.

I pulled the little girl to my heart and enveloped her in my arms. "No. It means the four of us will live together and be around one another a lot more. Your daddy and I will also spend more time together. I won't go anywhere. I'll be here with you all the time. And available anytime you need me. Not like a nanny, but more like your *extra* special friend."

Mikaella raised her eyes to mine. "Do extra special friends kiss too?"

I pinched my lips to refrain from laughing. "Nah, extra

special friends are best friends forever. They eat tons of pancakes together, sing songs before bedtime, dance in the rain, watch movies with a lot of popcorn on the weekend, and tell each other when they're sad…or afraid…or happy. Do you think you and I can be *extra* special friends?"

She bobbed her head, a hint of a smile grazing her lips. "I'd like that."

"Me too," I said, mirroring the tilt of her lips. "I'd like that very, very much."

I fastened my arms tighter around her, and she hugged me back.

"I love you, Maddie."

"I love you too, Mika. So much, you have no idea."

"Are you going to sleep in daddy's room now?"

I offered her a lopsided smile. "I will. Even daddies are afraid of the dark sometimes."

"It's okay. Daddy is less *grinchy* when you are here anyway. He smiles more. And doesn't burn dinner when you are around. He even sings in the shower or when he's doing the dishes."

"See? All he needed was his own special friend. I guess we've figured out how to keep his grumpy-bear attitude away then."

Her giggles filled my heart with a new sense of purpose, and a lot of calm.

She turned until we faced each other. "Do you *love* love my daddy? For real?"

"I do. Like a lot. So much my heart breaks when he's not around."

"Why did you stay away for so long if you missed us?"

"Because I had to get better so I wouldn't have to leave ever again."

We stayed like that until she broke the silence. "Daddy

was *grinchy* again. When you were gone. He only smiled around Justine and me. The rest of the time, he was unhappy."

"I'm sorry. I'll do my best to keep his *grinchy* side far away."

"Okay. Can I tell you a secret?" She lowered her voice, kneeling to speak into my ear. "Daddy has a hairy chest. And sometimes, he snores and sounds like a bear. Justine and I think it's funny."

I couldn't contain my laughter this time and tilted my head back as my eyes dampened. "I won't tell him you told me. Your secret is safe with me. *Extra* special friend safe." I held out my hand. "Think we should go see him and tell him we're not mad at him? I'm sure right now his heart is sad because he thinks he's lonely again."

Mikaella watched my hand, then her eyes traveled to mine, and after I gave her an encouraging nod, she moved to her feet.

The last bruises of my heart healed.

Her fingers snaked around mine. "Do you think Lisa will come back?"

My heart pinched in my chest. "I don't know. I wish I had an answer for you, but I don't."

She shrugged. "It's okay. Daddy is happier with you anyway. I think he loves you too."

"You think?"

She bobbed her head fast. "Yes. He has shiny eyes when you're here, and he keeps staring at your mouth like he wants to kiss you."

"Oh, I didn't know that," I said, doing my best to look surprised.

"I saw him do it. Many times. Daddy is not good at looking away from you."

I bent to kiss her hair. "I love you, Mika."

"I love you too, Maddie. Can Justine call you Mama? Because if you kiss daddy, she'll believe you're her mama. She already thinks you are. She doesn't understand you're not."

"If she wants to call me Mama and it's okay with all of you, then it's fine with me. Justine is still little and can't understand everything, but I don't want you to be mad at her if she does."

She reflected on what we'd just shared for a minute. "I'll tell her I'm okay with her calling you Mama. I won't tell her she's stupid anymore."

"That's really kind of you. That's your big sister's job. To explain things she doesn't understand to her, like I just did with you, and to reassure her. Emily is my big sister, and she always explains stuff to me too since she's older and knows more."

Glee painted Mikaella's face, and my heart swelled inside my ribcage at the sight, knowing everything would turn out just fine.

Side by side, with my hobbling on crutches and her supporting me, we went back to Sam and Justine. My man moved to his feet, relief loosening his features the moment we neared them.

"Sweet pea," he said, sauntering our way, his eyes asking mine if it was safe to proceed.

I gave him a subtle nod, and he looked at me with so much love and a lot more emotions. Respect, lust, affection, gratitude. The entire cocktail.

Squatting in front of his eldest daughter, he sucked in a jagged breath. "Can we talk?"

Mikaella shook her head, and Sam's face fell. "Sweet pea—"

Her eyes flew to mine, and with a squeeze of her hand and a nod, I assured her everything would be all right.

"Daddy, it's okay if you want to kiss Maddie because you can't stop looking at her mouth, and I think it's because you love her." Her voice dropped to a whisper. "She also said you're less *grinchy* when she's with you. And I agree."

"Did she?" Sam said, waggling his eyebrows when he glanced at me.

Mikaella bobbed her head. "If Justine wants to call her Mama, I won't call her stupid again." She shrugged. "Justine is little. She doesn't understand how mamas and daddies work."

Mikaella said something in her sister's ear, and both girls snickered, watching Sam and me.

"What is it?" he asked after a moment.

They held hands and asked together, "Can you kiss?"

Sam raised an eyebrow. "You sure?"

They bobbed their heads fast.

Before I had time to say anything, Sam cradled my jaw, and his mouth claimed mine, our lips meeting and my heart thundering in my chest.

The girls screamed, bounced on their feet, and clapped their hands, excitement radiating from them. Soon, their arms wound around our legs—careful around my bad one.

Sam's hand splayed across my lower back, steadying me, while he tugged me closer to him. *I love you, Maddie*, he mouthed, kissing me once more.

The girls cheered and hugged us again.

"Can you be my mama now?" Justine asked, and all laughter died down.

"Yes," Mikaella replied before Sam and I could utter a word. "It's okay. Maddie and I discussed it, and we decided it's normal for you to be confused because you are little. She can be your mama if you want her to be."

Justine's eyes brightened, and Mikaella offered me a thumbs-up.

"You're stuck with us now," Sam whispered against my mouth.

"There's nowhere else I'd rather be. Remind me of this moment when my thoughts go dark, please."

"Always."

47

SAM

We were about to cross into Oregon, where I had a series of concerts lined up along the West Coast.

With the woman I loved back by my side, I felt invincible, my level of glee reaching new highs.

Last summer, Riley and Devon had decided to get their own bus and tour the country with us. As my manager, Riley didn't have to be on the road with me, but I was grateful that he had chosen to. The more time we spent together, the more inseparable we all became. I loved having our friends around. For someone who had pushed everyone away for two years, I was now thankful for those who had stuck by my side. Things were running smoothly these days, and it felt like life had finally decided to give us a break.

Right now, my girls were with Devon in her bus, catching up on news about the crew and baking cupcakes, while my friend and I were in my bus, discussing business and going over the itinerary for the next few shows, interviews, and promo requests.

Madison had been back for almost two weeks now, and whenever I had days off, we made sure to spend time with the girls, showing them everything would be all right. That we loved each other, and they had nothing to worry about. Things wouldn't change for them—only get better.

Stud Burgess, Carter and Dahlia's ex-bandmate, had agreed to join me onstage for two songs tonight. He now lived outside of Portland with his wife Belinda and their children. Since he had retired from the music industry a few years ago, he'd been doing woodwork and had started his own business. The guy was one of the most talented musicians I had ever met in my life. He could play any instrument with ease and perfection. Or, I should say, he was talented with anything his fingers touched. Riley, being his ex-manager, persuaded him to make a comeback—for one night only—and he had agreed. We met through video chat earlier, and I had just finished putting together what we had discussed.

At the end of the afternoon, we parked the buses in a rest area, ready to pile ourselves into the SUVs Riley had ordered for tonight when Mikaella and Justine came running in. Dressed in matching silver skirts and white shirts, they halted near Riley, who spun them around and kissed their cheeks.

We were having a pre-show dinner in a fancy restaurant with our friends before Stud and I took the stage together later. Since Doris was still touring with us, she would babysit my girls tonight, so all of us, grown-ups, could enjoy the night together.

"You girls look like royalty," Riley said with a bow.

"*Royalality?* What is it?" Justine asked.

"It means we are princesses," Mikaella added, joy shining in her eyes. My little girl was back. All of her. Gone were the tantrums and bad words. She was glowing and appeared to have forfeited the grudge she had been holding against me for the last two years. Three days ago, we video chatted with her therapist, who had confirmed she was doing a lot better too. I shed tears that day. And kissed Madison senseless that night. Mikaella's victory was all ours. Madison's primarily. It was only thanks to her that my family could get the breath of fresh air it was starving for. The path to move forward, one that would leave the past behind. For good.

"Daddy," my daughters screamed when they saw me, running into my arms when I crouched down before them.

"You girls look stunning. And your hair, wow. It looks fantastic." They both wore some sort of complicated braid on one side of their heads.

"Devon picked our outfits," Mikaella said, twirling on herself.

"And Maddie did our hair," Justine added.

"Girls, I'll go to my bus to get ready. I'll see you later, okay?" Riley said.

"Bye, Uncle Riley," they both hollered.

Frantic energy permeated the air.

Armed with her crutches, the ones she now cursed at only every few days, Madison walked in, sporting the rose-gold sequin strapless dress I'd gotten delivered for her this morning. Tonight was a big night for all of us—our first as a couple and a family. It was also the first concert where Madison would stay from start to finish.

"Wow," I murmured, unable to tear my eyes away from her.

She discarded her crutches and walked toward me. I froze there, speechless. Even though she complained that physical therapy hurt like hell, I couldn't help but be in awe of her dedication and strength. Tonight was the perfect example.

"You look beautiful, Miss Prescott."

"And so do you, Mr. Stevens."

"One day, you'll be a Stevens too."

"Is that a threat?" she asked with one arched eyebrow.

"No, it's a promise."

She swiped her thumb across her phone screen, and music began playing from the portable speaker we kept on the kitchen counter. The girls started dancing around, giggling and singing. For an instant, we watched them.

"Dance with me?" Madison asked when the song switched to a ballad.

"Are you sure it's safe?"

"One song. Hold me tight so I don't put too much weight on my leg." She locked her eyes with mine. "I trust you."

"Then it would be my pleasure," I said, bringing her arms around my neck, my thumb grazing the soft skin of her cheek. "I love you. Thank you for not quitting on me that day at the nanny agency. I don't know what I've done to deserve your love, but you're the best thing that has happened to me in a long time. I can't believe I'm the lucky man who wakes up by your side every morning, and the father to the girls you love as your own. Tonight, I'll show you all over again how gone I am for you."

We kissed some more, and our focus traveled to the girls, carefree and happy.

"Sam, were you serious that night before the accident when you said you'd have more kids one day? With me?"

I drew the length of her spine with a finger, and Madison shivered against me. "Yeah. I want it all with you. Not now. But in the near future. When we're settled. If that's what you desire too."

Moving to the tiptoes of her right leg, she claimed my mouth. It was slow and tender. A pledge of our love. A promise of our devotion to each other. And the confirmation that our family would be a pillar of our relationship.

———

Thanks to Madison, I gave the performance of my life. Everything shone brighter, smelled better, and tasted fucking amazing when she stood beside me. Her eyes met mine as I sang the last verse, and I swore I could've blown my load right there onstage in front of fifty-thousand people, and no one would have been able to prevent it.

In the rose-gold number that sheathed her curves perfectly, she looked like a vision. My woman illuminated not only my heart, but also the lives of everyone around her. She wet her lips with a swipe of her tongue, and no matter how much I tried to look straight ahead, my eyes always returned to hers. I had never performed a show on this scale in front of her before, and it felt so damn right. I wondered if she had any idea how much better she made me. As a man, and as an artist.

Right now, I was stiff as a pole. Performing for over an hour with a hard-on was possible. I could testify. Uncomfortable, but doable.

Stud joined me for two songs, and together we rocked the stage. Memories of performing at festivals with Carter Hills Band years ago flooded me.

My friend was still the *über*talented musician I remembered him to be.

He clapped my shoulder. "Thank you for this opportunity," he said, before walking offstage. He joined Belinda, Madison, Riley, and Devon by the side of the stage as I played for another half-hour.

After the last song, I thanked the crowd for sticking with me after my sabbatical, then rushed offstage and pulled Riley into my arms. None of this would have been possible without his stubborn ass and his convincing talent. As it always did, emotions poured out from both of us.

"Thanks, man. You changed the course of my life."

My friend slapped my back, his arms still tight around me, and he repeated the same exact words he always did. "It was all you. Get ready, Stevens, it's just the beginning."

We broke apart, and the need to touch Madison, kiss her senseless, fuck her, and relieve the scorching tension that had been circulating between us all night made me angsty.

The way she watched me robbed me of all common sense.

I found an excuse to bring her to my dressing room, and without a warning, I plunged into her with abandon.

I could write an entire album from just the way she made me feel. How she colored the somber pieces of my life in vibrant shades and hung stars in my darkness.

How every word she spoke added lyrics to the melody of my heart.

"Downtown, our place, or yours?" Stud asked when we met him by the artists' entrance of the venue after I'd changed and we'd made ourselves presentable. "Where's the celebration tonight, Stevens?"

"There's none. I'd rather be home with my girls and be a father in the morning without a hangover than partying all night."

"Yeah, I get it," Stud said. "Where are the buses parked?"

"I've texted you the location," Riley chimed in. "Follow us."

———

Up early, I sipped coffee as I worked on a new song, a pencil lodged between my teeth, ready to note the lyrics that flowed from me as I adjusted the melody. At this rhythm, I'd have enough material to record a new album within a month or two. Creativity had been on my side since Madison came home. Every time we loved each other, a new burst of songs spilled out from me right after.

Tiny feet padded my way, and after kissing my cheeks and hugging me good morning, my daughters hurried to my bedroom where I knew they'd cuddle with Madison for at least another half-hour. Having a woman full-time in our lives hadn't just been beneficial for me, but also for them.

And love from the woman they both considered a mother figure had skyrocketed their confidence too.

My daughters were thriving. Emotionally, physically, and psychologically.

The sound of their chatter warmed my heart. I could hear them laugh as Madison told them something.

They joined me forty minutes later, all dressed and ready to go.

"Are we packed?" Madison asked with a kiss.

"Yes. The rental is parked outside, and our stuff is already in there."

She eyed the pad of paper on the table beside me. "New song?"

"Yep. New material. I'll sing it to you later. Since it's all about you anyway."

She cupped her chest with a hand. "I love the sound of it. But 'Kissed By An Angel' and 'Maddie' will forever hold the top positions in my heart."

Standing, after I put away my guitar, I faced the girls of my life. "Today's schedule includes a visit to the aquarium. I read somewhere they have a great white shark, and we can pet starfishes, then dinner at that dinosaur restaurant, and desserts under the stars. Who's ready for a day of fun?"

My daughters raised their arms above their heads and screamed, "Me, me, me."

"I made breakfast burritos that we'll eat in the car since it's over an hour's drive. Madison told me you each prepared a presentation. I can't wait to hear all about polar bears and walruses."

They both started talking over each other.

Madison watched me and shrugged.

"Ready?" I asked.

"With you? Always. Show me the way."

With her hand nestled in mine, I led her forward. "The song I wrote this morning, I came up with a dirty version, just for you," I whispered in her ear.

Her face lit up.

"So maybe you'll have another favorite by the end of the day." I winked, and her smile shook me to my core. Like it did every time.

"If it's good enough, I may reward you with a prize. A private show. Since you won't be able to get a music award for it, you better surpass yourself."

"I love you."

"You better because I prepared a presentation too. But it can only be appreciated without clothes on and with a very naughty mind."

I pushed my hardening erection down with a palm. "Now I can't wait for tonight."

"Let's enjoy this day out first. Family day is my favorite day of the week."

This woman, she'd never cease to impress me. Her dedication to us had no boundaries. I dropped a kiss on her shoulder as she buckled Justine in her car seat while I stored her crutches in the trunk.

"Daddy," Mikaella said, tugging at my shirt and putting the brakes on my train of thought. "I'm happy you found Maddie. And I love when you're smiling."

"Me too, Mika. I'm thankful she found us. And I'm happy you're smiling so much all the time too."

I hugged my daughter.

"I love you, Daddy."

"I love you more," I replied, kissing the top of her head and closing the door behind her.

My eyes found Madison's as we both settled in our seats. "Ready?" I asked, leaning forward to tattoo my lips on hers in a bruising kiss that left us both breathless.

"With you? Always. Let's go on our next adventure."

48

MADISON

At five, I woke up, ready to jumpstart my day. Sam's arms prevented me from moving. He spoke in a hushed tone, his eyelids still sealed from sleep, "Don't go. Stay with me. I need your warmth. Sleeping is pointless without you."

I turned in his arms and kissed him. His hands descended to cup my ass, grinding his morning wood against me.

"If you stay in bed for another hour, I'll make you feel good."

His teeth grazed my neck in a way that had my toes curling.

"Sleep some more. We'll have our fun later. The girls never wake up before nine these days. We'll have enough time. You'll need your strength," I mused.

With one last kiss, I tiptoed my way outside, a yoga mat tucked under my arm. For the last month, Devon had started practicing yoga with me three mornings per week, stating it helped her to rest her mind. Last night during

Sam's concert, we spent the evening together, and she had opened up about her past. The scars that had marked her heart for the longest time. I told her about mine. We hugged and cried together. Cursed and clinked our glasses at how her life had turned out and at the happy ending we both deserved.

The first signs of a new day brightened the sky with pink and orange glaze. We were in Virginia, and even at this time of the year, the crispy morning air wasn't too cool to prevent us from exercising. Still, the coldness stung when it reached my lungs.

Four months after the accident, I had returned to my yoga practice. Even though I still had to be careful and avoid some movements, I felt more like myself as it helped bring balance to both my mind and body—and boost my confidence. I wasn't back to my old self yet, but I was getting there. One day at a time.

My friend joined me, dressed in leggings and a hoodie, her hair messy and eyes still swollen from sleep. "How can you look so awake at this early hour?" she asked, laying her mat next to mine.

"Habit, I guess."

"Riley groaned because I got out of bed and he wanted to snuggle."

"Sam whined too. Said he couldn't sleep if I wasn't around."

"Last night, after he came back, Riley said we should get married," she confessed.

"Ohmygod, did he propose?"

She shook her head, her smile taking over her whole face. "Not yet, but I can feel it coming."

I took her hands in mine. "Do you want him to?"

"Yes. I told him I love the idea. I never thought I'd get

married one day. Sure, when I was a little girl, I dreamed of it. Thought some prince would save me and we'd live happily ever after together, but as I grew up, I never believed I was destined for such dreams. That I'd meet someone who would love me unconditionally. So, I kinda forfeited the entire thing. A piece of me has been wishing for it to happen lately. We've decided we'll start trying for a baby next year, but Riley says he's old school and wants to get hitched first."

"You guys have been together for a while, so it's like the next logical step. Baby or marriage. Whatever the order." I pulled her into a hug. "I'm happy for you…if you are."

"I am. Your turn will come next. I've seen how Sam is around you. It's almost animalistic how he watches you all the time. Like he can't wait to have his way with you."

A heartfelt chuckle left my mouth. "Mika once said he can't stop staring at my lips."

"Yes. Imagine, she's six and noticed. He has it bad. I'm telling you."

"He's already hinted about babies and marriage. We'll see how it goes after the tour. I don't have doubts. I know he's the one. I'm not even scared when he talks about the future. It just sounds so…so natural. We're in no rush, though. We must learn to be a family first, the four of us. It's still brand new and already more than what I've ever wished for. I'm ecstatic and perfectly happy with how things are right now."

Bare feet and with our arms stretched over our heads, tickling the clouds, we breathed in the silence and calm of the early hour. I led the session, and Devon followed my movements, her face waking up the more we got our blood flowing. We bent over to touch our toes, letting it all go. And started over. Until our bodies vibrated with new energy. Sitting, we raised our arms and legs into a boat pose, our toes and fingertips pointing upward. I relished the way my abdominal muscles engaged. Surgery had really thrown off my core stability, but now, I was slowly getting it back.

After a few deep inhales, we switched from one position to another, only to end up in a side plank. This pose hurt my bad leg the most, but I gritted my teeth, breathed deeply, and tried to relax as I counted to thirty.

A shadow hovered over me when I rolled onto my back, and for an instant, I sucked in a rickety breath until I realized who stood there.

"Morning," Sam said, bringing a camping chair next to where we lay, his eyelids hooded. He looked good enough to eat right now. "Mind if I join you?"

"You wanna practice yoga?" I sat with my legs stretched before me, massaging my cramped thigh, curious about his newfound interest.

"Yep. Heard it'd calm my overactive imagination. These days it goes to dirty territories. I share my bed with my favorite person every night, and my body and mind are restless. And you girls look great in spandex."

Seconds later, a barely awake Riley walked out of his bus and took a seat next to Sam. Had they called each other?

"Are you guys ambushing us?" Devon asked, unable to stop grinning at her man.

"Please continue what you're doing," he replied. "Stevens and I have decided we should have our own morning ritual. I'm sure I'm speaking for him too when I say the view is quite enjoyable from where we sit. In fact, it makes waking up at five a little easier. You girls do your thing, and we'll be right here, drinking coffee, in case you need us to intervene or be a partner to help you stretch."

I sighed, but I saw how he watched Devon. If she thought Sam had it bad for me, she was blind to how Riley was head over heels in love with her. "You guys are incorrigible. Next time, I expect you two to join us. It will be good for your stress level. Either that or you can watch from a distance. No more disturbing our moment with your naughty thoughts."

Sam leaned in and kissed my lips. "Oh, I love this business side of you, babe. Careful, Ry will want to snatch you up and bring you on his team."

"I already offered. She's better at working with kids," Riley said with a shake of his head before disappearing inside his bus, only to come back minutes later with two mugs of coffee and offer one to Sam.

Back on our knees, once the tension in my leg had receded a little, Devon and I moved to child's pose, stretching our arms in front of us on the ground and breathing in and out. Beside us, the guys sipped their caffeine, lost in their thoughts and the calmness of the morning.

In silence, later, once we were all done, we watched the night ceding its place to the day, relishing the beauty of nature as it offered a blank page to us—and to our souls

———

The emotions whirling inside me were hard to name. Pride and lust. Or joy and fascination. And love with a capital L. I was madly in love with my country music star boss. The man whose daughters I adored, and the one whose smile grew bigger when I stepped into his vicinity.

Sam strummed the first chord of "You're My Whole World," waiting for the images of the girls and him to start playing on the giant screen behind him. Mikaella and

Justine's voices filled the space, and his eyes darted to mine. All night, I'd been sitting on a stool by the side of the stage, my gaze glued to the man performing. He kissed two fingers and sent the gesture my way, though people might interpret it as being meant for his daughters. But I knew better. A mist clouded my eyes, and I pressed my chest with both hands, calming the chaotic throbbing of my own heart.

Kissing my fingers the same way he had, I blew the kiss back at him. My heart went haywire at the sight of the twinkles dancing in Sam's eyes.

In this silent conversation, we exchanged more emotions than any words could.

"He's amazing, isn't he?" Riley asked from my right.

I nodded. "I'll never get used to this. It's breathtaking."

He chuckled. "His *Legend* title fits him more than ever. He was at the top, walked away when he had to, and climbed right back up as if he never left. He's an amazing father, an amazing artist, but more than that, he's an amazing man. I'm glad he finally gave himself the chance to prove it."

Belinda, or Belle as they all called her, joined me. After the success of Stud's surprise appearance back in Portland, her husband had agreed to do a few more shows with Sam.

Our men hugged and performed together.

"They're just phenomenal," she said, watching her husband with so much pride. "I know he misses it. I'm glad he accepted Sam's offer to join him."

I looked at her. "Why did he retire? If it's not too personal."

"Short story. Dahlia quit the band and got married after she learned she was pregnant with Jack. The whole nine yards. It got us thinking. We had talked about having a family of our own and reaching for other dreams we shared. This life isn't always easy. Anyway, the opportunity presented itself sooner than we thought. We bought a piece of property and decided to go for it. During that time, Carter was struggling due to the band breaking up. Timing." She paused. "We never looked back. I'd follow him around the globe if he chose to give it another shot. Music is his passion, but woodwork fulfilled him. He's calmer, more focused, and he gets to be with the kids. I'll always respect his choices, but seeing him rocking a stage fills me with a mixture of nostalgia and elation."

I sighed. "I get what you mean. It's still brand new to me, but I see how Sam thrives. How happy he is when he steps onstage."

Her phone rang. "I'll be right back."

Once she left, I returned my full attention to my own rock star.

The crowd erupted in applause and chanted his name as he walked offstage, after an hour and a half of laying his heart and soul bare in his music.

My body thrummed with its echoes even minutes later.

After accepting a bottle of water and handing the technician his guitar, Sam walked to Riley and hugged him, torrent of emotions bursting out of him. I blinked to keep my own emotions at bay at the sight of this man, strong and hard-working, vulnerable and grateful, facing his friend. None of us would have been here tonight if Riley Burns hadn't made it happen. I was all too aware. Sam knew it too.

Once he collected himself and dried his face with a towel, Sam pivoted until we faced each other. His pupils dilated. Raw arousal radiated from him in waves. Even without touching me, Sam Stevens had total control over my body. It responded to every twitch of his.

With my finger, I pressed the rapid pulse point in my throat, talking myself into calming the fuck down.

I knew that version of Sam Stevens. I'd never be able to resist him when he stared at me as if I was his next meal. This happened every time he exited the stage on the nights I'd come to see him perform.

He neared Stud, and they clapped each other's backs, grinning like fools. Even tonight, I still had a hard time conceiving how I had ended up in the close circle of two of the most talented musicians in the world.

We parted ways, Sam leading me away after telling Stud we'd meet him at his hotel for drinks afterward.

Unable to stay apart, we reached the green room where Sam had gotten ready earlier. His fingers circled my wrist, and he pushed me inside the room, kicking the door shut and pressing my back against it. His lips crashed onto mine. Assertive fingers hoisted my dress up to my hips. Positioning me until my front pressed against the cold surface of the table, he sheathed his erection with a condom, and after ruining my panties with a flick of his wrist, plunged himself deep inside me in one possessive thrust. The earth opened underneath my feet. Every single molecule of air left me. My head whirled. Right and wrong, black and white, up and down, everything got mixed together.

With his hand seizing my ass, Sam pumped inside me, blurring my vision. My hands clutched the edge of the table, and with each piston of his hips, the room spun around, both of us intoxicated with each other.

Adrenaline surged through him, and it left me giddy and ravenous for more.

Our bodies met thrust for thrust. Our breaths mingled. Our hands sought blazing skin.

He turned me around and sat me on the table, positioning himself between my legs. My nails left marks on his shoulders as I gripped him tight, ready for the ride of my life.

This post-concert, aroused version of Sam was my demise. A euphoric demise. Growls—sounding more like guttural barks—blended with the sound of our skins slapping together. Sam rammed into me with purpose, breaking me and gluing me back together all at once. His hands cherished my flesh as he built me to his touch.

"Maddie, you feel so perfect. You are *my* perfect."

He leaned in, and I cocked my head back when his teeth brushed against my right collarbone. The words, *his words*, always brought a fresh batch of dampness to my eyes. Sam pulled me into his arms, spearing into me from beneath, harder, faster, branding me with promises and forevers.

With my arms around his neck, we melt together and reached our climax, our tongues swirling and our mouths starving.

"I love you."

He tugged me closer to his heart. "Maddie, you already are everything I could ever hope for in this life. I waited for you for so long..." His voice trembled. He blew out a hissing breath. "Everything I went through wasn't in vain if it meant I'd find you on the other side. I would do it all over again, just for a chance to be seen by you. To be kissed by you. And to hear those words."

Framing his face between my hands, I kissed the tears building up in his eyes. My beautiful man. Strong and brave. Real and oh so talented.

Sam glided out of me, and the withdrawal sent chills through me.

His lips connected with my bare shoulder. "This was

just the appetizer," he said with a wink. "To get the angst out until later when we're all alone."

My pulse turned into an orchestra and fireworks show.

Right now, I had a hard time remembering what my life was like before we became an us, and I wouldn't have it any other way either.

49

SAM

The girls rushed into bed, wrapping their small arms around Madison's neck and mine, laughing.

"We made breakfast," Justine announced as I ruffled her hair and nuzzled her neck, my eyelids still half-shut from sleep.

My eyes sprang open, and every remaining trace of sleep vanished. "You did?" I asked, exchanging a nervous glance with the woman who shared my bed, now snickering behind her fist.

"Yes. We made *cedredals*."

"Cereals, Justine. Repeat after me. Ce-re-als."

My baby girl's smile widened. "*Cerededrials*."

"We'll practice later," Madison said, nudging my arm.

I love you, I mouthed her way.

She flustered. *I love you too*, she repeated.

"Sorry. We never get a chance to cuddle in the morning when they're up early."

She shrugged, then grinned. She looked so beautiful, with wild strands of her hair spread across my pillow. "I'll check on that delicious breakfast of yours, girls," she announced, pulling away from me to get up.

"Can I ask something to Maddie first?" Mikaella's tone had turned serious. Since the day she'd gotten onboard with the idea of Madison and I dating, a permanent smile had taken root on her face. My little girl had never been happier.

The four of us were joined at the hips.

I had everything I wanted in life. For now.

It had been a month since the concert in Virginia, where Stud joined me onstage for a few songs. It was crazy how time flew when you were enjoying yourself, surrounded by the right people—and lots of love.

Mikaella fidgeted with the hem of her blue nightgown. Gone was the black. Now she dressed in colors all the time. I only had Madison to thank for this change. She brought sunshine into our stormy days and planted seeds of love into our hearts.

"What is it?" Madison asked, lifting my daughter onto her lap and wrapping her arms around her. "You can tell me anything. You know that, right?"

Mikaella nodded, her golden irises sparkling. Her eyes drifted to me.

"Whatever it is, sweet pea, you can tell us. We love you both so much. It's okay," I said, trying to encourage her to speak up.

"Huh, can I…can I call you Mama too?"

Madison's eyes rounded, and a pink hue covered her cheeks.

I was pretty sure my heart grew butterfly wings. I tried to talk, but words got stuck in my throat. My vision blurred, and when I cocked my head, Madison had tears shining in her eyes, and she blinked, trying to stop the flow from streaming down her cheeks.

"I already call her Mama," Justine said. "I always call her Mama."

"I know, baby," I said, trying to keep my composure.

Madison fastened her grip around my eldest daughter. "Mika, is this what you want?"

"Yes."

"Mama is fine with me. In my heart, you are my little girl, no matter what. And I love you."

Mikaella rose to her knees and looped her arms around her neck. "I'm sure I love you more."

Right there, time stopped.

How could I ask for anything else in life?

They hugged, and Justine and I joined in, our family bubble filled with so much love and respect for one another. It was rare, unique, and exclusively ours.

"Ready to go back home next week?" I asked once we all stopped crying and took our place around the kitchen table, ready to enjoy our…huh…whatever this was. It looked a bit like cereals after all.

Both girls shook their heads.

Mikaella tugged at my sleeve. "Do we have to go home? Vacations are the best. I love it here."

"I want to stay on the bus. I like the bus," Justine said, pouting.

"I think we should go on a real vacation. All of us."

"Like a princess castle vacation?" my baby girl asked, her eyes big as saucers.

"No, more like a beach vacation. What do you think?"

"I love the beach," Mikaella exclaimed.

"Me too," Justine echoed.

"Me three," Madison added.

I let out a loud chuckle.

"Me four," a voice said from behind us. We all turned to stare at Riley as he took a seat beside us. "So, what are

we having here, guys? Cereals? Hmm, that looks…well…
yummy." The girls snickered as my friend fixed himself a
bowl. "About this vacation, can I come too?"

The girls cheered.

I stared at him with a frown. "And you're crashing our
family breakfast because—?"

"Oh, yeah. We gotta meet. And it couldn't wait." His
gaze traveled between Madison and me and then the girls.
"Justine, Mika, do you want to go to the park with Devon?
Hope and she are kinda lonely right now. I think they miss
the company."

Justine jumped to her feet. "I'll be *Debon's* friend."

Riley ruffled her hair. "Good, that's the spirit. Let's
meet her. She's waiting for you. I gotta talk to your daddy,
then I'll come too." Riley lifted Justine in his arms and
spun on his feet to face us. "Hey, Mika, you coming?"

Mikaella moved to stand and entwined herself in
Madison's arms, who held my daughter in a caring
embrace. "I wanna stay with Mama."

Riley's mouth popped open.

His eyebrows bunched together.

He blinked.

"Wow, I never thought I'd see this day coming. Wow,
my heart is racing right now. This is huge. Are you guys
okay?"

I nodded as Madison dried fresh tears building in the
corners of her eyes with her fingertips.

I swallowed my own emotions. "It's new. From this
morning. It came from her." My heart bounced in my
chest. My daughters never stopped surprising me.

"Can we go now?" Justine asked, cupping Riley's face
with both hands. "*Debon* misses me."

"Sure. Mika, come. I'm sure your…Mama will join us
later too. We could all go for a picnic or something."

Madison leaned forward and pushed the hair away from Mikaella's forehead. "We'll be real quick, sweetie. I love you. Now go save Devon from her loneliness. I'll be right behind you."

My daughter bobbed her head and circled Madison's neck with her arms. "I love you, Mama."

"Love you too. Now go."

Riley left with both my daughters, and I pulled Madison against me.

My lips found hers, and when she parted them to let my tongue in, I dissolved under the strength of her love. I grabbed a handful of her ass with one hand, winding the other around her neck, keeping her as close to me as possible.

If I could spend my days buried in her warmth, I'd be the happiest man out there.

With her love, Madison not only salvaged my heart, but my soul too. "I want you naked. Now."

She raised her glistening eyes to me, overflowing with lust and love. "Can you at least wait until Riley is gone? He'll come back any minute. Ohmygod, I'm so wet I could drench the floor right now."

"Glad I'm having so much effect on you, babe."

I grabbed my phone and texted my friend.

ME

Don't come over just now. Wait.

My palms glided under her shirt, and I lifted it up over her head, exposing her black lace bra. "One day, I want a child who looks just like you, Maddie. Someone with your beauty, your intelligence, your heart," I said, kissing my way down her chest. "You're too good for me. I'll never understand how you can love all of me."

She pulled me up, her lips searching for mine. "Don't

ever say that again, Sam. I love everything about you. Your smile, your energy, the way you're a daddy to those girls, even your grumpiness. I want a child who looks like you too. We already have two amazing daughters, but there should be more people like you on Earth. Smart, generous, and strong." Her mouth feasted on mine. "I don't want to wait, though."

I leaned back, just enough to stare into the depths of her eyes. "We have all the time in the world. You're so young."

She shook her head. "Nah. I want our kids to be close in age. I want them to grow up together. To play together. To run around the house together. When you are ready. I know I already am."

"You sure?"

Emotions twinkled in her eyes, making her irises greener. "I've never been so sure."

Riley's words from a conversation we had a long while ago popped into my head. *If I do this, I'll do it right.*

"You know I'll have to ask you to marry me first, right?"

She shook her head.

"You don't want us to get married?" I tucked a strand of her hair behind her ear, wanting to see her whole face.

"Not now. We're good. When the day comes and our family is complete, then our kids—all of them—will cele-brate with us. It'll be a family thing. The last piece tying us all together."

I swallowed the lump in my throat. How could she be so selfless? And so amazing? How could she consider my daughters hers so easily? Without questions or demands?

"I just fell in love with you all over again, Madison Prescott. You're one hell of a woman. I'm glad you're mine because I'll never let you go. And I'm gonna get you a ring.

To symbolize everything we are. And everything we're about to be."

"Please love me."

And that's what I did. Until we were both panting, our bodies fused together.

"We should call Riley. He must be wondering what's taking so long," she said with a grin.

"Shit, I forgot about him. He must be seated outside, waiting for us to finish." Madison's laughter mixed with mine. "Maybe he'll think twice before playing matchmaker next time." I dropped a kiss on her bare shoulder, and she shivered under me. "Come on. Let's get dressed, or we'll be spending the day in bed."

ME

The coast is clear, man. Come over when you're ready.

Madison carried three cups of coffee and placed them on the table, then sat onto my lap. She could now walk without the crutches, a victory we had celebrated two weeks ago. Spasms still crippled her at night, but they were less frequent and painful. I locked a protective arm around her, keeping her close to my heart. I was nuzzling her neck when Riley peeked inside. "Everyone dressed and decent?" he asked.

"Yep. We're all covered up," I teased.

He stepped closer and studied us, his hands stuffed in his pockets. "Can you guys just break apart for a minute? I can't focus when you have your hands all over each other." He made a gagging sound, and we all burst out laughing.

Madison moved her arms around my neck. "See? My hands are where you can see them. No funny business, I promise. But I won't move because we're barely ever alone, and we don't get a chance to be all over each other often enough. So don't be the fun police—or rather the love police."

I smiled at my girl's wit.

"Sam, honey, show Riley your hands so he can see where they are."

"My arms are around her waist, don't worry," I said with a wink.

Riley huffed. "Okay, you two, you think you're funny." He sat in a chair across from us. "Here's the deal. We could extend the tour. By three months. Starting in a little over a month. Some pop band broke up, and we could get their dates. We have to move fast, though. The guy called me first because he owes me one, but we need to confirm by the end of the day." I began to say something, but Riley raised a finger. "Think about it. And gimme an answer by two."

My eyes drifted to Madison. She gave me a subtle nod, her eyes shiny.

"We've already decided, Ry. The girls aren't ready to go home just yet. And neither are we. We'll do it. But we'll go on that beach vacation we've talked about between the two legs of the tour."

"One more thing," my friend said. "I talked to Curtis earlier. We were talking about Anderson and his refusal to go on tour. All because of Alexi. Fear of missing out, I guess. Or to succeed at making it work. What if he opens for you? With you guys as an example, maybe he'll realize it's possible for him to combine his personal and professional lives on the road. And with Maddie there, it will help with the transition. I think it'll be the perfect opportunity. What do you think?"

"You talked to your father about your half-brother opening for me?" I bowed my head. "I'd like to have the youngest Burns brother around. See if he's anything like you. I just met the guy once, so it was inconclusive."

Riley sighed, barely hiding his crooked smile. "Stop fucking with me, Stevens. Officially, he's a Ford, and you're well aware. Anyway, Alexi will need some extra help if you don't mind sharing your nanny with him."

Madison's gaze drifted back and forth between us, trying to catch up on the conversation.

"Curtis Burns is Riley's father," I explained.

"*The* Curtis Burns?" she asked with wide eyes.

I nodded. "And Anderson Ford is his half-brother."

"Oh, I see," was all she replied.

My friend dragged a hand over his face. "Our relationship is complicated. Sam will fill you in later. So do we all agree to an additional three months of tour?"

Madison and I said "Yes" at the same time.

"Great. Let me call my guy, and I'll keep you posted. I won't be able to follow you on the road this time, though. Thanks, Maddie, for making this grumpy fellow happy and making my job easier. You should get a raise."

I kicked my friend's shin under the table.

"My heart is full," my woman said, glancing at me. "Money doesn't matter. It's just numbers."

We swam into each other's eyes and failed to notice Riley leaving.

My phone vibrated on the table, breaking the moment.

RILEY

We'll talk later. You two are disgustingly in love, it shouldn't be legal. I'll take care of your kids while you're busy with their mama. (I still can't believe Mika said those words this morning.)

I'm happy for you. You deserve it all.

I put my phone down, unable to tame the grin stretching my face.

"You really want to do this?" I asked.

Madison nodded.

"What about your job? I put you out of work…sorta. You don't need to get a job, but I'm pretty sure you'll want one, and I want you to thrive, not be an accessory to my life. You gotta fulfill your own dreams."

"Well, now that you've brought it up—and it's funny Riley mentioned it—I've been thinking for a while about teaching kids on the road. All these roadies, they miss their families. What if I teach their kids too or find a way to provide them with the curriculum they need when they join their parents for long stretches of time? We could make your tour and others' family-friendly so all those guys wouldn't have to choose between their children and their jobs."

A million thoughts swirled in my head. "Wow, I like that. Also, the girls would have friends. This could actually be great. I already knew you were amazing, but you just proved it to me all over again. You should talk with Ry. I'm sure he would be a great ally in helping you set this up."

"I know nothing about Alexi, but from what I gathered from your conversation, he could be the first one to benefit from this."

"We'll sit down with Riley. I'm sure he'll be ecstatic at the idea. Alexi has special needs. I'm not entirely sure what that involves, but helping him through his struggles could be a new challenge for you to tackle—in a positive and productive way. We'll ask Ry for more details." I kissed her lips, eliciting a moan from her. "Now that we have a few hours to ourselves, what do you have in mind?"

Madison shrugged. "Can we just watch a movie or do something boring together? You know, cuddle under a blanket and nap on the couch. Regular stuff couples do, that we never have a chance to indulge in."

"You want us to be boring, Miss Prescott?"

"My life will always be full of excitement with you guys in it. But yeah, we could be that couple for a few hours to see how it feels. Let's get naked and see how long we can resist each other under that blanket."

"Deal."

We stood up, undressed, and slid under the blanket Madison had brought to the living room section of our bus.

We were just getting comfortable when her body went limp in my arms, her soft breaths acting like a lullaby. My eyes grew heavy.

"Thank you, life, for putting her on my path. I'll forever be grateful," I said. Unable to keep my eyelids open, I capitulated and fell into a deep slumber, the woman I loved nestled against me.

EPILOGUE
SAM

Three years later

"Daddy, come see. Come see. Austin is making bubbles with his mouth. It's so funny. He can't stop laughing."

It took me all my will to crack my eyes open. What time was it? I looked to my right. Madison wasn't there. I was supposed to do the morning shift. We'd talked about it last night.

"Where's Mama?" I asked my cheerful daughter.

"With Austin, duh," Mikaella deadpanned, rolling her eyes.

"Come here, you," I said as she neared me and dropped a kiss on my cheek. "I love you, sweet pea."

"I love you too, Daddy."

I felt a rush of warmth in my chest. Seeing the joy pouring out my little girl was priceless.

"Now come and see Austin. You'll miss his show."

"All right. Let me get dressed first."

"Hurry," my daughter said. I was picking up a shirt from my dresser when her soft voice sent a shiver down my spine with her next words. The kind that felt good. "Are you and Mama going to get married one day? All my friends, you know, their parents are married. Why are you not?"

I turned on my heel and sat on the edge of the mattress to level my eyes with hers, weighing my words. "Does it matter to you?"

Mikaella nodded. "I don't want Mama to ever go away. I want her to be in our family forever. I love Austin too, even when he burps all over my shirts or when he stinks."

"Listen, you know the ring on Mama's finger?"

She nodded again.

"It's my promise to her to always love her. But I think you're right. We should ask her to marry us. For real this time. The wedding will have to wait until after the baby is born, though. That's what she wants. All her children here to celebrate with us."

A wide smile brightened my daughter's face. "Can Mama also be our mama forever?"

"She already is, sweet pea."

"But I want to be her real daughter. Like in that movie. Justine wishes it too. We talked about it."

"You did?" I blinked to keep my emotions at bay, not ready to let them out. "You two want Maddie to adopt you?"

Mikaella nodded again, seriousness written all over her face. "Yes, and be a real family. Austin has a real Mama. We don't. Justine and I choose Maddie. Can you choose her too?"

I pulled my now nine, almost ten-year-old, daughter into my arms.

It'd been almost six years since Lisa left, and to this day, she'd never contacted us or tried to make amends with her children. For a short while, I was tempted to hire a PI to keep tabs on her, but Madison discouraged the idea. What would it change in the end, except bring more pain to the girls, if she ever came back or approached them? She said she wouldn't want her own biological mother to reach out if she was given the choice. After she shared her point of view, I couldn't agree more with her perspective.

"That's all I've ever wanted, Mika. You sure you're ready, though?"

"Daddy, I've been ready for a long time. I was just waiting for you to make a move. Since you don't move fast enough, I've decided to help you out. We'll bake a cake later and ask Mama, okay? Justine said we should throw a party."

"Oh, I'd like that."

"We'll invite our friends. And Riley, Devon, and little Briana. And your other friends with their kids. All the people we love. We'll call grandma and grandpa and grams and gramps on video."

Madison's family had become ours too. Her parents loved my kids as their own grandchildren.

"Mika, right now, you're making me the happiest daddy on the planet."

"Now hurry. You'll miss Austin laughing."

She tugged at my hand, and I followed her downstairs and into the kitchen.

My pregnant fiancée sat there, looking at our one-year-old son with stars in her eyes. The same stars that appeared every time they landed on the girls or me.

I leaned in to kiss her lips, and like always, my heart shot fireworks in my chest. Contentment traveled in my bloodstream. These people were my entire universe.

"Oh, you taste good. I could eat you up right now. You know how hungry I am all the time. These damn pregnancy hormones," she said with a wink.

"Let's drop the kids at Riley's later. He still owes us hundreds of hours of babysitting. I might let you sample me afterward. To satisfy your appetite. Because I'm selfless like that. And maybe because I love you a little bit much."

Madison snickered behind her hand. "I love selfless Sam Stevens, always ready to share his essence. He's my favorite."

Austin laughed, bubbles coming out of his mouth. Just as Mikaella had described. He looked adorable in his highchair, clapping his hands before him, enjoying being the center of all our devoted attention.

"I think we've got another performer in the family," Madison said with a dramatic sigh followed by a small grin.

"Babe, you look tired. You should rest. I'll take care of the kids." I dropped my voice to a whisper. "I want you refreshed and relaxed if we wanna play later." I looped one arm around her and helped her up. "I love you."

She buried her head in my chest, the smell of her vanilla shampoo filling my nose.

"If you drive the kids to our friends'; don't go before I get a chance to kiss them goodbye, okay?"

"Never. Now go, take a nap. This baby girl in there is sucking all the energy out of you."

My eyes were trained on her backside as Madison climbed the stairs to our bedroom, my heart pumping heat waves through my veins, every molecule of me at ease—and at peace.

"Okay, girls," I said to our daughters once I heard the bedroom door click behind her. "Time to bake that cake."

———

I brushed my lips over Madison's. Hers still tasted like the blueberries she'd had in the morning. "Hey, babe. Time to wake up."

She stirred in her sleep, grumbled something, and rolled to her side. I grazed the side of her face with my knuckles, relishing the trail of goose bumps they left in their wake.

Her eyelids fluttered open and seconds later, she fastened her arms around my midsection. "I was having the best dream. What time is it?" she asked, her voice groggy from sleep.

"Almost five."

Her eyes sprang open, and she propped herself up on her elbows. "Sam, you didn't wake me up. I asked you—"

My mouth claimed hers, silencing her protests as she melted under my lips. Even after all these years spent together, we were still insatiable for each other. Our honeymoon period had just never ended. Our tongues danced together. I forgot how to breathe or to form words. The entire world started and stopped with us.

She locked her arms around my neck, pulling me closer and deepening the kiss. I was a gone man.

This woman could ask anything of me, and I'd say "Yes" without a second thought. Never in my life had I trusted someone as much as I trusted her.

Madison Prescott owned my heart and every bit of me, my present and my future.

"Are the children still here?" she asked once we broke apart.

"Yes. Downstairs. They wanna see you actually."

"They do? Wait. Aren't they supposed to be at Riley's?"

I shrugged. "No. He had other plans. He promised a raincheck, though." I waggled my eyebrows. "Let's get you out of those pajamas and dress you into something a bit more fashionable. I have great expectations for later."

She frowned. "Why? I love these PJs. They would make a great motherhood fashion statement."

"Suit yourself, babe. I'll never complain, but I thought maybe we could eat out or something." *And because there are people downstairs, and I'm pretty sure you'd kill me if I let you walk down there dressed like this.*

Without asking further questions, she put on the powder-blue cotton maxi dress I brought her. She braided her hair quickly and added a touch of gloss to her lips and a coat of mascara.

"How do I look?"

"Perfect."

Something I made sure to remind her every day. To me, no none had ever looked so beautiful as this woman. Inside and out. The one I still had no idea how she could love an old man like me. Well, not old, but older. Back when we'd started dating, she said age was just a number, and I couldn't agree more. Madison and I, we just fit. From the first time we saw each other, I'd never looked at another woman the way I looked at her. We were two halves of the same heart. If that made sense.

With her hand firmly in mine, we made our way down the stairs. My fiancée stopped on the last step, taking everybody in. Our children. Riley, Devon, and their daughter, Briana. Carter and April, Aisha and Gavin, and all their kids. Emily and Becks, who'd gotten engaged last summer. And some of Mikaella's and Justine's friends from down the street.

"What did I miss?" Madison asked, strangling my fingers as she squeezed my hand a little tighter. "It's not my birthday." Questions and surprise shone in her eyes. Without a word, I pointed with my chin to the banner the girls had painted earlier, now hanging over the back door.

Maddie, would you agree to become our mama?
For real. And forever.

The love of my life cupped her mouth as tears cascaded down her face.

"For real?" she asked in a small voice.

Justine and Mikaella, who was holding Austin in her arms, inched closer.

"We do," our eldest daughter said.

"All three of us," Justine added.

"Do you want to be our mama? Like in that movie you like so much? Where the couple adopted those orphan siblings?"

Madison bobbed her head, her emotions preventing her from speaking. She opened her arms and pulled our children to her heart. "Is it for real?" Her eyes met mine.

"Yes. We all agreed it was about time. Also, there's something else we've meant to ask you?"

She arched an eyebrow, drying her tears with her fingers.

"Yes," Justine said, clapping her hands.

I dropped to one knee. "Madison Prescott, I've been loving you since the day we met. I was stubborn and stupid back then and tried to push you away. To keep my feelings tightly chained. Luckily for me, I realized I was being an idiot and came back to my senses just in time. Now that we're about to have four children together, I think we should officialize our love. I know technically we're already engaged, but let's get married—with all our children—so we'll remember this night forever, the one where you agreed to become my wife and the mother of our children in front of all the people we love. Madison, will you marry me?" I took a steadying breath. "Please say yes."

She let out a cry. Then, through sobs, her shoulders heaving, she whispered, "Yes. Oh, Sam. I do. I love you all so much. Official or not, you're all already mine."

"We love you so much," I said as we kissed, her lips trembling under mine. "I love you so freaking much."

Opening an arm to welcome the girls, I lifted Austin from Mikaella's embrace, and we all hugged one another.

"I heard those guys even baked a cake for the occasion. At least that's what they said to convince me to come over," Riley announced with a wink.

"Cake. Cake. Cake. Yes, we baked a cake," Justine singsonged, her happiness still contagious even though she was older. "And we made you gifts."

Their mama squatted and grabbed both our girls' hands in hers. "Justine, Mikaella, I'll always be your mama. Whether or not I adopt you two officially, you'll always be mine in my heart."

"We wished for it. Many times. We asked Daddy, and he agreed we'd wasted too much time already. Do you agree to become our mama, Maddie?"

Another batch of tears filled Madison's eyes. "Yes. There's nothing that would make me prouder and happier. This is the most incredible day of my life. Gosh, I love you two so much."

They all hugged as I stood there, my son in my arms, wiping my own teary eyes, my heart racing in my chest, blissfully happy.

My fiancée moved to stand up. "Now let's taste that cake. I'm starving."

Carter and April joined us a while later. "Maddie, I got

your message. About helping out with our charity. When you're ready to discuss how you see things from your end, just reach out, and we'll set up a meeting," Carter said.

My wife-to-be clasped her hands before her. "I'd like that. My *teaching kids on tour* business is running smoothly. I'm ready to add another challenge to my professional life. Once the baby is old enough for me to resume work full-time, I really wanna help you guys. Be a part of it. Your foundation is doing something meaningful for young artists, and I really appreciate you two including me."

I kissed her temple. "They will be lucky to have you, babe. Please don't spread yourself too thin, though."

"Yes," April agreed. "We'll be happy to have you onboard, Maddie, but don't overdo it. I know how exhausting raising a house full of kids can be. Come on, let me help you out."

They both disappeared toward the kitchen.

"Congrats," Carter said with a smirk. "If only I had predicted it years ago, right?"

I backhanded his chest. "Yeah, yeah, yeah. Throw yourself some flowers, man."

"Are you happy, Stevens? You look happy."

My eyes caught sight of Madison, laughing with the girls about something Justine said. "Like I've never been before. I have everything I've ever wished for in my life."

"Did you put the girls up to this?" my soon-to-be wife asked as she exited the shower, enveloped in only a towel.

I neared her, Austin now deep asleep in my arms, sucking on his pacifier, his tiny fist clamped around my finger, and his dark locks brushed gently to the side.

"Nope. It's all their doing. They said it took us too long

to make a move, so they've decided to take matters into their own hands. I can't be prouder right now."

Madison rose to her tiptoes. "I never knew how much it meant to me until they asked me. I love our family. It's unique. It's us. We're perfect."

"No, you're perfect."

The towel billowed on the floor at her feet, and she grinned at me. The scar across her hip was still visible. Madison had undergone one round of plastic surgery before deciding she loved her scars because they reminded her of never losing hope and fighting for what you desire the most. The ones along her leg had healed better and faded with time. They were daily reminders that life could be unpredictable and that we should love with all our hearts when given the chance.

"You and I, we haven't celebrated yet. Care to love me, future husband?" she asked, her sultry voice sending electricity up and down my spine and waking up every part of me.

"Oh, you won't need to ask me twice. Let me put this little man in his crib, and I'll be right back." I did a quick tour, making sure all three kids were deep asleep before going back to our bedroom. I almost tripped over my own feet in my hurry to bury myself in my wife-to-be.

I locked the door behind me and prowled in her direction, ditching all my clothes in the process.

"I like it when you're happy to see me," she said as I moved closer, my throbbing hard-on now pressed between us.

I kissed the woman I loved with everything I had and lay onto my back on the mattress.

God, she was beautiful.

A chime on my phone broke the silence of our rushed breathing. Who would contact me at this late hour?

Holding up a finger to indicate one second before kissing her lips, I twisted my body to fetch my device from the nightstand. I blinked. And re-read every line to make sure I got it right the first time.

"Everything okay?" Madison asked, braced on her elbow and spreading kisses in the crook of my neck. "Sam, you have your business face on. Something's wrong. I can tell. Who is it?"

"It's Kiera and Edward."

She frowned. "What happened? Are they safe and sound?"

Eight months ago, we had fostered seven-year-old twins, whose mother had gone to rehab and father was unknown, for five months. A way for us to help children like Madison and Emily who'd suffered from their parents' neglect. Kiera and Edward had fit right in with our children. It was a tough adjustment at first, but we made it work, and it was one thing Madison and I were really proud of. That we brought some light and hope into those children's lives.

"Yes and no. Their mother. She relapsed and…huh… she overdosed. The social worker is searching for a home for them. She asked if we're willing to take them in since they know and trust us. They're affected. They found her unconscious and called 9-1-1 themselves."

"Ohmygod. That's terrible."

"Yep. She said it will be an even bigger challenge this time around."

"Poor babies. Where are they now? I'd never let them go to a stranger's house. They need stability. A loving environment. I want them home, Sam. With us."

"They're at a foster home. For tonight only. All temporary. They could come here tomorrow. Full-time, if we agree to do this."

"Do you?" Madison asked. "We're leaving on a seven-week tour in two months. I want them here, that's not even a question, but we gotta be practical about it."

I rolled to my back, and Madison shifted position until half of her was spread over half of me. "Yeah, I don't want them living with strangers either. I'm sure we can make this work. We'll talk with Shana, the social worker. Last time they traveled with us for a week. I have no idea how we'll do this."

"Raise six kids?"

"That. And making it all work."

Madison's eyes shimmered in the semi-darkness of our room, and her smile split her face in two. "Are we really doing this?"

I mirrored her grin. "I guess we are. They're already family. Imagine how scared they must be right now."

"This breaks my heart. Think we can go get them? Tonight?"

"Let me make a quick phone call and see what I can do."

Madison glowed as she kissed my jaw. Her heart would never cease to amaze me. She watched me with adoration, and I kissed her.

"Sam? I'm happy we're doing this together. It means a lot to me."

"Always. Perhaps we should consider expanding the house after all like we've discussed. We'll need a few more bedrooms."

"We'll look at the plans the architect drew tomorrow and see our options."

"Gosh, I love you so much."

"I love you more," she said in a breathless voice, the fire re-igniting between us as she coiled strands of my hair around her fingers.

A wave of joy washed over me.

Music had come back into my life, and I'd climbed to the top again. Nothing or no one would ever push me down again. Right now, I had everything a man could wish for and more. My life was about to get even richer in so many different ways and I only had Madison to thank for all of it. Together, we were unstoppable, and I relished every single one of our adventures.

"You're the best man I know. Don't ever stop loving me," she said.

My lips molded to hers in the slowest kiss, injecting her with all the passion weaving through me. "Never. You're my home, Maddie, you're my heart and my soul. And the best part of me. Let's go get those kids."

The End

———

Continue with Anderson Ford's story.
Read **Snowbound**

emmanuellesnow.com/products/snowbound

Thank you for reading
Sam and Madison's epic love story.

———

FREE bonus chapter
Want even more? Your bonus chapter awaits here
emmanuellesnow.com

———

Want more of Riley and Devon?
Read Last Hope: Riley and Devon's story
Read Midnight Spark: Aisha Jone's story

Curious about the rest of their friends?
Read False Promises: Carter's story
Read Cruel Destiny: Dahlia and Nick's story

WANT MORE EMOTIONAL LOVE STORIES?

WHICH COUPLE WILL YOU PICK NEXT?

False Promises

★★★★★ "The angst, the utter heartbreak, and protectiveness I felt for Carter during this book is unreal!"

★★★★★ "Emmanuelle Snow really knows how to tug at all of your emotions and does such a great job of bringing her characters to life!"

A gripping story of sizzling passion, lust, and the price of fame.
Start Carter Hills's story now

———

Sweet Agony

★★★★★ "If I could give more than 5 stars, I would."

★★★★★ "This is not a romance, it is a story about first love, first heartbreak and growing up."

A compelling tale of love, friendship, and self-discovery that will tug at your heartstrings.

Start Dahlia's story now

———

Cruel Destiny

★★★★★ "Wow. Just wow. If that could be my review, that is all I would write."

★★★★★ "Emmanuelle has done it yet again. She found a way to slip into my mind and heart with her words and the creation of characters you can't help but fall in love with."

★★★★★ "This book broke my heart in the first twenty five percent and sewed it back together."

A story of healing, second chances, and the risks of opening your heart to someone new. Can they trust each other with their hearts, or will their pasts keep them apart?

Read Nick and Dahlia's love story now

———

Wild Encounter

★★★★★ "This is by far one of the most well-written

book I've read this month. It is dynamic, intriguing, interesting, unafraid to go there and most of all touching."

★★★★★ "I personally wouldn't call this book JUST a romance novel because it's so much more. I 100% recommend it no doubt in mind."

A tale of passion and perseverance that will leave your heart racing and your spirit soaring.

Read Tucker and Addison's love story now

———

Last Hope

★★★★★ "This book was not only about the darkness but it was about pure love, hope, spice, family, and friendships on point with just the right amount without overpowering the storyline at all."

★★★★★ "Devon and Riley's story is a beautiful one with a lot of emotions. The subject matter is intense but it is handled very gently."

A tale of resilience and second chances in a world where love and danger intertwine.

Read Riley and Devon's love story now

———

Midnight Sparks

★★★★★ "The characters, the love, the humor, the steaminess, the emotions… it's everything I hoped and more."

★★★★★ "I think that is one Emmanuelle Snow's sexiest novels yet."

Welcome to the island where Holiday magic meets unexpected romance and a chance at a fresh start.

Read Gavin and Aisha's love story now

————

Fallen Legend

★★★★★ ""The love that grows, not only through tough angst but through unconditional moments had my heart. This is a spicy and riveting book"

★★★★★ "Emmanuelle Snow doesn't just tell a story, she creates an entire world."

A poignant and uplifting journey of hope, love, and the power of second chances.

Read Sam and Madison's love story now

————

Snowbound

★★★★★ "5 big stars from me for this amazing story. Absolutely loved it!"

★★★★★ "Emmanuelle Snow's stories are always full of angst, and Snowbound is no exception."

The intertwined lives of two strangers bound by fate in the midst of a snowstorm.

Read Anderson and Abigail's love story now

———

All available at emmanuellesnow.com

ACKNOWLEDGMENTS

Oh, wow! This book has turned out to be a greater challenge than expected. I have no words to express how happy I am it's now released.

Publishing a book is not a straightforward process, and it's hard to estimate from the first line you write where the characters will take you. And how much they'll complicate your job as an author. I'm a sucker for soulmates, realistic, and emotional love stories, and this book is living proof.

From the first time Riley mentioned Sam Stevens in *the Heart Song duet*, I knew I had to write his story. It was one that stuck with me and wouldn't go away. So, I started writing this book a long time ago. And up until now, it's the one that took me the longest time to complete. Because it had to convey the right emotions and complexities (Mikaella would love the usage of this word here!) to Sam and Madison's story. With Sam being a single father of two, he and Madison couldn't just jump into a relationship without second-guessing themselves in the process since it wasn't just about them. I wanted the story to feel real as much as possible. I wanted the children to play a huge part in their love journey because no matter what we tell ourselves, no parent can disregard the consequences of their choices when little kids are involved.

Sam and Madison's story is filled with uncertainties, challenges, hope, and a lot of love. The simple word, which comes with the greatest powers, can also spin your entire world upside-down when you least expect it.

Children being neglected, no matter the form, is a topic that's often disregarded because it makes people queasy, but it's real. And it's important we address it. Not all stories turn out perfect, but some stories really come with a happy ending. Because there are people who care.

This is not your typical single-dad, age-gap romance, but I hope it'll live in your heart for a long time.

I wanna thank my Snow babies for this one. We've been through hard and amazing times together, and I love you more than words can express. And no matter what, you're stuck with me. Because I'll always have your back. And I'll always cheer for you. To Mr. Snow, I love you. We've proven over the years we make a great team and that no matter what life throws at us, when we're together, I know that in the end, it will all be okay. Because we have each other's backs. You don't write me love songs, but I know that I can always count on you. Even when it gets tough.

Shalini. Where do I even begin? Once again, I'm impressed at the turn-around we succeeded to accomplish for this book. When I set the book up for pre-order a year ago, I had no idea my year would get crazy, and it would mess with my schedule. But you hung in there. With me. And for that, I'm thankful. I can't give you a hug right now, but I'm sending a virtual one. We did it! Hope you are ready for all my new projects lining up and filling your own schedule.

To my friends and family, thank you for encouraging me when I need a little push in the right direction.

To my Snowmate team, you guys are the best. Seriously. You're always so happy when I announce a new release, and you do awesome, sharing your love for my work. Thank you.

To the Bookstagrammers, YouTubers, TikTokers, bloggers, and everyone else who spread the word about my releases and love for my books, I'm thankful. This is the best feeling in the world when I see you posting, sharing, and supporting me. Every time someone tags me in a post for the book they have loved, I do a happy dance. It's worth the world to me.

And finally, to life. When you keep pushing, you should know by now I'll just keep pushing back. That's just how I'm wired. And I'm glad you tested me many times in the past because now I know how strong I can be.

This is a wrap.

To all y'all, cheers!

ABOUT THE AUTHOR

Soulfully Beautiful Love Stories

USA Today Bestselling Author Emmanuelle Snow is an author of contemporary YA and women's fiction love stories, who gives life to strong characters who'll fight with all they have to reach their life goals and find their own happiness. She loves her characters to be relatable and realistic.

Emmanuelle is in love with love. Especially complicated, deep, and passionate feelings that make a relationship extraordinary and complex all at the same time.

In her spare time, when she's not writing or reading, she likes to go on road trips—with her four kids and her own soulmate—watch movies, paint, or do some DIY, always with a cup of green tea in her hand and listening to country music.

She splits her time between beautiful Canada and the small US towns she adores.

Find all of Emmanuelle's books here:
emmanuellesnow.com

———

Want to connect with Emmanuelle online?

Website
Author's bookstore and merch store

Snow's VIP newsletter

emmanuellesnow.com

Readers' VIP group Snow's Soulmates

facebook.com/groups/snowvip

amazon.com/author/emmanuellesnow

goodreads.com/emmanuellesnow

bookbub.com/authors/emmanuelle-snow

facebook.com/esnowauthor

instagram.com/snowemmanuelle

x.com/snowemmanuelle

pinterest.com/snowemmanuelle

tiktok.com/@snowemmanuelle

ALSO BY THE AUTHOR

CARTER HILLS BAND UNIVERSE

(suggested reading order)

Carter Hills Band series

False Promises

HEART SONG DUET

Blindsided

Forevermore

Whiskey Melody series

Sweet Agony

SECOND TEAR DUET

Cruel Destiny

Beautiful Salvation

BREATHLESS DUET

Wild Encounter

Brittle Scars

Upon A Star Series

Last Hope

Midnight Sparks

Love Song For Two Series

EMMANUELLE

SNOW

SNOW
BOUND
a love story

PROLOGUE
ABIGAIL

My eyes hurt from the lack of sleep. I'd been up all night, searching the internet to find the one person on this Earth I didn't know the name of. I rubbed my heavy eyelids with the sleeve of my hoodie, hoping to clear my now cloudy vision. I swore my brain had decided to see everything in dual frames. A thick fog enveloped my mind, making it hard to think straight.

Every social media platform I could think of, I'd checked numerous times.

How many Andrews about my age lived in this country? Way too many. It was a lost cause. A conclusion I'd come to minutes ago. He could be anywhere around the world right now.

I sighed.

Soon, I would have to resign myself to my fate and go through this alone. *On. My. Own.* I scanned the space around me and took in the pile of boxes my best friend Ellie and I had emptied last week, and my eyes brimmed with hot tears. A wave of sadness washed through me. Exhaustion settled in.

I had promised myself I would find him. And I had failed.

Rivulets of my sadness cascaded down my cheeks, and I let them flow freely, too tired to even patch the broken pieces of my heart and the dam that had ruptured.

How had I become such a failure at nineteen? I wasn't even out of my teen years, yet my life seemed all set to derail—in more ways than I could count—and I was all alone for the ride.

Ellie had left before dinner. She had taken a flight back to campus.

She didn't have to come all the way to Tennessee for me after I'd broken the news to my parents that I'd withdrawn from college. For now.

She didn't have to help me set my new life on track either. Or even fly here once more to unpack my things after I'd moved.

Three months ago, my parents gave me an ultimatum and threw me out without a second glance. For eleven weeks afterward, I'd been living someplace I never thought I'd consider home in this lifetime. But what other options did I have? Zero to none.

Deciding not to let life have the last word in my future, I worked double-time—even when exhaustion got the best of me—and so far, it had paid off, because now I had a place to call mine. A home. Or more like the only non-dump I could afford.

Ellie didn't have to fill the refrigerator of my new apartment with healthy options. And she didn't have to stop by the store to pick up colorful decor items to give this place a little character and make it lovelier than it was. I had told her I'd pay her back. Eventually. One day. She'd brushed the idea away with a flick of her wrist. "My treat," she had said. Something that she often repeated these days whenever it concerned me. Or my screwups.

No, Ellie didn't have to do any of those things. But she did them anyway, out of the selflessness of her heart. And I would forever be grateful that she'd stuck by my side, because no one else did.

To add misery to my already complicated existence, I was now failing at the promise I'd made to myself: to get hold of the one person I needed to talk to, to confide in about everything. Be honest. And tell the truth. And yet, he was the one who didn't seem to exist. As if my brain had created him one night. And he'd evaporated in the morning light.

Fresh tears blurred my vision.

Pulling the fluffy purple blanket Ellie had gotten me to cover the not-so-pretty brown couch that came with the apartment around my heaving shoulders, I curled up on the worn wooden floor that must have looked fancy in its earlier years. Now it just looked old. And sad. Like me.

Even though I tried, I had no more fight left in me.

These days, every effort felt harder than it really was. I was constantly exhausted, but I always tried to push a little more because I only had myself to rely on. And being tired wasn't an option.

My body let go first. But even in my dreams, my mind was restless.

Images of our time together waltzed behind my closed eyelids.

"I'm sorry," I murmured through the raw lining of my throat. "For everything."

That was when my brain lost the fight too.

I would be all right. I had to be. What else could I do?

His name fell from my lips as his handsome face, brightened with joy, formed in my mind, the sparks in his eyes aimed at me. He smiled and whispered, "I'll never forget you, Abby." The last words he had spoken to me.

How I wished it were true. The image dissolved, and there was nothing left of the man I'd been thinking about for months now.

I begged my mind to bring him back. Not a flicker. Nothing. Even the dream version of him had abandoned me.

For the first time, fear made me a prisoner, its steel claws digging into my heart.

I wouldn't let it win. I had to fight back. To make it work. Somehow.

Oblivion filled my head, my heart heavy with tears.

CHAPTER 1

ABIGAIL

Present

All my life, I'd been wanting to work in the music industry and after everything that happened, I never thought I'd see this day coming. Or that my dream could become tangible one day. For more than three years, I'd worked my ass off as a virtual assistant while juggling home, college, and all the other responsibilities a twenty-three-year-old woman shouldn't have had to deal with all by herself. But hey, I was now ready to prove to Mr. Burns I could be the assistant he was looking to hire.

Three months ago, I had finally graduated with a dual degree in business administration and music management. One I'd worked my ass off for. Days and nights. Literally. I was overqualified for this position, but I didn't care. I would be an assistant any day if it meant I could prove my value. Climb up that career ladder until I reach my ultimate goal. Yeah, anything to bring me closer to my dream job.

In the full-length mirror in the entryway, I glanced at

my power outfit one last time—white blouse and red pencil skirt—my first impulsive buy and the most expensive one to date. Along with matching heels. Money had been scarce in the past few years. But I had always made it work somehow. I smoothed the fabric over my thighs with trembling fingers, doing my best to calm the jitters invading me.

Tears pooled in my eyes, and I felt a little pinch in my heart.

"I can do this. I will do this. I deserve this." I repeated my mantra over and over. Nothing like a little pep talk to put me in the right mindset.

I blinked hard to chase the moisture away. Now wasn't the time to think about every bump in the road, all the things that needed to be done to reach where I was today. Instead, I focused on Aisha Jones's country song "In Your Dreams" playing in the background. A reminder that the Holidays were seven weeks away. And a nod to the best night of my life.

Two weeks ago, I had celebrated my birthday with Mixchos—reinvented nachos—and the biggest mug of hot chocolate I could find. Ellie, my best friend, had sent me the new pair of heels I was wearing today as a present and told me they would bring me luck. I hoped she was right.

From my spot near the front door, I surveyed my small apartment, the single main room, two closet-sized bedrooms off to the side, and an open kitchen. My eyes caressed all the furniture and the mess around it lovingly. It had been hard, but totally worth it.

A hint of a smile peeked on my lips. If I'd come all this way, the interview would be easy-peasy. I crossed my fingers, hoping it wasn't wishful thinking on my part. I'd been learning all about CB Music for the last month, from the awards Mr. Burns had won over the years to each page of their corporate website. A girl couldn't be prepared enough. The guy was a household name on the international music scene. I wouldn't let his credentials and achievements intimidate me. I would be the professional he expected me to be. Even though, deep down, I was kind of amazed by his career and success.

Every day, I listened to each of his songs, just in case they quizzed me on them.

Back when I was nineteen, I used to be a music encyclopedia. I knew every artist, even the emerging ones, and could recite by heart every award they'd won in their careers and all their biggest hits. I could tell which songs would be chart-toppers and which ones would be misses. Over the last few years, I'd lost my magic touch, too busy with the numerous curveballs life had thrown at me. Now I was ready to take my power back—to get to the top of my game and dig up the version of me I had somehow lost along the way.

Looking in the mirror, I wiped the tears from my eyes with my fingers and swiped a hand through my hair. I was ready. I would get this job. I could feel it. Today was the day my life would change for the better. It was about time. I huffed. Yes, the stars would finally align themselves. It was my time to shine.

At the front door, with a hand around the doorknob, I closed my eyes. This job, this opportunity, would mean the world to me if I got it. I believed in the magical power of the holidays. A girl could always hope for the best. Growing up, my grandma had told me multiple times that all the best things happened around this time of year. I could tell she spoke the truth, because I had already experienced a Christmas miracle four years ago. Now I craved a second one. If it wasn't too much to ask.

Locking the door behind me, I exited the building with a pep in my step. All week, I'd been walking around my apartment in heels to get used to their feel and look confident wearing them.

On the sidewalk, I let a full breath out as I glanced at the sky. An immaculate blue canvas and glittering sunshine. Yes, today would be a good day. A great day. One to remember.

A prayer to the Gods above and I climbed into the backseat of the idling cab that would drive me to Nashville's tallest building where I would meet some of the most important music executives in the country.

Wish me luck. No, not luck. I knew I'd be the best at that job.

Go, get them, tiger. Yeah, much better.

I exhaled. This position was mine. I was ready to hustle for it. Whatever it took, I'd be the newest CB Music employee by the end of the day. I, Abigail Peña, would be a rising star on the Nashville music scene. One day, I would sign the biggest artists under my management and would become a household name in this industry.

———

One breath in. I passed though security, filled the logbook, hung the visitor pass around my neck, and made it to the twenty-sixth floor. Yes, I belonged here. I could feel it deep in my bones. Goose bumps spread on my arms, and excited flutters danced around in my stomach. This was my chance. And I wouldn't miss it.

I checked my outfit and makeup one last time and smoothed a hand over my hair in the mirrored wall of the elevator. Satisfied, I rubbed my clammy hands on my skirt discretely and steeled my shoulders.

A woman in her fifties with a businesslike demeanor

gave me a not-so-subtle once-over when I exited the elevator.

I cleared my throat softly before approaching her, hoping my voice wouldn't squeak.

"Welcome to CB Music. May I help you?" she asked, lifting a dark eyebrow.

I breathed out. "Yes, I'm here for the interview. For the assistant's position. I'm meeting with Mr. Burns and Mr. Jacobson at ten."

The woman tapped something on her computer before bringing her attention back to me. "Ms. Peña. You're early. That's good. Just take a seat. I'll call out your name when they are ready for you."

I nodded and sat on a white leather chair in the small waiting room, crossing my feet at the ankles.

To avoid freaking out, I grabbed a magazine and pretended to glance through it.

I had an interview with Curtis Burns, one of Nashville's most famous country music stars turned record label owner slash manager.

If he were as good a manager as his son Riley, this was promising. Riley Burns had signed many upcoming country rock stars over the years. He was as famous as his dad, even though they chose different career paths. One day, I'd play in the big leagues. Just like him.

The receptionist called out my name, and I jumped to my feet, adjusting my top before following her to the conference room. My breath hitched when I took in the view. The room had a floor-to-ceiling glass wall, offering the best view of the Cumberland River and the football stadium on the opposite shore.

Curtis Burns and Gregory Jacobson rose to their feet to shake my hand as I entered, and I took the seat they pointed me to, a genuine smile plastered on my lips. I finally had my chance to shine.

Deep down, I urged my throbbing heart to take a rest.

Confidence spread through me. It spurred me to talk slowly and show them I was the real deal. That I was the perfect—no, the only—valuable choice for this position.

The interview passed in a blur.

If someone had requested me to write down the questions they'd asked, I couldn't have done it. The words had flown out of me with ease before I could think them through. Every time the men exchanged nods and took notes, I high-fived myself in my head. I could do this. Excel and take the first step toward making my dreams a reality.

"Before you go, Ms. Peña, I want you to meet the first artist we've signed under our label," Mr. Jacobson said. "Being Mr. Burns's assistant means you'll work closely with our artists." He pressed a button on the speaker set in the middle of the table. "Laura, please send Mr. Ford in. We're ready for him."

Laura said a few words and hung up as we waited.

Moments later, a discrete knock resonated through the room, and the door opened to let the man in. I moved to my feet, ready to greet him and introduce myself. Longish brown hair, dark enigmatic eyes, nonchalant gait.

Our eyes met, and air froze in my lungs.

"Ms. Peña, this is Anderson Ford," said someone in the background.

I tried to speak, but words refused to make their way up, my feet glued to the floor and my arms hanging at my sides.

Then a rush of air along with a single word. "You?"

———

Read Anderson and Abigail's story,
Snowbound, now

emmanuellesnow.com/products/snowbound

Author's bookstore at emmanuellesnow.com

"I'll tell you this; if you're looking for a book that will make you ugly cry but leave you with your heart full – look no more; _Emmanuelle Snow_ is the right author for you."
(OMGreads)

"Be ready with a box of tissues because this is gonna tug at your heartstrings from every possible direction. I was ugly crying so much the whole day and even now." (OhMyWordMelly)

Snowbound is book one in the ***Two of Us*** duet.
Read the first part now